THE ESSEX CULT

RONNIE PATERSON

Copyright © 2023 by Ronnie Paterson

All rights reserved.

No part of this book may be reproduced in any form or by any electronic or mechanical means, including information storage and retrieval systems, without written permission from the author, except for the use of brief quotations in a book review.

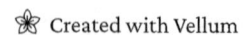

✸ Created with Vellum

FOREWORD

Although the action of the novel takes place in the Romford and Essex police area, the story itself and all the characters in it are entirely fictitious. This has been drawn entirely from the author's imagination to ensure no connection is made between any existing police station or personnel in the force and the content of the novel. I would also point out that I have used some poetic license in relation to the local police structure and some of the specific procedures followed by His Majesty's Constabulary to meet the requirements of the plot.

INTRODUCTION

The ESSEX CULT

Detective Chief Inspector John Jenkins, Romford Police is once again set a full list of challenges in these cases having just married and sadly lost his new wife in a road traffic accident. How will he recover from his grief? Will he succeed?

INTRODUCTION

This crime investigation was to discover the perpetrators of the atrocious and brutal murders of three young girls snatched off the streets and subjected to horrific sexual abuse and death which occur in a famous old church altar.

The Master of the Cult is a well-known personality in the local community, and a Lord of the Realm his accomplices consist of some senior corrupt police officers.

And, Jenkins is no stranger to this investigative work. He is this time fortunate to be accompanied by Detective Chief Inspector Bob Clarkson a former Army Veteran.

The criminal intent is also buried itself in drug barons of the USA and the UK, hitmen, and debauchery.

Jenkins and Clarkson are going to have to burrow themselves into a society that they are not too familiar with, To get the answers to permit success will be difficult. Both are going to have to achieve the impossible. There are hostile people involved, some of whom would rather die than reveal their secrets. Will Jenkins and Clarkson succeed with the professional help of Detective Sergeant Smith of Romford Police?

But, then as in previous cases, if Jenkins is on the trail and coming after you, you may be better off dead. Because you may just end up that way.

CHAPTER 1
TOW PATH MURDER

It was a typical Urban Romford Monday morning and white; fluffy clouds hung in the pale blue sky. The sun had awakened and was emerging through the hazy sky. The cloudy layer created a protective blanket from the early spring sun. Birds simultaneously tweeted out to each other in a chorus, singing a soothing, melodic tune. A graceful robin flew swiftly across the River Rom as the water flowed beside the Tow Path. The singular ancient oak tree stood proudly watching over the river. The fragile wildflowers having sat dormant all winter grew on both sides of the river.

"Not a pretty sight, I am afraid Sir."

Looking around him, Acting Detective Inspector Barrie Smith wondered whether the Uniformed Sergeant was referring to the surrounding area, or the body laid out on the towpath. You could say what you liked about the killer; he wasn't picky about where he dumped the corpse. The body of a young girl was laid out naked in the form of Christ's Crucifixion. Both arms were outstretched with her legs tied together. The red ligature tied around her ankles could have come from a set of window drapes. The remainder of the cord was around her neck. The riverside towpath meandered alongside the River Rom. Her right hand was missing, and the stump had dried. Some sharp instrument had severed it. Close examination of the left hand confirmed, subject to forensics that there was a hole in her palm. The River Rom may have been much more extensive in ancient times, but "River" was not a description that Barrie would ever have used, considering the small trickle of water inching its way downstream.

This area had once been part of a large estate. There had been a grand manor house construction, with a Workhouse for the poor. It now merely housed the Brooklands Estate and The Manney's private dwellings at the town side of the road. Previously this had been the location of 'The Workhouse,' which accommodated the poor folk of the town. In short, a dirty horrible existence within the confines of the walls. History reports that the residents were prevented from going outside the inner sanctum.

It was now a place where Supermarket trolleys came to die, and the dank stench of stagnant water trickling past did nothing to enhance this area. The Romford rats, awaiting the sound of The Pied Piper,' occupied it in abundance, as a home worth using as home. On looking at the corpse, it was clear to him that the rats had had a bit of a nibble. The body was that of a young girl, no more than twenty years of age, with dark blondish hair, cut into a bob. He noted, that aside from the crucifix posture and laying out of the body in this particular manner. There was also the sign of a crucifix branded into her forehead. It contained what appeared to be an ancient crown comprising two horizontal arms, with the lower shorter than the other.

Detective Sergeant Natalie Lewis knelt beside the corpse and examined the sign on the forehead with great interest.

Standing up, she turned to Barrie.

"Interesting the marking on her forehead, never seen anything of this nature before. Could it be a ritual killing and disposal of the body? Was it never intended to be found? She must have suffered incredible pain if she was conscious at any time before her death. Also, we need to consider, was the branding done post-mortem?"

Barrie responded,

"Well, this is not a path that's used these days, as the water disappears about two hundred yards further upstream toward North Street. The only occupants are the odd frog and the town water rats. And they are not of the acting fraternity!"

Natalie rose to her feet from the kneeling position she had assumed to have a closer look at the corpse. She then commented,

"Yet again, I wonder why here?"

Barrie responded,

He turned to the uniformed copper and inquired,

"Constable, when was the body found and who reported it?"

Police Constable Peter Carew, who had not been involved in the previous discussion, replied,

"Two small boys, who were playing truant from the Mawney School, had ventured down the path when they came across the dead woman. They ran back the 100 yards to the school in deep shock and reported it to the school caretaker who just happened to be closing the school gates. They had explained what they had found, and he had ventured along the path to find her. He then dialed the police and communicated the location of the body. I was contacted on my radio at…..he then took his notebook from his pocket……at 0945am by the control room. On arrival, I called for backup, and once they arrived, I suggested we cordon the area as best we could with only four men. Women Police Constable Amanda Knox went to the school to deal with the traumatised boys, and as far as I know, she is still at the school with them, Sir."

Barrie had a habit of chewing his lower right lip when in deep thought and at this point, it was evidentially so. Turning to Natalie, he inquired,

"Any news on when forensic will make an appearance?"

Natalie responded,

"They are reportedly on their way from the police station with a team to cordon off the area, erect the white Scene of Crime Officers, (SOCO) tent and commence their task of piecing together what evidence they can."

Barrie ceased chewing his bottom lip and said,

"Good lets you and I go and see these two young boys and find out if they have any information of use. I doubt it, but we must keep an open mind."

Turning to PC Carew, he said,

"Detective Sergeant Lewis and I are going to the school and will return here following that. Please inform the doctor to remain here until I return, as I am interested to know his thoughts on the sign branded on her forehead and why her hand was removed."

Carew nodded assent and just as they turned to depart, Peter Carew spoke,

"Excuse me, Sir!"

Barrie and Natalie turned their heads, and the Detective Inspector uttered,

"Go ahead."

Carew, was not short of confidence, stating,

"The cross Sir is a Latin Cross, The Latin Cross is when the vertical beam sticks above the two horizontal beams with the upper being longer than that below, it's known as the Crux Immissa."

Barrie was surprised to learn this from a Uniformed

Constable of little more than five years in the force and was suitably impressed. He replied,

"Where did you learn that son?"

Carew replied,

"When I was at University, my degree course was Religious Studies, and I assimilated lots of historical information on ancient religions and their symbols. The Cross and Crown Sir, the cross passing through a crown is a Christian symbol appearing in many churches, particularly Roman Catholic. Still, it is also used in the Knights Templar Order within the York Rite of Freemasonry. As the Knights Templar are founded purely upon Christian principles."

"Thank you...... very interesting indeed......perhaps you may be of further assistance Constable."

With that, they made their way along the path, turning right on the pavement and headed for, The Mawney School. The pair strode quickly with some purpose. Smithy turned to her and with a little forcefulness uttered,

"This Natalie, from what we know so far, is something from the dark side and may turn out to be some secret society with Dan Brown historical connections. Or it could be a single nutter seeking publicity. Whatever, we need to keep this well away from the Press."

The Head Teacher, Mrs Jean Barr, was awaiting their arrival at the school entrance to greet them and ushered them to her office where the two boys were sitting, guarded by WPC Knox. They looked, not surprisingly, terrified and had been crying at some stage. The Headmistress had arranged a cup of hot sweet tea in an attempt to calm them down. Natalie asked WPC Knox.

"Have the parents been informed and summoned?"

"Yes, they should be present soon, they only live in the flats around the corner in the Mawney's Estate."

"Good, as we mustn't interview them until a responsible appointed adult is present."

WPC Amanda Knox was in her third year of policing and familiar with the requirements regarding minors.

Natalie interrupted everyone's train of thought, suggesting,

"It may be as well to have a doctor present in the case that trauma may occur, as a result of having seen a dead body for the first time. It could well have long-term consequences. Better to ensure all the safety angles are covered."

In effect, it all went according to plan, and the mothers arrived as did the local doctor, David Hamilton, from the practice, not half a mile from the school gates. The interview threw up very little more than they knew already. The boys had come across the body and had immediately run back onto the road and informed the school caretaker, who had dialled the police emergency service.

Both Barrie and Natalie thanked the Headmistress.

Taking Amanda Knox to the side, Natalie whispered instructions to her.

WPC Knox was left with the children and their mothers. They headed for the River Rom path and returned to the crime scene.

The well-set operational procedure had kicked in by the time they turned left and hit the towpath again. The white tent had police tent had been erected, and the incident was being controlled by a uniformed Sergeant who had assumed the task of Incident Commander. As per their standard operational procedure, there was only one way. Barrie and Natalie were presented with a white disposable paper suit and latex gloves, helping to highlight the importance of protecting the crime scene areas and the significance of health and safety protection. They entered the tent to find Doctor Cyd Loveday, the forensic pathologist expert, on his knees, examining the body. He looked up upon their entrance.

Barrie inquired,

"Do you have you anything of note yet, other than what we have seen already, Doc?"

Doctor Loveday answered in his Northern English Cumbrian dialect,

"Early doors as yet and once I get her back to the morgue. I will be able to make a full assessment. However, the time of death was, I would say from my calculations, about five to seven hours ago. On average, the body temperature drops about one degree an hour. But as she is naked, it may well be she has been here a shorter length of time. My readings from arrival on my plotted graph, extrapolate to approximately five to seven hours as lividity is present, although the pallor of her face suggests perhaps longer. There are definite signs of Rigor Mortis in the face which again indicates about five to seven hours since the death. Mortem was I am pretty certain by strangulation, thereby depriving the lungs of air. With what I have gleaned so far. I asses ritually murdered elsewhere, and the body laid out here. The crucifix on her forehead is of a Religious and Christian nature. As for the absence of her right hand, I have no idea what that may indicate. Strangulation by ligature is a common method of murder. Inspector Smith this is your baby to investigate and find out. I have completed as much as I can here. Please have the body removed to the hospital morgue and I will see you both at the autopsy. This will determine the exact cause of death."

CHAPTER 2
THE WEDDING

Detective Inspector John Jenkins had experienced a hard life. He had finally found a woman that he loved very much, Dawn was a beautiful woman just breaching thirty and a qualified solicitor, with the local firm Hargreaves & Green. John had met her at Romford Crown Court where she had been prosecuting a local habitual thief for seventeen burglaries, the sum and total of his achievements over the seventeen years of his pathetic life. They had gelled immediately as, like her future husband she sported a shock of curly red hair and being over five foot, by six inches she was strikingly good looking with a slightly pear-shaped figure. It did not stop admirers gawking at her. She was in short, a head-turner, if for no other reason other than her long red locks highlighted against the demure black of her court gown.

John's adoptive parents were now gone, and his life had changed a great deal following the introduction at Ellis & Ellis, to his younger sibling, whose existence was revealed in his biological Mother's Will. He had inherited a substantial sum of money, more than he would make in the Metropolitan Police Force if he continued until natural retirement age. His share of his mother's will was one and a half million pounds, no less! He had a decision to make soon, as the Chief, while pleased with his sudden substantial wealth, would wonder whether this would change his ability and conscientiousness, working as a DI at Romford Police Headquarters.

In effect, it very much looked like his days in the police force were numbered. How on earth could he continue, was also opined by his number two and long-time partner, Detective Sergeant Barrie Smith. He was the kind of guy who was dependable and could come up with forthright views. Also never short of a joke when times were rough. It wasn't as though if John signed off, Barrie would succeed him as perhaps he had shot his bolt in that area due to age. After all, he had already had a career in the Army, more specifically, The Coldstream Guards. That indicated this was undoubtedly a dilemma for John. He knew if he stepped down, someone else would be appointed over Smith's head. In reality, John's loyalty was affecting his decision process and stopping him reaching his ultimate choice.

Spenser Junkins or Jenkins, along with five others were murdered on the day he had heard the news that they had both been bequeathed a considerable sum of money from their deceased mother. It was such a vast amount that it seemed as if they had all but won the National Lottery, well similar to the wealth bequeathed to both brothers. John had spent the entire afternoon discussing how their lives had taken differing paths, with his newfound brother. One had become a soldier, the other a policeman. Their in-depth conversation at The Top Oak Public House had been about the past and why they had never known about each other, since being separated as children. The disturbing fact that they both suffered nightmares on the same subject matter and how that had unfolded in the explanatory letter left behind by their mother. They had got on like a house on fire, being relatively too close to reality where Spenser was concerned. As historical nightmares showed, he liked a bit of fire.

John was to find out that evening that his brother had been taken away from him before he had the opportunity to get to know him. Having been given a ride to the Police Station, on Main Road, Romford, by Spenser, via his estate in Havering ate Bower. Spenser had turned down the offer from his driver to drive him up to his house preferring to get out at the security operated gate and make his way by foot through his well-tended gardens. When John was eventually informed of his brother's untimely death, the shock surprised even his authoritarian nature. He had seen it all and worn a few T-Shirts as the saying goes, though this was different in so many ways. Attending the funeral of the local, 'War Hero,' Spenser Jenkins as was now his surname, not as was Junkins, Military Cross, was much more harrowing than when he had attended his mother's paltry send-off. Because his brother left behind his wife Elizabeth plus two nephews with whom he never had and probably would never have the opportunity to acquaint.

Elizabeth was devastated by the untimely demise and the modus in which her loving husband was murdered. It became apparent during the detailed investigation that Spenser had been the boss of, "The Romford Boys," who had incinerated an entire family of twenty-three travellers in their caravans. John had at one time suspected he was involved as it took place on his newly purchased land but Spenser's wife, now his sister-in-law had provided an alibi which had sounded plausible and believable. It was the worst atrocity the Borough of Havering had experienced since the Second World War. Revenge had been sought and exercised by the only survivor Padriac Lafferty of that Sunday in June 2006, who himself was disposed of in rather unpleasant circumstances.

John and his CID Team had erred, in that they assumed that

the sole Lafferty boy was dead, so the entire investigation had less importance it was being run down. Alas, not so, as the travelling community never give in and person unknown took out his brother and five of what transpired to be the remainder of his gang including Mark Taylor who had driven him to the police station on that same autumnal Friday evening between five o'clock and mid-night.

All six died with an ice pick through the temple, duck-tape over their mouths, and twenty-four stab wounds to the rear torso. On assessment, this turned out to be one wound for each of the twenty-three Lafferty's burned to death and the final twenty-fourth for Padriac Lafferty. If one person carried out the copycat killings, he was to be admired; however, it was more than likely multiple killers. No trace of the vile wretch or wretches was found and to be honest the CID Team let it rest, closing the file. It was thankfully the last of that spate of murders suffered by the local community, and it was now over. However, it wasn't the last murder to occur in Romford and never would be!

His wedding day approached, and as expected, he had asked DS Smith to be his, 'Best Man.' It was a bit of a rushed affair as he wanted to have it over and done with and at the age of thirty-two, had thought marriage had passed him by. His future wife's younger sister couldn't make it to the wedding because she had an important meeting out of the country that had been scheduled for several weeks. Her mother was also not able to make the wedding due to a critical in-patient consultation she had at the hospital about an ailment. Her father had died in a Road Traffic Accident ten years earlier. The wedding was to be one of the most important days in his future wife Dawn's life, no one from her family could attend.

Dawn had asked Edward Stone, Queens Council, a close friend and member of her Law Firm, to give her away. The wedding took place in the Church of St Edward the Confessor, which stands in the heart of the busy marketplace of Romford. Dawn, the bride, was standing next to her, her groom. She was looking at the floor, her fingers intertwined with his and a nervous smile on her face. It was March 18th, 2007 the most ecstatic, lively, and joyful day in her life. It was her Wedding. All arrangements were assiduously prepared. And, here she was standing at the altar in a beautiful church. Her wedding dress was stunning, classic and her red hair cascaded over her shoulders onto the pristine white of her gown. The ceremony went off without a hitch and as the happy couple exited the church, their route was lined by policemen and women in their dress uniforms. White gloves and police truncheons forming an arch by raising the traditional John Peel batons.

At the wedding reception, Barrie Smith, as expected was Best Man and carried out his duty with remarkable aplomb. On being introduced by the "Toastmaster," resplendent in his traditional, Red Tail Coat, Black Dress Trousers, White Dress Shirt, White Tie, with matching gloves and finished off with immaculately polished black shoes. Barrie stood, commencing with the traditional Best Mans introduction speaking consciously with his unmistakable voice said,

"Good afternoon, ladies and gentlemen. If there is anybody here who is feeling worried, nervous, or apprehensive, you're either me (because I am) or you just married John Jenkins.

Ladies and Gentlemen: you are all about to witness a unique event in history. It is the very first and very last time that my wife Maureen, is going to let me speak on behalf of both of us. John has had some dodgy girlfriends over the years. Being a detective, I never forget a face, but in their case, I'd be glad to make an exception. Well, I do hope that John and Dawn enjoy their honeymoon in Wales. I assume that's where they're going anyway. When I asked John what he was doing after the wedding, he said he was going to Bangor for a fortnight!"

The room erupted in fits of uncontrollable laughter. Barrie let it die down and sipped a little from his wine glass. He went on,

"During the service today I couldn't help thinking it's hilarious how history repeats itself, I mean it was 30 years ago when Dawn's parents were sending their daughter to bed with a dummy.........and it's happening all over again today. Now I have a few cards to read out from those who couldn't make it today:

Dear John,

Thanks for the weekends lazing by the pool, I do hope you've made the right choice.

Love: Michael Barrymore.

More bursts of laughter.

Dear Dawn,

It was nice while it lasted, but I guess we'll have to call it a day now you're married.

Love: Brad Pitt."

Speaking of Dawn, I would like to say how beautiful she looks today in that fantastic dress."

The entire room full of wedding guests was in bits and Barrie thought to himself, he should quit while he was ahead. He raised his glass and said,

"Ladies and Gentlemen please be upstanding and raise your glasses in a bumper toast to a life full of joy and happiness and may all their troubles, be little ones, I give you the Bride and Groom."

Following the meal, the dancing was led by the Bride and Groom, and it all went off well. They had booked a room at the Heathrow Hilton hotel, before flying off on their honeymoon to a warmer climate. It was springtime, and they needed a relaxing time in the romantic setting of the Maldives.

Soon after the wedding reception, the happy couple was driving to the Hilton Hotel on the M25 motorway with not a care in the world and anticipation in their hearts for their future together as Mr & Mrs John Jenkins. He had bought her a new BMW Sports, in shocking pink. Dawn was driving at about seventy miles per hour with the hood down. It was a bright spring day the sun was in the late afternoon sky, and after all, it was a Beamer Sports, when their car hit a patch of oil on the motorway. The pink BMW skidded on the oil patch, careering off the tarmac onto the embankment slope and coming to a halt halfway up the camber. Dawn was conscious, and on focusing on the claret running down her head, she cried,

"John," I can't feel my legs."

She was unaware that her liver had been ripped in half and blood was rushing into her peritoneum. The abdominal cavity that supported her small intestines was ruptured to shreds and exposed to the air. It was little wonder she was unable to feel her legs; they were crushed and trapped under the driving wheel. Her seat belt had protected her and restricted her movement. The airbag on her side of the car had failed to inflate properly. John had a broken fibula; his inflated airbag also restricted his movement, he managed to remove his seat belt the inflation of the airbag was preventing him from working on getting to her. John, regaining his senses from the blow he had suffered on his head, crawled free of the wrecked car. He somehow, with considerable difficulty managed to make his way to the offside front door and manipulate it open. He said to her,

"Don't worry my darling, and you will be alright. I am here with you."

As he grasped her right hand, he noticed it was distorted at an angle, clearly broken in the road traffic accident. He could see she was poorly while his condition prevented any first aid, there was blood seeping out of her lovely body and running down and gathering in the well of the driver, clutch, and pedal recess.

The person who had been following in the vehicle behind them had pulled into the lay-by. She immediately called 999 for an ambulance. It was not to arrive in time! It was too late for the newly married Mrs Dawn Jenkins, and she died at the scene. John would no longer be up at the crack of Dawn!

A white handkerchief protruding laterally from the tailcoat pocket

CHAPTER 3
THE RIVER EXPERIENCE

It was evident from how she was driving that Detective Sergeant Natalie Lewis was one very pissed off woman. She changed gear jerkily and jabbed at the accelerator, even though it was her car, not a police car, and it was also her pride and joy - one of the few significant indulgences she had allowed herself in the whole of her life. The vehicle surged out of the rear yard of Romford police station with a screech. Natalie threw a right down at the roundabout and drove down North Street, followed by another right up the Eastern Avenue A12, London Road towards the flyover at, Gallows Corner. She had to slow to a stop at the lights which were on red. She braked, nearly upending the car, then took a deep breath and forced herself to relax into the comfortable driver's seat of the 1980 yellow, 'Corvette Sting-Ray.' Then she mentally reprimanded herself for getting so riled up about the plight and the 'up yours' attitude of just another of her police colleagues. No doubt about it: the job was getting to her. No, she had to bin that idea. The job had brought to her several good things in life, including her husband. She thanked the Almighty she had paraded in front of the Chief Constable, had been promoted to Detective Sergeant with effect from the following Monday. This meant she had only one week more to work on this boring role before she transferred onto the CID and became a Detective Sergeant. She couldn't wait to move into a more rewarding position. She angrily avoided the flyover taking the third exit through the six-ways junction and onto the A12 road heading towards Noak Hill, refusing even to acknowledge the person next to her. She then attempted to offer advice to the young offender.

"Look, Claire, let's face facts: you can't go around doing exactly what you want to do all the time. You're well old enough to realise that you need to consider other people's feelings besides your own. Your mum has been frantic and anxious about you."

Claire's lips curled cynically at Natalie's reasonable words. She continued to stare dead ahead through the rain, her eyes unrelenting pools of liquid steel. The little speech had gone in one ear and out the other. Natalie shook her head in frustration. The lights changed. She turned left - south - onto the A12, smack into the fiercely driving rain and howling gale-force wind which had virtually cleared the streets of almost all pedestrians. She had spent most of the last two hours trying to get underneath Claire's tough facade - in the presence of the girl's nineteen-year-old cousin, who had been as useful as a chocolate fire-guard - and failed. Natalie would have preferred to have had Claire's mother been present, but she had been uncontactable.

"You've gone missing from home six times in the last two months, on the last two occasions you've been nicked for shoplifting. You're bloody lucky we've decided to caution you again; next time we might put you before a juvenile court. Is that what you want? The court might even decide to place you in a home. Do you want to be sent away?"

Natalie knew it was only a remote possibility, but Claire

didn't need to be aware of that. Not that Natalie's words had much effect. The kid exhaled in a manner which suggested she'd heard all this garbage before, turned haughtily to face Natalie and with a sneer said,

"I don't fucking care."

She drew her right knee up and wedged her foot on the seat. Natalie had an urge to lurch across the gap between them and give the young runt one almighty slap across the chops. Instead, she snapped,

"Feet off!"

Claire insolently let her foot thud back onto the floor well of the car.

"Six times in the last two months, eh? Why? What's behind it? You unhappy at home?"

Claire winced and quickly looked out of the side window at the passing vehicles. The BMW was being lashed by a combination of the heavy rain and the waves of spray thrown up from the cars in front. Natalie missed the reaction. She exhaled an exasperated breath and thought, Sod you, you little cow! If you don't want to open up, I'm not sure I want to be bothered with you. And yet she was concerned, which is probably the reason why Natalie had been such a success on JJU, Juvenile Justice Unit.

She cared. Why should a kid like Claire, from a good, apparently stable background, doing well at school, popular, likable, suddenly veer off the rails? There was a multitude of possible reasons, none of which Claire seemed willing to divulge. It didn't add up. And Natalie Lewis didn't like things that didn't add up. The remainder of the journey was completed in deathly silence, Natalie knew from experience; that she was banging her head against a brick wall. To be fair, WPC Lewis didn't have the time or the energy to pursue things further. So instead of trying to draw Claire out, she concentrated on driving, enjoying her car, which despite its age handled and responded beautifully in the wet conditions. Claire, glad of the respite from the pressure, closed her eyes and rested her head on the window, apparently exhausted. A few minutes later, Natalie pulled up outside The Deer's Rest, on Noak Hill Road. The public house where her parents we mine hosts and which was Claire's home. 'Here we are,' she announced, and killed the engine.

"Home sweet home."

With a start, Claire opened her eyes. She had almost dropped off to sleep for the first time in thirty-six hours. She glanced - wide-eyed, like a rabbit trapped in headlights – at Natalie, who saw the expression on the youngster's face; but it was only on later reflection, much, much later, that she recognised it as fear. There and then, Claire's reaction to her arrival home did not register with the Detective. It just seemed to be a rude awakening. Nothing more.

"C'mon lass,"

Natalie urged her into action. Claire's shoulders slumped. The corners of her pretty mouth curled down, and she pouted with a quivering bottom lip. With resignation, she opened the door and climbed out of the car. Natalie unfastened her seat belt and got out too. The rain washed over her immediately, as if someone had thrown a bucket of water at them. Side by side, they walked across the paved parking area outside the pub towards the front door. Natalie knew Claire's parents were now home. Apparently, they had been out at the Cash & Carry warehouse when Claire had been picked up, which was why the police had been unable to contact them. Natalie was anticipating the genuine pleasure of depositing the uncooperative little brat back into Mummy's open arms. She looked down at the grubby missing person - by her side. Claire was dressed in ragged denim jeans, an 'Oasis' style anorak, and a pair of multi-colored Reeboks. By contrast, DS Lewis was dressed in a practical but elegantly tailored longline suit in colour described as 'soft-grape' and sling-back court shoes with three-inch heels on her feet. Ideal attire for office work as well as the wide range of other activities she carried out on the children's unit. However, completely inappropriate, for pursuing a young lady who decided on the spur of the moment that there was no way in this world that she was going to be returned home. About four yards from the door, Claire twisted unexpectedly. She legged it around a parked car and vaulted over the low wall separating the frontage of her parents' Public House from the bungalow situated adjacent to the car park. Then she shifted quickly into top gear. Natalie lunged for her, missed, grabbed an armful of fresh air. Swore with words from a vocabulary that could only have come from seventeen years' police service. And without a second thought, gave chase. 'You little bitch!' she screamed, yanked her skirt above her knees and cleared the low wall with only millimetres to spare. Claire was fast and agile, as a fourteen-year-old girl should be. But Natalie was determined not to lose her, even though she was not in the peak of physical condition. It was a matter of pride. She landed awkwardly, going over onto her left ankle, feeling it crick out of shape with a pop. She gasped, regained her footing and belted after the fleeing kid. Claire looked over her shoulder, saw how close Natalie was and reacted by veering right, skittering around the front of a parked car and bounding over the dividing wall onto the next house in the area. She lost her footing and, skidded over, rolled, and was up and running again. Natalie followed. This time she caught the top of the wall with the heel of her shoe, crashing down on the opposite side. Landing on her hands and knees in a deep puddle of rainwater. Her work attire was now ruined. The cuffs of her jacket sleeves were soaked in dirty muddy water, her skirt was completely drenched, and she had laddered her tights. Eyes burning with irritation, she scrambled to her feet, slithering and sliding, then was back in pursuit, determined not to lose her quarry. Seconds later, Claire realised she would have to do more than simply leg it to escape from Natalie. Despite her present lack of fitness, the Detective was built with the loose-limbed athleticism of a cheetah and, in days gone by, before the evils of cigarettes, booze and late nights, she had been a superb sportswoman who had represented the county at running, tennis and netball. She was still pretty good over short distances. Natalie lunged for Claire a second time. And would have had her if the girl hadn't glanced over her shoulder at that exact moment, seen Natalie's fingers stretching out for her, ducked left behind a car, then shot onwards. The road was busy, the traffic-heavy, the rain making it so much worse. Without even looking, Claire flung herself dangerously in the path of an oncoming van. Panting now, Natalie ran after her round the same parked car, only to hear an ominous ripping sound as her skirt caught on the bumper and tore. This, however, was not something which immediately bothered her because she had seen Claire's reckless dash into the road and the van bearing down on her. Natalie shrieked the girl's name. Claire stopped immediately. She became rooted to the spot on the tarmac and turned to face the van. Her mouth dropped open in a silent scream. Everything slurred down into slow motion. The driver had been motoring along, Noah Hill Road not concentrating mainly, listening to some loud heavy-metal music and exceeding the 30-mph speed limit by a dangerous twenty miles per hour. His windscreen wipers were working hard against the sluicing rain. The last thing he expected to see was the ghost-like apparition of a young girl darting out directly in front of him and stopping stone dead.

"Jesus!"

He gripped the steering wheel tightly enough to crush it and literally stood on the brake pedal, his backside lifting off the seat. The music pounding in his ears lost all form and substance, becoming a deafening, blare. The brakes slammed on. The wheels locked. The tyres vainly tried to grip the wet surface of the road which was a river of rain. The back end slithered round towards the front end as the vehicle entered a skid and lurched towards the petrified Claire. On the roadside, Natalie watched the scene unfold with a kind of morbid fascination. Even as she stared at the inevitable accident-to-be, her mind told her she would be the one to blame; she was the one who had chased a frightened fourteen-year-old into the path of a vehicle; the one who would have to answer all those awkward questions in a Coroner's court. Claire was only inches away from the front grille of the van. A fraction of a second from being mown down.

Then, amazingly, she moved. She leapt out of the way and ran across the road, over the road towards an empty field. Everything clicked back into real-time. The van shuddered to a skewed halt over the spot where Claire had been standing a few seconds before. The driver was ashen-faced with fear. His heart had stopped momentarily. His fingers were still wrapped solidly around the wheel, his knuckles white, drained of blood. His eyes bulged in their sockets like someone had whacked him with a spade on the back of his head. He wasn't sure whether or not he'd hit the girl and she was underneath the front wheels, whether it had been some sort of spiritual apparition or whether he needed to see an optician. With one last judder, the engine stalled. He watched in fascination as a tall, slim woman, drenched to the skin, hair plastered in mud to her head, dressed in a filthy suit with a tear right up the back of her skirt to her knickers, revealing her pink panties as she dashed past his vision.

The road was being bombarded by a fusion of crashing heavy rain, supported by the strong wind. Claire was running along, perilously close to the oncoming vehicles. Natalie was behind her, leaving more space between herself and the angry young girl. She was finding it increasingly difficult to make up any ground on Claire. The elements didn't seem to want her to catch up - running against the gale-force wind was like swimming against the tide - she was approaching the limit of her fitness and also by now her ankle was hurting like hell. All national thoughts were then purged when a massive gust of wind burst over her head and landed on her, almost drowning her in an ice-cold sheet of rainwater. For more than a few moments. Natalie had to fight against the terrifying elemental force of the rainwater as it surprisingly skewed. It tore at her, trying to unbalance her and drag her back, pulling at her legs and ankles. It was all she could do to remain upright against such force which had knocked all the breath and spirit out of her. She was worried about Claire: if the foolish youngster should get hit, would she be able to resist the strength of the sea? With that in mind, Natalie stopped chasing, allowing Claire to get away from her. Nothing was worth putting lives in danger. Up ahead, Claire ceased running. She turned and faced Natalie, looking like a half-drowned rat. Some thirty yards separated the two females. Claire shouted something which was blown away in the wind and the water. Natalie took several paces towards her and having withdrawn her Taser pointed if towards her assailant,

"Don't come any closer!"

Claire yelled in warning. Natalie stood still. She could see utter anguish on the girl's face.

"I won't, I promise,"

Natalie shouted in reply.

"Just come away from the edge, of the road it's perilous. Then we can talk."

"I'm not coming home. You can't make me go home. If you do, I'll fucking run away again."

"Okay, okay, just move away from there. Claire! LOOK OUT!" Natalie bellowed out the last two words of warning as she saw another massive truck build up inertia and then breaks like a vast water claw right over Claire. The crushing weight of torrential rainwater rammed the youngster to the ground as effectively as if a sack of potatoes had been dumped on her shoulders. She screamed and writhed in a fight against it, but it was no use. She was hauled across the concrete road surface and forced into the river running alongside the road. Her screams muted as the bitter rainwater filled her nose and mouth and lungs, choking her for the second time in less than two minutes. Natalie was compelled to watch in horrified fascination as the fate of the young girl was enacted in front of her eyes.

Then Natalie moved into action. Drawing on her last reserves of strength and energy, she flung herself towards the pathetic figure. She knew she might not make it. Claire was too far away and being pulled too quickly into the fast-flowing river. She would be gone in seconds and explain that one to Acting Detective Inspector Smith.

Not, now a fatal road traffic accident, but a drowning victim. Claire slithered towards the precipice of the river bank and was dashed sideways against one of the perpendicular posts of the railings - which she grabbed at instinctively - but still, the wind pulled her backwards and tried to unwrap her fingers from the post. She clung on desperately, but with failing strength and great pain inside her chest where she had slammed against the iron post. At the same time a new, even more, powerful gust of wind was building up behind her, one designed to finish the job started by its predecessor and claim a victim. This wind speed was increasing and resembled the vanguard of something more devastating. Natalie saw it rise. She also saw that Claire's progress had been halted by her collision with the railing post. But not for very long. She weighed up the odds. If she did reach Claire and grab her, the chances were in favour of them both being swept out of the river onto the road and under a heavy goods vehicle and into a grave. If she didn't, Claire was definitely dead. The low odds did not prevent her from flinging herself across the last few feet and risking her own life to save Claire's. At the precise moment Natalie got hold of her sleeve, Claire lost her grip, and her legs went over the edge as Natalie wrapped herself around the post and shouted,

"Hold on tight."

The next Windrush was like a monster from the deep and exploded. Natalie and Claire held grimly onto each other, their eyes locked in horror at one another, looks of solid resolve on their faces as they fought to live, whilst the weather did its utmost to separate them once and for all. 'Don't let go, don't let go,' Natalie chanted as much for herself as Claire. The water whooshed back past them, battering them, trying its damnedest to draw them into the path of the HGV and almost succeeding. Had it continued a few more moments, Natalie would have had to let go. Suddenly the water all drained away, leaving them clinging to the edge of the wooden field post. Alive, certainly. The wind had changed its angle ever so slightly and whipped out to a point further south. Natalie did not hesitate. She knew from past experience just how fickle that she was after all- she had pulled four bodies out water in her time - and this respite would only be brief. They had to make use of it, even though their natural reaction would be to stay put and get their breath back.

"Oh God, oh God,"

Claire spluttered.

"Come on; we've got to move!"

With one last effort, Natalie heaved Claire back onto the side of the pavement running alongside the river bed.

"Come on, get up, we can't hang around."

Claire was on all fours, coughing and retching up the water which had cascaded down her gullet. Natalie yanked her up.

"Run!"

she shouted. The howling wind changed again. The weather wind ghost was about to make another attempt on their lives. The burgeoning swell of river water looked enormous.

"I can't,"

Claire wept. Natalie grabbed her roughly by the collar and hoisted her bodily away from the edge. They reached the comparative safety of the concrete walkway just in time to turn and watch the next monstrous water swell explode against the river bank. Had they been underneath it, they would have been fish food for sure.

The driver of the second Heavy Goods Vehicle having observed the horror unfold before his eyes, pulled into the roadside and removing his emergency bag fought against the wind and sprinted to their aid. He handed out safety items, including blankets.

Natalie pulled a blanket around her shoulders, brushed her damp straggly hair back from her face. The driver wrapped a safety blanket around the younger female. She was shivering and quite clearly in a severe state of shock. He had called for an ambulance, and in the background, he could hear the siren approaching. The Emergency Crew were expert in dealing with this type of situation, and pretty soon Claire was on a stretcher, being lifted into the ambulance. Her parents had arrived and were shocked at the sight of their wayward daughters' distress.

Her mother, on seeing her daughter being uploaded into the emergency vehicle, made the understatement of the day,

"Claire seems to be unhappy for some reason."

The driver, looking at the two bedraggled females, plus the parents saying,

"I can't think why. God knows, they were both lucky to survive not only the river but also being hit by my lorry when she crossed the road."

Her mother, Deborah Cottage, began to sob uncontrollably and said,

"We give her everything she wants, and she's spoilt rotten,"

Her stepfather grunted, a tone of real nastiness underneath the words. Joe Cottage was a significant, brusque individual who intensely annoyed Natalie. She thought she knew him from somewhere - way back when - but could not quite place him.

"She's going through a rebellious phase, that's all. Needs it knocking out of her."

"And you're just the one to do it;" obviously Natalie nearly said. Instead, she ignored him, turned back to Mrs Cottage, and commented, "Well, Deborah; this phase seems to be pretty extreme, wouldn't you say? Shoplifting? Missing from home?"

Natalie then pulled Mrs Cottage to the side for a private word,

"When she is released from Queens Hospital, if you'd like to bring her down to the police station, I could spend some time with her, interview her again, maybe less formally. Perhaps that'd get to the root of the problem."

"That's a good idea."

The woman began, but her husband butted in rudely.

"There's no call for that," he interrupted.

"We'll sort her out. What she's short of is a good old-fashioned leathering. No need for you lot to be involved any further you've done enough. Family matter from now on."

He seemed to brighten suddenly and said,

"Thanks anyway."

Natalie shrugged. "Whatever."

But to Mrs Cottage she said,

"I'm always available if you need me."

And at the same time handed Deborah her Met Police Business card, qualifying this action by saying,

"My direct dial number is on this card as well as my mobile, please do use it if you require any assistance, and I mean any!"

By this inference Natalie made it crystal clear to Mrs Cottage that help was available for whatever reason, Mrs Cottage said a quiet thanks. Natalie got into the police car and was taken to A & E for a check-up. The emergency ambulance was escorted by the police car, on arriving at the entrance. Claire was wheeled into the hospital.

The three of them were sitting in one corner of the crowded waiting room in the casualty department at Queens Hospital. Claire had been creased double with agonising pain in her chest. Mr and Mrs Cottage followed in their car. After an interminable wait, an X-ray had confirmed two cracked ribs, caused when Claire had been smashed against the railing post. Natalie herself had been given a quick check-up by a very dishy doctor and been declared fighting fit. He had rather sensuously eased a tuba-grip bandage around her ankle which, from X-rays, was diagnosed as being sprained. All Natalie had wanted, though, was a double vodka-tonic and to get home to her husband, after all, he was a doctor and able to look after her if required.

A nurse was guiding the still-bedraggled young girl down the corridor towards the waiting room. Claire was shuffling rather than walking. Each step looked painful, because other than the broken ribs, she had suffered a multitude of other bangs, cuts and bruises during her ordeal. Claire looked exhausted and ready to drop. She needed a good meal and a rake of sleep.

"Sweetheart,"

cried Mrs Cottage. She stood up. Open-armed, she went to Claire and embraced her gently.

"Little cow,"

Joe Cottage muttered under his breath. He got up and put on a false face of concern.

"C'mon girl, let's get you home."

He rubbed her head with his hand in a fatherly gesture. Claire reared away from him, fireballs in her eyes. He withdrew his hand. His mouth became a hard line. Natalie rose wearily, aware that the tear up the back of her skirt was hanging open like a pair of curtain drapes. She didn't have the energy to care who saw her knickers any more. Claire walked up and murmured a meek,

"Thank you,"

to Natalie, who nodded. She could not fail to see the expression of absolute desolation on the youngster's face as her parents led her away. She looked as if she was going to the scaffold. Natalie heard Mrs Cottage saying,

"The first thing we'll do is get you into a hot bath and then. . .' Her voice faded. Natalie wondered how long it would be before Claire Cottage went on the run again. The Detective limped into the ladies' loo. After she had relieved herself, she studied herself in a mirror over a washbasin, stunned by her reflection. Talk about the witch from The Well. She looked appalling! Her pretty ash-blonde hair had dried like strands of thick, coarse string. Most of her make-up, which she always took great pride in applying, had been washed away. The remnants of her eyeliner and mascara made her look like the victim of an assault. Her suit was ruined beyond cleaning or repair, and she knew there would be no earthly chance of the police footing the bill for its replacement. Her tights had more ladders in them than a board game and her shoes, which had partly dried out, had gone all crinkly. But worse than that, she looked and felt her age. She was aching all over, having used muscles that hadn't been stretched for years when she'd chased and rescued Claire. This must be how an arthritic eighty-year-old feel, she thought. And frankly, you don't look much less than eighty. It was as if the river water had scoured away the last vestiges of her youth. She held up her chin and could see the lines of ageing running down her neck, giving her the likeness of a skinny chicken. There were also deep lines at the edge of her mouth, which seemed to put ten years on her and needed filling. Her shoulders sagged; she experienced a wave of nauseating depression. 'Darlin',' she said to herself critically,

"if you don't watch it, you're going to become a haggard old mother."

She blew out a long breath.

"Shit."

Then she stood upright, forced a smile onto her face and tried to be positive. The experience might have revealed Natalie underneath the make-up. But it also showed that her best features couldn't be washed away - her lovely slanting green eyes which were almost oriental; and her lips, which despite the lines at the edges, were full, soft, and very kissable. Nor had it done any damage to her figure. She still had firm, beautifully formed breasts which provoked many a second glance from passing men, a slim waist, and hips which were only just beginning to broaden. Suddenly the cloakroom door burst open, and a couple of noisy teenage girls entered, giggling when they clapped eyes on the state of Natalie. She brushed regally past them and stormed - limp and all - out of the hospital.

The rain was still bucketing down the wind had eased off. By the time Natalie reached the Taxi Rank, she was soaked to the skin again, hair plastered down her forehead. It was fortunate that she was returning home to her husband, and no doubt some TLC. That would make things much more bearable.

CHAPTER 4
PRESS BRIEFING

It was already 2 pm on Monday 22nd April 2017, and he was under the cosh in half an hour Barrie was to conduct his first Press Briefing since his promotion to Acting Detective Inspector. Yes, he had attended many of them with DI John Jenkins, but this was a whole new ball game, now he was to conduct the briefing. He thought to himself, 'I am hardly, Sir Simon Rattle conducting the BBC Symphony Orchestra with his baton in hand. during the London 2012 Olympic Ceremony. 'Although his version of 'Chariots of Fire' with Mr Bean on the keyboard.' Nevertheless, he was about to orchestrate the press announcement of the young female body found on the River Rom Towpath last Wednesday. Both he and his number two had enjoyed a delicious lunch and were ready for the expected confrontation with the Press.

Natalie his number two, was with him and would hopefully draw some of the attention from him when he opened the briefing. His primary purpose was to solicit the assistance of the public through the media. The general public may have information that would assist the inquiry into Jane Dow's identity and any further helpful information. Smithy was well aware that John often had a real confrontation with the Press bordering on anarchy on occasions. The main aim was to avoid that if at all possible. He had briefed, discussed and rehearsed with Natalie, and at agreed times, he would let her speak to the assembly to make essential points of interest. Between them, they had produced a written Police Report covering all the facts currently to hand.

At 2.00 pm the Press were assembling in the briefing room. This briefing room had had a complete makeover and as such ADI Smith and DS Lewis were fortunate to be the first team to use the new facilities. There was a new modern enclosed light oak table for the briefing team to occupy. It was raised one metre from the floor, thereby permitting an overview of attendees. The press seating was new and comfortable, much better than the previous wooden folding chairs. At the rear of the room, there was a further raised platform to accommodate electronic field production for both television and radio. This enabled remote broadcasting, never before in the provinces was such a facility provided. Outside the police station located on Oaklands Avenue, parking was available for at least five mobile outside broadcasting trailers with satellite dishes. The icing on the cake was a refreshments area where the vending machine provided coffee, tea and water. Romford's Chief Police Officer had certainly pulled out all the stops, and his vision was now a legend for his foresight for his progressive policing matters.

Barrie and Natalie were fitted with mikes to ensure diction was clear and audible. They had carried out a good sound test.

The was a very large two-way mirror to the left side of the briefing room which allowed the Police to observe the gathered assembly and the remote voice recorder picked up any conversation within the precincts of the place. In the adjacent room, Barrie switched the mike to live and announced.

"Ladies and gentlemen of the Press would you please make

your way to your seats as we are about to commence the briefing."

The assembled Press moved to their respective seats with notebooks and pencils to hand as well as digital recording gizmos. The television crews adjusted their cameras from the rear of the room making final adjustments ensuring they had good coverage of the briefing desk. The Metropolitan Police Flag was draped on the front to show the Met Police Logo.

Barrie checked the list of Press Attendees:

National Newspapers:

Daily Express, *Daily Mail*, *Daily Mirror*, *The Daily Telegraph*, *The Guardian*, *The Independent*, *London Evening Standard*, London *Metro*, *The Observer*, *The Sun* and The Times.

Local Newspapers:

Romford Recorder. Basildon Standard, Southend Standard, Brentwood Weekly News.

Television Crews and Mobile Vans:

Anglia Television, BBC News, ITN News, Chanel 4, Chanel 5.

As they entered the room, the chit-chat died as they took their respective seats occupying the centre area of the table. Barrie was first to speak,

"Good afternoon, Ladies and Gentlemen of the Press you will have received a printed Police Briefing notice informing you of the brief details of the body that was discovered on the towpath of the River Rom just off Mawney Road. The body of a young female was discovered by two young boys from the local Mawney Road, Primary School. It took place at about 09.15 am on Monday 13th April. The body was naked with no associated clothing available at the scene. We are at a loss to identify who she was. So for the time being, and until we can do so, she will hitherto be referred to as, 'Jane Doe.' The autopsy which took place this morning has confirmed that she was strangled and that there were no medical signs of any sexual interference. As stated, we are in the very early stages of the investigation, so there is very little more I can tell you. Once we have more information to hand Romford Police will call another Police briefing of which you will all receive due notice."

There was much muttering going on in the room by the press reporters which Barrie curtailed by speaking once more.

"I would like to introduce you to Detective Sergeant Natalie Lewis, who is assisting in the investigation and is second in command of my team. She has recently been involved in crime analysis for the last eighteen month and will be a great addition to the squad."

Natalie remained seated and said,

"Thank you for the introduction, DI Smith. I can inform the Press that this is by no means going to be an easy case. The crime scene yielded very sparse information for us to go on, given that she was naked. Also, the overgrown nature of the towpath provided no footprint of any note. As already briefed, the victim was very young between eighteen and twenty years of age. The initial assessment indicates she was killed somewhere else and then dumped on the sinuous, Tow Path, which if you are aware of the precise spot is infrequently used. The odd runner taking exercise may use it. Forensics has been busy, and the Scene of Crime Team has logged all relevant information. This will hopefully throw up worthwhile lines of investigation. I will now hand you back to DI Smith."

Barrie then announced that he would field any questions that the assembled company may have by saying asking them to state which part of the media they were from.

"Hello, Jean Bancroft, Romford Recorder."

DI Smith looked at the women, in her mid-fifties had raised her hand; her face was rather long with a pointed chin and a dimple housed in the centre. She wore bright red lipstick making her mouth look more like a slash rather than a mouth.

Her sombre black dress over a lumpy frame and silver coloured chain around her wrinkled neck, sporting a medallion, which rested on her ample breast bulge, done nothing to enhance her looks. He said,

"Please go ahead with your question?"

She cleared her throat and asked,

"Apart from truant children, and runners is there any further information as to the human traffic which may use the towpath?

DI Smith replied,

"No, but it has been the location where drunks and drug users frequent as it is not that public, as it's shielded from the public due to its location."

Jean went on,

"So, what you are asking us to believe is that the person or persons, who dumped the corpse, were knowledgeable that the path is isolated and discovery was highly unlikely?"

Smithy, smiled inwardly being careful not to show his emotions to the gathered News Hacks.

"It is without credible information to hand as yet, more than likely, that is why this location of choice. I doubt it was selected by shutting one's eyes with the street map of Romford laid out on a table, and a pin stuck in it. No, I dare say the site was fully researched in some detail before selection. That said, if the killer was hoping for the body to rot there for a long time, he or she failed in their assessment."

She, was determined to make her point, in her high pitched yet forceful voice, commented again from the red-painted lips,

"So, I was going to ask, Inspector Smith, how someone might gain access to the path carrying a dead body without Somebody not seeing this happen?"

DI Smith, the bottom lip was being chewed again as he held himself in check. And he responded in what can only as may be described as conciliatory. A shadow of a smile shot across his rugged face,

"My dear lady, the answer to the Dead Body being transported is, 'No!' Clearly, this is a public place and as previously stated it is not unusual for tramps, drunks and druggies to accommodate the area at any given time. That is a fact, which the perpetrators may have already taken into their plans. Also, it may well have been that a reconnoitre took place before the corpse was left there."

Jean replied.

"Thank you, Inspector, I much appreciate your candour."

As she had completed her question the Anglia Television reporter, Donald Dougall, with the cameras rolling raised his arm, wishing to question the chair,

"Hi Donald Dougall, Anglia TV, Inspector I wonder if I may direct a question to Detective Sergeant Lewis?"

DI Smith was somewhat pleased that the television would be showing Natalie on the regional evening news. Dougall was a handsome male of thirty-five years of age with loads of experience in local general Romford and Essex issues regarding criminal activity. On his feet, he stood a good six foot tall, immaculately attired in a dark blue pin-striped suit, with a silk bow tie of Dark Blue, a hint of Yellow thin diagonal stripe and Sky-Blue. Barrie recognised the bow-tie being that of a military nature, in particular, 'The Queens Regiment.' He nodded his head, giving permission and said,

"Go ahead please."

"DS Lewis, What about CCTV and has that shown up any information which may lead to some idea of how this unfortunate, Jane Doe arrived on the towpath?"

Natalie, replied to her, sweet and alluring, addressing the press tone,

"There are some images on the local street CCTV which is

currently still being analysed. However, as yet, no concrete evidence has been assessed, but it is early days, and we are hopeful that ongoing footage from various other town cameras will be forthcoming."

"Thank you, DS Lewis, very helpful."

Another hand shot into the air, it was a lady's, but due to the stature of the said hand, it wasn't easy to locate the personage. Barrie fielded it by saying,

"Hi, can you please stand, state your name, media source and question please?"

The woman stood, all five foot nothing of her. There was just something unreal and eerie about her. Her face, somewhat luminous, had a pale tone to it. The eyes were a piercingly sharp shade of grey. The eyebrows were arched over the curve before dispersing onto the bridge of her dainty nose. A little plump, her lips had the strangest curl to them. Using both hands, she straightened her hair, throwing it behind her smart red blouse. She was aware that television cameras were recording everything that went on. She threw a spanner direct into the works by saying,

"I am Adele Braithwaite, of The Basildon Weekly News. The question I have for you, is this murder in any way ritual? I have heard through the grapevine that Jane Doe was missing her right hand, and there was branding on her forehead?"

Barrie was shocked by this revelation in front of TV Cameras and the National Press. He had wanted these details to remain undisclosed at this stage of the inquiry. Now he had to think on his seat rather than on his feet. What to disclose had to be the dilemma. Adele Braithwaite knew some of the details. That leak must have occurred either from the Police or the hospital morgue. He favoured the latter. There is no way on this earth that any of his team would expose the details of the cadaver. The human remains were removed by forensic experts in a laborious process, meant to preserve evidence. Having gained a minute or so, and his thoughts he responded,

"I have to say it is a peculiar case we are dealing with and I would ask the Press and Media here assembled to refrain from publishing or reporting the ridiculousness of the detail you have just heard. Exposure of such acquisitions would produce panic among the good folk of Romford. Furthermore, this is a murder inquiry. As yet, we have no idea who the victim is, and it would be irresponsible of us all if the circumstance in which she was discovered were leaked. We, the Police, are exploring every angle, and we'd be remiss in our duty if we did not pursue every lead no matter how nebulous it may seem. That please also goes for the responsibility of Her Majesty's Press."

The room erupted and *en-masse* shouting questions at him and Natalie.

"Do you have any suspects?"

"Male or Female?"

"Young or Old?"

"Why?"

Then it came, the 'Coup de Grace!' Donald Dougall of Anglia Television when he yelled out at the top of his Scottish brogue,

"Was it a Masonic Ritual Murder? Perhaps a shade of Dan Brown type novels?"

The entire room which a second ago was no longer controlled and orderly erupting like a volcano then fell silent with this shocking question. The cameras continued to click and roll recording this.

Barrie was dreading this assumption and now knew things were about to become very messy. He, therefore, decided it was time to call this briefing to a close. He stood and closed his briefing folder stating,

"Ladies and Gentlemen of the Press it is my assessment that we have exhausted this briefing, and I now bring it to an end.

Thank you for attending and will notify you as and when we have cause for another of these meetings.

As the Press collected their thoughts and recording apparatus was closed down, the Newspaper and Radio Hacks muttered amongst themselves and shuffled out of the room.

CHAPTER 5
ROMFORD SAMARITANS

As she drew nearer to him, he saw that she was dressed in Lollapalooza as ever. Her Red Mercedes SL contained all the accoutrements he expected of someone of that standing. Having surveyed the car many times, he was now familiar with the accessories such as the Sat Navigation, the leather upholstery and the paddle gear change. Gwynn was now out of the vehicle and on foot. It was Friday afternoon, and Jim had decided that he would carry out his surveillance of the target. The training, while a member of the Special Forces would ensure that neither the target nor the public would be alerted. Jim Pratchett was a special operative in many theatres.

His transfer from the SAS to MI5 had been smooth. How he had been orchestrated in the nuances of observing targets without suspicion was paramount. The ten-year secondment had gone well. However, the fact he was not educated to what the desk managers termed, Degree Level, restricted his progress. Jim's posting back to the 22 Special Air Service Regiment had been frankly disappointing. This resulted in his resignation. He was financially sound and extremely wealthy due to his secret post-service life. He was pathetically unable to form any real, long-lasting relationships with the opposite sex as he thought, 'You reap what you sow'.

She walked with extraordinary grace, her figure near perfect for a woman of her age. Her face was not visible. It was hidden by the floppy hat she wore, but it was impossible not to see she was stunning. Gwynn walked briskly, passing so close to him. She symbolised the adventure of which his evenings were so empty – a more significant melancholy gripped him. He felt wretched as an inferior individual. He rounded his shoulders and lowered his eyes as he sat crunched. Presently he was unrecognisable, incognito, dressed like a tramp with his begging bowl and the sign hanging by a piece of dirty string around his neck – but not before casting one furtive glance at her. Raising the begging bowl held in his filthy hands, he begged. He used this accent often as part of his operational tours in Belfast which was more Ballymurphy than Shankill Road.

"Please help an old soldier on hard times, surely?"

(He would have been chastised within MI5 for the inadvertent error, highlighting the fact that the pathetic-looking character he portrayed may have had some relationship with the military.)

He was so astounded at what happened; next, he was shocked and stared into her face. Jim had made no mistake. She was smiling with what appeared to be a sympathetic yet curious look. Also, the lady hesitated, opened her handbag, and rummaged around inside. Withdrawing a five-pound note, she placed it in his bowl. He thought instantly: 'Whore only five pounds?' No, that was uncalled for she was hardly a lady of the night. Perhaps more, Florence Nightingale.

She was stunning maturely. He could not speak and swallowed some oxygen, but a growing joy gave him the power to smile at her as she then passed. With her glances, many subtle inflexions of teeth and eyes, she was inducing an intimacy that suggested much. He felt he must be careful not to expose his real persona. At length, he thought the best thing might be to evade her stare, but hell no, he desired this fine-looking woman, and in his warped mind, he would one day have her, come hell or high water. He was instantly reminded of the chorus of the Deep Purple hit song and hummed the tune and inwardly sang the words.

Come hell, hell, or high water.
Nothing's gonna hold me down
Come hell, hell, or high water
Nobody is messing' me around.

That night he dreamt of the possibility of a perfect encounter, following months of disillusion which never entirely killed off his desire. Within his mental capacity, his elation rose beyond control, and his mind was running wild. He believed she would succumb to him one day. Jim was confident of that, the perfections compounded in his head. His thoughts wandered. Mrs Robinson was before him, naked in a silken shift, he poured out his love, a love that was to be eternal, to be always perfect, as fabulous as this, their exquisite meeting was. Softly he thought to caress her but...wait......the real Gwynn was not here it was only the enlarged photo of her he had taken surreptitiously. The photographic shop assistant had blown it up to life-size, and now it adorned his wall. It was all in his powers of thought, however, and unfortunately as yet not real. The fact he lusted after this former Magistrate and Samaritan, from his point was quite frankly all-encompassing.

His covert following of her for the last six-month had provided a complete detailed knowledge of his fantasy woman.

She did want to be with him, but alas Gwynn was not aware of that detail. The calls to Romford Samaritans were numerous; however, on some occasions, he was fortunate, and she answered the phone. On such evenings he recorded the response on hearing her voice. By these constant actions, Jim was now able to recognise when she answered. When it was not her soft voice, he disconnected the call. She had a distinctly soft Middle England tone which was both endearing to the ear as well as authoritative at times. He absolutely loved when she was so strict and matronly on the phone to him. It did get him worked up. She was quite unaware of this resulting in an uncontrollable ebullition.

Gwynn had been having what was a typical Saturday night shift when the telephone on her desk rang. She was always neat, a mature, 68-year-old woman of medium build. Always well dressed and as a former magistrate, still took great care of her appearance.

From her days on The Leal Bench, she was quite used to dealing with people at all levels of humanity, and a volunteer as were her colleagues. They handled the phones of the Romford, 'Good Samaritans,' located at the end of Como Street as it meets with North Street. The Havering branch postal address was 107 North Street Romford. They received about 13,000 phone calls per year and almost 240 face-to-face visits for confidential emotional support. In short, it provided a service for those in distress. Gwynn took the phone to her ear, brushing her silver hair to the side, thereby enabling the phone to rest by her earlobe and supported by her chin and shoulder. With what she perceived as a friendly tone, answered the incoming call,

"Samaritans, how may I help you?"

There was no response from the caller, and the line went dead. It was not unusual, and Gwynn logged the call with the statement,

'Number withheld 10.30 pm.'

Just as she had completed the entry on her log book the phone went again, taking the handset to her ear once more she commented,

"Samaritans, how may I help you?"

This time a male voice spoke,

"Good evening......who is that there?"

Being well aware of nuisance calls from bored people who just wished to talk to someone to relive their personal loneliness, Gwynn, once more spoke into the green phone she held to her ear,

"Good evening......please, how may I help you?"

It was at that stage she could hear that the person on the other end was breathing rather heavily and clearly obtaining some sexual pleasure from her presence on the phone. Events and calls of this nature were not an unusual occurrence and remaining professional, she said,

"I think you should hang up if you do not require help from the Samaritans!"

The caller then began to speak as she was about to hang up.......

" Well I do have a problem, which I am sure a pretty lady like you could help with......are you able to do that.......?"

Gwynn had an idea where this was going, but her training course plus experience had implied the importance of slowly investigating what help the caller required. She permitted the heavy breathing which was going on in her ear. After a few minutes, she then put the phone back on its cradle and hung up, disconnecting the call. Shaking her head in disgust entered the incident in her logbook. Sympathy was not what this fellow was seeking rather more like some sort of sexual relief.

No sooner had she finished writing the details in the logbook. The phone rang yet again. On reaching for the handset, she hoped upon hope that it was a fresh caller. Alas, it was not to be! As soon as she answered in her usual manner, off he went again with the heavy breathing, however, this time he seemed to cease the heavy breathing and spoke,

"Can you please help me?"

Gwynn paused for a moment and contemplated putting the phone back on its cradle, but she was a dab hand at dealing with odd conversations and had experienced similar calls in the past. She once more recognised the voice. Her professional outlook would not permit that. So once more she uttered the opening phrase,

"This is the Samaritans; how may I help you?"

Again, there was a short pause, and he spoke once more,

"I am Jim, and I am so frustrated I needed to hear a women's voice; will you please accept my apologies?"

"Yes, of course, I will what is your problem, Jim, apart from the obvious? It is you again Jim, who has called three times in so many minutes?"

He responded,

"Yes, it is."

"And what can the Samaritans do to help you, Jim?"

Gwynn was cautious, not attempting to push the caller.

"So what is your problem, Jim?"

"I need a woman......one I can see regularly and fuck!"

She was a little shocked by this outburst but not that surprised.

"I really can't help you with that Jim, that's not what we do here. We are here to help people in mental turmoil, however not the type of dilemma you seem to have. I would continue buying the Kleenex."

He responded,

"I know who you are Gwynn. I have watched you walk into the office at 107 North Street. I have observed you for some time now, and I desire you, Gwynn. You are always fashionable, quite stunning. You are married and a former magistrate. I have seen you many times when you were a magistrate on the bench, dealing with local bad boys and women. By the way, none of the women has ever been as attractive as you Gwynn. I lust after you and have done so for a very long time,"

She should have hung up the phone there and then, but was intrigued and to be honest a little flattered that even as a sixty-eight-year-old grandmother, she still had an admirer. She became a little flustered, even thrilled and strangely gratified, she commented,

"Well Jim, you must know that we are here to assist those in distress and it seems to me that you are not in any way distressed, but more frustrated than anything. Is that not so?"

He responded,

"I just have the hots for you Mrs Gwynn Robinson and want to give you something that will satisfy both of us.......so let's meet after your shift, you finish about midnight, and I can walk you home?"

The shock that he obviously knew who she was and had clearly followed her at some time in the past raised a great deal of concern. How could she deal with this without causing him to throw a wobbly? Thinking quickly, she said,

"I am flattered by your offer to see me home Jim, but unfortunately we are forbidden to fraternise with callers. So, regrettably, I have to refuse your offer. I do hope you understand that rules are here to be obeyed. If you require assistance, I could call the appropriate service, and they could visit you and help sort out your problem. Can I please have your full name and address, so that I can arrange this help? However, regardless of the need, you have, to meet me, that would be a dereliction of our code of practice."

Silence ensued for some time yet again. Just as she thought, thank goodness he is gone, and she could hang up, he sang,

'And here's to you, Mrs Robinson,

Jesus loves you more than you will know.

"One way or another, Mrs Robinson. I am going to meet you someday soon."

The line went dead; she was thankful that it had. Gwynn thought what an abnormal caller. She had been chatted up recently over the phone......was it him......or was this someone new? She then entered a resume, of most of the conservation details into her log thinking, she had to defend herself, can't be too careful, but at least his voice had been recorded on the monitoring system. This included his rendition of a few lines from the Simon & Garfunkel, Oscar-winning song from The Graduate movie.

What she was unaware of was that he knew that her Red Mercedes C220, was parked in the locked caged car park behind the building. This lady would not be walking home as he had implied.

The remainder of her voluntary shift went with only two more calls fielded. Thankfully he never called back to bug her. At midnight with her six-hour shift finished, Gwynn closed down and completed her log page, then signed and filed it in the out tray on the desk of the workstation. Taking her mustard coat off the hanger placed it over her shoulder. She called to the others as she departed the building,

"Goodbye, you guys and gals see you Monday evening."

Her car was secure. It was parked in her regular bay where she had always left it. Walking to the locked gate she placed the key in the lock, turning it anti-clockwise to open it. Swinging the gate ajar, she provided sufficient clearance, for her to drive her car through the gap. Turning from the entrance as she clicked the automatic key fob to open the vehicle, a hand unexpectedly reached around her face from the rear. Her world went darker than the crepuscular midnight surrounding her. The chloroform-soaked rag induced immediate paralysis of faculties as she buckled to her knees. The dark-clad figure could have been an operative snatching Osama Bin-Laden as he easily manhandled her into the rear seat of the Mercedes. Recovering the key fob from the tarmac ground, he swiftly started the car and was off down Como Street to his lair.

Nobody witnessed the incident at that time of night, other than the small security camera affixed to the rear wall of the Samaritans building covering the car park area. Her abductor had catered for this; his previous training had taught him well. He was dressed head to foot in black and wore a black balaclava. The entire camera recording would reveal nothing more than what was a six-foot-tall figure of indeterminate sex kidnapping a delicate female.

CHAPTER 6
LORD PETER GENTRY

Lord Peter Gentry was neither paying attention to his breakfast nor to his late wife Olivia who had mysteriously committed suicide on a train entering a London Station. Her cat Pickles, was as ever scratching the leg of his large mahogany, triple pillar-legged dining table. He mused that he should have the cat either fostered out to one of the families living in Ingatestone, or better still have it put down.

He sat, taking breakfast in the grand dining room of Ingatestone Hall, his beautiful Grade One, and listed manor house in Essex, England. The Estate dated back to his family before the eighteen-hundreds. It was located just outside the village of Ingatestone, approximately five miles south-west of Chelmsford. His forefathers built the house during the 16th century. Peter Egbert Gentry was absorbed in reading the leader of The Times Newspaper which had been printed in stark, bold print. The article he was engrossed in was The Time's principal news headline:

CHIEF CONSTABLE STEPHEN JONES: MURDERED

IN CHELMSFORD

Now and again he tugged at his brown goatee beard to quicken his comprehension of the weighty phrases of the leader-writer, now and then he made noises, chiefly through his nose, expressing disgust and concern. For in his mind, he felt the exposure of his position as Leader of Ordo Templi Orientis. That confounded police detective from Romford was he felt on his tale. It was imperative that he either flew the nest or had the pain executed. He had just the man to carry out that task. James, aka Anthony Steel, would manage that task.

She also paid no attention to her favourite, pussy-cat Pickles, duly excited by the smell of grilled sole, as it was delivered to Lord Gentry by the butler. The cat rose on his hind legs and laid his paws on his Lordship's trousers, penetrating the fabric with his claws into his shin. It was no more than gentle, arresting pricks but this angered the already agitated nobleman. He sprang from his chair with a banshee-like cry and kicked with some violence, the cat's rear end, launching Pickles a full five feet into the air in the process. This action was accompanied by some squeals of protest from the flying pussy. And, while doing so, his Lordship stumbled and only just managed to avert falling over his chair.

Lady Gentry did not laugh, but sheraise her right hand to her mouth and did cough.

Her husband, his face a furious crimson. He glared at her with reddish and angry eyes and swore violently at her and the cat and screamed,

"Get that fucking moggy out of here, how many times do I

have to tell you he is not, repeat not permitted in the dining room woman."

Lady Gentry rose from her seat, her face flushed, her lips trembling, picked up Pickles, cradled the cat, commenced petting and stroking the animal and walked out of the room. As she gently stroked the cat and whispered so that her husband would not nuts again,

"Come on Pickles let's leave Lord Grumpy to himself. Such a naughty man, don't you think?"

His Lordship scowled as she closed door, sat down and carried on with his breakfast and The Times Newspaper.

James Brown, the butler, came quietly into the room, took one of the smaller dishes from the sideboard and Lady Gentry's teapot from the table. He went quietly out of the room, pausing at the door to scowl at his master's back. Olivia Gentry finished her breakfast in the sitting-room within her suite on the first floor. She was so attentive to Pickles, her affection for the cat was about the only love she was able to give. Her concern for its safety and her husband's behaviour weighed heavily on her mind. She was sure Pickles might lose one of his nine lives if she was not present.

During her breakfast, she put all consideration of her husband's behaviour out of her mind. As she smoked a cigarette after breakfast, she considered it for a little while. Too often of late, her mind had to consider her husband's rabid outbursts. Arriving at the conclusion to which she had usually come before, that she owed him nothing whatsoever. She further decided that she detested him. She possessed far too good a brain, not to be able to see the facts. Olivia wished more heartily than ever that she had never married him. It had been a grievous mistake, and it seemed likely to last a lifetime—her lifetime. She often contemplated whether his temper would snap, and she would suffer the consequences. The last five ancestors of her husband had lived to be eighty. His father would doubtless have lived to be eighty also, had he not broken his neck in the hunting-field at the age of fifty-four.

On the other hand, none of the Quinton's, her own family, had reached the age of sixty. Lord Egbert Peter Gentry was thirty-five; she was thirty-two; he would, therefore, survive her by at least seven years. She would undoubtedly be bowed down all her life under this grievous burden.

It was an odd calculation for a young married woman to make. Still, Lady Gentry came from an uncommon family, which had produced more brilliant, irresponsible, and passably unscrupulous men than any other of the leading families in England. Her father had been one of them. She took after him in that on occasions she was somewhat irresponsible. Moreover, Lord Gentry would have induced odd behaviour in any spouse. He had been intolerable since the second week of their honeymoon. Wholly without the power of self-restraint, furious outbursts of his vile temper had been consistently revolting. Once more she told herself that something would have to be done about it not at this instant, however. At the moment, there appeared to be months to do it. She dropped her cigarette end into the ash-tray and with it any further consideration of the infuriating manners and disposition of her consort.

She removed another cigarette from the packet, placing it between her lips and using the Zippo Lighter, inhaled the ignited tobacco and let her thoughts turn to that far more appealing subject, Colonel James Craig. What dreams she had, turned to him frequently and wholly? Instantly she was seeing his erudite face and hearing certain tones in his voice with fantastic clearness. Olivia looked at the clock impatiently. The time was now half-past ten. It would be almost three hours before her clandestine rendezvous. It seemed such a long while to her. However, she could go on thinking about him, and she did!

Olivia continued to consider her ill-tempered husband while doing so; her eyes had been stiff and almost shallow. While she thought of the handsome officer of the Guards, Colonel Craig, they grew soft and deep. Her lips set and almost thin, now they grew....well they felt, most kissable at this precise moment as the tip of her tongue licked her upper lip. Assured as she was of that, the gallant Officer and Gentleman would indeed plant his lips on her sweet mouth.

In the baronial Tudor dining room, Lord Gentry finished his breakfast, the scowl on his face fading slowly to a frown. He lit a cigar and with a moody air went to his smoking room. The criminal carelessness where the body was left still rankled. Not however as much as the front-page leader of The Times. As he entered the room, Mr Bert Mountfield, his secretary, bade him good morning. Lord Gentry returned his greeting with a scowl.

Bert Mountfield had one of those faces which began well and ended badly. He had a fair forehead, lofty and broad, a well-cut gently curving nose, a slack, thick-lipped mouth, always a little open, a heavy animal-like jaw, and the chin of an eagle. The shaggy fine, black hair was sparse on the temples. His moustache was thin and straggly. The ebony black eyes were that of an intelligent, observant, and alert fellow. It was plain that if his lips had been more delicate and his chin larger, he would not have been the secretary of Lord Gentry or anyone else. He would have been frankly, a masterless man. The one great attribute that Bert's possessed was his writing ability. The success of his two one-act plays on the stage of the local Towngate Theatre, which brought beautiful drama and much more to Basildon and Essex folk in general, was commendable. It had given him the firm hope of one day becoming a successful dramatist. This current post gave him the leisure to write plays.

But for the fact that it brought him into such frequent contact with Lord Gentry, it would have been an enjoyable post. The food from the kitchen, below stairs, was excellent, the wine was good, the library was passable, and the servants respected him. He had the art of making himself valued, (at far more than his real worth, some may comment) and his disposition of importance continually impressed others.

With a patient air, he began to discuss the morning's letters and ask for instructions. Lord Gentry was, as often happened, uncommonly captious about the letters. He had not recovered from the shock of the inconsiderate Pickles sinking his claws into his leg. The Times newspaper article concerned him much more than he cared to consider. His nerves at this moment were not good. The instructions he gave were somewhat chaotic, and when Mountfield tried to get them clearer, his employer swore at him as if he was an idiot. Bert Mountfield persisted firmly through much abuse until he did get them clear. Having concluded his employer's furies were an unfortunate weakness, which had to be endured by the holder of the post he found so advantageous. He bore them with what stoicism he might.

Lord Gentry, in an awful patina, always produced a strong impression of redness for a man whose colouring was merely red-brown. Because his fierce, protruding blue eyes were red-rimmed and somewhat bloodshot from the copious carafes of red wine and port he quaffed daily. During moments of emotion, they shone with a curious red glint, and his florid face flushed a deeper red. In these nanoseconds, Bert had a feeling that he was dealing with a bad-tempered Spanish bullfighter. Could he kill someone who angered him sufficiently? Mountfield considered he had a strong inclination to do so with little forethought. His employer made much the same impression on other people. Bert was pretty convinced that Lady Gentry always felt that way, whether her husband was ramping or quiet that she was dealing with a bad-tempered bull an English one at that.

Presently they came to the end of the letters. Lord Gentry lit another cigar and scowled thoughtfully. Bert gazed at his scowling face and wondered whether he would ever meet another human being whom he would detest as heartily as he excreted his employer.

A profound thought it indeed unlikely. Life at Ingatestone Hall would be so much sweeter if his master were gone, but then he would be unemployed and not able to spend so much time writing his plays. He was much better off continuing to cajole Lord Gentry. Still, when he became a successful dramatist, he would be such a famous writer, producer and director. Alas, his daydreams were interrupted when the brute interjected.

Gentry said,

"Did you tell Helena Green that, after September her pay and allowance was to be reduced to twenty-five-thousand and five- hundred a year?"

"Yes, My Lord"

said Bert Mountfield.

"What did she say?"

Bert Mountfield hesitated, and then he said diplomatically:

"She did not seem to like it."

"What did she say, man?"

Cried Lord Gentry in a sudden, startling bellow his eyes shone red again.

Bert Mountfield winced a little and said quickly,

"She said it was just like you."

"Just like me? Hey? And what did she mean by that?"

Gentry shrieked loudly and angrily.

Bert Mountfield expressed utter ignorance by looking blank and shrugging his shoulders.

"The cheeky, Brood Jade! She's had fifty thousand a year for more than two years. Did she think it would go on forever?"

His employer was now more red-faced than before. Goodness knows what his blood pressure was during these temper outbursts.

"I dare say she must have, My Lord."

Mountfield replied in an apprehensive could not care less tone.

"And why did she think it would go on forever?"

Said, Lord Gentry in yet another challenging tone.

"Because she mentioned that there wasn't an actual deed of settlement,"

said Bert Mountfield with a smirk on his face.

"The ungrateful, Jade! I have a good mind to stop it altogether!"

Exclaimed, His Lordship in an even louder tone!

Bert Mountfield said nothing. His face was blank, and neither showed that he no more approved nor disapproved the suggestion. He was well aware that his Lordships use of the urban terminology Jade is for a girl who is someone you are blessed to have in your life. She can go through hell but always gets back on her feet and shows the world she is strong enough of mind and character.

Lord Gentry scowled at him and said,

"I expect she said she wished she'd never had anything to do with me."

"No!"

Mountfield lied in his reply.

"I'll bet that's what she thinks."

Lord Gentry growled like a hound.

Bert let the suggestion pass without comment. His face was blank, best he thought, not to get too involved as he would blow a gasket if he were aware of his relationship with the lady under discussion. Even Sherlock Holmes, 'The Hounds of the Baskervilles,' never made such a noise as his master.

"And what's she going to do about it?"

Said, Lord Gentry, in a challenging manner.

"I believe she wishes to see you about it."

"I'm damned if she is!"

Lord Gentry replied hastily, however in a much less confident tone.

Bert Mountfield permitted a faint, sceptical smile to wreathe his lips.

"What are you grinning at? If you think she'll gain anything by doing that, she won't,"

Lord Gentry responded, with a blustering truculence.

Mountfield was aware that Helena Green was a lady of considerable force of character. His suspicion that if Lord Gentry had ever been afraid of a fellow-creature, he must at times have been fearful of Helena Green. He fancied that now his master was not nearly as fearless as he sounded. However, Bert was forever mindful not to reveal these thoughts.

His employer was silent, buried in scowling reflection. Bert gazed at him without any great intentness, and came to the conclusion that he did not merely detest him, he loathed him.

Presently he said,

"There's a cheque for your stockbroker for twelve thousand and forty-six pounds for the rubber shares your Lordship bought. It requires endorsing."

He handed the cheque across the table. Gentry dipped his pen into the inkpot; his eyes were transfixed by a struggling bluebottle floating in the Inkwell and doing all it could to escape this dark blue lagoon.

"Why the devil don't you see that the ink is fresh?"

He roared.

"It is fresh. The bluebottle must have just fallen into it, my Lord."

Bert said, in a could not care less and unruffled tone.

Lord Gentry cursed the bluebottle, speared the bluebottle with the tip of his pen and restored the dear insect to the inkpot. He endorsed the cheque and blew on it to dry the ink and tossed it across the table to Bert.

"By the way, your Lordship,"

Said Bert, with some hesitation,

"There's another anonymous letter."

"Why didn't you burn it? I told you to burn them all."

Snapped, his employer.

"This one is not about you. It's about Markham,"

said Bert Mountfield in an explanatory tone.

"Markham? What about Markham?"

"You'd better read it, your Grace."

He was well aware that he seldom used this title whenever speaking to his master, and then only when he was seeking something. Bert handed him the letter and commented,

"It seems to be from some spiteful woman."

The letter indeed was written in what appeared to be soft female handwriting, and it accused the senior butler. It was well written and wordily enough. That was having received a commission from Majestic wine merchants on the purchase of three dozen magnums of champagne, which he had bought from them a month before. It further stated that he had received a like commission on many other such purchases.

Lord Gentry read it and scowling, sprang up from his chair with his eyes protruding further than usual, and cried,

"The scoundrel! The blackguard! I'll teach him! I'll have him locked up in The Tower of London for this!"

Peter Gentry in a fit of temper dashed to the electric bell by the fireplace, set his thumb on it and kept it there. It's ringing transmitted throughout Ingatestone Hall. Indeed the villagers could probably hear them

Davidson, the second footman, came running. The servants knew their master's ring. They always ran to answer it, from experience as a permanent ring was clearly from their impatient master following some serious discussion as to which of them should go.

He entered and said:

"Yes, M'Lord?"

"Send that scoundrel Markham to me! Send him at once!"

Roared, his master.

"Yes, M'Lord."

Davidson said as he hurried away.

He found Markham in his pantry, told him that their master wanted him, and added that he was in a tearing rage.

Markham, who never expected his sanguine and irascible master to be in any other mood, he finished the paragraph of the article in the Daily Telegraph he was reading, about some poor girl being found dead in Romford. He put on his tailcoat and went to the study. His delay gave Lord Gentry's wrath full time to ferment and mature.

When the butler entered his master shook his fist at him and roared,

"You scoundrel! You are an infernal miscreant! You've been robbing me! You have been tricking me for years, you good-for-nothing wretch!"

Markham met the charge with complete calm. He shook his head and said in a surly tone,

"No; I haven't done anything of the kind, M'Lord."

The flat denial infuriated his master even more. Lord Gentry spluttered and was for a while, quite incoherent. Then he became articulate again and said,

"You have, you rogue! You took a commission a secret

commission on that three dozen of champagne I bought last month. You've been doing it for years."

Markham's, pouty face was transformed. It grew malignant, his fierce protruding, red-rimmed blue eyes sparkled balefully, and he flushed to redness as deep as that of his master. He knew at once who had betrayed him, and he was furious at the betrayal. At the same time, he was not greatly alarmed, for he had never received a cheque from the wine merchants. All their payments to him had been cash in hand, and he had always cherished a warm contempt for his master.

"I haven't, and I am confident there is no proof of such."

He responded fiercely.

"And if I had it would be quite regular, only a prerequisite."

For the hundredth time, Bert Mountfield thought of the homogeneity between Lord Gentry and his butler. They certainly had the same fierce, protruding, red-rimmed blue eyes, similar narrow, low foreheads, and identical large ears. The hair was of a darker brown than Lord Gentry, and his lips thinner. Nevertheless, Bert Mountfield was sure that, had he worn a goatee beard instead of whiskers, it would have been difficult for many people to be sure which was Lord Gentry and which his butler.

Gentry again spluttered, then he roared:

"A bloody prerequisite more like you received a reward for the order! What about the Corrupt Practices Act? It was passed for rogues like you! I'll show you all about prerequisites! You'll find yourself incarcerated inside of a month."

"I shan't. There isn't a word of truth in it or a scrap of Evidence.

Markham retaliated the now overconfident accused thief, fiercely.

"Evidence you say. I'll find Evidence all right!"

Cried his master,

"And if I don't, I'll discharge you without a character reference. I will get you one way or another, my fine fellow! I'll teach you to rob me!"

"I haven't robbed your lordship."

Markham uttered, in a less moody and more agreeable tone. He was more worried about the threat of discharge than the risk of prosecution.

"I tell you…..you have. You can clear out of this house. I'll email to town at once for another butler an honest butler. You'll clear out the moment he comes. Pack up and be ready to go and when you do go, I'll give you another twenty-four hours to clear out of the county before I put the police on your track."

Thundered the exasperated, Lord Gentry.

Nevertheless, Bert Mountfield observed that it was exactly like him to take no risk, despite his fury, of any loss of comfort from the lack of a butler. The instinct of self-protection was indeed strong in him.

"Not a bit of it M'Lord. You've told me to go, and I'm going at once this very day. The police will find me at my father's for the next fortnight.

Said Markham with a sneer.

"And when I go to London. I will leave my address with Mr Mountfield."

"A lot of good you're going to London will do you. I'll see you never get another head butler placement in this country,"

Snarled, Lord Gentry.

Markham gave him a look of venomous malignity so intense that it made Bert quite uncomfortable, turned, and went out of the room.

Lord Gentry shouted at him as he disappeared from view,

"I'll teach the scoundrel to rob me! Write at once for a new butler Mountfield."

He took some lumps of sugar from a jar on the mantelpiece.

He went through the door which opened into the library. On reaching the library, he stopped and bellowed back to him,

"If Morton comes about the timber, I shall be in the stables."

Then he went through one of the long window doors of the library into the garden and walked briskly to the stables. As he drew near them, the scowl cleared from his face. But it remained a formidable face; it seldom grew pleasant. Nonetheless, he spent a pleasant hour in the stables, petting his horses. He was fond of horses, they demanded respect, and he never bullied and seldom abused his horses as he mistreated and bullied his fellow men and women. He had learnt from experience that he might bully and abuse his human dependents with impunity. As a young boy, he had also mishandled and abused his horses. However, in his eighteenth year, he had been savaged by a young horse he had maltreated. The lesson had forever stuck in his mind. It was a simple, obtuse mind, but it had formed the theory that he got more out of human beings, more deference and service, by bullying them and more out of horses by treating them kindly. Besides, he liked horses.

BERT MOUNTFIELD DID NOT SET about answering the letters at once. He reflected for a while on the likeness between Markham and his master. As a consequence, he thought the physical resemblance of little interest. There was a whole clan of Markham's in the villages and cottages within the woods around the Estate and Ingatestone. He was much more interested in the resemblance in character between Markham and Lord Gentry. Markham, probably under the pressure of circumstances, was much less of a bore than his master, but quite as much of a bully. Also, he was more intelligent, and consequently more dangerous. Bert would on no account have had him look at him with the intense malignity with which he had looked at his master. Doubtless, the butler had far greater self-control than Gentry, but if ever he did lose it the result would be uncommonly bad for Lord Gentry for Markham was ferocious. But was he not sacked this morning? Surely that put an end to the two bulls going at one another in the future. It would be interesting to find in the family archives, the common ancestor to whom they both cast so directly back too. He fancied that it must be the third Baron.

His task now was to set about reading and sorting out today's post. When he had finished them, he took up the stockbroker's cheque and considered it with a thoughtful frown. Then he wrote a short note of instructions to Lord Gentry's bankers. The ink in his fountain pen ran out as he came to the end of it, and he signed it with the pen with which Lord Gentry had endorsed the cheque. The dead bluebottle was still floating around in the Inkwell. Using the pen nib, he speared the wretched thing again, saving it the pain of drowning. He put the cheque into the envelope he had already addressed, put stamps on all the letters, carried them to the post-box on a table in the hall, went through the library and out into the garden. Following this, he went to the library and took up his task of cataloguing the books. He often paused; he did not believe in hasty work.

Bert was quite unaware that Lord Gentry's mood had commenced as he had read the Times Headline article. The Ritual Murder of a girl in Romford had everything to do with him, and his friends and members within the cult. The French, 'Ordre De La Rose,' did not suffer errors and Lord Gentry the Master had to deal with this one, which had made the National Press.

CHAPTER 7
THE CHAMBER

James Pratchett rented a four-bedroom detached house with a rear garden located at Number One, Dorrington Gardens, Hornchurch. It was owned and managed by Syed Tajammal Hussain, a British Citizen, who was born and raised in Karachi, the former Capital of Pakistan. James had managed to secure an excellent letting arrangement with little or no background inquiry. It was made simple and attractive by the fact that he had offered to rent it for twelve months and paid cash.

Following his abduction of the Samaritan, Mrs Robinson Gwynn was now his and his alone. She was currently incarcerated in his specially prepared love nest. It had taken six long months to ensure it was acceptable and substantially soundproofed. The air-conditioning had been a significant challenge. Testing had proved difficult nevertheless; now, he was confident it was safe for his beloved. The lightning was a scintillating feature of the auto-changing movement-controlled system. The video surveillance setup was in his estimation superb, and he could watch and record her at his behest. However, there is no way a woman could live down below ground without two essentials, water and a toilet! So he purchased a luminous seated bathroom waste device coupled with a macerator and drainpipe attached to his household waste. The bed was the most comfortable, 'Silent Dreams Orthopaedic Mattress,' he could purchase. She would be very comfortable. That was essential for such a beautiful mature lady after all Gwynn deserved the best. He had contemplated installing a shower. However, that would have proved too difficult. As for lighting, he had established an overhead red lamp that would not interfere with the Video recording.

She was on the bed, having recovered from the sleeping agent he had used. Confused and tearful of course, what else would you expect in her circumstances? It took her some time to regain all her faculties; slowly, her eyes became accustomed to the surroundings in due course. In the bleak single red light located in the center of the room, it was gradually coming to her that she had been abducted. The last recollection was clicking the car fob.......then, nothing, blackness. The sudden realisation resulted in her screaming at the top of her voice. In an attempt to alert someone, any person in the vicinity?

"Where am I?"

"Where am I?"

Gwynn screamed at the top of her voice she was frantic and oh so afraid.

Alas, it was all in vain as he had insulated the walls by firstly erecting four by two-inch wooden vertical posts floor to ceiling. Also using Acousiblok rock wool between each upright, he finished it off by applying similar acoustic half-inch thick material of a decibel rating of 25db. The best professionally used and guaranteed to cut out all sound even that of a piston air-handling machine or, to put it more forcibly, the Rolling Stones with Mick Jagger singing his head off, would not be heard on the other side of this insulated construction. So, a whimpering, almost naked woman had no chance of being listened to.

He viewed her on three fifty-inch screens located in his control room, and he could ensure complete predomination of her environment. She did look rather attractive with only her bra and panties as clothing. With one flick of the Pressel switch, he was able to speak into the Professional Condenser Microphone. The distortion facility converted the audio sound to anything but human. almost similar to the voice in the movie, 'SAW,'

"Hello Gwynn, please do not be terrified, you are safe here in my home."

She reacted to the message by curling up in the fetal position with her knees under her chin in horror.

He communicated once more through the device,

"You are going to be a good girl now Gwynn, are you not? I have not invited you here for you to misbehave. You know how you like folk to behave, don't you Gwynn?"

Remaining in the curled-up position on the bed, she remained quiet but continued to whimper. Her stress was apparent on the screens. Leaving her to continue to snivel for a full 5 minutes until she settled down again just as she was breathing evenly once more, he voiced in a whisper,

"You are going..... To enjoy this experience, Gwynn. I promise you will want to remain with me forever once we are married!"

She was horrified by this statement, but on appraising it as she had during her Samaritans Induction Training, it gave her a little confidence that at least she was not about to be killed, whatever else her captor had in his sick mind. Was it a man, the voice distortion made it challenging to appraise. Indeed, it had to be male as it spoke of marriage and that surely would hardly come from a female.

The voice again interrupted her train of thought.

"Gwynne darling, if you require something to drink it is in the receptacle box which you should locate with ease. There is a bottle of Evian water. Also, if you look to your right, there is a small cubicle, and inside there is your very own toilet. Please do remember to flush it or the smell may become severe. Now proceeding on, I have no doubt you may be feeling hungry, are you?"

She remained silent for some time bewildered if she needed food. Seeking the opportunity to engage with whomever this monster was, she replied.

"Yes, I am."

"No Problem, I will place some food on a tray for you, would you prefer coffee or tea?"

"Yes... Yes, Tea, please."

"No Problem, Gwynnie, give me five minutes while I rustle something up for you."

The room again fell silent. It was deafening, the complete absence of sound as she contemplated her dilemma. What was to be her fate, would she escape, how was he to marry her, would he want sex, was she to be violated and raped and so it went on and on and on. Just how long had she been a captive, she had no idea as she evaluated her situation. The chamber only had one red light, one toilet, one box containing drinking water and this comfortable bed. With great uneasiness and foreboding Gwynn lifted her feet and gingerly placed them on the floor. To her pleasant surprise, it was covered in a relatively lush carpet. She made for the box and opened the lid, inside as her captor had stated, was a large sports bottle of Evian water. Flicking the top and taking it to her mouth, she gulped down almost half the contents. Ambling towards the cubicle devoid of any door for privacy, on entry, she noted that it was immaculate and clean with the initials on the top, RAK. Suddenly her memory kicked in. Were those initials RAK stand for one of the United Arab Emirates, yes that was it, Ras Al Khaimah she remembered that from a holiday many years ago she and her husband visited the Emirate when holidaying in Dubai. They had visited the Ceramic Factory, where these toilets we manufactured. She used the ablution and remembered his command and flushed it.

She made her way back gingerly to the bed and sat with the half-full bottle of water in her right hand. Her mind was not unexpectedly racing. Not unnaturally, she felt rather exposed clad only in bra and pants and without thinking folded her arms across her breasts in a sort of protective manner. Just as her mind was wandering once more, the awful twisted voice disturbed her train of thought.

"Gwynn, darling if you go to the receptacle by the door you will find some food. I trust it is to your liking. Please do enjoy it and I will speak to you later once you have eaten."

James was careful not to mention whether it was breakfast, lunch or dinner as such an error would assist her to determine the time of day. The imbibed lack of time was all part of the dissociation process before interrogation. The training course within his special forces combat survival and interrogation had not been wasted.

Once more she made for the box, and sure enough on lifting the lid, there was a paper plate containing two buttered crumpets, a polystyrene cup containing hot Tea with milk added. Removing them from the box, she made her way back to the bed. The Tea was acceptable and tasted fine; she ate the two crumpets. They were delicious, and the liquid gave her a feeling that perhaps, she may survive this ordeal. As she finished drinking the Tea, suddenly the room seemed to be spinning, and a sense of light-headedness and disorientation abounded. At that moment, she managed to place her head on the pillow before blacking out. He observed the drug had induced the unconsciousness he sought.

On entering the cellar room via the concealed door, he gained access to the room. James was buck-naked except for a black face mask with appropriate holes for his nose and mouth. He had been taught that an operative no matter what the role-play should not be too careful. James made his way to the bed, removed the breakfast items, and placed them in the box that contained the secret door enabling him to deliver food and drinks to his captive. James returned to the bed; he lay beside Gwynn, removing her scant clothing, and then commenced, kissing and caressing her luscious body. She certainly was a cougar but a beautiful one at that. The definition of this being a powerful tawny-brown cat was apt for her. The 'Venus Mound' was certainly awaiting exploration. Well aware that Pop Culture stated that a cougar woman was predatory and pathetically desperate. However, he was aware that women have recently begun fighting this stereotype: cougars, they argue, are confident, successful, women over the age of 50, and she was certainly all of that.

The Tea containing the date rape odorless Flunitrazepam, commonly known as Rohypnol, had the desired effect. Such was the effect it could last for two hours and may even persist for up to eight hours. Gwynn would have no memory of what happened while under the drug's influence. To think that the tablets he purchased only cost him five pounds each, it was twenty pounds well spent on the black market in Romford. Anyway, he was hoping that two tablets, when ground down to powder and mixed with Tea, would be sufficient for her to be unaware of what occurred while fulfilling his sexual need to be satisfied.

He carried on kissing her, letting his tongue search into her soft, tasty mouth, but the lack of response somewhat perturbed him, he wanted a reaction, and none was forthcoming. Nevertheless, he carried on fondling her breasts which for a woman of her age were surprisingly firm. He tweaked her nipples between his forefinger and thumb and was surprised to notice that her nipples became erect from his soft touch. That affected him, and his penis began to become aroused and stiff. He was whispering in her ear how much he admired her for such a long time. He so wanted her to be aware of his lust over the last six months. His numerous failed telephone chats to the Samaritans were about to be fulfilled. It culminated in this passionate embrace. Of course, Gwynn was blissfully unaware of these sweet mutterings. His hand slid between her legs and probed her vagina, which not unsurprisingly, was dry. He reached for the lubricant casually reading the label. He had no idea why he did this, but the name on the plastic bottle was, 'Durex Play Tingle Lube!' James was not about to use a Durex sheath for protection. After all, at her age, she was hardly going to end up with a child! He was going to enjoy fucking her as many time as he wished. Squeezing sufficient lubricant into her cunt he assessed it would make her easier for penetration. As he took hold of his bulbous manhood guided it and entered her vagina with great delight, having achieved his conquest. The rhythm commenced slowly, but it was a one-horse coupling as the filly beneath him was not responding to his verbal instructions. His movement quickened, and his breathing surpassed this action and pretty much in no time at all, he had practiced his Roman Catholic upbringing. 'Coitus Interruptus,' occurred as he removed his penis from her and ejaculated over her breasts. It was a crying shame she was not awake to appreciate his expertise in fucking.

Was he satisfied? He thought so but felt he would have liked her to be a little more awake so that the reaction would have been better. He thought perhaps next time I will reduce the portion of tablets to one-and-a-half if that was feasible. He proceeded to wash her down, ensuring that he cleaned her vaginal tract as he did not wish her to know what had happened when she came around. He replaced her bra and panties, placing Gwynn on her back with the head placed on the pillow.

Checking that everything was as it was before his almost satisfactory sexual session, he left the room and made for his control room. On running back, to the VCR, he sat on the brown leather armchair with a cold beer and watched himself perform what in effect was his own, 'Pornographic Movie.' He mused I must do better next time. Next time this had to be corrected.

CHAPTER 8
LADY OLIVIA GENTRY

Lord Gentry following the problem conveyed so prominently in that morning's 'Times Newspaper,' had left instructions that he would be out for the entire afternoon. He was therefore not expected to return to Ingatestone Hall until well after six in the evening. The chef was informed that he would have dinner with his wife at eight that evening. His driver had prepared the Rolls-Royce Phantom 6.7 litre - four-door luxury on wheels, for the trip and was awaiting his master as instructed.

Amongst the collection of portraits at Ingatestone Hall, is one of a former, 'Earl of Gentry,' standing proudly in his uniform. The caption on the plaque at the base of the enormous gold frame was that of Colonel (The Lord) Fredrick David Charles Gentry, 44th Regiment of Foot (East Essex) 1890. Connoisseurs of the nineteenth-century art ascribed it to Leonardo da Vinci. The next portrait adorning the wall was a quite alluring head and shoulders portrait of a beautiful young woman. It was between two older paintings of former Lord's Gentries. Lady Gentry's parents had gifted this portrait. The art historians of the twentieth century ascribed this one to

Bernardino Luina, the master of fresco work. Apart from the colour of the hair, it might have been a portrait of Lady Gentry, albeit a slightly faded image. It was such a resemblance to Olivia and was one of her actual ancestors. The appearance was a lady of an ancient Tuscan family origin, and Olivia had inherited her looks. It was not uncommon for the servants to comment that she was 'La Bella Figura,' literally saying, 'the beautiful figure!' She indeed sported a delicate frame.

Be that as it may, Lady Gentry had soft, dark, dreamy eyes. They were set relatively wide apart, her straight, delicate nose, the alluring lips, promising all the kisses, available. The broad, well-moulded forehead and the faint, curving eyebrows were similar to the girl in the picture. Above all, when Lord Gentry was not present, the mysterious, enchanting, lingering smile was always apparent. That smile, which is perhaps the chief charm of Luini's women, nearly always rested on her face. Bernardino Luni was an artist during the same era as Leonardo Da-Vinci. Known primarily for his graceful female figures with elongated eyes, however, while the hair of the girl in the picture is a deep, dull red, the natural curls of Olivia's hair were blonde with glimmers of gold in it. The colouring was warmer than that of the girl in the picture, and her alluring charm so much stronger.

At a quarter to three that afternoon, she came out on to the east lawn in a silk blouse and floral summer skirt and hat of green, rather sombre for the summer day. She had been advised by a fashionable fortune-teller never to wear green, for it was her unlucky colour. But that tint had so given her colouring its full values and her dark, liquid eyes so deep a depth; she had paid no heed to that warning. Olivia preferred pastel colours in the fabrics she chooses to wear. Pastel coloured clothing was her favourite for they highlighted her stunning beauty. There was a bright light of expectation in her startling blue eyes, and the alluring smile lingered on her face.

She walked quickly across the lawn with the comfortable, graceful gait akin to the accomplished golfer she was, darting quickly into the shrubbery on the other side of it a few feet along the path she looked sharply back over her shoulder. Observing no one at those windows of the East wing which looked on to the lawn and shrubbery, but a movement on the property itself caught her eye. The cat Pickles was following her. She did not slacken her swift pace, but for a moment, the smile faded from her face at the remembrance of her husband's outburst at breakfast. Then the smile returned, subtle, yet expectant.

She did not wait for her moggie. The cat frequently followed her as a dog would. Others perceived it as being somewhat strange for a cat. She knew that if she displayed no interest in him, the cat would probably come no further. Olivia carried on at the same brisk pace until she came to the gate in the East wood. Opening the ring handled gate latch, she went through, shut it gently, paused and again looked backwards. The entire path through the shrubbery that all that could be observed was empty. Turning as she walked briskly along the narrow way, passing through the wood, she came into the long, turf-paved aisle which ran at right angles to it.

The wheels of the numerous carts deeply rutted the middle of the aisle. These carried away the timber from the spring thinning of the woods. The lavender was commencing its first growth. She turned to the left and sauntered carefreely up the smooth turf along the side of the aisle, with a brighter light of expectation in her eyes, her smile even more mysterious and alluring. The scent of lavender in the air abounded. She had not gone fifty yards up the aisle when Colonel James Craig, VC, came limping out of the entrance of a path on the other side of those mentioned. The Guards Officer quickened his pace as he crossed it.

The Victoria Cross is the highest and most prestigious award for gallantry, in the face of the enemy. It was only awarded to any of the United Kingdom, British and Commonwealth forces. Lieutenant Colonel James Craig was a serving officer in the Scots Guards. His limp was caused by the gunshot wound he received while going to the aid of his wounded Sergeant in Afghanistan. The high-velocity round had clipped his left gastrocnemius muscle, ripping it almost to shreds. Recovery was a protracted affair, and it had been touch and go, whether he would ever be able to continue his career. His determination, coupled with the intense long months of physiotherapy at the rehabilitation centre, as well as two months in the Swiss Alps, had succeeded. He reflected the whole period was made more bearable due to the location of Headly Court, in the leafy lanes of Surrey.

She stood still, flushing faintly, gazing at him with her lips parted a little. He looked so very young to be a Lieutenant-Colonel and uncommonly fragile for a V.C. At any time, he would look delicate, and he was the paler for the fact that at times he still suffered considerable pain from his wounds. But there was a force in his soft yet rugged and distinguished face. His lips were set very firm, his chin was square and highlighted in the middle was a dimple. His nose had a rather heavy bridge; his eyes were cold and very keen. He gave the impression of being wrought of finely-tempered Sheffield steel.

His eyes were shining so brightly at this particular moment. They had lost their keenness with their coldness exposed during the war in Afghanistan, and some may say they wept for the men he had lost in battle. Of course, some assessed this was as a result of his chronic pain. He joyfully noted the flush on

Olivia's face and did not know that he was a little aglow himself. When he was about five feet away, he stopped, gazing, or rather staring, at her, and said in a tone of earnest conviction:

"Heavens, Olivia! What a beautiful and enchanting creature you are!"

She smiled, blushing more profoundly and stepped forward, taking his hand, and holding it very tightly.

"Goodness, James! But I have been impatient for you to be with me!"

"I'm not late, am I?"

He said in a welcoming manner as he took hold of her delicate hand and staired into her eyes.

As he let go of her hand and said:

"But you saw me for three hours yesterday,"

she said in her low, sweet, rather drawling yet teasing voice

"I don't know why it is, but I've been as restless as a cat on a hot tin roof all morning. I'm never sure that you will be able to come, and the uncertainty worries me. Yesterday, that was twenty-four hours since I enjoyed your presence."

"Yesterday feels like an eternity away. I wasn't sure that you'd come today."

"Why shouldn't I come?"

He said, falling into step with her.

"Gentry the cad might have got to know of it, and stopped you coming."

"Fortunately, he doesn't take enough interest in my doings. Of course, if I didn't turn up at a meal, he'd make a fuss, though why he should make such a point of our having all our meals together I can't conceive. I should certainly enjoy mine much more if I had them in my sitting-room, or better still with you."

She said in a dispassionate tone, for the entire world as if she were discussing the situation of someone else.

"I am so worried about you,"

he said with a harassed air.

"Ever since that evening, I heard him bullying you during the baccarat drinks party. I've been simply worried to death about it. Had the wonderful, Duke of Buccleuch, Michael Scott and his charming wife Duchess Veronica not been present, I dare say his behaviour would have been more outrageous. As it was, he caused great consternation to all present."

"It was nice of you to interfere, but it was a pity,"

she said gently.

"It didn't do any good as far as his behaviour was concerned, and we see so much more of one another when you can come to Ingatestone Hall. It's good that he spends so much time away with his secret society stuff, which incidentally, I still have no idea what it is all about; however, to be frank, I could not care less."

"Then you do want to see more of me?"

He said teasingly.

Lady Gentry lost her smiling air; she became demureness itself, and she said:

"Well, you see—thanks to Egbert's vile temper—we have so few friends."

Craig frowned; she was always quick to elude him. Then he growled:

"What a name! Egbert, it's no wonder he uses his second name, Peter! It's so old-fashioned, and it was Egbert, King of Wessex who fought and lost his land to the Vikings."

"He can't help it was given him, by his parents, and that name has run along with his family for generations. Besides, as I say, it's but a family name,"

she said in a tone of fine impartiality.

"What if it would be Eardwulf, I believe it's the old Anglo-Saxon term for the land wolf. That would suit him perfectly, snarling and bad-tempered!"

Said Craig contemptuously.

They went on a few steps in silence both in deep thought, then she said:

"Besides, I don't mind his outbursts. I'm used to them."

"I don't believe it! You're much too delicate and sensitive!"

He said.

"But I am getting used to them,"

she protested.

"You never will. I think that Gentry has been bullying you again?"

He commented once more, looking anxiously into her eyes.

"Not more than usual,"

she replied, in a wholly indifferent tone.

"Then it is usual! I was afraid it was,"

He muttered in a miserable voice.

"What on earth is to be done about it?"

"Why, there's nothing to be done, except just grin and bear it,"

she said bravely enough, with the conviction of one who has thought the matter out thoroughly.

"Then it's monstrous! Just dreadful and I dare say perhaps violent at times. It does concern me daily. That you the most charming and loveliest creature in the world should be bullied by that infernal brute!"

He exclaimed as he put his arm around her.

The Countess was deep in dreamland when her faithful cat came out of the bushes a dozen yards ahead of them, and with a small furry creature between its teeth. Then came a very distinct and ugly vision of Lord Gentry's flushed, distorted, and revolting face as he swore at her during breakfast that morning. She did not slip out of the encircling arm. James bent his head and kissed her lightly on the lips. It was the gentlest, lightest kiss, the kiss he might have given a pretty child, just a natural tribute to her beauty and charm.

As he withdrew from her lips, his admiration was full of wanting, could he control his deep desire? James could not have contemplated what was about to occur. With force, he had failed to anticipate, without warning Olivia, enveloped his torso and sank to her knees onto the lush grass. His only option was to buckle with her. Presently she was on her back and him in a prone position on top of her.

There eschewed but a nanosecond before their mouths were entwined in a most passionate kiss. Colonel James Craig was attempting to be an officer and a gentleman. Nonetheless, his unbridled passion knew no bounds. The scent of the Lavender pods was heavy in the air; it surrounded them; it was palpable. He was like a rampant panther, slowly encircling its prey as his tongue, like that of a spitting cobra darted into her mouth.

They were as one, oblivious to their surroundings! Swiftly, they manoeuvred, groping each other with prying desperate exploring hands, searching in haste to remove the impeding restrictive clothing. Her fragrant aroma heightened their excitement. The thrill of wanting, the tingles of excitement, the jittery nerves, and the infatuation was with them both. Olivia did not know what made the change.

Nevertheless looking up at his handsome face, she felt herself becoming wet. It came from inside, and felt her vaginal mucus flowing, giving out that secretion liquid. He smiled down at her, and it was clear to both that there was no turning back.

James opened her blouse slowly, twisting each button with his thumb and third finger, and then running his finger along her breastbone. When her dress top finally fell open, he studied her, and then gently caressed her breasts. Licking her nipples and then moved his tongue slowly down her stomach. Olivia couldn't have cared less if he was not her husband; she could not remember the last time she had experienced such warmth. James lifted her skirt then removed her silk panties and kissing her just above her pubic bone; he slipped two fingers inside her, she was moist, ready. Olivia moved into his hands until he stopped suddenly, removing his fingers as if he had thought better of the whole thing. She propped herself up on her elbows to see what had happened. James got up and opened his wallet. Was he moving to pay her? Before sex, surely not? Or worse and now she thought of Midnight Cowboy; that film had so scandalised her. Indeed, he was not expecting to pay her? With that, he removed a protective sheath placed the cover between his teeth and ripped the top off, exposing the lubricated Durex.

With real professionalism of an experienced suitor he applied, the sheath to his erect penis in the blink of an eye. Her legs were still akimbo awaiting deep penetration, and he did not disappoint. Her exclamations of sheer pleasure were audible until she climaxed in a writhing wreck of passion. Anyone passing would have been aghast at this disgraceful public behaviour. However, that was unlikely as this was private land. Their rumpy-pumpy had not gone unnoticed. James was at that moment, letting his semen fill the bag as his final thrust took place. Immediately it caused her to climax once more with a whimper of joy. As the officer and gentleman, he was. His sensual expertise having provided her with complete accomplished satisfaction. They embraced and kissed; she was so satisfied that she thought how lovely it would be to repeat this as soon as humanly possible.

However, the harm had been done. The population of Great Britain cannot be more than one and a half persons to the acre. The great majority, of them, live in thousands to the acre, in towns; yet it is indeed challenging to kiss a girl during the daytime in any given acre. However thickly wooded, without being seen by some superfluous sojourner on that acre; and whether or not, it was that of the green frock and hat that the Countess wore. She was well aware it was her bad luck colour. The fortune-teller had foretold this several years ago. Alas, there was a witness to that kiss and unbridled love-making. When you're riding the height of love, your smile always meets your ears, and you have that warm, tingly feeling in the pit of your stomach. In Olivia and James case, this digression would come back to haunt them both.

Undoubtedly, too it was not only Pickles her cat who sat close during the entire sexual intercourse, Unfortunately, but it was also not the right kind of witness. If it had been an indulgent elder not given to gossip, or a polite young man not averse to kisses himself, all might have been well. But William Roper, under-gamekeeper, was a young man without a spark of chivalry in him, and he had been soured in the matter of kisses by the steadfast resolve of the young women of Ingatestone Town and the surrounding villages. He was an unattractive young man, not unlike the ferrets he kept at his cottage. He was the last young man in the world, or at any rate in the neighbourhood, to stay silent about what he had just witnessed.

Even so, no great harm might have arisen. He might have blabbed about the matter in the village pub. The whole village and the servants of the Hall might have talked about it for weeks and months or even years, without it ever reaching the ears of Lord Gentry. But alas, William Roper saw in that kiss and open-air sexual activity, what he thought was a wealth of an Olympic proportion. It was to be his royal road and gold medal to wealth. Ambitious for sure, but he was not content with his post of under-gamekeeper; he desired to oust Bob Hutchings from the position of head gamekeeper. Though there were two other under-gamekeeper's senior to him with a more extraordinary claim on that post, he would occupy it himself.

For here was the way to it. His Lordship could not but be grateful to the man who informed him of such goings-on. Undoubtedly, he could not but award and promote him to the post he coveted. Gratitude was not one of Lord Gentry's attributes, but how could he fail to elevate such a loyal subject and employee?

Olivia slipped out of Craig's arms, and they walked up the grass aisle. But they walked along, as completely changed creatures—trembling with spent excitement, a little bemused. Colonel Craig was after all the proud holder of the Victoria Cross for bravery, but cheating on Lord Gentry with his wife in the open air was sure to lead to drama, both within and without his beloved Scots Guards.

William Roper, the ill-favoured minister of nemesis, continued to follow them at a reasonable distance.

At the top of the aisle, they came to the sumptuous Pavilion, a small white marble building in the Classic Indian style, standing in the middle of a broad glade which would in a few months, would be covered in the colour of deep purple and the scented lavender.

As they went into it, Olivia said wistfully:

"It's a pity I couldn't have tea sent here."

"I did. At least I have brought it with me,"

said Craig, waving his hand towards the pre-positioned basket which stood on the table.

"I knew you'd be happier for tea rather than champagne in the afternoon."

"No one has ever been as thoughtful of me as you are,"

she said, gazing at him with grateful, yet slightly troubled eyes.

"Let's hope that your luck is changing,"

he said gravely, gazing at her with eyes no less troubled.

Then her pussy scratched at the door and meowed. Olivia

let him in. Purring in the friendliest way, he rubbed his head against Craig's leg. He never treated Lord Gentry with such friendliness. Little wonder as he frequently became a 'Flying Cat!' Little aware that Pickles the cat was having similar thoughts about Lord Gentry, 'I am dreaming that one day that man joins me in having a boot inserted onto his fat arse!' That's if cats could really think as humans did!

William Roper chose a tree about fifteen yards from the Pavilion and set his gun against the trunk. Then he filled and lit his pipe, leaned back comfortably against the trunk, hidden by the fringe of undergrowth, and, with his eyes on the door of the Pavilion, waited. For Craig and Olivia, never dreaming of this patient watcher, the minutes flew; they had so many things to tell one another, so many questions to discuss. At least Craig had, Olivia, for the most part, listened without comment unless the flush which waxed and waned should be considered a statement, to the things he told her about herself and the many ways in which she affected him.

For William Roper, the minutes dragged. He was eager to start briskly up the royal road to his fortune and future as, 'Head Game Keeper.' He was a slow smoker, and he smoked an intense, slow-burning Amphora Full Pipe Tobacco, which produced a fragrance of oranges. Still, he had nearly emptied the pipe which held it before his observation target exited the door of the Pavilion.

It was a still late afternoon, but some drift of air had carried the rank smoke from William Roper's pipe into the glade, and it hung there. Colonel Craig had not taken five steps before his nostrils became assailed by it.

"Damn!"

In a quiet almost soft whisper he said,

"What's the matter?"

Said Olivia.

She was too deeply absorbed in Craig for her senses to be alert, and the reek of William Roper's twist had not reached her nostrils. Olivia was oblivious of the spy.

"There's someone about,"

he exclaimed.

"Oh, Bother!"

Olivia softly commented, and she frowned.

"Can't you smell his vile tobacco?"

Olivia did not respond as she contemplated this turn of events. They tiptoed on. Craig was careful not to look about him with any show of earnestness, for there was nothing to be gained by letting the watcher become aware that he had perceived his presence. Indeed, he would have seen nothing, for the undergrowth between him and the glade was too thin to form a good screen, and William Roper was now behind the tree trunk.

Thirty yards down the broad aisle Craig said in a low voice:

"This is an infernal nuisance!"

"Why?"

Olivia exclaimed.

"If it comes to Gentry's ears, he'll make himself devilishly unpleasant to you, and the consequences could be disastrous."

"He can't make himself more unpleasant than he does,"

she said, in a tone of quiet certitude and utter indifference.

"But why shouldn't I have tea with you at the Pavilion? It's what it's there for."

"All the same, Gentry will make an infernal fuss about it, if it gets to his ears. Worse still should the spy have observed our actions before taking tea? The fallout could well be detrimental to you. The swine, he'll bully you worse than ever,"

he said in a melancholy tone, frowning heavily.

"What do I care about Gentry—now?"

Lady Gentry said, smiling at him, and she brushed her fingertips across the back of his hand.

He caught her fingers and held them for a moment, but the frown did not lift.

"The nuisance is that, whoever he is, he had been there a long time,"

he said gravely.

"The glade was full of the reek of his vile tobacco, as I mentioned,"

"Suppose he saw us making love? Then followed us to the Pavilion?"

"Well, if you will do such wicked things in the open air,"

she said, with a smiling tease.

"It isn't a laughing matter Olivia; I'm afraid we may be in a comprising situation,"

he said rather heavily and frowned.

"Well, I should have to consider your reputation and say that you didn't. It would be awful for your career if it became known that you did such things, and Egbert would never rest till he had done everything he could do to injure you. I should certainly declare that you didn't, and you'd have to do the same."

"Oh, please leave me out of it, darling Olivia! It's you I'm thinking about, more importantly, you're standing in society would be appalling. "

He muttered, with deep concern.

"But there's no need to worry about me. I'm not afraid of Egbert,"

SHE SAID, and her eyes, full of confidence and courage, met his steadily. Then, resolved to clear the anxiety away from his mind, she went on:

"It's no use meeting trouble half-way. If someone did see us, Egbert might not get to hear of it for days, or weeks—perhaps never."

She did not know that they had to reckon with the ambition of William Roper.

"Lord, how I want to kiss you again!"

He tried to enunciate each word slowly and act normal to deflect the dilemma of the dilemma swimming around in his head.

"You'll have to wait till tomorrow,"

Olivia said, with a rather teasing smile.

It was as well that he did not kiss her again, for fifty yards behind them, stealing through the woods, crept William Roper, and he was all eyes. Roper already had quite sufficient to tell. He was, however unaware that Colonel James Craig VC had seen him and scrutinised his appearance and most importantly, his face and the fact he was carrying a shotgun. Regret abounded for Mr Roper.

CRAIG WITH OLIVIA strolled through the wood and nearly to the end of the path and the splendid shrubbery. She spared no effort to set his mind at ease, protesting that she did not care a rap how furiously her husband abused her. A few yards from the edge of the East lawn they stopped, but they lingered over their parting. She promised to meet him in East wood at three tomorrow.

She strolled across the lawn and up to her suite of rooms, thinking of Craig. She showered to remove the love juice which yet lingered within her. Then changed into a peignoir, lit a cigarette, lay down on a couch, and went on thinking about him. She gave no thought to the matter of whether they had been somewhat impulsive and lacked discretion. Lord Gentry had become of less interest than ever to her; his furies while disturbing now seemed trivial. She had a feeling that he had become a mere shadow in her life, past tense. In her thoughts, she was, to be precise, in the first throes of love with an Officer in the Guards Brigade.

As she lay smoking that cigarette William Roper had gone into the Stables to mull over the shocking news he was about to impart to Lord Gentry. This afternoon was to be memorable, and soon Lord Gentry would elevate him by way of reward for information received of his wife's infidelity. As he attempted to exit via the stable door, James Craig barred his exit. Roper said, with an air of great importance,

"If I were you, Sir, I would make lots of distance between Ingatestone Hall and wherever you are stationed in London. His Lordship is very particular about who fucks his wife. When I tell him of your little banging session in the woods, he will have you."

Colonel Craig responded in a condescending, even begging, verbal manner,

"Please, please don't do that, it will cause Her Ladyship such serious grief. I am wealthy and prepared to pay you a handsome sum to maintain your silence on this matter."

Roper immediately saw a way of making some real cash but was he willing to give up his undoubted promotion to, 'Head Gamekeeper,' from the grateful Lord Gentry. He turned to the Colonel saying,

"How much would you pay me for keeping quiet?"

James, instantly knew he had succeeded in assessing that this was a greedy individual and monetary gain was sufficient to stop his blackmail attempt. He mulled over what he should offer. How much was this blaggard willing to accept? He made his proposal,

"I have five hundred pounds on me now which you can

have, and I will meet with you tomorrow and pay you another, ten-thousand pounds. But you must swear never to divulge this secret to anyone, ever again?"

William Roper had a sudden thought of wealth he could only have dreamed of, responding to the offer, eventually saying,

"That will be alright, but I swear if I do not receive the balance of cash by tomorrow afternoon, his Lordship will be informed."

"That's absolutely fine. I will let you have the five-hundred pounds now, and as I am returning the morrow to call on Lady Gentry in the afternoon, that suits me, if it is acceptable to you?"

James removed his wallet from the inside pocket of his jacket. Opened the flap and took out a wad of fifty-pound notes. He gestured to Roper to hold out his hands to accept the bribe. Roper turned toward the horsebox and leaned his shotgun against the wooden barrier. Colonel Craig commenced placing the notes one at a time, saying and counting as he went along,

"Fifty, One-Hundred, One-Hundred and fifty, Two-Hundred, Two-Hundred and fifty,"

and so it went on until almost the full amount was in the dirty palms of the blackmailer

Roper with a broad smile on his face and his hands outstretched received the notes, as James called the sum. He accidentally dropped the remaining notes, and as they fell to the floor of the stable William Roper bent down to pick them up. He just never saw it coming. James brought his right knee up connecting with Roper's head with such force that he capitulated his entire frame backwards. Craig was on him like a crazy banshee. Taking held of his head in a half-nelson and with one twist snapped his neck severing the atlas and axis vertebrae. These are the first two bones going down from his skull. His brainstem luxated. It was a swift action, and death occurred in an instant.

Colonel Craig had attended the United States, 'Marine Corps Martial Arts Program,' before being deployed to Afghanistan and he was well-schooled in silently killing the enemy. Dragging the body out of sight and covering it with a tarpaulin. James then carefully rolled both Roper and the tarpaulin together and secured the bundle using some horse leather straps hanging on the stable walls. He remained in the stables until it was well after dusk. Once confident that darkness would cover his movement, James lifted the now weighty body bundle using the well-practised fireman's lift and proceeded to make his way to his car. He dumped the body into the luggage boot. Disposal would be a simple task.

CHAPTER 9
POLICE PROGRESS

As Barrie Smith sat in front of Natalie, they ran through the evidence, collated during the ongoing investigation of the Romford Row Path murder. Barrie sipped from a glass of water and said to Natalie,

"It is my considered opinion that the perpetrators of this heinous crime are involved in some organised secret cult society. It is too well structured to be anything other than that. We are well aware that the branding sign on her forehead is quasi-Masonic. Nevertheless, I do not believe it is standard English Masonic, but my mind is currently open. Both of us agree and consider that Jane Doe's body was subject to ritual execution in another place before being transported and discarded. The River Rom Towpath, while a quiet location to discard a corpse, it was still risky. It would be feasible to assess that disposal could have been disturbed. We have to ask, what type of depraved individual or cult would first of all commit this atrocious murder? Be assured, that this was no single person murder but that of perhaps a coven consisting of several members. I also do not rule out that there may well be females involved; however, this may turn out not to be so. Also why, the removal of the right hand, this also beggars' belief!"

DS Lewis before speaking gathered her thoughts, then proffered her response,

"You may well be on the right track but let's consider this if it is a cult killing and they can dispose of the body in such a manner, that would require some excellent pre-planning. Also, they would first need a solemn oath of allegiance and the ability to hold such rituals. The location for such to take place would require it to be well out of the public's, all-seeing eye. What type of cult would carry out this barbaric and monstrous act of depravity?"

Natalie then chipped in her penny-worth,

"Quite frankly, I'm hedging towards a large storage facility or an old disused factory. Come to think of it there is no reason why we could not find it to be a large private dwelling or as I said, an old disused factory."

DI Smith bit his lower lip. He had as yet not considered this option. Having thought it through, he then offered,

"I would say that the length of time taken for this dreadful murder must have been between eight and twelve hours. My reason for this assessment is the written autopsy report. It affirmed from the duodenum contents of Jane Doe that she had consumed and digested food. The forensic pathologist reported that he found, a half-digested tuna sandwich assessed to have been eaten, some four hours before she died. Additionally, from the 'Toxicological Report' following the removal of 150 grams of her liver and kidney, also reports that she had consumed excessive quantities of red wine. It goes on to state that contained within the liquid was a trace of midazolam, which is part of the generic heading term of Benzodiazepines. These work in the brain but have different potencies and duration of actions. It can produce general anaesthesia. That together leads me to consider, that she may have been using one of the local wine bars before her eventual mishap and was slipped the drug during alcoholic consumption. It may well indicate that she partook of the alcohol in the company of those who administered the drug."

Natalie considered this for a few minutes. She was shifting through the papers and reading the report which Smithy had passed over to her. Holding it in her right hand, she read the contents with interest, then said,

"The dental investigation shows that she had undergone a root canal treatment within the last month from the presence of the dental amalgam. It showed it was recent, less than a month old. The local dental and other, further afield practices are currently being trawled to see if we can identify her from her teeth."

DI Barrie Smith was delighted with this excellent move forward in identifying Jane as it could well lead to further investigative leads. It was imperative identity became established soon. Already they were well behind expectations. The Murder Display Board to date was sparse.

Natalie went on:

"Another blinding revelation is that there are no foreign DNA traces on the body, but in her fingernail, a minuscule fragment of a cotton thread was discovered. It has been examined under the microscope and proves whomsoever the perpetrator of this murder was, he, she, or them, may have been wearing white gloves. I would opt for the decision that this could be conclusive evidence. Albeit I believe we can rule out the assumption that it was anything other than a ritual killing."

Barrie was pondering on the problems faced by this case. After taking his time to run what evidence they had through his mind, he addressed Natalie again,

"As much as I'd like to be wrong. I am pretty content that

our assumptions, for the time being, are on the right path. It could well be a one-off murder. But because we have never had a case of this kind in Romford does not necessarily compute to being singular."

DS Lewis was silent for a few minutes as she contemplated all the facts before them and reviewed the discovery of the unfortunate young girl. After all, Jane Doe was someone's child and daughter. The pain this would cause was devastating. Natalie then commented,

"It may even have been the accidental killing of this young woman. However, I remain open-minded. It stays pretty conclusive that she did not arrive on the towpath without some pre-planning. Also, it's clear to me the manner of getting rid of her was difficult. The dismembered body must have been transferred from the murder site in either a car or van. The site remains a strange selection for the disposal of the corpse. Those involved in this crime could quite easily have been spotted by the local police, and if that were so, we would not be having this conversation. You and I would be questioning the perpetrators at this stage. It remains for us to find proof of where and why? It may have been something that went too far and ended in the demise of Jane Doe."

Barrie Smith replied,

"Not that old potato again. It has been peeled, sliced, chipped, and used on numerous occasions by Her Majesty's finest detectives!"

Natalie laughed loudly at his statement and commented:

"Let's pop into the Major Incident and Murder Squad room and see how the team has been progressing with the investigative tasks we left them with."

Leaving his office, they walked along the long grey corridor sporting several small doors, leading to various department sections. As Barrie held the door open, Natalie entered into a vast open-plan room with individual workstation desks. Each desk and workstation possessed all the functionality required for the modern-day police investigator.

The incident murder board - was already being set up. There was a single picture that commanded the centre spot. The naked body of the deceased young woman with the right hand missing. Located on Board Number Two is also an enlarged photograph of the area of the Romford Tow Path. Even on the second board was a street map of the site. A red circle highlighted the area in which she was found.

At the top of the board, an artist had sketched the opined route that the killers may have taken to dump the body. It was appended with the distances involved from ingress to egress of the Tow Path. The Palisade Tulip Wooden Garden Gate was visible in the photographs but had produced no specific forensic information.

DI Smith was using a red laser pointer to trace the route on the board and said:

"Right folks, gather round the Murder Board and I will summarise what we have so far, which incidentally is not a lot to be going on with."

There was much shuffling around of chairs scraping on the floor, and in due course, they settled down with their police notebooks and pencils to the ready.

DI Smith once the chatter had abated spoke:

"Listen out, before we get into what's going down today, let me remind you all that the forthcoming Romford Detective Squad's big annual black-tie dinner dance is only a couple of weeks away. Saturday 23rd May during the bank holiday weekend, at the 'De Rougemont Manor Hotel.' You can't miss it as it's in Great Warley Street, Brentwood, right opposite the pub, 'The Thatcher's Arms.' If you don't have your tickets booked, then you'd better get on to it as soon as possible, or you'll lose out."

A young DC held his hand up and spoke:

'It's a bank holiday, isn't it, Guv? Only I was booked to go on a fishing trip. Can't they change the date?

Polite laughter rippled through the room like a Mexican wave from spectators at Twickenham Rugby ground when the match is so dull that the crowd had nothing better to do. Smithy looked at him ignored his foolishness and said:

"Don't be an idiot, Morton! It's always on the second last weekend of May because it is a bank holiday and the squads are at minimum strength over the holiday weekend. Just cancel your bloody fishing trip. It's a right old knees-up and worth getting your dickie bow out for."

DC Douglas Morton was a little embarrassed by his DI's comment and realised he should have kept his mouth shut. He had made a bit of a plonker of himself in front of his colleagues.

Natalie smiled at Barrie and was rewarded with a cursory nod. She doubted that she would be able to remember all their names on her first case with them and realised that the Romford Murder Squad, was unlike the glamorous Flying Squad she had previously been part of. She stood and moved to the centre and addressed the room:

"Now moving on to the investigation. Firstly, as yet, we have not been able to identify Jane. It is deduced, from the plaster casts of the footprints taken from the Tow-Path, Both the ingress and assumed egress routes. What has been revealed from forensics, is that there were two individuals involved. There are two full sets of differently-sized footprint castings. They indicated that the individuals had not returned along the same route once the body was discarded. Indeed, they had carried on down the path to Mawney Road and presumably entered the same vehicle that had facilitated the drop off with the body in Como Street leading to the Tow Path."

With that, she dimmed the lights using the automatic

control and immediately a VCR began to run on the vast television monitor screen. It was of the recording of a white Ford Transit Van coming to a halt in Como Street and the time clock on the recording dated Monday 13/05/ 22 at 02.05 am. Two males of medium build wearing what appeared to be tracksuits and caps conveniently covering their faces. On alighting the vehicle, they moved to the rear and opened the double doors. They removed what appeared to be a bundle and together, carried it towards the Tow-Path. Then disappeared from view, as the camera did not cover the entire area nor did it cover all of their movement. The white van was seen to leave the scene of the drop off heading towards the North Street roundabout. Unfortunately, there was no recording of the driver, which would permit identification.

The screen was blank for a brief moment and then burst into play again. The time clock showed Monday 13/05/15..02.15 am. However, this recording was of Mawney Road, showing what appeared to be the same two individuals briskly walking to the exact white Ford Transit, which was parked facing towards the A12 and boarded the vehicle. Once on board, the white van sped off down the road towards the main junction and turned right at the traffic lights. It was then shown some two-minutes later at the Crossways Roundabout take the third exit and on to the empty A12 at that time in the morning driving towards Brentwood/Ingatestone/Mountnessing. Again, the screen went momentarily blank and returned when the vehicle pulled off the A12 onto the B1002, and then the picture went blank.

DI Smith then took over and spoke again,

"Well fellow sleuths and sleuthettes, here is the dilemma. The recording finished as the white van came off the A12, and here we have a very rural area on which to concentrate. As you can see, the descriptions of the possible the two suspects are pretty poor and difficult for us to work with, there are no real distinguishing features. So once again, up the proverbial river without a paddle. There is also an added problem in that they left our policing jurisdiction. Brentwood, Ingatestone and Mountnessing, all come under the command of the Essex Force. DS Lewis will make contact and liaise with them regarding this evidence from the VCR. It could turn out to be a joint inquiry unless we are permitted to be the lead investigation team, given the murder took place on our patch or certainly culminated in Romford. You will all be aware of the absolute debacle experienced during the joint operation at the Travellers Site last year commanded by the Hertfordshire Police. Do any of you bright sparks have any blistering good ideas as I am right out of them?"

Silence ensued for a few minutes then DC Ken Trotter, an experienced detective with thinning close-cropped greying hair raised his hand. He had been part of the investigation team that handled the now-infamous case of the 'Lafferty Traveller Family,' who were incinerated by the gang now known as 'The Romford Boys.' Ken indicated he wished to make a suggestion.

DI Barrie Smith raised his eyebrows in a gesture of surprise or perhaps disbelief. His lips were stretched out, forming a straight line, and his teeth were not visible. He had in effect what one might describe as a tight-lipped smile. Detective Inspector Smith beckoned Ken Trotter to come to the front of the room and impart his thoughts from that position. Ken stood up from his chair all six foot of him with his slight beer gut leading. He wandered forward as directed; arriving at the location suggested and pointed to by Barrie's outstretched hand. Trotter was quite used to interviewing suspects, so this presented little concern to him. He cleared his throat and began,

"This may seem off the wall Gov, but I believe that we will discover that Jane Doe was a lady of the night. I perceive that she worked for a private agency that hire out the available good-looking woman to satisfy the creepy desires of others. I would suggest that we turn our investigation and scrutinise such agencies in the Havering and Essex areas. I am well aware it is a vast area to investigate. However, I have a hunch it will bear fruit. For that reason alone, I have drawn up the list of agencies, with contact telephone numbers. I humbly urge that we distribute this to the team and make appointments to visit and question the agencies at the said locations."

With that, he looked toward Barrie to establish whether his idea was workable and worth progressing. He remained at the front of the assembled Romford Number One Murder Squad. Ken stood with his legs apart and the palm of his hands facing forward. His stance indicated a trust me a signal and said,

"I do know what I am talking about, trust me, I am a policeman."

There was abject laughter that echoed throughout the room as he staggered back into his office desk stumbling as he went. As quickly as he tried to get away from the spine-chilling laughter from his colleagues, he had to accept the noisy banter.

DI Smith was sure that DC Trotter had put a great deal of thought into this proposal. He then spoke,

"As this would impinge on the local Vice Squad Team. We will have to clear this part of the investigation with them. Natalie, can you and Ken please contact Detective Chief Inspector Bryce, arrange a meeting with him and explain what our proposition is?"

He knew that Jane Doe's death was going to cause more significant problems for the team than anticipated. Turning to address the entire team he commented,

"Look, folks, we are getting nowhere fast. Let's now call a halt to this briefing and progress the inquiry as swiftly as we are able. Number one priority is to discover the identity of the unfortunate young lady, currently being kept in cold storage in the morgue."

Natalie was contemplating how attractive DCI Smith's mature manner was. She also noticed how much respect he had from the squad. As they headed out of the room, a tall, baby-faced female officer stood beside Natalie and commented.

"Don't worry; I'm pretty new to this Murder Squad as well. I'm DC Jane Dunston, but they all call me Blondie."

Jane Dunston was indeed a new member of the team but had been on board for about six weeks, and she had an empathy for the modern female DS. She wanted Natalie to feel welcome.

DS Lewis was well pleased with this offer of friendship and smiled at Jane in a thank-you manner.

Smithy and Natalie left the room as the squad was busying themselves around their workstations.

As they strolled back the way they came, accompanied Natalie commented,

"Do you know of any progress regarding the disappearance of the Samaritan lady two weeks ago?"

Smithy turned toward her and replied,

"Afraid not I read about it that as we are rather preoccupied in this case. I left it on the back burner. I have no idea if it is under investigation!"

CHAPTER 10
CHEATING GWYNN

Gwynn Robinson remained trapped in the secure room where her abductor had detained her for the last ten days. Continually, she was being kept in a state of drug abuse. Jim had his evil way with her without redress. She couldn't ascertain how long she had been in captivity. However, in her mind, Mrs Robinson, like most mature females, suspected that she had been sexually interfered with. As an experienced woman, the realisation that her captivity individual had a rather strange voice.

It always came through the speaker system; It was clear it was that of a male, it figured therefore that he was perhaps obtaining some pleasure, either by holding her prisoner or sexual activity while she was comatose. Otherwise, why was she being held interned within this plush and darkened room with the only illumination being a solitary red lamp above the bed? Of course, it had not escaped her thoughts; she may well be held prisoner before being killed. If the latter was indeed the case, she had had an eventful and enjoyable life. Her abductor most certainly was causing her severe physiological problems. Peter Robinson had been a dutiful and supportive husband.

Gwynn had borne him one son. Her handsome son had excelled, and his qualification as a Barrister and being called to, 'The Bar,' was a satisfying occasion for her and Peter. In the United Kingdom legal profession, it is the second-highest level of advocate or lawyer in the country. That and the fact he had joined the oldest Legal Chambers of John McDonnell Q.C, originally dating back to 1893. In these moments of reflection, her mind was consumed by various occasions. Gwynn's flighty and unfaithful nature had manifested itself. In particular the most recent with the wonderful, handsome Melvin Harris.

These reminiscences helped her to discard her fears, and as she drifted off into the land of Nod, her last liaison with him came into her mind. It sweetened her to remember that discrete and fulfilling night in Sussex and assisted in relieving the apprehension that invariably haunted her. In the dream, his manful voice spoke softly,

"See,"

he said playfully and raised his eyebrows like the raised eyes of the door attendant of, 'The Moulin Rouge Paris.'

"Admit it."

He moved his mouth so close to hers that she could practically feel it moving when he spoke. He could sense and almost taste her breath.

"Admit what?"

She said with an almost sexy tease in her voice; she was well aware of driving him loopy as he drove into her. Looking up his flared nostrils with her deepest 'Gina" Lollobrigida,' a voice whispered,

"Admit that you like my kisses and yes to going out with me, even though you're cheating on your wife, Melvin?"

Melvin Harris was shocked by the frankness of her statement while admitting to his inner self she was correct on both counts. He did like the taste of her sweet ruby red lips and well aware he was committing marital hara-kiri, should his wife ever discover just what he had been up to during his away days in the village town of Albourne, West Sussex. The sleepy village lay only an hour from London by a fast car. It was once described famously, being eight miles north of Brighton, as 'compact, virginal and exquisitely old-fashioned.' There was nothing virginal about Gwynn beneath him. She concealed secrets between her thighs like napkins and folded memories in the valley of her breasts. She was an attractive mature woman who did not disappoint between the sheets. Her husband of over thirty years had lost his impetus and was frankly of no use, in the sexual and fulfilling way. Gwynn had, for many years, played away from home when necessary to satisfy her lust for sex. Her tactics in this field were faultless. It was little trickier now that she was no longer a Magistrate, but she still maintained her monthly liaison with Melvin. He was that little bit younger than Peter and oh so attentive, plus he had loads of money and knew how to treat a lady.

Their joint tryst on the fourth Monday of each month was, in short, becoming somewhat habit-forming. The Wickford Hotel and Spa was well secreted and the staff excellent. Though they must have suspected his regular attendance was not to sample the waters of the Spa but the beautiful dark-haired companion with the appearance of a slightly aged, doll-like creature, with similar looks of the famed Italian actress, 'Gina" Lollobrigida.' She was quite a fair bit older than his 52 years. As she climaxed with multiple orgasms shuddering in deep pleasure, he withdrew, planting a kiss on her forehead. He made for the bathroom to shower so that he could dress and make his way to the office. As Head of Personnel, he would have numerous interviews with the back-office staff, and the fourth Tuesday of the month was his day for visiting the back office.

Melvin entered the bathroom, and with that, his thoughts

turned to the previous evening, which encompassed the perfect antidote for stress. They always commenced with a long and sensual bathtub game. He found it just as sexy as skinny-dipping in the private pool, only far more intimate and beautifying to boot. They always set aside time for a hot, steamy tub session for two before going down to dinner. Their use of therapeutic rubs plus luxurious scrubs and oils was instrumental in getting each other squeaky clean and silky soft and gloriously uninhibited. They were aware of their shared experience as when you're in the tub with someone, you've let down all of your defences, so each touch becomes all the more intimate. Melvin would scan the spa-inspired lotions left by the hotel chambermaid for their personal use. Following the aqua cavorting, they would dress and proceed downstairs to sample the delicious, outstanding menu accompanied by a vintage bottle of 'Bollinger 2002, James Bond 007, Collector's Limited Edition.' Melvin habitually washed his meal down with a large glass of, 'Remy Martin Louis XIII Cognac.' The hotel had a well-stocked cellar and never failed a guest request, no matter how expensive or obscure the client sought. These habitual actions set a boundary between the pair of cheats and the rest of the world. As his thoughts drifted, he knew for sure that the afternoons and evenings with Gwynn were quite remarkable.

Melvin vacated the bathroom and was replaced by Gwynn as she passed him, he planted a loving kiss on her lips. Gwynn permitted him solitude to dress alone, ready for his day at his office. She was quite unaware that he was attending the back office of his London City Bank. This information he was careful never to divulge. Once he checked his apparel for neatness, he entered the bathroom once more.

He admired her laying in the tub with bubbles up to her neck with a confident smile and an erect nipple protruding the water level. Kissing her gently on the forehead saying,

"What a beautiful lady you are Gwynn Robinson. I shall dream of you until we meet in four weeks."

As he reached the door, he glanced over his left shoulder and blew her a farewell kiss. His monthly review meetings at the back office in Haywards Heath, are the ideal excuse for his absence from home overnight. As almost an afterthought he silently mouthed,

"Love You!"

The door automatically closed behind him as he made his customary exit via reception having already settled the room charge in cash. He was meticulous in leaving little trace of his presence other than his deposit of semen inside Mrs Robinson.

At this point in her dream reality set in and she awoke becoming well aware of her current imprisonment and surroundings and tears flowed.

CHAPTER 11
JANE DOE REVEALED

The Chief wished to see them at eleven and warned that he required an update on the investigation of the Tow-Path murder. One full week had passed since Monday 13th with little tangible information on the identity of the Towpath female.

It was just turning eight o'clock on a bright and sunny April Monday morning. The Investigation team was assembling in the briefing room. The tea and coffee were being enjoyed. There was general chit-chat, on the progress or lack of it—of the ongoing Tow-Path Murder which was being investigated by the squad. The main topic of conversation was the failure, so far, to identify Jane Doe. All this despite the door-to-door inquiries using what was a single photograph of her face. The mortician had done a fantastic makeup of her, despite being in death. The photofit of the unfortunate young woman had been produced to try and discover her identity. All the Public Houses in Romford had been trawled with no tangible evidence forthcoming. This result was disappointing for the team.

Both DI Smith and DS Lewis entered the room, and the murder team settled down awaiting the morning briefing, known colloquially among the police as, 'Morning Prayers!' Natalie sat down on a chair provided at the front of the room. As ever on taking her seat, she brushed her skirt flat with both hands. Her continual tendency to do this manifested her fastidious nature. Barrie, in turn, went to the small table provided at the front which was offset to the left of the current, 'Murder Board.' He then opened his police folder and addressed the assembled detectives,

"I have some good news on the identity of Jane Doe, which requires to be confirmed by a visit to her alleged parents in Collier Row. Her dental records have come up trumps which were held on record at The Collier Row Dental Practice, located at 21 Collier Row Road which is opposite the Costcutter Shop. Please note the telephone contact number is 01708 888888 as two of you will be visiting to have a chat with the dental staff and recover the dental record. Her full name which we have to confirm was Christine Mary Pearce, aged 21 of 69 Bellevue Road, Collier Row, Romford RM5. Her parents have lived at the address for decades, and she had been conceived and born into this house. They have not reported their daughter missing so that will need to be further explored."

There was a visible sign of relief among those present. At last Jane Doe had a name and identity subject to confirmation. Personal chit-chat ensued between the members of the team. DI Smith allowed this to carry on. Barrie reached for the glass of cold water on the table and took a sip of the refreshing liquid. He then went on,

"I would like DC Paul Thompson and DC Archie Archer to take on this task. Paul, as you are the senior by several years, you will take the lead with Archie as backup and witness to the interview. However, I should not have to stress this point, but I will, please treat them gently. As I have stated, they have not reported their daughter missing and as far as we are concerned

and so they are unaware of her demise. Have either of you any questions on this task?"

Paul decided to answer for both of them,

"No problem Gov, we will get on with it pronto following this meeting. We will sign for a covert car and keep you informed of developments, Sir."

"Good DS Lewis and I have a meeting with the Chief at 10.30 am to brief him on the progress of which there has until this morning, been nothing to write up about."

Responded Barrie,

Detective Constable Josie Bunton raised her hand to intimate she had a question.

DI Smith said,

What do you want to say, Josie?"

DC Bunton dropped her right arm. She was a dowdy and unremarkable woman of forty with grey hair parted in the centre and knotted into a small bun resting on the nape of her neck. She completed her appearance wearing a black sweater with a floral skirt. Her feet he noticed were encased in a pair of sensible black shoes. Nonetheless, despite her appearance, Josie Bunton was an outstanding detective with many years of experience and success. Her frumpish appearance permitted her the ability to make folk less intimidated when being interviewed. When she spoke, people noticed how euphonious her voice was. Distinctive for sure and not dissimilar to the actress Dame Helen Mirren. Okay, she was no Jane Tennison, but she did get results. Clearing her throat, she raised a point not thus far discussed,

"Sir, have we managed to trace yet, where the white Ford Transit van travelled to after it headed up the A12 Colchester Road? I am aware it left our jurisdiction, nevertheless, wherever it departed the A12 could perhaps lead us to where it completed its journey and who owned it?"

With that DC Pat Shovlin chipped in,

"I received the tapes this morning from the Highways Agency Romford and intended to analyse them later and before mid-day. I am confident they will provide us with a steer to where the murderers are perhaps hiding if indeed they are the perpetrators or just the body individuals. The note attached stated that the 'Automated Number Plate Recognition,' was unable to provide the Vehicle Registration as the front and rear plates had been doctored to prevent identification."

Barrie answered this statement,

"What a pity that is. I will leave you to go through what you have Pat and let me know if anything of note transpires. If possible, I would appreciate any information to be communicated to me before our meeting with the Chief. If there are no further points, I will end this meeting with you folks, with a little aside,"

"What do you call an alligator with a vest?"

The room fell silent, and before anyone could chip in he said,

"An In......vesta.......gator!"

The room filled with genuine laughter and as it drifted, Barrie commented,

"That is what we require, an outstanding Investigator to crack this case. Let's do it!"

With that final statement and joke, the assembled team broke and made their way back to their specific desks. Barrie and Natalie then returned to his office to prepare for their meeting with the Chief Super. As they entered the office, the telephone was ringing. He went to his desk and lifted the handset to his ear.

"DI Smith, can I be of assistance?"

"Boss, it is DC Shovlin here. I have quickly concluded my appraisal of the recorded footage of the Ford Transit suspects. I can confirm to you that the vehicle used the A12 from the six-way roundabout and headed toward Colchester. When it left our governance, the Essex recording picked it up and showed the van leaving the A12 headed towards Fryerning, a suburb of Ingatestone. It then turned into a leafy lane, which then continued to a large country house. The name and details of which as yet I do not possess. As soon as I do I will forward it by secure email to you, Sir."

DI Smith responded,

"Well done Pat, yes please email me but would you please also message me on my mobile? As I said at the briefing, Natalie and I have a meeting now with the Chief Super. It would be great if I could supply more precise details of the potential van location."

Pat, responded,

"Wilco, Guv."

Barrie turned to DS Lewis and commented,

"We have a lead on the white transit vans potential location. DC Shovlin will message me the details once confirmed."

"Tremendous!"

The Chief was sitting in one of the comfortable chairs around the square mahogany coffee table accompanied by the Chief Constable of Essex who had made the journey from his Police Force Headquarters in Chelmsford, Essex. Stephen Jones, The Chief Constable, was sitting opposite. He was balancing a saucer in the palm of his left hand and drinking coffee from a small delicate cup using his right thumb and forefinger.

The Chief Constable of Essex had arrived with his cashmere coat which was now hanging on the hat and coat stand next to the door. He wore a blue pin-striped suit, which contrasted with his silver hair, and a Balliol College, Oxford striped tie with matching gold clip and cufflinks. He had never actually been a student at Oxford University, but that was simply a minor lie in an entire world of falsehoods. He said to the Chief Police Officer of Romford,

"And this DCI Addison doesn't know about my involvement?"

"She is simply following my orders."

Responded the Romford Police Commander with much assurance, he went on to say,

"I have told her to get rid of Acting Detective Inspector Smith soonest. That is what she is doing."

"Without questioning why?"

"I have information that she would not want to be made public. Therefore, she does what she is ordered to do."

"Ah, I see..... Of course,"

He thought the lovely Matilda knew a thing or two on how to advance up the promotion tree, and how to achieve the advancement she wants. The Essex Chief Constable had served with her several years before in Norwich. He was well aware of her ability and zest for promotion.

The room fell silent while the pair of senior officers together contemplated their next step. What they must achieve was that this case is shut down as soon as possible as it stretched too far into the senior members of their secret society. Further investigation and revelations would shock not just Essex, but the entire United Kingdom, in general, was it ever made public. It was rooted in the occult which many seniors, both in the police force and Government. Let's face it; nobody wanted that to come out, least of all David Bagley and Stephen Jones. Even more importantly, least of all Lord Peter Gentry, the Grand Master.

Meanwhile, both Barrie and Natalie arrived in the Chief's outer office, which was staffed by his Personal Secretary, Tania Sachdev. She was a bouncy, energetic little woman. The combing of her hair was similar to that of a Barbie Doll that had seen better days. She had the habit of prancing joyfully along to a Bollywood soundtrack when not at her desk. You could witness this as you approach her; however, the change that comes over Tania as soon as she occupies the front of her boss's office was terrific. She grows suddenly still, focused, her large ebony eyes solemn and unblinking. Total efficiency as you may expect from a university-qualified personal assistant. Some of that boisterous energy exudes in her smile and winning laugh bubbling up throughout while addressing them.

"Good morning DI Smith and DS Lewis you are here for your appointment with the Chief. I should let you know that he is not alone, the Chief Constable of Essex is with him. Can I offer you both a coffee or tea?"

Barrie answered for the pair of them,

"No thank you, Tania, we have just had coffee at our morning prayers meeting."

"Great if you will please take a seat? I will let them know you are here."

She said, pointing to the reception sofa."

With that, she picked up her desk telephone, depressed the Chief's button, announced who sought admission and instantly received a positive response. Rising from her desk, she ushered them both towards the door and gave a gentle knock, opened it and let them proceed through.

Both inhabitants stood, and Chief Superintendent David Bagley introduced the Commander of Essex Police, Chief Constable Stephen Jones. Barrie and Natalie proffered their respective right hands. Formalities over, the Chief pointed towards two chairs on either side of the square mahogany coffee table while he and his principle guest sat on the comfortable chairs. Barrie noted RHIP, (Rank has its Privileges) with a slight smirk on his face which was not lost on Natalie. She as ever sat with her knees together, and Barrie watched her with the most sedulous care, brush her skirt smooth. He mused to himself, "she never misses a trick to impress."

The Chief commenced the conversation,

"The Chief Constable of Essex is here because of the identity of Jane Doe and who she may or may not have been associated with before her demise. This Tow Path Murder has far-reaching consequences with our Metropolitan Borough for which you are to be aware. I am responsible for the policing of our Met Borough and answer upwards to New Scotland Yard. Following the excellent work of your team Barrie, I have received the hard copy briefing from you this morning, which is excellent. Thank you. It should reduce the snarling press and media."

Barrie then responded,

"We now know her identity. She was as anticipated from Romford. I have two detectives currently visiting her home to confirm her details and inform her parents. They have not reported her missing despite the fact she has been dead since the fifteenth of April. That perhaps reveals why we have taken so long to reach this stage. Her body was dumped on the Tow Path, and the two peoples who removed the corpse from a white Ford Transit Van parked in North Street rejoined the vehicle in Mawney Road. As it sped off towards the A127, it was picked up heading out of our area heading towards Colchester on the A12. The Essex CCTV provided evidence of it leaving the main A12 and driving towards the village of Fryering as the suburb of Ingatestone. The leafy lane The leafy lane which the van took leads to a large country house which is owned by a billionaire whose only uses of it, is when he is back in the United Kingdom. His regular residence is in Dubai. His business, from what Essex Police investigation has revealed, is offshore finance."

Chief Constable Jones will nominate one of his leading Detective Superintendents to take overall control and you

Barrie will come under his command. They will join us on their arrival."

Natalie, stared at DI Smith expecting the worst from her Boss, she had read his response. Barrie held himself in check before his comeback to this shocking statement by his Chief Super. He would have expected to be the lead detective in any investigation of a murder that had seemingly occurred in the Havering area. What went through his mind was that he was being shafted or the senior policeman had knowledge he was not sharing. Quite clearly, some off-the-table deal had been done between the two senior officers, and, a mere Acting Detective Inspector was being sidelined for reasons unknown. However, he was determined to find out what it was. Natalie noticed that he was biting his lower lip, and that was in her experience, not a good sign. Barrie took a sip of water from the glass on the table. He then looked at both senior officers with a determined stare. Then he addressed the pair of seniors as he had handled many in his military career with resolute firmness and said,

"Sirs, while I understand the wish to share this investigation as a duology operation between both force locations. I have to say that due to the nature of the state in which Miss Christine Mary Pearce was discovered with her hand severed and the branded etching on her forehead, we perceive must have been the work of some sort of cult. I would urge you both to reconsider this decision. It's all very well working in tandem with another force. I would remind you, Chief Jones of the absolute Horlicks that occurred when a similar decision was made with the 'Hertfordshire,' sorry Hertfordshire police. (*He had made his point strongly he thought.*) The lack of regular communication resulted in the escape of the murder suspect followed by dreadful headlines the following morning in the national newspapers. It was derogatory for the police and resulted in the suspect escaping, and resulted in the Number One Suspect incinerated in a log cabin. Not the outcome we were all striving to achieve. I would lobby against such a move as bi-lateral policing, as it seldom works. We in the Metropolitan Force have a standard, dare I comment, slightly higher than those out in the sticks."

The face of both senior policemen was palpable; you could have cut the air with a knife. It was clear; neither was happy with this forthright statement by DI Smith. Chief David Bagley, was the first to address this outrageous verbalisation which he considered an open criticism of the Essex Force, especially in front of Chief Constable Jones. In a most forthright manner and tone which left nothing to the imagination, he directed his comment directly to Barrie saying,

"DI Smith, I have to inform you that the decision has already been agreed between Commander Jones and in the interest of inter-force operations which incidentally at your pay grade is not in your remit to decide. You will work together with the nominated Investigation Leader who will be DCI Matilda Addison who is as you know, located here in Romford, so it is not as if the overall command is being levied out of London. Is that crystal clear Inspector?"

Barrie was shocked at this statement; chewing his lip, this was turning out to be a nightmare meeting. It was well known in the Romford Police Station that DCI Matilda Addison was termed as, 'A Piggy Back Officer,' interested in using others for her advancement. The stories were a legend about her sleeping around with seniors.

The Chief of Romford then continued,

"I have arranged for her to join us, and when she arrives, you can articulate the current level of progress. I hasten to add it has not been that promising; it took over a week to reveal who the unfortunate murdered young girl was. Now, I am aware that

DCI Jenkins is recuperating from his unfortunate road traffic accident, but we need to do better.......much better are we clear on this ADI Smith?"

Natalie remained silent; however, in her mind, she was well aware that this was not a discussion on the way ahead but a railroaded order. In her training days at Hendon Police School, she and Matilda had been quite friendly. She could observe Barrie fuming but controlled, and he responded accordingly,

"That Sir is your command prerogative, and as ever I will adhere to your instruction. I look forward to working with DCI Addison. I was wondering if the Essex Force had nominated their representative in this joint operation.?"

Before the Chief could answer this pointed question, the phone on his desk rang. He fielded the call via the extension apparatus located in the centre of the mahogany table. Removing it from the cradle, he mouthed into the phone,

"Hello,"

There was a pause while he assimilated the call, then said,

"Please show them both in!"

The Chief got up and moved towards the additional chairs and moved not one but two seats to the area of the occasional table. He was intimating that not one but two people were about to join the meeting. Barrie did not assist as he was so pissed off at this time, helping was the last thing on his mind.

The door to the office opened and in waltzed DCI Matilda Addison. There was just something unreal and eerie about her. Her face, somewhat luminous, had a pale tone to it. The eyes were a piercingly sharp shade of grey. She possessed eyebrows that were arched over the curve before dispersing onto the bridge of her dainty nose. She was a little plump; her lips had the strangest curl to them. As for her face, it was framed by wavy, ebony-coloured curls, falling to just above her shoulders. Her prominent breasts jutted out before her and challenged the strength of her undergarment, brassier which certainly lifted and separated her breasts.

Overall, Barrie had to admit; she was indeed an impressive-looking woman in her mid-thirties. Matilda was accompanied by someone whom neither Barrie nor Natalie had met before. Detective Inspector Larry Donegan was blade-faced, six and a half feet tall, and had a body of whipcord from the marathons he ran, in London and Manchester. His scalp glistened through his shaved head; his energies were augmented rather than diminished by the two hours a day he spent on a Stair Master at the police headquarters gym. The local press always referred to Larry as 'charismatic,' and 'clean-cut.' God helps the man or woman Larry had in his sights. He was on his way up in the sweet sewer of police politics, and he had long ago decided it was better to be first in Chelmsford rather than second in London.

The Chief permitted Stephen Jones to shake hands with the joiners before introducing them to Natalie and Barrie. Once the overtures were complete, and they were re-seated he commenced,

"Now that we are all present, I wish to make it clear that this will be a joint operation to investigate the reason why this young girl was murdered and dumped in our patch in Romford.
 I hasten to add that from information so far derived; it appears that perhaps the murder took place in Essex and disposed of in Romford. Also, we are all adults, and I do not wish any self-effacing policing. Egos are to remain intact and in no way are to interfere with this investigation, is that clear?"

The detectives agreed and acknowledged this by nodding their heads in approval. The Chief went on,

"I want you, Barrie, to update me daily on the progress of this joint-murder inquiry. I would also like a weekly meeting, say on a Friday at 10.30 am with the joint team leaders ADI

Smith and DI Donegan being present unless of course there is a pending operational reason, why either of you is unable to be here. In those circumstances, your deputies will please stand in. DCI Addison will be the overall liaison coordinator of both investigation areas and will ultimately report directly to me. I will take the responsibility of keeping the Chief Constable and Commander of Essex in the frame. Do any of you have any points you wish to raise at present? We will commence with you Barrie and move around taking any other points from the assembled team?"

ADI Smith, Romford CID, was not a happy puppy and it was apparent on his face. His eyes had almost turned to the colour black he was fizzing mad. Barrie's lower lip had reddened from the number of times during the last half-an-hour he had chewed it. This was nothing more than an insult by the pair of senior police officers. He considered binning the investigation altogether. He counselled himself that would be an error of judgment, and there had already been a garbage bin full of poor decisions made during this meeting. Alternatively, was he being ploddingly railroaded from this case? Did the Commander of Essex from his plush office in Chelmsford have information he was not sharing with Romford? It certainly seemed so. He offered,

"May I commence with the fact that as previously highlighted, joint operations can only go so far. I honestly do not feel that the correct decision has been taken. The patch where the body was discovered is where the investigation should remain. I see no mileage in Essex Police being involved."

Detective Inspector Larry Donegan chipped in with his smooth baritone yet clear and calm voice saying,

"I somewhat disagree with that Barrie, as there are numerous cases in the past where joint investigations have enhanced the inquiry, leading to successful completion well ahead of estimated time frames. I also welcome the opportunity of working alongside you and your team."

It was quite evident that Larry spoke and presented himself most succinctly. Both the senior officers were pleased that DI Donegan was more than happy to work together with the Romford Team. However, it left the impression that Barrie was less than content. Natalie had remained silent and had made no comments up to this point, however, she decided it was time to interject and save the Havering, Romford and Redbridge Metropolitan Police situation. Her cough attracted the necessary attention she wished. Natalie noted the meeting had turned slightly sour and the wheel wanted greasing, she said,

"I would like to make the point that albeit Jane Doe, who we now have identified through our local door-to-door inquiries as well as the numerous agencies trawled as being one Christine Mary Pearce, aged 21. She lived with her parents in Collier Row, which is only about 4 miles from this station. We are aware of where she was found. Also, we now know the type of vehicle that brought her to the River Rom Towpath. Her body was discarded in an overgrown graveyard for Supermarket trolleys. A worse place, you would not wish to have your daughter left dead and alone. So, can I ask us all to pitch together and find the killer or killers of this young lady? I know we are all a little fraught as to who will command the investigation but does that matter? Inter-police rivalries aside, Essex Police hardly found her corpse, drove it to Romford, and discarded her to save money on budgets. I have heard stories of bodies being dragged over borders to save time and money. But seriously and to return to the business at hand, may I please urge, we all work in our operational ways to solve this crime?"

Her point well-made and Natalie brushed and smoothed her skirt conscious that perhaps she may have ruffled a few feathers, in particular, Barrie's. However, in glancing at him, he had a smirk on his face. Not all that visible to others present, nevertheless he looked relieved that she had extracted him from the mire he was digging.

The Chief was pleased that the assuage had been diverted by this oh-so-creative Detective Sergeant. He then said,

"Ladies and Gentlemen, I feel we have chewed the fat over this and think it's time we get on with our task in hand. No doubt you will all have sub-meetings following this, and I wish you all success. We will reconvene as I stated at 10.30 am on Friday."

The assembled meeting arose from their respective seats and began to mutter with colleagues as they departed the Chief's office. However, Commander Stephen Jones remained behind. When the office was clear, he turned to David Bagley, being aware that the office may be bugged and whispered into his left ear,

"David, we cannot let this case expose our society, and it must not be so revealed. That we, the members of, 'ROSICRUCIANISM,' are depending upon you, is sacrosanct to ensure this happens. I would add as previously discussed in private; Smith must be dealt with and removed. He is dangerous. Please remember the fame of the brotherhood which has been in existence since 1614 in Bavaria. We are the brethren of the Hermetic Order of the Golden Dawn."

David moved toward the coat stand removing the cashmere garment sporting a blue velvet collar which was the preferred daily garment when not dressed in the White Mantle Shroud with the Red Rose Croix, emblazoned on the front of the garment. He assisted the Commander who resisted placing his arm into the coat preferring to have it over his shoulders. He looked more like a gangster in Chicago than the Chief of Police of one-thousand-five-hundred and forty-two square miles of Essex. Even though Essex had been founded during the 6th century, covering a vast area of the East of England. The former previously covered Essex, Hertfordshire, Middlesex and Kent. The last king of Essex was Sigered, and in 825, he ceded the kingdom to Egbert of Wessex. A direct descendant was perhaps Lord Egbert Peter Gentry of Ingatestone Hall. History records that, 'Egbert of Wessex,' was overthrown by The Vikings.

CHAPTER 12
DISTRAUGHT HUSBAND

It was late; almost Grouse Whisky late and Barrie felt he could do with a wee dram of the golden nectar as he sat at his desk on the third floor of Romford Police Headquarters. It was Monday 4th May and still a while before summer arrived on the 21st of June. The late spring sun was setting as he gazed out of his window it grew smaller as the sky began to darken. Slowly, ever so slowly, the Sun disappeared behind the horizon. The dawn has its splendours, but it brightens out of secret mists and folded clouds into the light of day when his working policing burden must be resumed. But the sunset in Barrie's mind wanes from glory and majesty into the stillness of the star-hung night, when tired eyes close in sleep, and rehearse the mystery of death; and so the dying down of light, with the suspension of daily activities, is of the nature of life in general.

As he turned from his desk to his small occasional table, he reached out for his Coldstream Guards Chrystal tumbler. Removing the glass from the table, transferred it, and placed the empty receptacle on his ink pad. He withdrew from the bottom right drawer of his pedestal a litre of the famous Grouse Whisky. He remembered being told by his old buddy Ronnie

Paterson that the head of the MacGregor Clan, Gregor MacGregor of MacGregor had stated that there was nothing better on a cold winter evening bur a glass of the Low Flyer. (Scottish Grouse from the Highlands of Scotland.) Then he proceeded to unscrew the cap decanting a considerable measure of the golden liquid. Barrie raised the glass to his nose, pretending he was a connoisseur of blended Scotch, and sniffed the aroma. This particular bottle was a special edition of, 'The Famous Grouse,' aptly named, 'Black Grouse,' this blend was otherwise known as, 'Blackcock.' As the glass met his lips, so he swallowed a sip to appreciate its taste. The balance was all that it was meant to be with a distinct peat, smoky, and caramel flavour. Barrie Smith was now in a relaxed mood with his feet up on his desk and a large glass of instant refreshment in his right hand. With that there was a knock on his door, he answered,

"Please enter at your peril, adult male enjoying a dram."

The door opened and in waltzed Natalie. Immediately she clocked him in his relaxed mode and said,

"Do you want to be disturbed, or shall I come back later? As a matter of interest, you being English, why do you recite the Scottish term for a glass of whisky, a dream?

DI Smith smiled and beckoned her to draw up a chair as he opened his pedestal drawer, removing a crystal glass and proffered it to her. He removed the cap, and slowly poured a fair measure into the tumbler, then passed it to her, then said,

"I call it a dram because I used to be a Gin and Tonic man. When I was in the Guards serving in Dungannon, Northern Ireland. I met a fellow who introduced me to, 'The Famous Grouse,' and he instructed me that the correct terminology when drinking whisky was to use the word, 'Dram.' So, my dear that is the reason I call it a Dram."

Before Barrie could take another sip, DS Lewis interrupted him and said,

"If I were you Gov, I would hold on drinking that second glass of Scotch as there is a gentleman in the reception area. He is Mr Robinson, who is the husband of the missing Samaritan lady who happens to be his wife. He confirms that she has been missing for over a week and nothing has transpired as yet. He has not even had a visit from the police. We have not been allocated this investigation as this is the first the police have been made aware of her being missing. It was logged on Sunday morning 26th April the day after she failed to return from her shift. As I and I are the only two detectives left on duty, I am afraid we have the call. The desk sergeant has asked that we speak to him."

Barrie nodded his head in assent, placed the tumbler on his table moved his chair backward, stood up, and made his way toward the door. He removed from his pocket a,' Taveners Mint Humbug,' sweet placing it in his mouth to prevent the whisky breath. Just as Natalie took hold of the door handle to open it, Barrie inquired,

"Do we possess any documentation in this case, or are we flying blind?"

DS Lewis held a buff manila folder which had printed in large bold print, 'Gwynn Robinson – Missing Person.' She handed it to Barrie, and as he took hold of it he said,

"Gee whiz, thanks a million, there can't be more than two sheets of paper in this folder, it's hardly a great deal for us to be going on with. If only John Jenkins were not on sick leave, following his wife's fatality, he would love this. I have heard the update on his progress. His broken bones are on the mend. He could be back soon and deal with this missing person inquiry. It would be right up his sleeve."

Natalie spoke as they took the stairs to the ground floor,

"All we have is the completed missing persons form by Mr Peter Robinson, the husband; it contains his address and contact telephone numbers. There is also a brief resume' of what he knows of his wife's last movements as well as what she was wearing and the registration number of her car, a Red Mercedes SL.

Together they exited the stairway on the ground floor and entered the interview room Number One. They both took a seat and while he read through the flimsy evidence sheets. Natalie checked that the recording systems were in working order. Assured that they were, she turned to DI Smith and said,

"The audio and VCR systems are working fine, so when you are ready, we can summon Mr Robinson."

Barrie nodded his assent and said,

"Let's do it."

DS Lewis, rose from her seat next to him and headed for the door leading to the Reception area. As she entered the waiting room, Mr Robinson rose from his seat, and as he did so, Natalie put out her hand and said,

"Good evening Mr Robinson I am Detective Sergeant Natalie Lewis, and in a moment, we will be going into one of our interview rooms. The purpose of this is merely to establish what you know and what we can hopefully do to set in motion the investigation into your wife's disappearance. In the room, I will introduce you to the best detective we have here in Romford. He is DI Barrie Smith."

She took his hand and shook it firmly attempting to convey an air of assuredness. Natalie nodded her head to the Desk Sergeant, who then activated the electronic release unlocking the door. Escorted him through it and turned right to the ever-slightly ajar door leading to the signposted, Interview Room Number 1.

Barrie was standing awaiting Mr. Robinson's arrival, he held out his hand and said,

"Good evening, Mr Robinson, I am Barrie Smith, please take a seat. So as not to alarm you, I must first inform you that whatever we discuss in this interview will be recorded. The reason for this is to ensure we can refer to the details which you will kindly supply us. I have to ask you to acknowledge this verbally for the tape. Can I please inquire are you clear about this?"

Patrick Robinson responded,

"Yes, I am."

Barrie, then went on,

"I note from the information received that your wife, Gwynn Robinson, left home about six o'clock on Saturday 25th April, which was last Saturday. It is now Monday 4th May, and to date, you have not received any contact either by telephone or through a third party. Is that a true summary of the facts as you reported them to the desk Sergeant last Sunday 25th April 2015?"

Peter Robinson's face looked pinched, his eyes glassy. He was a mature adult male, but his emotions acted like he had been distraught and in severe turmoil. It was now over a week since his wife of 35 years had failed to return home. She was on shift at The Samaritans. It looked as if he was going to cry, but as yet hadn't. His eyes darted around the room. These were the emotions of an extraordinarily distressed husband. He cleared his throat with a nervous cough and said,

Gwynn is a predictable person, we have been married for over thirty-five years, and she has never once been away without telling me where she was going. She is a former Magistrate here in Romford. Following her retirement, she volunteered to assist at the Samaritans in North Street and only attended three nights a week."

Barrie interrupted,

I assume you have spoken to the manager at the North Street, Samaritans office to ascertain whether she had made contact with them? When was the next scheduled shift following Saturday?

"It should have been Wednesday evening, she started at the same time, seven in the evening and finished the shift at midnight. Gwynn always drove there from our home parking her car in the secure compound. Oh, she as a matter of habit, I would receive a call at about eleven fifty-five to say she was leaving the office on her way home. That was the last contact we had with each other."

Mr Robinson's eyes glistened with emotion, pulling his eyes brows down, his lips were now trembling as if he were to let out a sob, but he never did. His nose twitched as his mouth suddenly became agape, and he drew in a breath of air, sharply, turning his neck. He was doing an excellent job in extraordinarily difficult circumstances of keeping it together. His teeth nipped his upper lip and at that point, lost control of his emotions. The tears flowed like a river from his eyes; all self-control had vanished. The man was in bits, sobbing uncontrollably.

Natalie reached for the box of paper hankies which every interview room possessed as invariably they would at some point be required to stem the flow of tears. Extracting a handful, she passed them to Peter Robinson who accepted them with grace. He took a few minutes, but eventually control returned, and he went on,

"There is no way that my darling Gwynn would not contact me or our son Robert. I have spoken to him, and he confirmed his mother had not called him. I am worried sick, about what on earth could have occurred which prevents her from contacting her family. Yes, the thought did pass through my mind, perhaps she was having an affair of which I am unaware. But it would be quite out of character."

Natalie then chipped in,

"Have you checked with the office in North Street, to confirm she has not been in contact with them or had taken a leave of absence which was unknown to you or Robert, your son?"

He wiped his moist nose once more with the paper hankie before speaking,

"Yes, I have, and they affirmed she was due on duty on Wednesday evening, however as she failed to appear they assumed she must have been ill."

"Did you not think it very peculiar that they did not call your home to ascertain whether she intended to honour her shift?"

Natalie was searching for some glitch in his manner, but none was forthcoming. He continued to snivel, and his eyes remained puffy and wet from the previous tears. She was holding and reading the completed, 'Missing Persons Form.' As experienced detectives, both Barrie and Natalie had witnessed loads of crying and whining during interviews. Sometimes it transpired that the incumbent was the guilty party.

She then asked him,

"May I please confirm that she was wearing a mustard-coloured coat and black shoes with a small black Mylockme BB, Louis Vuitton handbag? Is that correct?"

Natalie thought to herself my goodness, being aware of how expensive these bags were. They cost in the region of £2000.00. It has a relaxed schoolbag" shape in a trendy small size and makes a big fashion statement. Crafted of soft calf leather. A brilliant choice for women with money. Natalie felt that she would never on her police salary be able to afford a bag of similar ilk. Dream on girl she mused to herself.

Patrick Robinson responded,

"Yes, she was."

Barrie, then came back with,

"Did your wife have any enemies or someone who would wish her harm?"

Mr Robinson responded,

"None of which I am aware of. Gwynn was on the Romford Magistrate's Bench for over 20 years. I have no doubt there would be folk she sent down who took an instant dislike to her. Nonetheless, we never suffered from any sort of intimidation or sick mail either electronically or by post that I am aware of."

Barrie responded,

"I believe you have given us everything we need to know at present Mr Robinson and thank you for coming in to see us. I will have her posted as a missing person and will appoint two of my best Detectives to investigate the case further. They will be required to visit you at home and with your permission have a look into some of Gwynn's personal effects. Is that okay with you, Mr Robinson?"

He has managed to cease the tears and had wiped his nose dry. Patrick Robinson responded,

"Of course, I have inserted my home and mobile telephone numbers on the form that the Sergeant on the desk asked me to complete."

Barrie stood up and said,

"If anything comes up no matter how small please call either myself or DS Lewis. Oh, and would you please inform your son Robert that they will wish to have a word with him? You never know he may have information that could assist us in locating her."

He then handed over his police business card and Natalie did likewise as she escorted him back into the central police reception area.

Mr Robinson shook her hand, and as the security door clicked open, he walked through it. Natalie noticed that his head was drooped as the pain of his wife missing was obvious.

Returning to the interview room, she noted that DI Smith was seated, writing into the paper log. He had ejected the tape recording of the interview, dated and numbered it. She pulled up the seat next to him, saying,

"Is it not a little absurd that he waited for a little over a week before coming to the police station to report his wife's absence?"

"Yes, I immediately picked up on that. It may be that there is some dirty linen in the Robinson laundry basket that he omitted to mention. Our investigation team will turn up evidence if his wife has been playing away from home. I was not surprised when he broke down as his wife of many years being absent from the home with no equitable reason. We have both handled cases in the past, which at the outset seem to have a third party involved to discover in due course that it was the spouse who was guilty!"

Barrie, then went on to say,

"Let's repair to my office, and I can finish that dram of fine Blackcock Grouse whisky and perhaps you will join me for one?"

CHAPTER 13
CATASTROPHE DI SMITH

DCI David Thompson entered the office of Acting Detective Inspector Smith and placed three envelopes on the table face up, each marked in large bold black ink with the numbers, One, Two, and Three. This was his warped way of giving DI Smith a choice of which crime to deal with and investigate. Turning to ADI Barrie Smith he uttered,

"Take your pick Barrie, and hopefully you will select the one you like?"

Barrie to say the least was surprised by this as he already had the ongoing case of the Tow-Path murder. 'The naked murdered girl with the severed hand.' Looking up from his desk he responded,

"I already have a case which I am involved in and attended a co-ordinating meeting yesterday, with the Chief. The Chief Constable of Essex is also involved now; he too attended this meeting. There is also Detective Inspector Larry Donegan from Chelmsford assigned to the case as it involves both the Met and Essex Police. I am to report directly to the Chief on this matter.

DS Lewis and my Team are deeply involved and have collated progressive evidence. I am also to update the Chief on developments."

DCI Thompson was a bit of a problematic individual and would instead put junior investigative officers off guard and immediately under pressure. He was well skilled in this but was not dealing with some sprog police officer. Barrie, as a former guardsman and mature detective, had seen it all and bought the proverbial T-Shirt. He was, in short, unruffled! Rising from his seat to his full six-foot-four-inches, he dwarfed Thompson by some eight inches. He looked at the envelopes and decided, for the time being; he would go along with what he thought was a charade. He then asked,

"I assume one of these three is my current case, and you are having a lark teasing me a little?"

The Detective Chief Inspector's face gave nothing away. He was a legend in the Metropolitan Police for his lack of humour and humanity. Thompson was well known for his strict abrupt disciplinary manner. Barrie was well used to dealing with this from his military days. He then looked Smithy in the eyes, well not quite in his eyes as due to his lack of inches it was more like his chest and said,

"I am sorry to tell you that the Tow Path murder of the naked girl, Christine Mary Pearce case, has been removed from this force and Essex police and handed to Scotland Yard for their examination and further inquiry. This case is quite a bit further up the food chain than you are chummy. You are to report to New Scotland Yard this afternoon and hand over the entire case file, to the 'Serious Crime Directorate 9. That, if you are not aware, is The Human Exploitation and Organised Crime Command, or SCD9.' You will personally take the evidential file to New Scotland Yard this afternoon and hand it over to Commander Mary Ward. Is that clear DI Smith?"

Barrie was astounded at this revelation. He was about to respond when DCI Thompson held up his hand to stop him from doing so. Thompson went on,

"You are booked in to meet with Commander Ward at two this afternoon, so if I were you, I would get my skates on grab the appertaining file, and take a fast train out of Romford for Liverpool Street and the London Underground to Saint James Park and New Scotland Yard."

Barrie was not happy with this shocking news and uttered but one word of one syllable,

"WHY?"

Thompson responded with almost similar brevity,

"Because Scotland Yard says so, do you have a problem with that Inspector?"

Barrie certainly did have a problem with this as his mind went back to the meeting in the Chief's Office and the attendance of the Essex Police Chief and the others involved.

Thompson went on,

"You will have to hand over the entire case file and murder book your Team have compiled so far to SCD9. So you are off that one I am afraid. Now is your opportunity to pick a replacement investigation for your analysis and action by you and Romford's Number One Investigation Team."

Smithy's eyes narrowed, he bit his lower lip, a frown creased his forehead, and he said,

"Brilliant Sir! What about the Essex Police side of the investigation? Detective Inspector Larry Donegan is dealing with that end of the investigation. The white van, and those individuals who were seen dumping the body in our patch and the driver whom we have a fairly good photograph of him. We also have the registration number of the van and the location where it ended its journey from Romford. Are you seriously stating that this case is no longer under our inquiry?"

Thompson, if not before, now realised that he had a very disgruntled DI on his hands who was not about to accept this decision lightly. There was not much, 'Ode to Joy,' from Smithy. He had a weary, resigned look of an elderly family pet who knows that the next visit to the Vet would be a one-way trip, all turned down mouth and rheumy eyes. In short, he was not a happy chappie with a cold, wet nose. On the contrary, he was quite clearly fizzing mad at this pronouncement and the reassigning of the murder case from on high was well, about the last straw.

With his right hand, he turned the envelope with the emboldened number 2 face-up; there was no point in shuffling them! ADI Smith thought to himself,

When in doubt go down the middle and select the centre one.' He lifted it deliberately slowly from the highly polished desk surface, opened it, and before reading the contents placed it on his desk.

DCI David Thompson liked to offer the three murder teams at Romford Police Station the possibility of winning what in effect was a lottery of available murder investigations. Yes, it was a blind choice but it also a bit of self-indulgence. DI Smith had a feeling that the DCI was not quite himself today and wondered why. Just a hunch, but a suspicion must be pursued! After all, that was sometimes the way crimes were solved when deadlocked. Perhaps it was the dishevelled appearance of his superior who, in former meetings, had always been immaculately turned out. His suit trousers looked as if the last time they had seen an iron was weeks rather than days ago. The tie around his shirt collar was crooked, and his black Samuel Windsor loafers hadn't been cleaned for some time. His eyes on closer examination were, unless Smithy was mistaken, a little bloodshot. Of course, he could have been on a bender with alcohol, but it seemed more than that. For sure he had a perception that all was not well with Detective Chief Inspector David Thompson, holder of. 'The Queens Police Medal.' Barrie decided that once he returned from his trip to New Scotland Yard, he would have a word with him when the opportunity afforded.

"Well go on tell me which murder you have selected?"

DCI Thompson said with a little devilment in his voice.

Barrie picked up the envelope with the hand-written number two on it. He proceeded to extract from the numbered envelope a card which he observed also had the number two on the reverse. Turning over the card and browsing the worded content. It had emblazoned in large red print;

NUMBER 2: A HUMAN MALE DEAD BODY WAS FOUND BEHIND THE

The disused Gasometer located in Crow Lane Forensic Team on site.

Barrie looked up at the DCI and said,

"That's rich, you just informed me that I have to be at New Scotland Yard in Victoria London this afternoon so how on earth do you expect me to deal with this charade?"

The DCI looked at Barrie and said,

"Is your second-in-command not capable of initiating the first steps of the inquiry?"

Barrie Smith took the point on board and nodding his head said,

"Yes, Sir, she is more than capable. I had better brief her and the Team sharpish and prep myself for the meeting at New Scotland Yard."

DCI Thompson replied,

"I would inform her to get their post-haste as forensics are already on their way."

With that, Thomson turned on his heel, leaving Barrie not a little dumbfounded. He left the office of ADI Smith who sat back in his chair, shocked and puzzled at this turn of events, the envelope still in his grasp. Recovering his composure, he picked up the telephone and dialled Natalie's mobile asking her to come and see him immediately. He removed the Coldstream Guards tumbler and Grouse whisky from his desk drawer, poured himself an extra-large dram, sniffed its aroma, and then swallowed it in one gulp. He was sorely pissed off at this turn of events.

On DS Lewis's arrival, Barrie gave her a short resume' and asked her to collect a pool vehicle. They agreed to meet in the Romford Police Station Car Park located behind the building on Main Road, Romford so that he could at least be present for the first look at the crime scene. DI Smith having put together and collected all the evidence on the Tow Path Murder including two fairly slim files containing what evidence they had collated. Removing a security briefcase from his cupboard, he inserted the manila files. He then snapped the lock on the Gladstone Bag and punched in the security code, thus rendering the reopening of the attached liable to be by him only.

As Smith left the office, locking the door, a familiar voice from behind him spoke,

"Is there a chance you may allow me to enter my old office?"

Barrie swiveled and embraced his old Boss, who looked remarkably well considering what he had been through, both personally and medically. Saying, to John Jenkins,

"Oh my God what a wonderful surprise John, I had no idea you were coming back so soon."

Barrie, looked him up and down making a swift appraisal, and commented,

"You look absolutely a sight for sore eyes. Only joking, you look in excellent condition."

John replied,

"Are you in a hurry? We could have a cuppa and run through my return to work!"

"I would love to catch up, but I have to be at New Scotland Yard for a meeting with Commander Ward of SCD9 at two this afternoon. I also have a new case that has been unceremoniously hoisted upon us. My number two, DS Natalie Lewis, is waiting for me in the car park. You won't know her; she is a fairly new transfer into Romford. She is mega efficient and a good detective. So please forgive me, Boss!"

John Jenkins smiled and said,

"Barrie no problem with that. May I accompany you and meet the Detective Sergeant?"

Smith replied,

"Of course, let's do it."

On arrival at the car park, Natalie noticed that Barrie had company and while she had never met John Jenkins, she recognized him from the photograph in Barrie's office. He was quite unmistakable with his shock of red hair and a slight limp from his road traffic accident. Natalie mused to herself; John Jenkins was a man who had returned from the preverbal death following his road traffic accident on the motorway which had killed his newly betrothed.

She was aware of the meeting her Boss had in London, and the leather Gladstone Bag confirmed this with a lock and chain around his right wrist. He was traveling by public transport and security of highly confidential evidence and statements had to be maintained, even by a courier as senior as DI Smith as they walked along the ground floor corridor, towards the pool vehicle car park.

Introductions were completed between DCI John Jenkins and DS Natalie Lewis the three of them walked toward the car. As they did so, John offered a solution to Barrie's dilemma of catching a train from Romford Station to Liverpool Street in good time to make his 2.00 pm meeting. John Said,

"Barrie, why don't we drop you off at the station and Natalie and I can attend the site of the body? I promise to take due diligence, ensuring that the correct procedure is adhered to, and both of us can brief you on your return?"

Smithy was well aware of how efficient John was; he was confident that the case would be in good hands and off to a flying start. He replied,

"That will be wonderful. I would hate to be late for Commander Ward."

On unlocking the Police Audi A3 3.2 Litre Quattro, they all climbed into the top-of-the-range car. Natalie sat in the driver's seat with John beside her and Barrie in the rear. The police security gates opened as the front of the vehicle approached and on clearing the entrance road signalled and turned right proceeding down Main Road passing the Bus Stop where Smith's old police buddy, 'Peanuts Graham,' had lost his head and his life last year. 'The Texas Home Care Massacre,' as it was now historically termed included the massive injuries to the response team within the vehicle. There were still a few wreaths adorning the Bus Stop location in remembrance of Peanuts. The incident resulted in an entire Traveller Family except one male member being massacred that early Monday morning. Both John and Barrie who knew Peanuts well looked out of the car window and bowed their heads in honour of a past police comrade. It took a mere seven minutes to arrive behind the station. Barrie got out of the police car he proffered his had to John saying,

"Thank you for this, and perhaps we can catch up when I return from New Scotland Yard, have a pint when you can brief me on the Gasometer body?"

As an after-thought, he said to Natalie,

"It would be good if you could join us in the 'Top Oak Pub,' for a noggin and catch up that way we will all be in the Rembrandt, on this one."

Barrie, having said his goodbyes and strode off to catch his train.

On arrival at the Gasometer in Crow Lane, the area was sealed off with police tape and an Incident Control Point had been set up permitting entry and exit via one location only. The old Gasometer was, as it had been for many years, bereft of gas and as a result, there was only a small piece of the circular round iron and rusty storage tank visible. The discovery of the body had necessitated the closure of the rear entrance in Crow Lane into the new NHS Queens Hospital. For good measure, access to the cemetery was also blocked by the cordon of blue and white tape. They were ushered through the cordon and Natalie parked the Audi as indicated by the policeman on duty. On leaving the vehicle, they were greeted by the uniformed Sergeant currently in charge of the site until someone more senior arrived to take over the task of Gold Commander.

He knew DCI Jenkins well. On introducing himself to both, he mentioned that as yet the operational tent had not arrived, so the scene was open to public view from the road. A small curious crowd had gathered. Fortunately, the body was behind the Gasometer and out of sight. The uniformed Sergeant pointed to the direction of the corpse and went back to the policed entrance.

John and Natalie now clothed in white suits and plastic over boots wearing blue gloves stepped towards the site. The Criminal Investigation Team,' consisting of two forensic scientists who had already completed their initial assessment of the site to check for obvious evidence that may be lying on the ground. Doctor Cyd Loveday was also present as he had very little distance to travel. The hospital was but one hundred yards away. He was examining the body to ascertain the cause and time of death if possible. Vital information of this nature was so helpful to the police investigation,

John then took control of the scene by approaching the on-site doctor saying,

"Loveday you old devil good to see that Her Majesty Police Force is still keeping you gainfully employed!"

They would have shaken hands, but both were wearing the crime-scene protective gloves, so they touched knuckles in salutation. Therefore, they made do with a smile and nod in each other's direction. Doctor Loveday then made a statement which confirmed just how well this pair knew each other,

"Well, as I live and breathe, the National Health Service has done a great job in putting you back together. You look well, and the hospital food has not made you gain any obvious weight. You still have that shock of Red Hair which confirms your nickname, 'RED ANT!' I am so pleased to see you back on duty, John."

This friendship greeting complete, John turned to Natalie saying,

Natalie this is Doctor Cyd Loveday, the person charged with assessing the time and if possible the cause of death. Have you met him before?"

She responded,

"Yes, for sure we met during the Tow-Path Murder which is now out of our hands, the details of which are currently in the briefcase DI Smith has chained to his wrist."

John further commented,

"You need to know if he likes you. He only wishes for you to use the title, 'Loveday!' This, he informed me is the way he is addressed when visiting his beloved holiday location, Kenya. The locals love him, and to them, he is, 'LOVEDAY.' To them."

Cyd smiled saying,

"Welcome to the not-so-pleasure dome."

"Have you any assessment yet Cyd?"

"Not yet. I think this may take some time as there are no obvious weapons about it, but the CSI Team has marked several pairs of footprints leading from the road to the body. Those as you will observe, have already been numbered from one to thirteen with the yellow plastic identification markers. Unlucky for chummy here."

Loveday, continued to support himself on both knees while examining the corpse for clues of the manner of lividity, and for the suspected cause of death, plus any other clues he may discover on this site. He then looked up saying,

"Hold on a minute; there is what appears to be a white substance just on the edge of his lips almost not apparent."

Loveday removed a swab from his bag and ran it over the moist mucous on the dead man's lip, placing it in his plastic evidence bag, marking the date time and circumstances of the gathered swab. He then lifted the cadaver's eyelid to inspect the eyes. It was evident that death had occurred sometime within the last twenty-four hours. The eyes were white and vacant. Cyd then pressed the body's forehead with his right index finger, counted ten seconds, and released.

Natalie then interrupted,

"Dr Loveday, may I ask, what you were doing there when you pressed his forehead?"

Sergeant Lewis, it is a way of determining the approximate time of death. It is only a guide. Confirmation by other means will be carried out during the postmortem. However, by releasing the pressure after ten seconds, the imprint and colour of his skin returned to almost normal. From this simple finger test, it tells me he died less than eight hours ago."

John Jenkins always liked a bit of humour in these situations and said,

"Elementary, my dear Watson! Oops!, sorry, Elementary, my dear Lewis!"

Barrie sat comfortably on the train heading toward Liverpool Street station. He felt it a relief to have time to himself, notwithstanding that he was sharing the carriage with others. Seldom did he, during his working day, have the opportunity to sit alone and contemplate life in general. His beloved wife Maureen was with him from the days they met when he was a Sergeant at the Guards Depot in Pirbright, Surrey, through his various tours in Northern Ireland during the "Troubles." They had two wonderful sons, grown men now, of course. One had followed his grandfather into the police and was a uniformed Sergeant and the other a Warrant Officer in the army having followed in his father's footsteps. He had opted not to join his father's regiment as he did not wish comparisons to be made with his father. Matthew Smith was his own man!

Before, Barrie could realise the train had completed its twenty-five-minute run, pulling into Liverpool Street mainline station. So that he was not too conspicuous with the briefcase chained to his wrist, he waited for the other occupants of the carriage to leave. He then rose from his seat and alighted the train. Barrie was well aware that it was a short journey from this station by underground to St James Park, which was the nearest tube station to New Scotland Yard. He walked with purpose through the concourse and made his way to the Circle Line; it would take him a mere 20 minutes to his destination. By experience, he knew the distance is roughly three miles by underground; however, if he had decided to walk, it would have taken him over forty-five minutes. The tube was a no-brainer.

He arrived in good time for his meeting with Commander Ward at 8-10 The Broadway, Westminster. SW1. The glass-fronted building was most impressive and fitting for its title, 'New Scotland Yard.' The building was adjacent to Victoria Street, and a stone's throw from Westminster Abbey and the Houses of Parliament. He had visited this location numerous times when he was a serving Sergeant in the Coldstream Guards. He suddenly remembered as he marched up to the policeman on duty outside the building why it had the strange title, 'New Scotland Yard.' The name Scotland Yard came from its very earliest days, soon after the establishment of the police force in London in 1829. The first Metropolitan Police station was opened on 6 October 1829 in the street called Great Scotland Yard. It was at the rear of 4 Whitehall Place which served as the office of the two newly appointed police commissioners. The Old Scotland Yard, following the move of police headquarters to its current location in Victoria, it became the recruiting office for the British Army in London. To this day it is still located just off Whitehall in the St. James's district of Westminster, London.

He also recollected an old tale once relayed to him by a retiring Inspector, that Charles Dickens was very friendly with an Inspector Freddie Fields of Old Scotland Yard and evidently went on patrol with him and constables on their nightly rounds. Dickens wrote a short essay on Fields, and it's reported he used him as the model for the all-knowing and charming Inspector Bucket in his novel, Bleak House.

Barrie booked into the reception on the ground floor and escorted to the lift. It was sign-posted, the sixth floor SCD9 only. He entered and pressed the only button available which he assumed would take him, to the sixth-floor. As the elevator arrived and the doors opened, he was challenged immediately by a burly uniformed armed policeman, who demanded,

"Identity or Warrant Card please?"

Having already proved his credentials on the ground floor, he was surprised by this further demand for proof of identity. He produced his warrant-card which received a nod from the inquisitor, and he uttered,

"Thank you, Inspector Smith, may I please ask you to remove the briefcase from your wrist and prove the contents?"

Barrie did not reply; however, he entered the security code on the front of the briefcase and presented the open receptacle containing several manila folders. The sixth floor SCD9 reception constable, pointed to the blue sofa with his right hand, saying,

"Thank you, Sir, please take a seat, and I will inform Commander Ward you are here."

He knocked and disappeared through the door marked, 'Commander M W Ward SCD9.'

Reappearing he beckoned Barrie saying,

"Commander Ward will see you now, Sir."

Barrie entered the office as she arose from her desk and proffered her right hand saying,

"DI Smith how lovely to meet you and thank you for coming."

He responded with a firm handshake and replied,

"The pleasure is all mine Mam. I am likewise delighted and greet you well."

Mary Wilhelmina Ward was no beauty; she sported drab hair which was neither brown nor blonde, best to describe he assessed, as mousy with a fair splattering of grey in a short bob-cut to facilitate wearing of her police hat. Barrie observed she must have been all of six-foot-tall as her blue eyes were level with his chin. Although no longer at the peak level of her life cycle, appeared by her build to be fit. The four decades and ten she had been on this mortal coil had taken their toll; with the result she sported a few crows-feet around those piercing blue eyes. Nevertheless, while she was not a raving beauty, she had a specific look of charisma about her. Barrie was aware that because of society's emphasis on youthfulness and physical appearances, middle-aged women might sometimes suffer from diminished self-esteem. Not this lady. She exuded confidence. Her voice was surprisingly mellow,

"Well, Inspector I believe that you have brought all the files pertaining to the unfortunate death of Christine Mary Pearce, whose body was found on the Tow-Path of the River Rom in Romford?"

He released the briefcase chain from his wrist, extracting the buff folders and handing them to Commander Ward saying,

"We were quite a long way down the road Mam, with the assistance of Essex Police, of identifying the white van and those who dumped the body in Romford. That was until this morning when I was shocked to be informed that the case was to be handed over and investigated by you and The Human Exploitation and Organised Crime Command," or SCD9. I must make it clear that I am not at all happy regarding this order. However, like all good officers, I am doing as instructed. Nonetheless, you will find the information contained in these manila files in their entirety has only been seen by myself and my number two, Detective Sergeant Lewis. However, several of the reports have been compiled by members of my Team. They have not had sight of the collated evidence. I should also mention that there is also another piece of the jigsaw which is not included."

Mary Wilhelmina Ward's blue eyes looked directly into his; she was clearly alarmed by what he had said and responded,

"Can you please expand on that statement?"

Barrie remained silent for a short time then revealed information that had hitherto not been shared even with his Chief."

"As I intimated to DCI Thompson this morning during his briefing of me you were now responsible for this investigation. I was to keep my Chief briefed daily. However, due to the case being removed from my investigation this morning, I did not see him to impart this new development. A snitch informed me yesterday evening that there is a religious coven involved in a large stately home in Essex of a Peer of the Realm, with Government Ministers also involved. He alleges that they meet monthly. They dress up in what he describes as white cloaks. He also stated serious cavorting goes on with young females, one of whom is always sacrificed. I think that my dead young girl was the result of this, and it was a cult killing. The informer went on to state that he had photographic evidence which he was prepared to part with for £20,000! I have not revealed this to anyone other than yourself. I did tell the Snitch that I would meet him at an agreed place and provided he produced the photographs he would be handsomely reimbursed. You will read the information concerning the religious mark on Christine Mary Pearce's forehead and the fact that her hand was severed and as yet still missing. This coupled with the snitch information, implies that some sort of religious cult activity is going on in Essex which needs to be investigated soonest."

Commander Ward frowned when she had assimilated this information and expostulated regarding the evil deeds done to this young girl. Then asked,

"Do the files contain the name of this so-called Lord, his stately home location and the informant's contact details exist in these buff files?"

Before he answered her Barrie could tell by the manner of her voice the deep concern, she had regarding this new revealing information.

"There is no reference, Mam, in the files as to the name of the Peer or Members of Parliament. Plus, the address which the informant suggested these meetings took place. As informed, I am to receive that tonight for the sum of £20,000. However, given it is no longer my shout, I dare say your department will wish to deal. The rendezvous is to be given to me sometime this afternoon. He was to call my mobile to arrange the location of the meeting."

Commander Ward was not relieved at this response and decided to insist that Barrie gave her his police mobile in order she could field the Snitch's call. She brought the discussion to an abrupt end saying,

"Inspector Smith, you will forget this case and the evidence you have discovered so far. It is sub-judiciary and not to be mentioned or discussed beyond this office. Some seniors in very high places. Have deemed this. Do you understand Inspector? I will require you to swear that you fully understand that this case goes no further!"

He was not at all happy about this order and command. His bottom lip was being chewed frantically. He stood up, all six-foot-four-inches with his chest expanded and a ramrod back saying,

"I do not concur with this course of action and will have to take it up with my Chief when I return to Romford. However, for the time being, I give you my word that this meeting and the contents of the files I have handed over to you will remain secret. You Mam, in turn, will I hope to understand that it will be my duty to inform my Governor of the actions you have instructed this afternoon and that will be my final comment on this matter."

She also stood and said,

"Thank you for the information and for bringing the files to me. Rest assured it will be dealt with at a much higher level. This case is way above your pay level Inspector."

He shook her hand and left the office of Commander Mary Wilhelmina Ward, of New Scotland Yard's, Human Exploitation and Organised Crime Command SCD9.

On the way to the ground floor reception where he booked out of the building, his mind was understandably racing. Why, oh why, was this case causing such drama and now being put to bed? Commander Ward had not disclosed the reason for the removal of his Romford and the Essex murder teams progressing the investigation. His informant had supplied revealing information if it was fact and not fiction. A Peer of the Realm and several members of Parliament were supposedly involved in a cult that may or may not have resulted in the death of Miss Pearce. This was the second occasion today that he had been informed that the case was above his pay scale. Barrie chewed his lower lip and assessed over in his mind he might. He understood to obey the command and ignore this murder investigation or should he surreptitiously progress the research under the carpet?

Barrie headed for the tube as he commenced his return trip to Liverpool Street from St James Park underground station. He was just passing the public house when he decided to pop in for a swift half-pint before boarding the underground. He felt that ten minutes of reflection and enjoyment would not go amiss. Barrie approached the bar and ordered a beer of his and John Jenkins's enjoyable Guinness. As he sipped the foam on the top of the glass, he failed to notice the chap who had also entered the bar at the same time as he did. Barrie removed his private and personal mobile phone and called Maureen at home to inform her was on his way home. The home phone rang for about a minute then it went directly to answer phone, where he heard his own voice requesting the caller to leave a message. He spoke,

"Hi, darling I have been at New Scotland Yard for a meeting and will be home at about six. I may have to go out for an hour later. Oh, by the way, John Jenkins is back at work. He looked well. I love you lots…Barrie."

The glass did not take long to consume; he thanked the barman left the pub and headed toward the main entrance to the tube station. Barrie was blissfully unaware that the chap who had followed him into the pub was only sixty seconds behind his exit.

On his arrival at platform two, he noted from the digital time screen that his connection to Liverpool Street was due in five minutes. The next train into platform two was for Aldgate East and would not stop at Liverpool Street. Delighted that he did not have to spend ages waiting for the train he opened the free Evening Standard newspaper he had collected from the entrance and commenced to read the front-page article. The Jacksons will headline this year's BBC Proms in the Park, to be held in Hyde Park on Saturday 12 September 2015. He found this not such a startling headline for a London Evening Newspaper. Sure it would please a lot of people but hardly front-page news. As he flicked to the back page for the sports news, he heard the announcement to stand back from the platform edge as the next train was not stopping. He ignored this advice, and as he listened to the noise of the approaching high-speed tube train, he ignored it at his peril. For as the train was speeding through St James Park, Platform Two, the driver was aghast as suddenly a body was pushed from the edge of the platform in front of his locomotive. Barrie Smith felt the full force of the push on his back, but that was the last thing traversing his mind. The leap of death had not been voluntary, Barrie Smith was hit by the tube train traveling at its maximum speed of 50 miles an hour. His body took the full force resulting in catastrophic, instant death. In that expeditious moment, he had joined the Coldstream Guards Battalion in the sky.

Tomorrow London Evening Standard almost certainly would run the headline,

Police Inspector dies in front of Tube Train

ST JAMES PARK STATION.'

What it would not report is that DCI Matilda Addison had achieved her aim of satisfying her seniors as instructed. The means were irrelevant, but the manner in which it was executed would cause a furore in the press, which would soon blow over.

The hired killer, Adolf Straffen was a level below your top-notch hitman and often took on those contract kills that required a bit of finesse. He was well aware that he could demand higher fees, but then that would expose him to a broader clientele, for sure he neither wanted nor desired that fame. Straffen had been contacted by a woman who had said her husband, a policeman, had been cheating on her for the past two months. She had confronted her husband. However, he had continued with his womanising. Adolf agreed to meet her to receive details of the target. The location was not that familiar to him as it was, Weald Country Park, located in Brentwood. It was sufficiently far enough away from Romford to prevent any casual onlooker, who may recognise DCI Matilda Addison.

On the encounter, he was not that surprised that her husband had it away with someone else. She was rather plump and her face, well nothing to excite even him never mind her spouse. The chubby women were dressed in a drab, nondescript coat, and had blonde hair with quite ebony eyebrows. Adolf was unconvinced the colour of her eyelashes did not combine with her fair hair which led him to believe she was wearing a syrup of fig, wig.

They say perfection is a moving target, a mirage; she was none of these a bit of a plain Jane, which he assessed was why her old man was dipping his tool elsewhere. They agreed to half the fifty-thousand pounds in cash fee up-front followed by the balance at the same meeting point following confirmation of successful execution.

Blondie, Matilda Addison handed over an envelope containing the payment agreeing to meet at this spot to make the final payment. At precisely 2.45 pm forty-eight hours later was the last liaison meeting Adolf Straffen would ever have. The excellent point was that the country park was such a lovely place to exit this mortal coil. The cleaning contract had already been arranged; his demise would be imbued with a sense of calm and serenity. DCI Addison would receive the plaudits of the Chief Constable of Essex and her own Romford Police Chief. However, she was unaware that these two prominent policemen were leading lights in the cult, 'Ordo Templi Orientis.'

The criminal who produced the 'Force Majeure,' that catapulted DI Smith into the other world did not survive to spend his ill-gotten payment.

CHAPTER 14
ORDO TEMPLI ORIENTIS

It was a lovely spring afternoon on Friday the 29th of May 2015 while the gathering was assembling cloaked in white mantles; the chapter met at the grand temple which was an old church secreted in the grounds of Ingatestone Hall. The surrounding woodland afforded its ability to be there but hidden away from most of the county of Essex. The geographic location was sufficiently near London so that it was accessible in less than an hour.

The monthly meeting historically took place on the last Friday of the month, and it was about to commence. As the members of the 'Ordo Templi Orientis,' assembled in the outer changing room, various general conversations ensued. The Tyler, who was in effect the Outer Guard of the assembly, James Martin, called those present to order by saying,

"Brethren of, Ordo Templi Orientis, The Academy of Alpha and Omega except for our Master, Lord Gentry, his Wardens and Officers, please sign the attendance book and make your way into the inner temple."

As instructed, they lined up and applied their signatures to the member's attendance register. There was thirty-five present including The Master and his officers. There were never more than thirty-five, as an entry to this secret society was by invitation and then only when one former member had passed into the 'Black World.' They were attired in their traditional white mantles sporting a small red cross bearing the ever-open eye, that same symbol which adorns the United States of America, dollar. What was not visible to the casual observer, if there had been one, was that they were naked underneath the robe.

In all, it took some time for them to complete the registration, enter and take their places which surrounded the floor, which was carpeted with dark blue and red squares. In the centre of the church was located a white marble plinth, of about six foot in length by three-foot-wide with small traces of blood around its base from previous sacrifices. (Order of the Temple of the East,) had the exalted position in the history of secret societies of being listed as number six of the most secretive in the world.

The Master and his Wardens lined up behind their escorting officers. The Director of Ceremonies was in charge of the procession. Those in the inner temple were called to order, and the procession commenced around the room, with the satanic rite, the organist played the Death March from Saul composed by Handel, while members chanted in unison. Once perambulations were complete, Lord Peter Gentry was then led by the hand and placed in the chair of the 'Perfect Pontiff of the Illuminati Rosicrucian doctrines of the Hermetic Brotherhood of Light.' On the wall above his head, was the 'Five-Pointed Star,' known as the pentagram. It is probably the most blatant occult symbol in use today. The five points of mystically represent the elements of nature, earth, fire, water, and spirit.

The meeting commenced with various chants, minutes were read to the assembly and duly authenticated by the signature of the Master. Those present included several members of Parliament and were true, the Illuminati of British Society.

People often fear what they don't know, and they should, for what was about to take place was genuinely shocking. In due course, the lights of the temple were dimmed, and only three candles burned, one in the East by the Master, Lord Peter Gentry, in the West by the Senior Warden, Stephen Jones, and in the South next to the Junior Warden, David Bagley. There were fifteen loud knocks on the temple door which was fielded by the Inner Guard carrying his ceremonial sword. What was to follow was debauchery of the worst kind.

The large bronze doors were held open and supported by the Outer Guard. Framed in the doorway was a petite skinny naked girl of no more than eighteen summers. She was drugged and supported by Deacons either side, as she was led into the temple. As was their modus operandi, she had been snatched from a Romford Bar on Thursday afternoon. The snatch squad had slipped her a spiked cocktail of the odourless Gamma-Hydroxybutyrate. Once she was the worse for wear, the perpetrators acted as if they were assisting her out of the bar. The bar was bustling, with loud music and numerous young folks in various states of over-indulgence, dancing and cavorting.

Nonetheless, this was no more than a regular Thursday, Friday or Saturday evening in Romford where the youth descended on the town to basically, get stewed on either alcohol or drugs. Therefore, her inebriated and drugged state was of no consequence to the two doormen on security duty at the entrance. In fact, they facilitated her egress by holding the doors ajar. The inebriated looking girl was then bundled into the black Jaguar car and conveyed to Ingatestone to await the Friday meeting, to be sacrificed on the altar of depravity.

Her hair was the colour of a raven's wings, it cascaded like a waterfall down her back, reaching almost to her waist. This was no more striking than her sapphire-like eyes, set symmetrically into her nearly colourless face, brimming from the induced drugs to the point of overflowing, with peace, wisdom and compassion. The female figure, slender and pale like a porcelain ornament and seemingly as fragile, also looked to be as light as a feather. Indeed, she appeared to glide as she was moved swiftly across the blue and red squared carpet with the Deacons either side, arms under hers, for support. Her induced imbued and desensitised state meant her feet swept over the carpet as though she were floating an inch or so above the ground. Her eyes held a distant, dreamy look within them, yet her head seemed to scan her surroundings with inquisitive purpose. Whenever her eyes met those of the others present, they held within them, an eerily knowing look as perhaps the opiate was wearing off. It was as if she could see right into their minds and knew exactly what they were thinking. However, she couldn't conceivably understand what was going on because she was drugged up to the eyeballs. The Master did like his slave girls to be a little aware of what was occurring as it made it all the more enjoyable for him. He was aware that some of the more depraved members were homicidal necrophiliacs.

The ebony-haired girl was placed on the altar, the ceremonial braid with impressive crimson tassels was bound around her hands and ankles as she was spread-eagled naked on the altar. The marble altar was in the form of a crucifix. Once in position, the Deacons, taking hold of the urns of water, proceeded to wash her body, including her vagina and anus. They then towelled her dry in preparation for the sacrifice, when complete, they stepped aside.

The Senior Warden moved to the Grand Master's pedestal and taking hold of Lord Egbert Peter Gentry's right hand, escorted him from the chair towards the unfortunate female. He was 'Master of, 'Ordo Templi Orientis, The Academy of

Alpha and Omega.' She was a votive offering at the shrine of the Master of this secular cult. On arrival at the altar, Lord Gentry removed his mantle, allowing it to drop to the floor, thus revealing his nakedness. He climbed aboard the young girl. His now bulbous penis was roughly inserted into her vagina, and he violently fucked her, while being applauded by the other thirty-four male members present. Part of this ceremony, which dates back to the Bavarian ancestors of this cult, stipulates that they are required to relieve themselves during this ceremony. So, after some brief applause, hands went under their mantles, and they duly masturbated to ejaculation without embarrassment. As Peter Gentry, a Lord of the Realm, naked on top of this unfortunate female in an enfeebled state, reached his crescendo, he joined his fellows in ejaculating. This debauchery was enjoyed and participated in by Right Honourable Members of the United Kingdom Parliament, The two supporting senior members of the cult other than Gentry were none other than Jones the Chief Constable of Essex and Bagley head of Romford Police. They were members and participants in this evil deed. However, what Peter Gentry did not know, was that at that same time, his wife was in a suite in The Ritz Hotel, London, also on her back enjoying the penetrations of one Colonel James Craig VC.

Then the thirty-four rose to their feet, allowing their mantels to drop to the ankles.

Then to a man, those in attendance stood and beseeched,

Satan represents indulgence instead of abstinence!

Satan represents vital existence instead of spiritual pipe dreams!

Satan represents undefiled wisdom instead of hypocritical self-deceit!

Satan represents kindness to those who deserve it instead of love wasted on ingrates!

On completion of the chanting, the Master was assisted in

re-cloaking. He was gifted by the Inner Guard a beautiful handmade ceremonial sickle which had been constructed from brass with ruby and diamond encrusted handles similar to those used by ancient Egyptian artisans. The Inner Guard then took hold of her right hand as she lay on the sacrificial altar semen dripping from her vagina. The curved blade glinted in the candlelit temple as it came down with force severing her right hand. The Master was well skilled in this action, having completed this maneuver on numerous similar ceremonies. Instantaneously the ulnar artery containing oxygenated blood gushed claret over the white of the marble accentuating its colour. At the same time, The Senior Warden had driven a wooden spike using the heavy maul into her left hand in the depiction of The Lord Jesus Christ being nailed to the cross. At this precise moment of the sacrificial lamb symbol, the wind came in chilling gusts on his left side, whipping against his legs, it made him shiver. The Junior warden then approached the altar where the now corpse of the young girl lay. He took hold of the brandishing iron from the heated stove from the opposite end of the alter and branded her forehead with the sign of the cult, the two horizontal and one vertical Latin Cross. The monthly sacrificial lamb had been slaughtered as required. Her fresh blood was decanted from her severed right hand and was collected into the ceremonial Chalice.

The Grand Master Lord Peter Gentry attended by his Wardens, Jones and Bagley, was presented with the ruby-encrusted Chalice by the Inner Guard. The Chalice was nearly full of the nubile wench's lifeblood. Lord Gentry turned toward the East where above the Master's chair was displayed the 'Ever Open Eye,' symbol. *(Their history claimed that Joseph of Arimathea used the cup to collect and store the blood of Christ at the Crucifixion.)

He held up the cup in both outstretched hands and announced to the assembly,

"Hoc Facite in Meam Commemoration.....Do this in remembrance of me!"

The Inner Guard took the cup from him, and wiped it with a pristine white linen napkin which was now stained by the red blood of the unfortunate sacrificed maiden. He handed it in turn to the Senior Warden to his right who repeated the process, his chant was,

"Et Multo Sanguine Comeditis, Eo Magis Consistit Manifestatione Christus Locum Capit in Yobis.....The more blood you consume, the more the manifestation of the Christ takes place within you!"

The Chalice was wiped clean.

It was in turn presented to the Junior Warden who held it above his head and cantillated,

"Touto Esti Elixir de Vita......The Elixir of Life!"

The skinny girl with hair the colour of raven's wings was well and truly flying without wings, DEAD!

Her body would be similarly discarded as those who had gone before. Her feet were bound by red cord taken from the drapes of the temple. The Inner Guard wrapped the corpse in a white muslin cloth. The blood seeping from her severed right wrist immediately stained the fabric. This practice was in reverence to mirror ancient Egyptian burial practices.

The meeting concluded, and the members left the temple. They would now disrobe and dress in daywear. The festive celebration board would now take place where much merriment and quaffing of quality wines would ensue before dispersal back to their abnormal, humdrum lives.

CHAPTER 15
ITALIAN SUPPER

Detective Chief Inspector Matilda Addison walked into the 'Bertoli,' Italian restaurant located on the High Street Hornchurch. It was sufficiently well away from Romford that the visit would go unnoticed. A member of staff greeted Matilda. inquiring, where she preferred to sit. She intimated a table at the rear of the dining room.

She took her seat, which allowed her a full view of the entire expanse of the room, including the entrance. The manner of her selection had taught her on her initial detective course; always having a view of the entire room when dining was an excellent lesson learned. She'd arranged to meet Natalie at eight and had arrived a bit early to ensure they could get in. The tables were covered in red-and-white checked tablecloths, in the center of each was an empty Chianti bottle with a new white candle stuck into the top. It was evident from the wax-covered bottle that they had been in use for quite some time. A very long counter display of bread and sweet pastries, together with a vast array of cheeses. On the other side of which a dark-haired man was busy cutting wafer-thin slices of, Prosciutto, Italian dry-cured ham. Matilda opened the extra-large menu card.

There was a lunch menu on one side, then the dinner menu and specials were on a thickly laminated page on the opposite side.

It was precisely eight when Natalie walked in. Seeing Matilda sitting at the rear of the room, she waved and walked over to join her. She tossed a stylish thick, woollen jacket over the back of her chair, and tucked her soft leather clutch bag under the table as she sat down.

"It's not very posh,"

Matilda offered in a somewhat embarrassed manner.

"It's fine... I love Italian food. Have you decided what you want to order?"

Natalie said as she took off her silk scarf and placed it across the back of the chair. Matilda noticed the quality of the Gucci silk head-square with the distinctive blue, red, blue outer and the Bugs Bunny rabbit in the centre of the scarf.

"I love your head-square,"

she said.

"It's Gucci, isn't it?'

"Yes. Christmas present from an old flame. I never spend that much money on accoutrements. You either have the looks, or you don't."

Matilda replied to Natalie's question on the menu,

"I think I might have the tomato and basil soup, followed by spaghetti Bolognese... unless you do not have a starter?'

As Natalie looked over the menu, Matilda admired her dinner guests pale denim shirt, tight jeans which highlighted her pert derriere; the cowboy boots set the tone of her outfit. Matilda thought to herself that as well as getting DC Josie Bunton to cut her hair she'd do some clothes shopping. It was apparent that she needed to spruce up to compete with Detective Sergeant Natalie Lewis. Of course, her figure was nowhere near as impressive as her companion as she was a little on the plump side.

"I'll have the minestrone, and then the chicken with garlic and mashed potatoes. . . or maybe the cannelloni."

Natalie turned to attract the waitress's attention.

"Excuse me, Miss, is the cannelloni freshly made on the premises?"

"Yes, we make all the pasta dishes here my father is the chef.'

The waitress nodded to the dark-haired tubby fellow behind the counter.

They ordered their food and a bottle of Pinot Noir. Natalie smiled at Matilda.

"Isn't this nice! On my way here I was trying to calculate just how long it's been. You don't look all that different. I remember Mam; you used to have very long hair."

Matilda smiled,

"Oh, God, yes! I had this terrible perm, and it went like a frizzy mop, so I had it cut short, you know that sort of bob cut. But it didn't suit me, so I've let it grow a bit. Also, we are off duty, so please cut out the Mam business."

Natalie returned the smile saying,

"I was thinking of getting my sister to cut mine and give me some highlights. I've not taken that much interest in my hairstyle, and always used to put it in a pleat under my police hat. But it was a relief when I came out of uniform. Those police issue hats are not very flattering, and the uniform was continually having to be dry cleaned, shirts starched, tie in place, of course. You are well aware of the need for we girls to remain smart, clean and tidy while on duty."

"And those black stockings and awful police-issue shoes," agreed Matilda.

Natalie paused and looked to be deep in thought and then said,

"But you know, I was heartbroken when I was kicked out of

Hendon. Truthfully, I don't think I would have made the grade as a police officer or detective back then.

Natalie then asked Matilda,

Where were you posted to when you left the detective's training course at Hendon?"

"Hackney. . One of the toughest areas. I didn't have too much time to think about it as I was thrown into the deep end. There was only one other uniformed Inspector there."

Natalie smiled and said,

"That's amazing! I also served at the Hackney Police Station once I had rejoined. I was seconded to the Vice Squad there. I had to deal with some seriously perverse criminals."

Matilda was relieved when the waitress came to the table and uncorked the wine, as she didn't want to get into a discussion about Christine Mary Pearce's death in front of the waitress staff. She had already had her instructions from The Chief regarding the removal of ADI Smith and loose talk on the case in hand would not have been advisable. Matilda took a small sip of the wine to taste it and nodded in approval. Turning to Natalie announcing

"This isn't too heavy. . . light and fruity."

The waitress decanted the wine into both their glasses and departed from their proximity. Matilda then took the opportunity to alter the subject matter by asking,

"So what did you do when you left Hendon and the police the first time?"

Natalie was silent for a few moments then responded,

"I did a course in accountancy. I worked in a couple of firms at a low level, but remember when I was a probationer, it felt like I was nothing more than the wallpaper. Only useful for making teas and coffees. I was also eye candy for the male accountants. I stuck with it for a few years, but I yearned to be a police officer, so I rejoined and went through the Hendon

Course this time seeing it through to the point when I won the Baton for Best Recruit. Then I had a few years in various Metropolitan Police Stations as I mentioned including Hackney, before moving to Redbridge where on one evening, I was summoned to the local NHS Hospital due to a serious incident. That is where my life changed. I met my husband, Doctor Richard Lewis, who just happened to be on Emergency Department Duty that evening. We now have two children; a boy and a girl. My son is named after his father Richard and my daughter I named after the women I most admired."

Matilda commented,

"So was that Joan of Arc? I seem to remember you were quite keen on, 'The Maid of Orléans.'

Natalie responded without hesitation,

"No you would be quite wrong and at the same time surprised I hope, in a positive manner. I named my daughter after you, Matilda."

The DCI was astonished at this news and said,

"Wow! That is a great compliment."

There was silence for what seemed an eternity and Natalie blurted out,

"I did have a serious crush on you at the time. That is why I came out and admitted I was a lesbian at Hendon, which resulted in my leaving the force at that time. It broke my heart but was the turning point in my life."

Matilda was shocked at this revelation; it took her by surprise. She responded,

"Well, I never suspected you were hot on me at that period of our lives. Of course, I felt we both had empathy for one another but not in a sexual way. That has shocked me."

There was another almost embarrassing pregnant pause when Natalie reached across the table with her right hand and gently placed it upon Matilda's left hand saying,

"It's better now I'm am married to Doctor Richard Lewis, back on the force, having been promoted to Uniformed Sergeant and eventually attending the Detective Course, qualifying as a detective. But it's still there when you appeared in the Chief's office. My heart went all aflutter when I saw you during that meeting. Oh, please don't worry, I can control my lesbian urges these days; however, they do reappear from time to time."

At this point, the waitress arrived at the table and removed the starter plates. This was the break that Matilda required from the startling revelation just imparted. Natalie was on a roll and continued,

"It was the same at the bank as it was at Hendon. Some of the clerks and bank managers I've had to deal with would make your hair stand on end. So rigid, and obsessive timekeepers. God forbid that you should make the smallest error all hell breaks loose and I decided banking was not for me. It was another turning point, so I applied for a job on a cruise liner."

She laughed again.

"I thought it would be a cheap way of seeing the world. But, my God, they worked my socks off. I saw the West Indies, and the Bahamas and the Virgin Isles, but nothing ever prepares you for the pettiness of the crews. Also, most of the guests onboard treat you like a glorified waitress and cleaner. When I was on the cruise ships, I was quite naughty."

At this point, the main course arrived. The restaurant was still only a quarter full. As they ate, Matilda gave a brief outline of how she had moved to Bow Street and succeeded in qualifying for CID. She rambled on about the fact there's a lot of discrimination in the Met. However, she learned how to deal with it.

Natalie interrupted her,

"How do you mean?"

Matilda was silent for a few minutes, then offered,

"Well, women officers often get sidelined or given incredibly boring inquiries. Even on murder cases, you end up doing tedious paperwork. I found that senior male officers had a penchant for casual sex. It proved that a little while on my back between the sheets with my legs akimbo almost always paid off,"

Responded to the DCI.

Natalie was grilling her with question after question; good detectives always have a particular way in which they converse with others.

"So, do you live with someone? Are you married now?"

Natalie inquired in a sort of husky manner, attempting to portray her sexy voice.

"I have lived with a few men, but haven't found the right one yet. There's nobody special. I've just rented out the spare room in my apartment to a fairly wealthy girl. "

They swapped stories of previous girls they had both shared. Natalie made Matilda laugh when she told her about one girl who had so many boyfriends coming and going, that eventually, she found out she was a complete nymphomaniac. She went on to describe Amoretti Radcliff and her vegetarian diet. She relayed the story about asking her if she had many belongings and how the spare bedroom now looks like a book depository. Matilda went on,

"Her name was as I mentioned Amoretti, which incidentally means, 'Little Love!' She comes from a very upper-class family they owned vineyards in the Amalfi Coast. she always had loads of money. She did not work; however, she still paid her rent on time. She made model Pigs and suspended them from the ceiling in her room. I asked her what the significance of these was; she said they represented her lovers! Anyway, one time she brought back this handsome chap and kept on saying that he was the one. We had loads of wine, and one thing led to another resulting in a 'ménage à trios.' So the three of us had what was mind-blowing sex. He was the handsome six-pack body type of guy and was well able to satisfy us both. I never touched her during the sex as I felt uncomfortable."

DCI Addison had just unwittingly revealed to Natalie that she did have the odd, unnatural sexual orientation from time to time. This fermented in the Detective Sergeant's mind.

By the time their main course arrived, they had drunk almost the entire bottle of wine. Natalie was very complimentary about her cannelloni, explaining how difficult it was to roll the light pastry around the meat and make the creamy tomato sauce.

"I love cooking, and I have to say that I'm not too bad. I even did a Cordon Bleu cookery course while I was on the cruise ship. The Head Chef was most helpful and did teach me a few things if you get my drift! I like experimenting and trying out new dishes. Do you like Indian food?"

Matilda shrugged, expressing that she was embarrassed at how hopeless she was in the kitchen.

She then commented,

"When I was at work or when I was living in the section house, I always ate in the canteen. My mother's a good cook; she did it all when I lived at home. You know, big roast dinners on a Sunday. I can just about boil or scramble an egg with some bacon. I've never tried anything fancy."

Natalie smiled and said,

"Well, I am going to change that, Matilda Addison! I'm going to give you a beginner's course in some basic culinary dishes. What are you doing this weekend police duty aside?"

The Detective Inspector smiled and said.

"Not a lot."

"Why don't you come over on Sunday? I'll do a grocery shop tomorrow, and we can cook lunch together. Richard is taking the kids away for the weekend to his parents in Bournemouth. Provided we don't receive a 'SHOUT'. Would you please come and join me?"

Natalie was a wonderful person and good company. Matilda realised that she had never had a close girlfriend. However, felt so at ease with her; nevertheless, caution was required. That aside, she readily accepted the offer of a cooking lesson. By the time they had both had coffee and a deliciously sweet honey pastry, they had agreed to meet on Sunday. Natalie wrote down her address on the paper napkin and insisted that Matilda come by early so she could start the cookery lesson commenting,

"It's a detached gated house on Sylvan Avenue, Hornchurch which is not too far from here. There is ample parking at the front. I have an indoor swimming pool, sauna and steam room in the basement, which the children love. So bring your swimming costume with you unless you fancy a bit of 'Skinny Dipping!' No pressure!"

Matilda, quickly realised that the fastidious and prim DS Natalie Lewis was hitting on her. She may well be married with two children. Despite this, the lady was into something she was not convinced was a good idea. Frockoling and participating in lesbian sex with a junior officer was dangerous. But she did nonetheless ponder in her mind what fun it would be.

Natalie then piped up again,

"I'm going to insist I pay for our dinner tonight, and you can pay the next time we eat out. But I'm hoping you'll be able to invite me to your apartment sometimes once we reinstate our former friendship, police duties aside. Your flatmate, Amoretti certainly sounds like a fun girl."

The entire evening was going not quite how Matilda had anticipated, and there was a real feeling of being very uncomfortable. Even so, she felt that it was better to go with the flow.

They were the last customers to leave the restaurant, and

the restaurant closed information was flipped over at the main door. As they headed out into the pavement towards the main High Street, Hornchurch they paused at the traffic lights.

"This is where I head back to my flat, thank you for a wonderful evening and the catch-up."

Matilda said.

"I had a great evening too. See you Sunday."

Natalie replied.

She hugged Matilda and kissed her on the cheek before hurrying across the road. Natalie was turning away when a highly polished black Jaguar pulled up before the red traffic light. She wouldn't necessarily have noticed the vehicle, and its occupant had it not been but for his face. She was unable to put a name to the individual, but somewhere in the recess of her mind, she recognised the man. Matilda boarded the Jaguar, and as the lights turned to green, it drove off in an easterly direction.

Natalie could hardly believe what she was doing; she flagged down a passing Black Taxi. As she boarded the cab, she said to the driver,

"Can you please follow that Jaguar, and don't lose him.?"

"Lost your boyfriend, have you luv?"

The cab driver smirked as Natalie got in.

"I'm a police officer."

She produced her warrant card as proof of statement which the cabbie recognised in his rear-view mirror.

"Right, luv, doing an Agatha Christie, are you? I'll follow it."

From the back seat, Natalie watched as the Jaguar drive along Hornchurch, High Street turning right into Bowden Drive eventually turning into Butts Green Road. The Taxi Driver seemed to understand that he had to keep a reasonable distance between him and the black Jaguar car.

The cabbie turned his head to the left as if speaking over his left shoulder, and said,

"This luv is a costly area to reside in."

She replied in a rather stern manner,

"Just stay with them."

The taxi driver did as instructed by the police lady. He preferred not to upset the female who seemed a bit temperamental.

The cab driver once more half turned his head towards Natalie in the rear of his cab,

"Do you know where your friend is going, luv?"

"No, I don't."

Natalie said, wondering if the driver of the Jaguar suspected he was being followed or was unfamiliar with the area.

"Well, I hope they're not in an evening sightseeing tour! That Black Jaguar looks like a courtesy car."

"Just keep following, please."

Part of Natalie was uncertain she had even recognised the driver who had collected Matilda. As they approached Parkside Avenue and headed into Nelmes Way, they were directly behind the Jaguar. When it stopped abruptly outside the gated property, the cab driver would have driven into the back of it had he not been alert and a reasonable distance behind. He did, however, manage to avoid a collision bypassing the Jaguar and pulled up some short distance ahead. The cab driver uttered,

"Did you see that? No indication he was stopping!"

It was evident that an automatic key had been operated as the metal black and the gold-coloured tipped gate opened. The Jaguar drove up to the house and came to a halt. The vehicle lights extinguished, and the man whom Natalie was by now fairly sure she had recognised got out of the driver's side and went to the rear of the car. He opened the rear passenger door, and DCI Matalida Addison slid out. They embraced, and arm in arm made their way to the front door.

Natalie had a much better view of the male driver and was

now able to put a name to the face. She knew he was almost certainly a West End Club Owner whom she had come across in the past when she was part of the Vice Squad, Hackney. He was the head of, 'The Clerkenwell Crime Syndicate,' known as the Boyd Family. He was the principal financier and enforcer respectively of one of the nastiest gangs in London. In the past, it was apparent that he had various gaffs. Seldon did he remain in the same place for more than a few days when he moved to another,

Why was Alan Boyd entering the home, DCI Addison? Also more importantly, why was he arm-in-arm with her? Alan Boyd, 'Drug and Crime Barron,' his reputation for developing alleged connections to Metropolitan Police officials. It was also rumoured that his syndicate had a British Conservative MP in their pocket.

When the door closed behind them, Natalie turned to the cabbie and said,

"Please take me to Romford Police Station?"

CHAPTER 16
THE IMPRISONED COUGAR

There was a movement within the room in which Gwynn was held captive. His view of her on the screen was almost as good as being with her in person. He knew what she was going through her mind as he had experienced similar deprivation and loneliness when he was attending one of the several, 'Escape and Evasion Courses,' while serving in the Special Forces and also during his undercover training for MI5. He had to admit that he was never in a drug-induced state as Mrs Robinson was subjected to. However, as part of his training, he was tortured with several bouts of waterboarding. On one such instance, as his head was removed from the water trough and he struggled for breath, ejecting the fluid from his nose and mouth, without warning, his interrogators immediately wrapped cling film around his head. This violent action induced further oxygen deprivation by preventing the flushing of carbon dioxide from his lungs. He did not dwell on this memory as it was torture to toughen his resolve should he ever be placed in peril.

He was well aware of the painful emotion she was undoubtedly feeling in his experience caused by the belief that it was all of her own doing. Of course, it wasn't, but she would never be sure that was indeed the case. It was over three weeks since he had abducted her that Sunday night from her voluntary workplace. So far there had been no clue in the press, neither had he seen any noticeable police presence searching for her in his residential area. James had been careful not to be observed purchasing excessive foodstuffs for someone who would have been assessed as residing alone. That would have been poor tactics, and if nothing else, he had learned his lesson from painful experiences in the past.

The untrained like Gwynn couldn't assess how long she had been a prisoner. In reality, it was almost four weeks now, alone in this room with minimal illumination from a single red lamp burning continuously above the bed. However, she was well aware it was a very long time since that fateful night. The thought that one day she would be killed burdened her with great fear. Be that as it may, she was still alive. Her mind was perplexed due to the lack of conversation with any living being. Other than the infrequent falsified audio announcements. It was driving her mad.

Nevertheless, she was aware that there was nothing she could do to change the situation. She prayed that somehow she would be rescued by a 'Knight in Shining Armour.' Alas, that was but a fantasy! Forcing herself to exercise, Mrs Robinson stood up from the bed and commenced walking around the four square walls of her prison cell. She fantasised trying to pretend she had a lovely walk around Raphaels Park, feeding the ducks in the lake on a pleasant Spring Day, by singing while she walked. The song she sang summarised her current desperate situation. Remembering the words of the Miley Cyrus hit released in 2010

THESE FOUR WALLS: THEY WHISPER TO ME

**They know a secret
I knew they would not keep
It didn't take long
For the room to fill with dust
And these four walls came down around me**

It was now late afternoon, and she was feeling peckish. Deliberately her captivity, James had kept her hungry, so that when offered food, she accepted it gratefully and would consume it with gusto. In doing so, blissfully unaware it contained a small portion of the odorless and tasteless Flunitrazepam, thus enabling him to satisfy his desires no matter how depraved they were. Throughout her captivity, he refrained from giving her too much of the drug so that she could be a little more responsive to his amorous advances. It had been a success as occasionally in a few sex sessions; it did result in coital enjoyment for him. Also, now and then she was almost cognizant of the sexual activity. These times brought about for him, the most happiness. In reality, during the majority of the sexual cavorting, Gwynn had no real recollection. There were times when on recovery, if the sex had been enjoyable, he presented small rewards, by placing a plastic champagne glass of Prosecco on her food tray. She always seemed to delight in this act of kindness.

James switched the Pressel to active his voice corrupted by the audio.,

"Gwynn I have just loaded your food tray, there is a small glass of bubbly for you to appreciate. Please do enjoy it."

A girl had to eat to survive. She rose from the bed and walked over to the now-familiar receptacle in the corner of the room. Almost naked as he only provided her with a Victoria Secret, Chantilly Lace Baby-doll slip in crimson. He had bought seven of them, thus ensuring that his Cougar was not only dressed for bed in a sexy camisole but had one for each day of the week. James if nothing else ensured she was kept in pristine condition.

Removing the tray, she made her way back to the sanctuary of the bed, sat down, and ate the small ham salad provided. Once she had finished eating, she took hold of the plastic glass, presented it to her lips, and gulped the prosecco in one movement. It tasted delicious and warm feeling, and with it, she then drifted back to the Miley Cyrus lyrics,

**It must have been something to send me out of my head
With the words so radical and not what I meant**

NOW I WAIT: FOR A BREAK IN THE SILENCE 'CAUSE IT'S ALL THAT I HAVE LEFT

Just me and these four walls again

Well aware that the isolation was sending her mad, she arrived back at the lonely bed and broke down. Once that first tear cut loose, the remainder followed in an unbroken stream cascading like a waterfall, dripping off her chin onto her almost naked breasts. Gwynn bent forward where she sat on the bed with her palms pressed into the mattress and sitting on them; she cried with the force of a person vomiting on all fours. Just at that moment, the spinning in her head began again, She felt overwhelmed by the words she had just sung, the tears still escaping from her eyes. Mrs Robinson placed her head on the pillow and drifted off into oblivion. Her dreams were swirling around inside her head.

JAMES OBSERVED the drug had induced the unconsciousness he sought in her. Entering the room via the concealed door, he made his way to the bed. There was no longer a requirement for a mask to hide his appearance. She was going nowhere, now or anytime soon! Gwynn Robinson was his woman now and would remain so until he became bored with her.

THE DRUG he had deliberately reduced in dosage, resulted in her becoming almost semi-conscious during the ensuing sex, which pleased James. Her participation in the love-making was paramount to his enjoyment. However, unbeknown to James, Gwynn was in her mind collaborating in the sex, her subconscious thoughts were of her monthly love meetings with the handsome oversexed Melvin Harris in the village of Albourne, West Sussex. James was shocked!

Surprisingly this was a first, as Gwynn whispered to him in her very sexy sounding, Gina Lollobrigida, Italian voice,

"God, Melvin, you're great. I so love you, fuck me hard?"

It did not surprise James, more like aggrandised his feeling at this precise moment, more startled and dismayed by the reaction of the Cougar- Gwynn Robinson below him on the red satin sheet and the soft glow of the same coloured lamp above the bed. Nevertheless, it merely enhanced his erection to further heights.

The cheating, Mrs Robinson, as she contemplated in her dreams arched against James when he moved to her other breast. Two fingers worked inside her, a little uncomfortable but nothing she couldn't handle. Just so long as he kept his mouth on her lips with his tongue darting like a serpent in and out of her mouth. James thought Gwynn had more mouth on you than anyone he'd ever known. He continued to lavish her breasts with attention. His thumb rubbed around the sweet spot of her vagina; her eyes slightly glazed from the drug rolled back into her head. The strength of what was building inside her was staggering, 'Mind-blowing.' He had never experienced such excitement on the numerous other occasions when she was unconscious. Her body was going to be blown to dust, atoms when he ejaculated. She begged him for more in her sexy imitation Italian voice,

" Don't stop, Melvin, Don't Stop!"

James wanted to keep going, but as most men know, there are times, well, when you can't hold on any longer, and the spunk just had to flow. Losing control, he committed the heinous act of coming inside her. At that moment Gwynn was thinking she was making love to Melvin and she climaxed more than once, groaning, every muscle in her body drawn taut. It was almost too much. Almost!!!

Gwynn Exclaimed in a very audible shriek,

"Please don't fucking stop I'll cry if you stop!"

The stud gently extracted himself from her, the end of his penis was quivering and spent, and he was tormented as to what he should now do.

Gwynn exclaimed once more in her best Italian dialect,

"Oh, Melvin Harris sei un Ragazzo cattivo lasciando un accattonaggio donne per più!"

(*"Oh Melvin Harris you are a naughty boy leaving a woman begging for more!"*)

At this, point, she was kneeling on the bed, and the role reversal occurred. The dominance was hers. James put his hand out to restrict her.

With that, Gwynn grew desperate. She pushed his hand

away, took his organ into her mouth again, and with her two hands, she encircled his sexual parts, caressed him and absorbed him until he came again. Falling backwards, onto the bed, she gulped as his second burst of sperm disappeared over the back of her throat. He recovered from the excitement to observe that once more she was oblivious, eyes closed, naked and at peace with the world. He guessed she was content in her dreams with Melvin. Whoever he was?

It took him over an hour to clean her private parts so that, when she eventually came around, there would be no evidence of the activity that had prevailed. He had completed his task when he remembered the final sex act. James went to her toilet returning with a toothbrush and toothpaste, and cleaned her teeth, ensuring there was no trace of his juice, left in her mouth.

The soiled bedding he exchanged for clean sheets, and eventually laid her on her back on the clean red satin sheet. He had to admit; that she was a real cougar! He had been one hundred percent correct in his initial assessment of Mrs. Gwynn Robinson that day when she had placed coins in his begging bowl. His disguise was impeccable that day. As he looked down at her, he could swear she had a contented smile on her face. She was beautiful and more importantly, 'All His!'

CHAPTER 17
FAREWELL DI SMITH

It was Wednesday, 6th May 2015. The church of St Edward the Confessor stands in the heart of the busy market town of Romford. It was packed with mourners, and Barrie Smith's widow Maureen together with his two adult sons occupied the front pew. The first five rows on either side of the main aisles were occupied with policemen and women resplendent in their dress uniforms. The Commissioner of Police of the Metropolis, Sir Bernard Hogan-Howe, who, two years earlier had been controversially knighted, was at the centre of a dispute over a confrontation between armed officers and the Conservative Member of Parliament, Andrew Mitchell in Downing Street. It was all about who was telling, 'Porkies!' His elevation to Knight of the Realm did not go down well in Parliament or for that matter the country.

Nevertheless, one of his own had been murdered, and it was his responsibility to show face and attend. Thereby he provided the public and Barrie's widow with a fitting farewell. After all, Barrie Smith had served his Queen and Country. The Coldstream Guards, then as a dedicated police officer. Someone unknown had killed him in the line of duty. His body had been laid in the church overnight and had a full ceremonial, 'Casket Watch.' It took place from dusk until daylight. His colleague police officers in blue stood vigil throughout the night in honour of their fallen comrade. Barrie Smith's casket was open all night. Barrie laid out in his police uniform. His military medals adorned the left chest. His feet were facing toward the altar in a customised manner. To the right of the casket was an easel containing a large photograph of him in full Red Tunic Order wearing his Bearskin Cap with the distinctive Coldstream Red Hackle. Above the picture was the statement:

NO DAY SHALL ERASE YOU: FROM OUR MEMORIES

DI Smith's final destination would be the Corbet's Tey Crematorium, Upminster, which John Jenkins knew ever so well as that was where his mother was cremated last year with him and only one other in attendance. It was to be a grander send off with the attendance being in the hundreds. The Council Buildings had their flags lowered to half-mast in respect. This was in respect for his service to his country. Early in the morning employees of the Town Council had been sent around the various business buildings with the instructions that black crepe paper streamers were to be attached to the flag poles just above the Union Jack unfurled flags. It was a splendid gesture of acknowledgment of a local hero. As the service was completed, a Burglar from the Coldstream Guards sounded the, Last Post followed by two minutes of silence and remembrance. The entire congregation fell silent. Suddenly, the mournful peace was broken by, the sound of Reveille.

The casket was borne out of the church by a squad of eight men, four police officers in Police Dress Uniform and four Cold-streamers dressed in Home Service Clothing. (Red Tunics) They were commanded by the Garrison Sergeant Major of The Household Division, one Perry Mason, Coldstream Guards. He had insisted on controlling them as he and Barrie had been instructors together at the Guards Depot, Pirbright.

With a precise drill and ceremonial, the coffin was placed onto the Horse Drawn Hearse with a pair of Black Horses with matching carriage. The Bearer Party then lined up behind ready to step off in slow time following the hearse.

The Smith Family boarded the limos and the column of vehicles containing mourners followed at a hastier pace to the crematorium.

On arrival, they dismounted the vehicles and entered the chapel it had seating for two hundred. Once the congregation was in position., the coffin containing the remains of Barrie Smith was carried into the chantry by the four police officers and four Coldstream Guards. The casket was then under the direction of the GSM; Household Division placed on the catafalque. At the rear of the pews, the sunlight filtered through the small stain-glassed window and beamed on a relatively robust-looking fellow by the name of Robert Titus Clarkson, holder of The Distinguished Conduct Medal awarded for gallantry in 1971 during the troubles in Northern Ireland, where he had served with the Scots Guards. It was the oldest British award for gallantry until 1992. It was discontinued and replaced by, 'The Conspicuous Gallantry Cross.' This very tall and rather handsome mustache fellow had entered the building behind those who had attended the church service in Romford. He squeezed into a seat next to a rather plump female in a police uniform, unaware that she would become one of his team. His sole purpose was to pay his condolences to a fellow police officer and guardsman, as Bob had also served Queen and

Country as a member of the elite Brigade of Guards. The lady who occupied the seat next to him, Josie Bunton sat cramped next to this burly fellow, and observed he had a lot of faith in the medicinal qualities of garlic. While thoughts rushed swiftly through her mind, the lonesome fellow tapped his fingers gently as if he were playing each key on the organ as it played the 'John Williams Imperial March,' from one of the Star Wars movies. She was unaware that he had been a military musician before leaving the military services and joining the police some ten years since. Little did she know that he would become the puissant man in the investigation of Barrie Smiths demise. Nonetheless, she smiled at him, encouragingly in a sort of friendly way despite the odour emanating from his mouth when he exhaled.

The service concluded just short of twenty-five minutes. Following the committal, the sway of the blue velvet drapes automatically and hermetically sealed the view of the casket and brought the procedure to a conclusion. The farewell to DI Smith was all but over. The remaining process before he occupied his very own, 'Amphora,' however, this one would contain his ashes rather than fine wine.

The car park, full of police vehicles and private cars soon became congested with mourners, having offered their sympathy to Maureen at the chapel door, mounted their vehicles and returned to Romford Police Station. Those free of duty were invited to attend his wake being held in the police station canteen. This was a fitting location for not only was it secure from prying eyes it happened to be where Barrie had spent many a useful lunch-time with his colleagues. DI Smith always liked having lunch with a member of his team as it fostered good working relationships. Also, they appreciated that he took time out of his day to have lunch with them. They liked learning about the on-going cases and those coming up. The advanced notice ensured good personal relationships. That is why he was respected by those above as well as below. All at the Romford, Nick would sadly miss Barrie Smith.

At 07.00 in the morning, John Jenkins was in his office, having reoccupied it following the sudden death under suspicious circumstances, of his great friend, best man at his wedding and drinking partner. John was convinced that it had not been an accident, nor suicide for that matter as some had suggested. He greeted the knock on the door with an authoritative,

"Come in."

The door opened, and if there had been sunlight behind the individual, entering it would have been automatically blocked by the person who took up most of the door's aperture. It was none other than Detective Chief Inspector Robert Titus Clarkson, DCM, QPM. He had been posted into Romford by Scotland Yard to investigate the death of DI Barrie Smith specifically by none other than Commander Mary Wilhelmina Ward. Hence the reason he had attended the funeral without announcement was that he could observe all present. For, without doubt, this was a case that required some serious and in-depth consideration. There was no way that the push that caused his demise was anything other than murder! But by whom and if so who ordered the killing?

As the Detective Chief Inspector entered the office, John stood and advanced from behind his desk to offer his hand. Given that he had to look upwards indicated just how tall Robert Titus Clarkson was. This colossus of a man was nothing under six-foot-seven tall with shoulders not quite as big, but almost to match. John's eyes traced his tall, muscled figure, assessing he must be in the region of fifty-four years of age. The closer Clarkson came to him, the better the view! Clarkson's eyes were warm and different colours. His left eye was brown and his right blue. John thought this strange! Lilac bags hung under them, ageing him a bit and revealing the many late nights he has spent carrying out successful police investigations. He found himself sniffing the scent of, 'Old Spice,' aftershave, which caused him to smile. However, there was a faint smell of garlic in the air. DCI Clarkson was as old-fashioned as he was. His hand outstretched to meet John's, he uttered in a mellow Yorkshire accent,

"Bob Clarkson, very pleased to meet you, John and I am so sorry that your friend and colleague's murder is the reason for this acquaintance."

DCI John Jenkins immediately felt his hand engulfed in what he could only describe as a garden shovel. For Robert Titus Clarkson, had 'mitts' which would have required specially made police gloves. His Physique, Health and Fitness had the appearance of someone who took great care of himself. John responded,

"I am delighted to meet you, Robert."

His visitor responded with a laugh, which seemed rather loud to John.

"Please call me Bob that is one of the less derogatory names I am saddled with."

John replied,

"Nevertheless, regardless of the circumstances, I am pleased to meet you.....Rob.... oh sorry I mean Bob!"

Bob had a grin which stretched from ear to ear and had a welcoming and friendly effect. He said,

"John, we very much have to get to the crux of this investigation. I wonder if would it not be fruitful if we worked together on this. Are you heavily involved in another investigation?"

The Red Ant responded,

"I do have an ongoing case. However, I am sure that Barrie Smith's, former number two, DS Natalie Lewis can continue that case investigation."

Bob, said in his Yorkshire dialect,

"Okay and 'Ear all, see all, say nowt. Eat all, sup all, pay nowt, and if ever thou does owt fer nowt – all do it fer thissen!"

John was bemused but understood most of what he was referring to;

'Hear all. See all. Say nothing. Eat all, drink your beer, pay nothing and if you ever do nothing for nothing, only do it for yourself.'

He replied,

"I agree full-heartedly with that Bob, let's work toward getting to the bottom of this dreadful crime."

Bob, who had access to secret information which currently he was loathed to reveal until he was one-hundred-per-cent confident in John Jenkins official security clearance, responded,

"I fully agree with this assumption, John. However, there are those in very senior positions who may or may or may not be responsible either in part or entirely for the murder of Detective Inspector Smith."

John was immediately shocked by this statement but decided not to force the issue by furthering the conversation. He then said,

"We live in dangerous times, Bob, and I well understand your resolve."

DCI Clarkson lifted his right forefinger to his nose, tapping it twice in an obvious sign of keeping 'shtum'. He then commented,

"Can we discuss the finer details of this investigation at a later time?"

The Red Ant fully understood the inference and said,

"Absolutely correct Bob, shall we retire and have a cuppa?"

They both left his office, and the listening device secreted by others picked up the closing and locking of the door. They were correct in the assumption that this case was of an ilk, way above what they were aware of currently. They walked along the wide grey corridor on the second floor of Romford Metropolitan Police Headquarters, made their way to the open space of the car park when Bob turned to John saying,

"I have certain evidence that quite a senior bunch of peoples are involved in something sinister. Barrie Smith was unfortunate that he had uncovered evidence which was about to be revealed and he was exterminated thus ensuring that did not occur. It is my belief from what I have been privy to, so far. I have reliable information that he possessed non-corroborated evidence from a snitch that perhaps members of Parliament may be involved. There is a 'D Notice,' on this. That is why the case of the Tow Path Murder was transferred and handed over to Commander Ward of SCD9."

Jenkins dwelled on this revelation before speaking,

"If that is the case, you and I must do our utmost to solve this difficult conundrum."

Bob, nodded his head and replied,

"Chummy, between us we will solve this case and bring those responsible to their just deserts."

As Bob was communicating this revelation, he removed a sheet of A4 white paper from the inside pocket of his suit jacket, opening it to its full length, he proffered it to John Jenkins to view.

John took the sheet of paper and observed the list of five names in bold red type. He was shocked at those listed, paused to take it in, then with a distinctive two-note wolf whistle sound exclaimed,

"This Bob is dynamite, be warned light the fuse paper and stand well back!"

DCI Jenkins smiled and did just that. He mused to himself this would be a tremendous relationship in many ways similar to the former with the sadly now departed Smithy.

CHAPTER 18
HAPPY BIRTHDAY

In Romford, it was a bright and cheerful morning despite the funeral of Barrie Snith yesterday. DCI John Jenkins entered his office at eight a.m. and,
"Seriously, I don't want much,"
John Jenkins mumbled to himself.
"All I want is a solid clue to who the killer is."
DCI Jenkins continued his mutterings, but as he was alone, it mattered not. He continued to study the photographs and the report which stated the facts, which produced a lively interest and a growing sense of its importance. For one thing, it settled the question it was murder for sure. The killer had worn gloves! This came from the forensic report. The Forensic Scientist, James Neil reported fragments of the dark blue thread on the bodies of Mr & Mrs Brown. They were minuscule and found on both their necks, presumably as the hit man checked that his work had been successful. Now, DCI Jenkins was being run ragged by this case and to add insult to injury he was getting nowhere fast! He had come on duty at eight o'clock, and now he was roped into this fiasco, baffling him and his team. He was nevertheless pleased that he now had the assistance of Bob

Clarkson. All be it he was not entirely sure where he would fit into the investigations of both Barrie Smiths' murder and the Browns.

Also, it strengthened the case against the mysterious Postman. He to all intents and purposes, looked to be just well, what he was, 'A Postman,' with his Royal Mail blue sack over his shoulder, presumably full of letters for delivery. This information had come, apparently, from the CCTV footage which captured the male-like figure as it crossed the field to the Brown household on foot. Also, he had been wearing blue woollen gloves. Only a person concealing his identity, and DNA would be likely to be wearing gloves on a warm late April morning. Indeed that gloved hand had been the hand of the mysterious man captured on the CCTV recording of that day, at a similar time entering the underpass. The blue threads found on both was perhaps an indication of whether the postman was pucker or not.

The murder had been premeditated, and the liquidator had worn gloves with the deliberate purpose of leaving no trace of fingerprints. However, the forensic report had stated that a minute strand of hair which was not related to the Brown family had been found on the hall carpet. As yet, no trace of the DNA had come up with a match. It had nonetheless confirmed that it was male. John Jenkins was aware that the most straightforward thing which DNA can reveal is whether the sample came from a male or female. Apart from some sporadic cases, that doesn't even involve looking at their DNA sequence - all you need to know is whether they have X or Y chromosomes. The latter indicates it came from a man or a pair of XX's, which makes them female. The initial report showed a male.

John thought in all probability to take out two individuals in such a professional manner; the suspect had to be well-experienced. The killer was quite capable of taking care of extermination and was no novice but someone adroit in such matters.

Then his sub-conscious mind began to jog his intellect. Somewhere in his memory, there was a fact he had noted about gloves, and that was clear, it was now necessary in its bearing on the case. He set about trying to recall it to his mind. He was not long about it. All of a sudden he remembered that he had been a trifle surprised to see that the CCTV showed the upright figure wearing the apparel of a postman with a cap covering about seventy per cent of his facial features a, wearing blue gloves. Also, he remembered that he was of reasonable height but looked to be of a physique which was exercised and fit from its upright bearing. He reached for the telephone and dialled Natalie's number; the phone rang several times but received no reply. Having failed to make contact, he got up from his seat, took his sports jacket from the stand and slung it over his left shoulder as he left the office. As he approached the main murder incident room, the door opened, and Detective Constable, David Torrance came out of the opening. John raised his hand halting his steps and asked him,

"Have you any idea the whereabouts of DS Lewis?"

"Yes Gov, she has gone to meet DCI Addison. I believe in her office on the third floor, Boss."

Dave said with a broad smile nodded and continued with his animated face flashing his white molars, producing a sort of malicious smile. It seemed he knew more than he was revealing and went on,

"Could be business, but then again Sir, it may be social. I think they are quite close and friendly."

John, returned the smile with a smirk saying,

"Thank you very much, Dave, and I shall, therefore, proceed in a northerly and upward direction to the third floor."

He ignored the lift and swung the door to the stairs open,

taking them two at a time his leg was much better and healing well. He arrived at the third floor, exited the fire-escape stairwell and made his way along the corridor to DCI Addison's Office. He knocked on the glass door with her name and title in gold lettering. There was a slight pause when he heard the giggling announcement,

"Please enter!"

John entered the room to observe what to all intents and purposes, could have been the 'Mad Hatters Tea Party.' There, set out on Matilda's office desk was a floral bone china teapot, accompanied by china cups and saucers and a similarly designed plate containing the remains of a birthday cake. Both incumbents were wearing paper party hats.

With a massive grin on his face, he asked,

"Who's the lucky girl then?"

Matilda responded,

"Why John it's my birthday, but at my age, I tried to keep it a bit secret from the remainder of the police station!!!"

He smirked again saying,

"You know what they say about birthdays?"

She replied with,

"What do they say about birthdays, John?"

DCI Jenkins recited his little ditty,

"Forget about the past; you can't change it.

Forget about the future; you can't predict it.

Forget about the present; I didn't get you one."

Both women burst out laughing in encouragement at his feeble joke. Matilda spoke,

"What can we do for you, John?"

"I was looking for Natalie and was informed she was here with you, hence my interruption to your birthday tea party. Please forgive the intrusion?"

"No worries, would you like a cup of tea and a piece of birthday cake?"

DCI Jenkins was always up for a bit of cake and nodded enthusiastically. He then pulled up a spare chair from the wall and joined the birthday tea-party. Once he had bitten into the cake and sipped some tea, he then said,

"I have been running through the CCTV, which shows some footage of the suspect dressed as a postman. If you would both please bear with me, I will explain a theory that I have. I have assessed the type of individual we are looking for having run through the tape countless times. In my experience, we are looking for a former military person or policeman. His stature was that of a physically fit individual and a male, of medium build. I would judge him to be about six-foot-tall, but that is all I can say at present. There was a human hair found on the carpet near the bodies it had a Y chromosome. It could have been brought into the house by their pet dog, but I am ruling that out."

Natalie spoke first,

"It is unlikely he was a postman, and your theory that he may be former military or police force could account for the lack of any real evidence at the murder scene, other than the strand of hair you mentioned. This was someone who was adept and knew exactly what he was about. However, why was this particular couple targeted and for what reason were they killed? It seems that it was well planned, but what was the motive for their murder!"

John was about to reply when Matilda interrupted,

"What do we know about Brown's family history, have either of them any criminal form? If so, then that may throw some light on the why's and where fore's of their deaths?"

"I have researched Jim Brown; he had a history of being a bit of a hard man and able to look after himself. He was a self-employed labourer, mainly working on building sites. The home was well decorated but not ostentatious. The investigating team found nothing to indicate any criminality in his past. No cash pot stashed, drugs or suspicious circumstances. No police convictions and looks as if he pretty much kept himself to himself. There was one assault investigation when he was alleged to have been attacked in Romford one evening. Possessing a mean disposition, defending himself resulted in the two perpetrators ending up in hospital. The case sheet states, 'following interview and investigation, no charges were made against him.' So while not squeaky clean, nothing to raise our hackles."

Natalie chirped in,

"This does seem rather strange as two seemingly innocent residents of Romford were murdered in their home. Not only murdered but seemingly as a result of a planned 'hit.' The investigation and questioning of neighbours resulted in little or no information with no one hearing any gunfire that morning. There was no apparent theft and no crime as far as we are aware, exists from the history of the Brown family. So why on earth were they murdered? That is the crux of this case, and unless and until we discover the motive for their deaths, we will be groping in the dark. The killer, dressed as a postman, has disappeared in town, without a trace. So the sixty-four thousand dollar question is; 'Who is he'? A professional hit man, or as you said John, a former military man with some sort of grudge?"

John with his shock of red hair now becoming a little greyer by the day said,

"I went through the CCTV countless times, and the figure dressed as a postman is picked up on camera as he walks along Mildmay Road, presumably following the murders. The figure turns right into Cottons Approach, next to the park, then turns right into Yew Tree Gardens, eventually into the main St Edwards Way then he walks down the slope into the underground walkway. Then he disappears, and there is no further trace of him or his egress from any of the five exits near the underground walkway. So, Natalie, we have to investigate if there is another exit from that location. Perhaps there is a maintenance walkway we are unaware of? It will require an early site visit to ascertain this."

Matilda realised that her private office birthday tea party was over and commented,

"I dare say you will want to be getting on with the investigation. Thank you for coming up and wishing me happy birthday with tea and cakes Natalie, perhaps we can carry on the celebration later and John, it would be lovely if you could please join us?"

Natalie stood up from the chair as John did likewise. They left her office and made their way to the police carpool to collect a vehicle; They aimed to investigate the underground walkway for any little known or secret passage. Not exactly a location they would be familiar with or frequent as invariably it was a location for the homeless to gather and sleep. It was a covered walkway and therefore protected from the elements. Intriguing for sure, what would they discover?

CHAPTER 19
JUST DESERTS

It was Wednesday morning. Jim Pratchett had enjoyed his contract execution of Jim Brown, the executioner of the person who had pushed DI Barrie Smith to his death at St James Park underground station. It was, in his mind, that it was incidental and a pity his missus was at home, but then the hirer received two for the price of one. The contract payment had come from an organisation which, due, to his thorough investigation. It provided information about deeply rooted men of some standing. Indeed, several were known members of parliament, and surprisingly not all Conservatives.

Further delving came up with the name of its Leader, James now knew him to be Lord Gentry of Ingatestone Hall. He mused I might have to visit his Lordship sometime in the not-too-distant future. He assesses that he is clearly a very prominent person and will wield loads of power both financially and politically.

On arrival at home, he checked that Gwynn was in her rightful place, which she was, lying comatose and prostrate on the bed. The breakfast had contained sufficient drugs, thus ensuring she slept most of the day. The imperfect love was at his mercy, and there was nothing anyone could do about it for his tactics were exemplary. He showered swiftly and dressed in only his bathrobe entered his well-constructed soundproof lair. On approaching the bed, he noted that she was naked just as he had left her before departing on his mission. Well, it had all gone according to his plan, he felt that he deserved a little fun with this cougar. He rolled her onto her back, slowly parted his legs and ass he removed his robe and let it fall to the floor he was already erect.

James entered her and for the umpteenth time had his evil way with the woman admired. And now due to her abduction, Gwynn was his. She was after all a 'Good Samaritan,' and he was only exercising his right to enjoy the fruits of his labour. As he thrust into her, she moaned which excited James even more as it seemed she knew what was occurring and was enjoying his sex. Satisfied he withdrew and wiped himself clean with the paper towel he had brought into the den with a small bowl of water which would be used to clean her. Pratchett was careful never to leave any trace of his semen as that may alert her during her short times of consciousness. Of course, he wished he could have her fully awake to enjoy the rapture that engulfed his mind during these sessions — the attempt to reduce the amount of the drug resulted in her once calling him Melvin and begging for more. However, this proved too dodgy; he therefore ceased experimenting with the dosage.

Once more left her again still in her state of deep sleep and removed all items that could be discovered and therefore alert Gwynn to what had occurred.

He was content he had taken out the problem of Brown as requested in the contract and would in turn bank the cash paid in small deposits in the seven bank accounts he had under his assumed identity. If MI5 taught him never to leave loose ends, and he never did.

He was aware that another hit would be contracted at some stage in the future as his reputation guaranteed success, plus complete confidentially. The feeling of power and exhilaration always made him feel rather randy. He viewed the large observation screen and saw that Gwynn was moving around her captivity cell, the cougar that she was. He suddenly became erect once more the thought of again another kill had stimulated him. She stood by the bed and allowed her baby-doll lingerie to fall to the floor, exposing her overgrown mop of pubic-hair. There she was on the screen naked and her pert breasts which required no pencil to remain upright. For a woman of her age, she had a magnificent body. He was aware he would not have sufficient time to drug her again and have his evil way with her despite wishing he could. Laying backwards on his five-star base chair, he took himself in hand and commenced masturbating while imagining he was inside her. As his right-hand movement increased, he could hold no longer, hold himself back and his spunk shot out the end of his penis. It was so forceful that it landed on the keyboard and created a dreadful mess. It took him some time to clean the mess which had a familiar odour. When he had completed his cleaning task, he switched on the Pressel switch and spoke into the mike. The audio as ever was not his voice but distorted,

"Gwynn bonny girl, I have made some supper for you which will be delivered to the usual location. Please enjoy it."

Mrs Robinson made for the deposit box and removed the tray with the food and a small glass of white wine which she would consume with glee.

In the afternoon in London. Lady Olivia Gentry went to meet Craig VC, in a mood very different from that of the previous afternoon. Then they had enjoyed an afternoon of unbridled affection and lovemaking. Lord Gentry was allegedly once again, at one of his many meetings. She did not care anymore, what he was up to, as now she had the handsome and virile James Craig to look after her needs. Her stomach was churning as she rang the bell for Flat 2. There were no names listed, but she remembered that he lived on the ground floor. She rang the bell three times and was just about to turn away when the main front door opened. James was barefoot, wearing only a pair of tracksuit bottoms.

"Olivia!"

He exclaimed in surprise, as he did not expect her to visit him here in Chelsea and certainly not without his knowledge that she was to appear at his apartment. James kissed her gently on either cheek just in case anyone external was observing her arrival. With his right hand, he ushered her into his instead plush living quarters. If an observer were watching, it would look like he was a friend and indeed not her lover. Olivia entered his bachelor apartment just off the King's Road and not too far away from his barracks. She was dressed for London in a perfect and spectacular outfit of stunning soft pink Christian Dior tulle, with the bustier dress which proved her ample bosom is forcing it forward and the cleavage prominent. She would not have looked out of place at one of the numerous London Fashion House exhibitions. Lady Olivia Gentry was attractive alright, ostentatious perhaps but oh so beautiful to the eye. How could a virile male not wish to explore her every curve and Colonel James Craig was the current beau who frequented her pleasures. He led her to the sitting room and using his right hand in a flamboyant manner guided and placed her in a comfortable chaise-lounge saying,

"My dear Olivia, I must say that you look absolutely stunning in that dress, exquisite beyond belief. May I offer you a cold glass of something sparkling?"

Lady Gentry smiled, knowing that time was not wasted getting attired for her trip to London. Olivia responded in her usual manner oozing sexual contestations as she let her tongue run across her top lip,

"Darling, James that would be tipper."

She knew exactly how to work a man never mind an entire room, which she had achieved on countless occasions. He left her sitting with her legs crossed on the sofa showing just enough leg to tantalise her host. The Colonel re-entered the room with two Edinburgh crystal glasses in one hand and a bottle of Bollinger 67 in the other. With a swish, he placed both glasses on the occasional table next to her. He decanted sufficient into both glasses allowing the effervescent bubbles to settle before passing one glass to her. She remained seated, raising her right hand which held the glass, upwards toward him. He encompassed her right arm with his so that they were entwined. James offered his drink to her mouth and intimated her glass to his. They both took a sip of champagne and dropped their arms to the side; their lips met in unison in a warm, loving embrace. It was seconds later that the glasses were laid to rest on the table and he swept her into his bedroom. Their lovemaking was, as always, passionate and noisy. Lady Olivia did like to express her delight on climaxing in a rather robust and loud manner. James hoped to hell that he was the only person who heard the exclamation as it would have stopped traffic had it been in public.

Their passionate lovemaking was over and she was fully satisfied. Lady Olivia dressed and returned to the reception room as he poured another glass of Bollinger into her crystal glass. He looked guilty as he lifted his left hand and observed his Omega watch. It was now well after five in the afternoon.

He was well aware that this evening he had a Regimental Dinner Night to attend in the Officers Mess. Lady Gentry was suddenly aware that something was disturbing him, so she spoke first,

"I sense my darling that you have an appointment from which my unexpected arrival is keeping you?"

He continued to look somewhat guilty, but replied,

"Olivia darling, your arrival was somewhat unexpected but nonetheless delightful. I have an Officers Mess Dinner tonight which I am unable to escape."

She smiled at him and then commented,

"James Craig, Victoria Cross, Colonel Scots Guards, you simply must be there. I would never dream of asking you not to attend. You must present yourself at dinner, my darling!"

He smiled widely and responded,

"Darling Olivia, you are a dream I never thought I would ever have the honour to meet such a woman as you and experience parallel warmth and affection. I fear, however, for your safety, as your husband that cad Lord Gentry may if he ever discovered our affair, would be uncontrollably violent. So I ask you to please take every care when visiting me as I do when I visit your Ingatestone Hall."

Lady Gentry responded,

"My dear James fear not. I take every precaution to ensure my movements are not easily tracked. Today, for instance, I had a previous meeting with my good friend Lady Penelope Tennant, who you have met and may recall resides in Pimlico. My chauffeur, Albert, delivered me there and I instructed him to return and collect me at six this afternoon. I now have more than forty minutes to return via her rear gate entrance for him to arrive and collect me. You see, it is not only you military officer types who can employ fiendish tactics. Anyone paid to observe my movements would assume I was all afternoon in her presence."

Lady Gentry was indeed a lady of some conniving James assessed. He embraced her around her slim waist, kissing her gently on the lips being careful not to disturb the newly applied lipstick. Olivia withdrew from his hold and patted him on the shoulder saying,

"When will I see you again, kind Sir, soon, I trust?"

James smiled thinking she has such an old-fashioned English way of speaking and replied,

"Is next Saturday available for yet another dalliance Olivia? I could well be invited to a Baccarat evening at Ingatestone Hall as I believe that your husband has invited the Royal Prince to attend as he so enjoys a card game. As I am known as a bit of an expert in the format, I have been requested to be the dealer."

"What a lovely surprise you have laid upon me, James. Will you stay the night or do you have to return to the barracks for duty on Sunday? If you were to arrive early afternoon perhaps, just perhaps, we could have tea in the pavilion. However, we should have to be more careful as we do not wish to be spied upon again by that dreadful William Roper, the under-game-keeper. However, he seems to have either been let go or went of his own free will. I swear I have not seen him since that unfortunate afternoon discovery."

Lady Gentry was indeed a lady of some conniving James assessed. He embraced her around her waist, kissing her gently on the lips being careful not to disturb the newly applied lipstick. Olivia withdrew from his hold and patted him on the shoulder saying,

"I will return to barracks for duty on Sunday. If you were to arrive early afternoon perhaps, just perhaps, we could have tea in the pavilion. However, we should have to be more careful as we do not wish to be spied upon again by that dreadful William Roper, under-gamekeeper. However, he seems to have either been let go or went of his own free will. I swear I have not seen him since that unfortunate afternoon discovery."

James decided it was better not to say too much concerning

Roper, the gamekeeper who was now into cement. Well, rather a great deal of it, as it had become his tomb. He commented,

"Perhaps he has gone on to better employment."

Olivia, is completely unaware of Roper's unfortunate error of attempting to blackmail James, which led to his strangulation and disposal. Nodded and said,

"I must keep you no longer my darling."

She planted a small affectionate peck on his right cheek as she opened the door and was gone from his presence. Her Channel Number One perfume however lingered.

As Olivia exited into the street and hailed a black taxicab she instructed the cabbie of the address and requirement to be taken to. Explaining it was the wicker gate rear entrance, she required to be dropped at. She was quite unaware that her entire movement from arrival at Lady Penelope's, being delivered to Chelsea and return to Pimlico had been observed and would be reported upon. The agent of her husband's friend had been instructed to keep a fair distance but to record her entire movements. The facts and details are to be reported to the Leader of the House of Commons, who was acting in the best interests of his Lord and Master, Lord Peter Egbert Gentry.

CHAPTER 20
DELINQUENTS CHATISED

James just made the train as it pulled out of platform eleven from Liverpool Station, London its eventual destination Romford. He managed to open the train door, while it was in motion despite the warning shout from the platform attendant. Taking a seat with little attention to anyone else in the carriage. He tilted his head against the window so that he could see through the reflection of the brightly illuminated carriage.

His mission in London had been successfully completed. However, he was concerned by how he had left Gwynn alone in her captivity suite. She may be in a panic with the lack of contact or food. He had little idea that she was in a panic most of the time she was compos mentis. Of course, this was seldom the case as he tried to keep her just on the edge of sanity. In effect, she was being held against her will in what effectively was indeed a 'Panic Room!'

His former career ensured that he adopted the initial assessment procedure. James looked around the surrounding area, checking for escape routes if required or folk that may cause him disturbance. The training, plus habitational actions were ingrained in his mannerisms. The only other person in the carriage sitting on the seat adjacent to him was this old chap. He must have been in his late seventies. He wore a veteran's badge on his dark blue blazer which he recognised as the Grenadier Grenade. He smiled and nodded at him. The old soldier's trousers were grey with a crease you could cut your hands on. He also noticed that his shoes were as shiny as humanly possible, he suspected spit and polished over many years of use, his shirt a sparkling brilliant white with his tie of blue, red, and blue diagonal stripes. It was apparent that he was a former Grenadier Guard.

He permitted the time-lapse as the train gained speed departing the busy Liverpool Street Station terminal. His destination in his case was Romford. He smiled at the well-dressed elder gentleman and again with a friendly smile commented,

"You were in the Guards then? I recognise the badge."

The old soldier, returned his smile replying with what he assessed was an accent that was sort of Middle England based,

"Twenty-two years in the Grenadiers, 1961 to 83. What about you, have you ever served in the forces?'

"Yes, I did. I'm out now; I left four years ago. I did nine years, loved it."

"How come you got out, then?"

James was tempted to expand on his time in the services and then MI5 but thought better of it. Too much information as far as he was concerned, He then deflected the question replying with a question,

"It's a long story! Twenty-two years, I bet you've seen a thing or two"

That was it. It was pulling up a sandbag for half an hour at least that's what he thought. He told James his name, Stuart Davis. He reminded him of Derek Murray a really tough guy from the highlands of Scotland whom he had buddy-buddied with while serving in the Parachute Regiment. He soon discovered that his new best friend, Stuart, boy, he had some stories to tell. It sounded like he'd been through some shit.

The next thing he knew they were pulling into the main large East London station, Stratford, which was the planned location for the Olympics. He had almost fallen asleep listening to the old boy, it was now twenty past eleven, and the old fellow was still rabbiting' on with his stories of yesteryear. As the internal announcement stated, 'Stand Clear of the Doors!' Just then, as if from nowhere, three youths entered the carriage.

Their faces were covered in darkness until they entered the carriage. The features of all three could be seen outlined by scars and wounds on each face, no doubt, from previous gangland fights. James' heart was in his mouth; he could feel the blood pumping through his veins, and the pace of his heart began to quicken. He was more than ready to deal with whatever he pulled. The leader reached into his jacket pocket; he fumbled around James waited for the inevitable knife or handgun. Neither appeared, he extracted a large handkerchief and disgustingly blew his nose.

One sat next to, the other two opposite. They'd obviously either been out on the piss or some sort of spiked drug, they were noisy bastards. James wasn't happy they'd disturbed his chat with the old soldier. It wasn't long before they started on Stuart, he thought that they were attracted to his immaculate persona.

The one with the long facial scar that ran from his right ear to almost his lips.

"Fucking hell lads can you smell piss?"

said the guy sitting next to the veteran of the Guards Division.

"It' must be that coffin dodger sitting next to you, Andy."

One of his friends replied.

"Fuck me; it is you! You, dirty old bastard. When was the last time you had a bath? You fucking stink. You old bastard!"

Stuart the old man just sat there taking the abuse, staring out of the carriage window. James was already weighing up his options, should he intervene now, he thought. Nevertheless, James decided to bide his time. They continued between them and carried on giving the old boy more verbal abuse, then the one they called Andy, a six foot nothing, streak of piss, took Stuart's hat and put it on his head. He was smiling with a broad grin full of malice.

Stuart Davis, former infantry and guards, spoke out,

"Can I have my hat back, please?"

"What fucking hat... do you mean this hat? This is my hat you old prick."

"You better give it back or..."

"Or what old man, what are you going to do you old bastard?"

The one called Andy blurted, as his chums sat giggling at his antics.

Pratchett had quite sufficient of this situation he interjected, finally in a controlled and threatening tone,

"Please give him his fucking hat back and get off the train at the next stop,"

They all three looked over at him, surprised by his intervention outburst. Most people would turn a blind eye to their antics, but he couldn't.

"You fucking what. twat?"

The mouthy one countered threateningly.

"You heard. Give him his hat back please and get off the train."

"Who the fuck, are you? You get off the train. Because, if you don't, we will turn on you, not this old geezer.!"

James was breathing deeply and preparing himself for whatever may occur. He then slowly said,

"Last chance saloon guys, please take off this gentleman's hat and return it to its rightful owner."

Meanwhile, James contemplated the next course of action he would have to negotiate, obviously, it was not going to be a peaceful outcome. Speed, Surprise, and Violence were the keys to this situation. In other words, keep it quick, keep it a surprise, and make it hurt like hell.

The noisy one Andy, stood up took the hat off threw it at Fred, and headed for the toilet, leaving the immediate seated area, passing James he commented,

"I suggest you keep out of it you fucking knob. You better not be around when I get back."

James, let him leave the carriage. Then he stood up and headed in the opposite direction; his two friends smiled at him thinking he was heeding their mate's advice. The train had pulled into the next stop, which was, Maryland, Leaving the carriage, James walked down the platform, and jumped back onto the train opposite the toilet the evil nerd was occupying, As this piece of shite came out of the loo, he grabbed him, put one hand around his throat and forced him back into the toilet up against the wall. He started to squeeze his throat using his well-developed bicep, removing the ability to breathe. This one whom he now knew to be Andy began to kick out. Pratchett buried his knee as hard as possible between his legs. He assessed his bollocks were now in his gullet because he attempted to talk but in a higher pitch, more like a painful screech. He took out his mobile phone with his other hand and took a picture of his distorted painful face. And, by necessity released some pressure on his throat permitting him to say in a choked manner,

"What are you doing? Why are you taking a fuc.....argh.....picture of me?"

"It's just a little hobby. I like to take pictures of my victims before and after, they die."

He looked worried and once more managed to painfully say something,

"After what?"

"After I've fucked them up and finished with them. The pictures are just my little trophies. Well,........ fucking smile then you low-life shitebag, picking on vulnerable old soldiers!"

For the next thirty seconds, he made this guy pay, he'd disrespected a veteran, someone who put their life on the line for their country. You could say James was personally doing his best to educate him with respect. Sadly, it was not to last too long as he reapplied more pressure to Andy whoever he was, the ability to breathe and recuperate was fast disappearing. He was now turning red in the face his rasping a warning that his lights were being extinguished. James released his right hand from his gullet. The rough, tough, insulting vagabond was in one word, 'DEAD!' He slipped to the toilet floor at the same time he expended the remaining urine in his bladder down his right leg and it seeped onto the toilet floor. The eleven-twenty-five from Liverpool Street pulled into Forrest Gate station which was where the corpse of Andy would be eventually discovered. Pratchett opened the toilet door the smell of urine from that expended Andy's last gasp of life expired it had run down his right leg soaking his denim trousers. He double-checked that nobody had boarded the empty carriage at this stop. It was clear. He took hold with both hands under his arms dragged him out through the carriage, sat him on the waiting bench seat with his legs crossed placed a copy of the London Evening Standard in both hands, and swiftly moved back to his original location where he had previously existed the train at the previous stop. He mounted the step discovering the two irks still taking the rise out of the old veteran. He sat down when they both began to look for Andy to appear from the toilet; they realised that their companion was still absent. The two yobs looked puzzled; they looked around to see where their buddy was. Realising that this fellow had done something drastic.

"Where's Andy? What have you done with Andy?"

James thought, perhaps he'd gone too far, he intended just to give him a good slap, but he couldn't stop strangling him. Two kills in one evening, and he was only being paid for one.

"Unless you want some of the same, I suggest it would be prudent to fuck off this train as soon as possible."

The stood up immediately, and one pulled out from inside his jacket what appeared to be a Bowie Knife with at least a twelve-inch blade as long as his forearm. He moved the blade in hand towards James in a thrusting manner. He was way too slow, Pratchett with Speed, Surprise, and a lot of Violence, crossed his hands thereby trapping the knife between his wrists, in one movement twisted the attacker's hand forcing him to drop the knife to the carriage floor. He then received a 'Glasgow Kiss,' which caused his nose to burst open and blood to profusely gush from it. Almost in synch, James with his spare elbow hit the third member of the team on the right temple which brought him to his knees. For James, this was just like the milling he had experienced while completing this Parachute Regiment 'P Company,' course. Both men whimpered at the sheer brutal violence that had been dished out.

As the train started to pull into Manor Park station, the two reprobates nursing their wounds couldn't leave quickly enough, they got up and left the carriage not wishing to endure any more punishment. As the train pulled out; he noticed the two individuals clearly licking their wounds following their exiting the train onto the platform. As he rather expected they were brave in his absentia as the train passed the bleeding youths, they raised their right hand with the ubiquitous, two-fingered, Churchill salute, mouthing Up-Yours as the window protected them from James and the old soldier Stuart were sitting again opposite one another.

'Thanks, son,"

Stuart Davis said.

'That's an okay pal; they deserved it. They should have had some respect. I've probably done them a favour; they'll hopefully think twice next time they pick on a veteran."

The former Grenadier then asked,

"What happened to their accomplice? He seems to have heeded your advice and got off the train at the last stop."

James smiled and responded,

"Yes, he did leave the train with a little persuasion from me!"

For the remainder of the journey, James returned to staring blankly out of the window; old Stuart also remained quiet perhaps being extremely grateful that this chap had managed to board the train at Liverpool Street station. For, without, his presence, he may have suffered badly at the hands of these three badly behaved, obstreperous delinquents. They had been well and truely chastised. James had been aware that the investigation of the corpse on the platform, the Platform CCTV may reveal a single individual probably male, as he dumped the dead Andy and arranged for him to have fallen asleep reading the news. As it transpired Andy would be featuring in the Evening Standard. He had kept his head down in a bid to avoid recognition by not showing his face toward the platform security camera.

As the train was about to pull in at Romford station; he looked over at the veteran, his new friend he stood up offering his right hand and Stuart Davis grasped it with a warm shake. James mused what a nice old fellow. He then said,

"I am getting off here Stuart you be careful and look after yourself, I suggest you take an earlier train rather than be exposed to the likes of errant youth."

CHAPTER 21
PROMOTION SOUGHT

Detective Chief Inspector Matilda Addison was a firm favourite of Chief Superintendent David Bagley the Met Police Borough Commander of Havering, Romford and Redbridge so much so that perhaps as suspected their relationship may just be other than professional. The Chief had available to him not only a detached four-bedroom house within walking distance from the police station should he be held up and unable to return to his wife, Shani, and his three sons. He also had at his behest a luxury bedroom suite fitted which was just two locked high-security doors from his main office in the police station. Not surprisingly, he was the only key holder to that suite except for the security-cleared cleaner. Her access was always through his office and only when he was present.

He had restricted furnishing the police house as it may have encouraged his wife to move in with the children. He liked to keep them well away from the job. He was informing Shani that she plus the kids should be safer at arm's length from the police station.

As he sat at his desk opposite him was Matilda. She could

have a seductive, yet eery scent and look about her that makes men unsure, something secreted in the deep folds of her eyes, so they are blank yet still stunning. It is almost as though she floats across the room, so gracefully. In his view, people were amazed by her beauty, yet could not seem to force themselves to go near her.

A cold and mysterious vibe emitted from her. She had her legs crossed and exposed a fair bit of thigh. It was not lost on David, and she was well aware that he had a wish to bed her. However, that was never going to happen unless she had what she wanted. It was not hot sex with her superior but another step up the ladder of Metropolitan Police appointments.

David was very keen for this to happen post-haste. In his mind, he felt that she would look incredibly naked on the altar of Ordo Templi Orientis her being the sacrifice, but, no, that would not be possible. He commenced the conversation with,

"So you wish to be put in command of the Missing Samaritan, an investigation which has seen two senior detectives in the form of the late DI Barry Smith and also DCI John Jenkins who currently is in charge. Why do you feel you would do a better job than either of those?"

Matilda exposed the tip of her tongue and slowly guided it across her top then bottom lip exposing a little more as it traversed left to right sensually. As she withdrew it back into her mouth. She now saw that she had obtained his full attention before saying,

"Both have failed in solving that crime over the last three months. The press and television have been all over it like a rash overnight; it has been the feature on the Newspaper front pages and this morning's Breakfast television, 'Sky News, the 'BBC Breakfast, and ITV's, This Morning,' where Piers Morgan has vented his disgust at the failure of the Metropolitan Police to solve the missing Gwynn Robinson Case. I need not remind you,

Sir, she was also a former serving, 'Justice of the Peace,' on our Romford Bench."

David Bagley, (DB) was well aware that it had dragged on without success as many cases do from time to time where no credible information was forthcoming. Lots of Females disappeared for no apparent reason, never to return. The fact she had been observed on VTR being dumped into her car was beside the point as far as he was concerned. However, to remove the case from the hands of one of his best detectives, investigators would be equivalent to stating that he had failed. Jenkins had outstanding success as the lead detective in Romford. His record showed that he had solved and brought to prosecution over two hundred cases with a failure rate if it should be termed as such, which was numbered at five, a mere two-point-five percent. In short, John Jenkins was outstanding. Matilda had nothing like that experience or success rate in anything so far. That, aside, he wanted her and was determined to have his evil way. Quite often, his penis ruled his brain, and this was no exception. After all, he could explain the change of crime investigative leader by stating that Jenkins was better involved in the more important, 'Romford Tow Path – Murders.' After all, there had been little progress on that investigation front.

This is mainly due to the fact that he had just assumed command of that investigation post the demise of Barrie Smith. Perhaps it was now time to appoint a new lead into the absentia case; of Mrs Gwynn Robinson so that he could concentrate on the Tow Path Murder's alone. Yes, he was sure that would be acceptable to John without causing too much of a stir

Matilda had not reached senior rank without stepping on or sleeping with a few on the way up the promotion ladder, and David Bagley was unaware that he was the next stone for her to plant her tiny feet upon. She was desperate to become a Superintendant by whatever means she had to exert.

Matilda walked across the small room and without hesitation, cocked her legs and sat astride the Chief. She wriggled her legs provocatively now astride him. The Chief gasped yet again, and he could feel movement in his groin, his man of war was beginning to fill with lustful blood.

DB uttered in a croaked voice of excitement,

"Imagine Matilda I did appoint you, however, I have to consider that you have only done short secondments to CID. You would be way out of your depth. I need someone of at least the rank of Superintendent to head it over the top of John Jenkins."

"I have given that some consideration."

She smiled and continued,

"I could be appointed Acting Superintendent....and anyways, running it wouldn't be that difficult. It's simply a case of being, a good manager. After all a woman's view and perspective may be the change in direction, this almost cold case requires after three months, unsolved!"

Before David had a chance to respond, she kissed him. It was long and wet with lots of tongues. She also swayed her hard nipples across his chest then she ran her hand down inside his trousers and y-fronts, grasping firmly his now erect penis. She extracted it from the comfort of his trousers. As she knelt before him, her hands moved up and down his shaft. Matilda let her lips encircled his manhood running the tip of her tongue up and down it. He gasped in uncontrolled ecstasy. She came up for air, then smiled at him and commented,

"How about it, Boss?"

David Bagley, the Met Police Borough Commander, chided himself. He wished at this moment he was big enough to say no. But she was bargaining from a position to total strength. He was nevertheless sufficiently large to enter her. He pushed her to the floor and gave her a right good fucking.

John Jenkins and Robert Titus Clarkson had their joint eyes peeled on the playing VTR. The technological experts had enhanced the picture. A police drone had, fortunately, picked up the van, and the operator back in the control room had followed the White Van. The Drone followed the route of the vehicle from Romford onto the A12 heading towards Chelmsford. It was not possible due to the flying height of the Drone to have a good shot of either the driver or his associate alongside him. However, it was possible to track the white transit van when it turned off the main A12 road heading towards Fryerning, a suburb of Ingatestone. It then turned into a leafy lane, slowing down to a stop by a large country house. It was highlighted on the bottom of the screen as, 74 Fryerning Lane. They could see it was a large country house; Further information confirmed that it was from where a suspected drugs business was being orgnised and distributed. No confirmation of the official business of the company. Companies House, merely recorded it was export and import. However, the location was well off the main routes and could quite easily hide a multitude of sins. The vehicle was then viewed on the VCR outside a very large outbuilding, the up and over doors opened, and the van moved into the building with the cantilever door closed. The vehicle was then out of sight to John and Robert. The information trail had ceased.

John turned to Bob and commented,

"Bob, now we do have something firm to investigate. What we do need to discover is where this is all leading the inquiries will eventually end."

Bob, smiled replying,

"Well John, I am pretty sure that it's not a garden path! I believe we need to have a good look at all buildings in this area which could hold a murder of this type. After all forensics confirmed that coital sex had occurred some short time before death."

DCI Jenkins looked perplexed and responded to Bob's well-made points.

"And, when we discover the answer to this conundrum we may be some way to discovering, why she was murdered in that horrific manner. Removing her right hand and brandishing a double-barred cross of her forehead, was nothing short of barbaric. In my view, it was most definitely, ritual."

It was nearly midnight as officers from Romford CID moved into the rancid concrete stairwell of Highfield Towers, House, Romford RM5 It stank of urine and weed, and used crack vials crunched underfoot. The walls surrounding them carried the names of the local gang, heroes. Their names are recorded in prominent black graffiti.

CHAPTER 22
THE COLLIER ROW, YOUNG GUNS,
ADIO WHITE DIED GSW

Badrick Jones Died Knife Wounds
Flamingo Williams Died GSW
D'Andre Campbell Died Strangulation

The Special Response Officers Team was carrying their Heckler-Koch G 36 semi-automatic carbine rifles. They were attired head to foot in their black boots, gloves, balaclavas, and Kevlar helmets. As they moved purposefully to the bottom of the stairs, awaiting instruction. Their goggles and ballistic body armour gave them an eerie, futuristic appearance. Detective Sergeant Natalie Lewis took no chances as she motioned silently for CID officers and the AROs to head up the stairs to the eighth floor. She heard the thudding of her pulse in her ears and felt the grip of anxiety in her stomach. She adjusted her tight, heavy ballistic vest. Even though it was there to save her life, Natalie cursed how uncomfortable and restrictive it felt. It's worse than her friend Janet's bloody bridesmaid's dress, she thought. Thirty minutes earlier, Romford Police

Station had received a call to say that someone had heard a gunshot in Flat 811 of Highfield Towers, House, Romford, East London – a notorious hive of drug gangs, violence, and murder. Natalie knew the flat was home to Oboh Imasogie aka Imas, a drug dealer and member of the infamous, Collier Row Young Guns linked to murders and crime for decades. Oboh had been on CID's radar for a while now, even though he was only a minor dealer of crack cocaine on the estates. However, Natalie was more concerned that Oboh lived in that flat with his wife Blessing and their two young children. She prayed that none of them had become collateral damage in a deadly trade. Already that year, Romford witnessed the deaths of four innocent members of the public, caught up in the crossfire of gang warfare in Romford Market Place on a quiet Sunday evening. The once quiet market town was fast becoming a violent town due to the influx of foreign immigrants. The Council has succumbed to the National Government's wish to be known as welcoming migration of souls from less advantaged countries.

The officers tiptoed along the concrete walkway and arrived outside the innocuous red door to Flat 12/4. Natalie motioned, and one of the AROs stepped forward with what they liked to call 'the big red key' – a steel battering ram that would break down the door in one hit. Natalie knew that a dry sense of humour was the only way to survive in the job. Natalie clicked her radio Pressel switch and said,

'Three-seven to Gold Command. Officers in position at the target location, Over.'

The radio crackled back.

'Three-seven received. Gold Command order is 'Go!'.'

Natalie paused, her mind racing through the various dark scenarios they might find behind that door. She uttered,

Right, let's go.

She nodded at the AROs and moved back against the wall.

'Bang! Bang!'

Natalie flinched as the door crashed to the ground with an almighty thud and the officers moved in, weapons trained in front of them.

"Armed police!"

"Armed police!"

They screamed at the top of their voices as they stormed into the flat.

"Armed police! Everyone get down!"

Natalie followed, heart pounding in her chest. The flat was tidy, and she noticed African wall hangings and the smell of spicy cooking. Natalie spotted children's shoes neatly lined up in the hallway, and two yellow coats hanging from hooks. It didn't look like the usual squalor she had come to expect of a drug dealer's home. The officers spread out throughout the flat, searching the rooms. In the hallway, Natalie carefully stepped forward, awaiting the Clear Signal. She had a sinking feeling in the pit of her stomach. Please let the kids be okay. Then she heard an officer cry from the next room the order,

"Armed police! Drop the weapon!"

It was followed by what was a woman's scream.

Following the noise, Natalie went into the compact living room and immediately saw a male body, she assumed it was Oboh Imasogie

His white shirt was blood-soaked; there was a wound entry in his upper chest from which the grume was beginning to amass. He was dead. Natalie turned to see the AROs training their guns at Blessing Imasogi. There was a shocked expression on her face. She was covered in blood, but very much alive. She held a 9mm handgun, but her hand was shaking uncontrollably. Her box-braided hair, fashionably held by a brightly coloured scarf, belied the look of terror on her face as she stared wildly at the officers who'd just stormed into her home. Blessing's, eyes flicked from one stranger to another. Then she looked at back to her dead husband spreadeagled on the floor. But her stare was blank. She was in shock. Something appalling and horrific had happened here. Natalie glanced at the ARO, raising her left hand to depict what she wanted him to hold. Natalie in a soft, reassuring voice calmly said,

"It's okay, Blessing."

She moved forward, looking at the blood-stained woman holding what she perceived was the weapon used to kill Oboh Imasogie establishing eye contact.

"Blessing I am Natalie, and I want to help you love!"

The senior ARO interrupted her compassionate attempt talk down and, in a concerned tone addressed DS Lewis,

"Mam, you need to be so careful here, this woman is armed and dangerous and has just killed her husband."

Natalie ignored him. She knew what she was doing. '

Blessing? I'm a police officer,' she said in a well-rehearsed and gentle tone. The now recently widowed Mrs Imasogie suddenly came out of her trance, looked up at Natalie, and then down at the gun in her hand.

DS Lewis was about to address her again,

The ARO commander in his black boots, gloves, balaclavas, and Kevlar helmets a fearful-looking figure also said,

"Drop the weapon!" t

but Natalie once more gave a hand signal to provide her with a moment saying,

Shouting at her isn't the way to do this! It would be sod's law if she also died tonight.

The widow then spoke in a thick Sierra Leonean accent,

"dis one common dis year nasty bassa to em kids an dem kill am me!"

It was the first utterance from Blessing all be it that nobody present understood a word of it other than,' an dem kill am me.'

DS Lewis now felt that she was getting through to the women, then requested in a very soft voice,

"Blessing, I need you to give me the gun?"

There was a pregnant lull while the woman made her mind up,

Yet again Natalie posed the question which if not complied with may result in another death in Flat 12/4, similarly quiet voiced she repeated her previous request,

'Blessing? Can you pass the gun to me?'

Blessing looked at Natalie but was still in a partial daze. Then she nodded, put the gun down and slid it across the table.

One of the AROs came forwards, took the gun away and made it safe. They had the gun, but they had a new problem. Natalie crouched down and looked at her. "Blessing. Where are your children?"

Blessing shook her head, her eyes suddenly wild and in understandable English uttered.

"I ... I don't know!"

Natalie looked at her and then said to the ARO Commander,

"Phil, can you please check the flat?"

Natalie glanced at a female detective constable who had appeared in the doorway.

"Keep her here until we find the kids."

She didn't want Blessing trying to roam around the flat in a frenzy. Natalie quickly manoeuvred herself out of the living room, accompanied by Phil; He led the way with his weapon at the ready should they meet further trouble. They moved down the corridor and found what looked like the children's bedroom —two small single beds with pink princess duvet covers. There were dolls and teddy bears neatly lined up on the pillows. She checked, but there was no sign of any children. Where the hell were they? Then another black-clad individual hurried towards her down the hallway he said,

"Nothing, guv. No sign of them."

"'Shit."

Natalie muttered.

She thought were they lying somewhere dead? Or had they fled and were now out there on the estate, terrified and alone? It was obviously not right. Then, from inside the children's bedroom, there was a whimpering noise and some movement. Natalie turned and walked over to where she thought the noise had come from – a narrow, pink wooden cupboard that had been self-assembled into an alcove. She carefully opened the doors and immediately saw two young girls cowering, looking utterly terrified. Natalie looked at the WPC and thought then relief came over her face. Thank God! Kneeling, Natalie looked at them.

"It's all right girls. No one's going to hurt you, okay! We're going to look after you."

The elder-looking girl blinked, then shifted herself and slowly rose to her feet.

"Good girl. Come here."

The girl's face was streaked with large crocodile tears as Natalie took her hand and gently guided her towards the WPC. Her little fingers were icy and still shaking with fear.

Natalie wiped them away gently and passed her cold hand to her colleague saying,

"This is Jane; she will look after you."

Natalie turned back to the alcove and smiled at the younger daughter asking,

"Do you want to come with me, darling?"

The little girl nodded, held out her hand, and Natalie helped her out of the cupboard.

"There we go. You're safe now."

Natalie watched as the girl wandered over to her sister, still lost in the trauma of what had happened. WPC Jane Andrews proffered her free hand which the girl took. She now had one in either hand. They were still shaking, nervous after all that had occurred in their infant lives today.

What would the events of the last hour do to them as they grew up? She had seen it so many times before. The ongoing cycle of crime, poverty, and addiction in places like this. There was Nothing they could do except try to hold it all together. Lives can be ruined in a split second, especially in Romford, RM5.

CHAPTER 23
HEAVENS RELEASE

As Natalie entered the CID office, she saw DCI John Jenkins with about twelve uniformed officers, who were all male. She spotted DCI Clarkson in a separate office through a window, having a conversation with DCI Dave Torrance. Jenkins was standing beside a table with guns, bullets, and shoulder holsters laid out on it, some of which he was handing to the uniform squad, none of whom she recognised. There was a tense atmosphere, and everyone had a solemn look on their faces as they signed for their Glock 17 pistols and commenced checking them for safety and loading them. Jenkins turned to Lewis,

"Are you an authorised shot, Lewis?"

Jenkins asked, his eyes scrunched tight as if anticipating danger ahead. Her response was in the negative.

"Right, we had better not arm you for this operation. One, which I believe you will be delighted to join."

"So, what's the mission Boss?"

John responded,

"We have certain tight information of an address in

Romford, which indicates that Mrs Gwynn Robinson is being held captive."

Natalie was excited to hear this news, coupled with the fact she was about to be part of the rescue. However, it puzzled her that firearms were at this point being issued for the raid. She turned towards John, and asked,

"Why on this earth do we require to be tooled up for this operation?"

"Well, the individual we have discovered is a former member of the Special Forces and a well-trained killer. He has a record of having executed for payment. It is, therefore, important that we can nullify him if necessary. When we raid his property, we will be ready for whichever eventuality occurs. Our main task is to prevent any mishaps. We believe he is a gun for hire, so he has little or no contact with the underworld. Needless to say, he will have contacts that we are unaware of."

DS Lewis, had seen and experienced many raids in her time, she was aware of the necessity for a swift entrance, disarm any threat immediately, and rescue the principle person. That was always the Metropolitan Police's Modus Operandi, (protection of the public,) without loss of life. She then asked John,

"What then will be my role in the operation?"

Jenkins smiled saying,

"Well your task will be once the house is secure and all fireworks cease, you my dear will be to deal with the principal person, Mrs Gwynn Robinson. Our electronic eavesdroppers are sure it is her that is being held. However, it is not one hundred percent certain. The audiotape recordings are not brilliant as it appears that the target is being retained in a location within the house, which is soundproofed. The fortunate revelation only occurred as he seems to have a recording studio that is not secure to sound detection. He has had the habit of replaying recordings and having his fun with her. It is this which has led us to the discovery. He replays his cavorting with his plaything which is rather disgusting, to be frank, it's pornographic, certainly on the sound recording."

Natalie was concerned that the planned rescue raid would go, pear-shaped. She had been involved in only two when she was in the central London Police Station, and one was successful. However, the other was a complete disaster with the 'Principle,' was shot dead by the person holding her captive. It was a concern to her, and she felt that it was essential to utter her apprehension.

"Boss, are we certain that he will be armed? And, if so, I request that I am immediately authorised to carry a firearm for my self-protection?"

John responded,

"Very well, I will arrange for a sharp, short period of instruction and have the authorisation license certificate issued in your name so that you may carry a pistol, post haste'."

Natalie spoke,

"But if the operation is tonight then how will that be possible?"

"We will delay it for twenty-four hours as we are observing the house if there is a necessity the observation team can move promptly when required in the interest of protection of the principle."

By mid-morning Jenkins arranged a suitable observation point in a house in Bruce Avenue opposite the target address. The owner, a professional photographer, had agreed to allow his home to be used as he travelled to Edinburgh to shoot various assignments in preparation of a glossy magazine publication featuring the world-famous Edinburgh Festival. By nature, he was a curious sort of fellow and wanted to know all about why the police wanted to use his flat. John explained to him there had been a spate of daylight robberies in the street and he would be compensated for the use of his flat and any calls made from his landline telephone. The owner told Jenkins he would be back in three weeks and left.

The police observation post was made all the more secure as it was directly opposite the target in Hornchurch. The entrance to the apartment was from the rear, thereby protecting it from the street view. Thus, ingress and egress are protected from public view.

His best officers operated the observation point. Team One, was DC's Paul Thompson and Pat Shovlin, and Team 2 was Mike Day and Jane Dunston, although new to the team the latter had proved her worth already, he was confident in her abilities. The apartment had all the amenities one may expect from a single man living on his own.

Paul had a proper search around the apartment, thus ensuring that the owner had not left an eavesdropping device in the location to record the police conversation. He discovered in a small room next to the toilet, and he mused, it was as dark as the earl-of-hells waistcoat. He searched with his right hand for the light switch, pressed it downwards, and was surprised when all that happened was a vintage Paterson darkroom lamp slowly came on. It was painted in a dark chocolate brown colour. Once fully powered the mix of brown and red reminded him of when his pet fish had the lamp in the fish tank turned off. It also reminded him that he had read somewhere in the past that experts thought it to be the ugliest colour in the world. Paul's eyes were brown!

The apartment was frugally furnished but nonetheless comfortable. However, the photographic dark-room was state of the art with a dry and wet sink area on the corner of the room and a small water tap. The room's centre has a square table at a comfortable height, containing around the edge ample power sockets, thus enabling him to work on his developed prints.

Immediately above was a photographic pully for hanging the wet prints to dry. Also, on the tabletop were his enlarger and tools. A cabinet underneath contained developing trays and a second locked repository that Paul assumed included set dry pictures. He tried the four drawers one by one, but they were all sealed. The contents interested him, however, would wait for further investigation in due course.

Paul and Pat took the first shift and were seated behind the drawn drapes opposite the house being observed. The surveillance equipment to record the target address was activated, and the camera lens was hidden to the human eye should anyone look up at the apartment windows. Pat double-checked that the recorder was operating and recording in real-time evidence should it manifest such.

The eavesdropping device planted against the rear garden window was so sensitive that they could hear any movement in the target house. All be it they were located some 20 yards away and across the road from their observation post. The audio was switched on to record, however, would not activate until something was either said or sounded. In effect, while they had to be on the ball at all times, it was somewhat dull.

For eight hours, Paul and Pat had kept themselves vigilantly observing but all to no avail. Absolutely nothing of note was either seen or heard from the target. Nobody had entered the property which was rather strange as reports had intimated that the owner James Pratchett was a consistent entrant daily. All be it at irregular times during the day. James was reported to be over six-foot-tall; his build was depicted as a Caucasian male adult with a round face.

There were no other detailed facts regarding the suspect. The Metropolitan Police had no information appertaining to his previous life. All this was due to his involvement with MI5 for his military record had been expunged. His new name was just that, and he was in short regicidal. In effect, he had no history nor any form of having lived at all. He was as it was recorded on the homeowner's local papers, one, 'James Pratchett.' He was to the police an enigma. Neighbours that occupied the house adjacent to his thought of him as someone who worked in the City of London. He was always immaculately dressed and always wore a necktie come summer or winter. His only identifiable point of interest was that he kept a cat, not an ordinary cat as one may expect. He had a pure white Persian cat somewhat similar to the one that, Blofeld had in the movie, 'You Only Live Twice.' He was widely considered to be Bond's greatest enemy. (Blofeld that is.... not the White Cat.)

DCI Jenkins was disturbed by the report he had received from his observation team. The fact that no entry to the house had taken place in the last twenty-four hours concerned him immensely. If as suspected there was a woman held captive and unattended to for that length of time. It was of concern that she could have been killed and abandoned. However, undoubtedly his priority was to safeguard life, and for that reason, he decided, caution would be thrown to the wind.

He picked up the telephone neatly positioned at exactly sixteen inches to his right and ten inches from the left edge of his desk. He was a stickler for uniformity in all its forms. He heard the phone ringing at the other end, which was Bob Clarkson's, his fellow DCI office. The answer came with Bob's usual authoritarian voice,

"Clarkson, here,"

"Bob, I believe we can wait no longer for confirmation of the arrival of the suspect. We must move now if we are to think that Mrs Robinson is being held captive therein."

Clarkson responded,

" I fully agree with you, and the sooner we get on with the

raid, we will perhaps save her. However, if we continue to sit it out until Pratchett appears it may be too late."

"I will rev up the teams again, which are in standby and proceed the operation from pause to go!"

As John replaced the phone into the cradle, he was concerned that they would be too late even now. His team had observed no movement or noise other than the dammed cat for over sixteen hours. Already, they were in trouble, he thought.

The briefing had already been completed in advance. So it was only a matter of final confirmation, and the police vehicles mounted by those involved left the Romford police station in convoy.

On arrival at the target address area, Bruce Avenue, Hornchurch they dismounted well short and secretly stealthy to the various assembly points. All that was now required was the command to, 'Go, Go' Go!' It was first absolutely operationally necessary to check that all were in position and ready to proceed. John Jenkins noted his throat became dry, and he swallowed with some difficulty. A bead of sweat scuttled down his temple like some insect, leaving a glistening silvery trail in its wake.

He could smell it in the air - sense the unnatural quietness, the electric tension which pervaded the order to, Go. They were coming Again. Suddenly it was sweltering. His throat became dry, and he swallowed with some difficulty. This operation could not fail, or his career would be ion the line. He mused, was this not what he had been trained over many years.

Then he heard the footsteps. Distant at first ... rather like listening to a piece of music and honing in on the bass line, separating it from the rest of the musical instruments. The footsteps became more loudly as they mounted the steps and reached the landing on which he was situated. On looking around, he noted it was Dave Torrance. John was surprised by this arrival, as Torrance was meant to be in the observation post, ensuring that Pratchett had arrived in situ or not. He turned his body towards him, saying,

"What are you doing here?"

Dave Torrance was panting and either fighting for breath or in dire need of some fitness training. He kept his head down to not expose himself above the small wall that contained a single column of police. DCI Jenkins, the Gold Commander, behind him was DS Lewis, (the only female), then Paul Thompson and finally in the group of four, DS Norman Bates who had been part of the original investigation of the Gwynn Robinson's kidnapping.

"I wanted you to know. There has been some noise within the house. Alas, we are unable to decide if its human or not, Sir!"

Torrance was too late to change John's mind or his action, and he must now throw caution to the wind, He depressed his radio Pressel and gave the command,

"Go, Go, Go!"

With that command, the Entry Team clad in their issued Kevlar Body Armour, Gas Masks avoiding identification other than the number on each helmet. Their security camera mounted on the helmet identified by the Metropolitan Police black and white dicing rim. Armed with Heckler Koch MP5 assault weapons were led by the policeman holding the issued battering ram approached the rear door. The leading individual halted the rush, and smacked the door with the ram device causing the wood to crack and splinter as the ingress was sufficient, providing access for the armed squad. The thunder flash which had been thrown into the house exploded with deafening loudness, thereby causing disorientation. The noise was deafening, and smoke bellowed around the breached entry. The remainder of the armed team entered the house, all shouting,

"Armed Police, Armed Police, get on the floor."

Once the smoke emanated, they systematically commenced to search each room, and when complete, the bellowed command was heard,

"CLEAR!"

They entered a room containing many large television screens with recording devices. They had OLED ability; Organic Light-Emitting Diodes, able to produce the best picture quality among flat-panel displays, hands-down. John Jenkins was following the entry team, and as he entered the room, he noted a still picture on one of the fifty-inch screens. There in full view was a petit woman laying on a bed, while he could hear nothing, it was apparent she was in sheer distress. Not surprising given the forced entry portal.

He turned to the team commander, saying,

"Find the door to this room before she expires from shock,"

The helmet-clad Sergeant nodded in assent, but said, nothing in response. DS Lewis entered the viewing station, John turned to her quickly pointing to the screen, and commented,

"We have to find her soon, or we may well be too late to save her and all will have been in vain."

Natalie nodded in acceptance of the statement. Just as she did so, another bellow emanated from the stairwell that led to a door in the basement.

The Ram Man rushed down the stairs pushing past his colleague; he smashed at the entrance, but, due to its reinforcement construction, the device bounced, making minimal impression, as he fell backwards. He then had a second and third attempt when eventually the door collapsed, thereby permitting access. Two members of the team entered the room to secure safety for others. Once satisfied they called loudly,

"Clear!"

DS Lewis is on that command. Immediately rushed into the

room and made for the bed where Gwynn dressed only in what was a sheer lace open bra and crotchless lingerie baby doll nightwear. Her legs curled beneath her in a foetal position. She was screaming in total anguish as Natalie approached the bed. This weeping woman stood out firmly as an iconic denouncement of the atrocities and inhumanity she had suffered. Her green eyes bloodshot provided a strident palette of acid green and hot purples, allowing no forgiveness-only protest and accusation of her torment. Natalie placed her arms around Gwynn to offer comfort. She pressed her against her yellow blouse as she was not in uniform like her colleagues. In effect, her attire's manner was to hopefully assist in making Mrs Robinson relax, feel warm and rescued. An NHS Ambulance Crew entered the cellar accompanied by a doctor. Following his thorough medical examination, Gwynn was loaded onto a stretcher, carried up the stairs, placed in the ambulance, and was still accompanied by DS Lewis. The yellow and green London Ambulance Service vehicle was parked in the main road of Bruce Avenue with the doors ajar awaiting the traumatised patient. Once inside and secured, Natalie sat with the ambulance attendants and the doctor as the vehicle took off for Queens Hospital, Romford.

After six-hours of thorough searching of the house, the result was in the negative, apart from the television control room which contained several large viewing screens. There was no evidence of recorded VCRs or any historical material in short nothing of any use.

No clothing was found in the entire house, and it was as if it had never been occupied except for the unfortunate Mrs Robinson and the white cat.

CHAPTER 24
ASSASSINS JOB OFFER

James Patchett had supplied his car registration number by telephone as requested. The automotive recognition system ensured the vehicle and driver's identity was confirmed. The gates automatically opened. Pratchett entered the estate driving through the sixteenth-century driveway opening which sported a unique, Clock Tower. He drove up to the house over red stones gravel that popped and pinged under his tyres. Once he had parked his car, opened the door and exited. His shoes landed uncomfortably on gravel stone chippings. He grabbed his briefcase off the passenger seat and got out to take a look around before ringing the bell. 'Money comes to money,' his mother used to say. Judging by the impressive parkland stretching down from the house's formal garden to a lake, Lord Peter Gentry must indeed be a very wealthy man. Behind him, the massive front door opened with a faint creak. A man's voice broke the silence.

"You must be Mr Pratchett; Lord Peter is expecting you. Please follow me."

James followed him inside. The interior of Ingatestone Hall smelled of lilac blossom. There was a massive spray of blooms in a tall glass vase on a table in the reception area's centre. Then towards the rear of the entrance, he was amazed at what he saw. The staircase swept up and round in a graceful curve before splitting into two. He had known of Lord Gentry and Ingatestone Hall for some time. Indeed, he had felt in the past that it required investigation. He was nevertheless shocked when he received the call asking him to attend for a chat with His Lordship. The caller specified that he must come alone.

"This way please, sir," said the butler.

They walked a few paces down a wide hallway before the butler opened a dark wooden door and motioned for James to enter. It was a library. Apart from the door and a large multi-paned window looking out on to the gravel drive, lined by floor-to-ceiling bookshelves. There was even an old-fashioned wheeled ladder on rails that would slide around to reach the higher shelves. The room smelled of cigar smoke and worn leather, a very male smell similar to some of the Turkish Bar's he had frequented during covert and clandestine operations with MI5. As he sat on one of the sofas a butler entered holding a silver tray above his left shoulder, he placed it on the small table adjacent to where James sat. he then proceeded without a statement to pour the coffee from the pot into the porcelain cup. Following this, he placed the cream jug next to them and asked,

"Would Sir wish anything else?"

James smiled and said,

"Thank you very much."

The butler remained silent and left the room..

James lifted the cup to his mouth and took his first sip.

The library door opened, and with a regular, purposeful pace entered Peter Gentry. James noted that he settled down each foot before the other, never quite having both of the carpets simultaneously. Pratchett, from his former experience, assessed that this was a man full of confidence.

"You have coffee, I see," said His Lordship.

James, got up from the seat as he approached him. They were level in height, and their eyes met. James spoke first as he was taught to always make the first statement when meeting a stranger.

"Excellent, thank you, Lord Gentry."

"Oh, please. None of the forelock-tugging. I insist you call me Peter."

"The coffee's excellent ... Peter," James said to appease the request,

He was struggling to match this man's relaxed, almost jovial manner. He pointed to a painting above the fireplace – a female nude picked out in almost abstract blocks of cobalt.

"Is that a Matisse, Green Stripe?"

"Yes, it is."

James was up on French modernistic art. He knew that Matisse was universally regarded, along with Picasso as one of the artists who best helped to define the revolutionary developments in the techniques throughout the opening decades of the twentieth century,

"I believe it is entitled Green Stripe."

Lord Gentry responded,

"Well done you, Sir, you know your artwork."

Patchett could sense a lucrative contract, a big plus in a world of insecure freelance assassins' income; yet, deep in his stomach, a worm was twisting and coiling this way and that as if trying to escape. It was an early warning, perhaps he thought! It prompted, James, to ask the obvious question.

"Dedicated to what?"

James decided not to oblige. There was an awkward pause, then Gentry cleared his throat and continued.

"Yes. We are dedicated, dedicated to a rebirth of national pride, James. I'm sure you can appreciate the need for an influential nation in these exciting times. Globalisation, terror on our streets, godlessness, unchecked immigration: they're threats, James, and we need to meet them. I intend to galvanise not just Parliament but the whole country.

Peter Gentry was silent for a minute, thereby allowing what he had mentioned being understood. Then he continued,

"We must reassert our values and declare England a place where people conform to our beliefs, not browbeat us into accepting theirs. There are intolerable stats which reveal that we have become what we know as a 'Snowflake Country!' James, this Nation of ours, requires reform."

James, pondered this startling statement and, just as he had gathered a response, Peter Gentry went on,

"I asked you to see me as I have a proposition to put to you. I require a top-notch, Communications Director, who has an outstanding impeachable track record in dangerous missions. My researchers are the best James, and they include very senior police personnel and a former head of MI5 JTAC (Joint Terrorism Analysis Centre) who knows your ability; you are very highly recommended from other such sources."

Pratchett was flattered by this opening statement, for sure his interested was captured. He was about to speak when Lord Gentry carried on,

"Before you make your mind up, let me continue with what is on offer. I will make you a full member of my board in the position of Director of Communications. The task will not be simple; however, for the salary I am offering is phenomenal, you will have a signing on fee of fifty-five-thousand pounds sterling. And your monthly remuneration, one-hundred thousand, and all expenses, and I reiterate, all expenses. Of course, due to your personal skill of disposing of the unwanted, you will be required to do just that. Also, let me inform you that your little plaything, Gwynn Robinson, whom you have kept in your cellar will have to go, Vamos, however, my contacts will deal with that for you. No risk is to be taken in the employment of you to this pertinent role in my organisation."

Again, James was trying to come to terms with this situation, and Gentry went on,

You will cease to exist as James Pratchett, your home in Romford will also disappear. I have secured a new abode for you so that you will be untraceable. So, for that, I requite total loyalty, that same fidelity and obedience you had to the Special Air Service before you moved onto MI5."

Lord Gentry, unlocked the desk drawer on the red leather topped mahogany table and removed an envelope. He walked over to James and handed him the envelope. Pratchett opened the seal and emptied the contents which he gave to James. They included two-passports, one red in colour, British and the other blue with the unmistakable, 'Great Seal of the United States,' in the centre, and in block capitals at the top, 'PASSPORT,' followed at the bottom with the italic words, 'United States of America.

He opened the British Passport to discover a photograph of himself, which was most recently from his assessment; however, his blood immediately ran-cold. The name on the passport was, 'Anthony Maitland Steel!' It was a thunderbolt out of the blue. He then opened the USA Passport; it was no surprise that the name remained likewise. Tony Steel. It suited him. His former life and history were about to be eradicated from existence or trace. James rummaged inside the brown envelope and extracted two separate wads of monetary notes. One contained unsurprisingly nothing more than the highest denomination issued to the public of red-inked, fifty-pound notes. The second was a somewhat more massive wad of US dollars, in the form of one-hundred-dollar bills. Each had scribbled on the surrounding paper seal the figure, fifty-thousand. He was staring at the joint sum in the region of eighty-thousand pounds give or take the cost conversion of the day.

As James contemplated the incredulity of this proposition,

There was a knock at the door, and a young woman in her early thirties entered. Lord Gentry stopped mid-sentence and looked round in annoyance; his lips clamped together.

"What is it, Olivia? Can't you see I'm busy? I gave strict instruction I was not to be disturbed?"

James took her in with a glance: a secretary or personal assistant of some kind. She was fairly tall, curvy. Cream silk blouse with the top two buttons undone; with tailored black trousers snug against her thighs; and emerald python-skin loafers. The strap of the caramel leather messenger bag she was carrying had pulled the blouse tight against her breasts, so the pattern of her bra was visible. The woman wore her blonde hair in a sort of, French Pleat against the back of her head and had a heart-shaped face with just a hint of pink on her cheeks – an 'English Rose,' complexion. She pouted.

"Oh, don't be such a grump, Darling. My car won't start, and I'm meeting Lottie and Imogen in town for coffee. Can I borrow one of yours? Please?" She placed her hands flat on Gentry's lapels and stroked them down the soft wool fabric as if pressing the suit.

"Pretty please?"

James watched as the stern wife warred with the what appeared was her indulgent Husband. The female charm won the argument.

"Very well. But not the Conti. I need it later."

"As if!" she said, winking at James.

"Bentleys are such old-man cars. And they're as big as tanks."

"Yes, well. Speaking of tanks, I'd like to introduce you to my new communications consultant. Anthony Maitland Steel, my wife, Olivia. Anthony used to work for Ronnie Mackenzie, at JP Morgan and before that, he was serving Queen and country."

(James in the past had gone into operations under assumed names, this was nothing new.)

He stepped towards the gorgeous woman; hand outstretched. She met him halfway, and they shook hands. She held onto his hand for just a second longer than he expected.

"How do you do?"

He said.

"Oh, I do very well, thank you, Anthony. Tanks, eh? How very ... very hot."

"Actually, we were on foot. Part of Combat Arms not much like the Cavalry and the Royal Armoured Corps, but separate. Airborne, if anything."

He paused, aware that military terminology might not be to the woman's taste.

"Anyway, no tanks, and please call me, J....Tony, much less formal?"

He finished.

James was unaware of her current affair with one James Craig VC., who was very much infantry and recognised, teeth arm troops.

She turned to him and said,

"Know anything about cars? I saw your Maserati on the drive. I'm surprised Lord Gentry my Husband didn't have you shot for parking there. Nobody's allowed to leave their cars in front of the house. Certainly not with the exhaust pipe towards the wall as they have a habit of leaving black smoke marks on the wall. Didn't you see the sign?"

That explains the butler's death-stare when I arrived, James thought.

Gentry intervened.

"Now, now, Darling. No need to embarrass our guest, Anthony. I'm sure we can show him where to park when he comes to work."

Husband and wife were playing well-rehearsed roles. James hadn't agreed to the job yet but felt he was being outmanoeuvred all the same. He tried to regain a measure of control.

"To answer your question, yes. I know a little about cars."

He was ever so slightly dishonest. As a B Squadron's Mobility Troop (The Bears Paws) member in the SAS, he'd been taught a great deal about cars, trucks, and wheeled vehicles of all kinds. More especially how to start them, without ignitions keys if required.

"Well, perhaps you'd like to look under my car bonnet then have a fiddle about. Because I couldn't change an air filter, let alone diagnose a fault in a 911."

She beckoned him with a slender index finger tipped with nail polish the same colour as her shoes. Tony, observed how thin her talons were, in his view, pianist-shaped, long and graceful, with a gentle soft pinkness poking through her skin. Her nails were the same colour as her ruby lips. She was, in short, a beauty! Her left hand's third finger was decorated with what could only be described as three rocks of diamonds. In his view, this was wealth on wealth. It was a decadence he was unfamiliar with.

"Come on. I don't have all day. You can help me choose what to drive from my Husband's collection."

James looked at Gentry. The other man nodded his approval, extracted rather than bestowed. Maybe he didn't want to cross his wife. Certainly not in front of James, anyway. He followed Olivia from the room. They left the library into the hall, then through a huge kitchen that would have swallowed the whole ground floor of James's modest house in Romford but nor perhaps his self-constructed lair. Where one might have expected in the kitchen décor, distressed or painted wood cabinets, in a colour of Sparrow's Wing or Silt, there was brushed stainless steel and bright-grained satin-finish timber. It was a central island topped with a shiny black marble work surface, veined with red like excellent trails of blood. He brushed past bunches of dried thyme, marjoram, and rosemary tied to a hook on the island, and the kitchen was instantly alive with the aroma of Italian cooking. It mixed with Olivia's smell – clean hair, sunlit skin, and a fresh, floral perfume – and made James glad to be following this attractive woman to help her choose a set of wheels. She opened the door at the far end of the kitchen and then stood aside to let James go ahead of her. Not far enough apart, for him to be able to walk through without brushing against her with his shoulder. He was holding fast to ideas of gentlemanly behaviour instilled in him by his father and the army. He didn't turn his back on her. Instead, he turned to face her and side-stepped into the room beyond the kitchen, the distance between them narrowing to a hand's breadth. The smell of her perfume was more pungent now, and he couldn't help but glimpse down at her cleavage for a split second, gentleman or not. And let's face it; he was neither. She caught him doing it of course, and followed his gaze, then looked into his eyes, saying nothing, but letting the tip of her tongue appear as she slowly and sensually ran it long her ruby lips. Olivia, flirted with him, returning his gaze at her heaving breasts. Immediately he averted his eyes.

She closed the door behind them. Apart from a handful of small red LEDs blinking and pulsing at about hip height, the room was dark. James heard her click on a light switch. As the neon strip lights on the ceiling pinked and flickered into life, James gasped. Facing them, gleaming in the harsh light of the fluorescent tubes, were two rows of cars that together were worth somewhere north of £2 million. The winking red dots were their security sensors. In the front row, the 'Conti,' a British Racing Green Bentley Continental GT, sat, squat and purposeful between a gunmetal BMWi8 and a wasp-yellow Porsche 911, its roof lowered to reveal matching upholstery.

But it was the two cars book-ending the trio of modern supercars that caught his eye. On the left, is a toffee-apple-red Chevrolet Corvette. On the right, is a primrose Jaguar E-type. Behind these icons, another five: two single-seater racing cars in old-school tobacco company liveries; a Ferrari and BMWi8, deep strakes carved into their sides; a lime-green Lamborghini Miura; and another American muscle car: a late sixties Chevrolet Camaro Z28, in what looked like its original metallic grey and black paint. He stood, quite still, and inhaled. Petrol, leather, and car polish. He commented to Olivia,

"Your husband likes cars, then?"

It was all he could manage.

"Oh, not just Peter. We all do. The Italia belongs to his Private Secretary, the 911 you probably guessed is mine, and the rest belong to Der Fuhrer."

She mimed a moustache with two fingers of her left hand and raised her right in a Nazi salute, its offensiveness undercut by the cross-eyes and tongue poking out.

"He's a meanie, won't give me the keys to Baby."

She said, pouting and pointing at the E-Type.

"Well, I guess that restricts you to the other eight."

"Four. That Corvette is a widow-maker, and I'm not permitted to drive it."

She paused for a second and leaned towards him,

"And the racing cars are Peters, hobby. Track use only. Hmm,"

she said, trailing the fingertips of her right hand along with the mirror-smooth bonnet of the Bentley,

"What shall I drive today? You choose, please!"

She spun on one foot and sashayed the length of the front row of cars like a catwalk model, twitching her rear with each step and pausing at the far end to cock her hip and glance at him over one dropped shoulder.

"Well?"

She called.

"Come on; I haven't got all day, Mr Communications."

James walked behind the Corvette and Lady Gentry, wandered between the first row of cars' boots and front bumpers of the second. He stopped in front of the second Ferrari, in Rosso Corso – Italian racing red.

"The BMWi8," he called. "It suits you! Fast and stylish. Temperamental, too. Am I right?"

"I don't know what you mean."

She joined him in front of the car and ran her manicured fingertip – red to match her lips – down the swooping bonnet.

"I have my opinions, and I like to get my way,"

She continued, running the same manicured fingertips along the thin silver scar that connected the outer corner of his left eye to his cheekbone.

"But I can be very steady, very ... measured. If I feel like it."

She twirled away from him.

"You see the phone over there?" She pointed to an old-fashioned wall-mounted phone with a curled cable connecting the mouthpiece to the main body.

"Pick it up, would you please?"

"What number?"

"No need. It rings in Markham's little man cave automatically. He'll bring it round to the front for me."

James did as she asked, held the hard-plastic handpiece up to his ear and listened to a distant burr as the phone system routed the call. After four rings, Markham picked it up saying,

"Lady Gentry?"

A deep voice, a man in his late forties or early fifties, James estimated. Not a smoker. Too clean and clear for that. And a slight German accent, a Swabian from the sound of it.

"I'm Anthony a friend of Olivia's,"

James said, figuring that the unclear nature of their relationship wasn't worth explaining at his point.

"She wants you to bring the BMWi8 round to the front?"

He couldn't help adding,

"Please."

"Certainly, Sir. I will meet Her Ladyship out front in a few minutes."

The line went dead, and James clicked the receiver back onto its cradle.

"He says—"

She interrupted,

"I know, 'Ziss vill take ein few minuten, Ja?'" she laughed.

"Come on, and I'll show you round to the front."

"Won't your Husband be expecting me back?"

"Well he might be, I suppose. But Anthony,"

she purred, coming closer again,

"where's the fun in jumping when the Old Man calls? He's not your commanding officer, and he certainly isn't mine, merely my Husband. Come on!"

James thought it odd that she was so informed in the British Army rank structure.

She shimmied between the cars to the far door, the soles of her shoes sloshing on the ribbed metal floor tiles. The steel roller shutter opened. It led onto a sweeping gravel drive that curved around the rear of the house on both wings. They both walked, their feet crunching over the shingle, past ancient climbing roses pinned and wired to the walls, arriving at the front of the house just as the ornate front door opened and Gentry appeared.

"Ah, Anthony," he said.

"Something's come up, and I need to leave for my next meeting a little earlier than expected. I'd very much like you to start as soon as possible. I assume you're happy now I've agreed to your terms."

Again, it was phrased like a question, but it carried no serious doubt in the speaker's tone of voice. James looked at Olivia and back at Gentry. He thought of cars and the smell of her skin as he'd squeezed past her into the garage. Then he thought about the man's rant about immigrants and the nervous churning in his stomach.

"I don't think so, Lord Gentry,"

he said.

"I'm not sure about the fit between us. But thank you for asking me. I require a little more time to consider?"

Gentry blinked. His lips tightened into a line. His face was immobile, and his eyes never left James's. He swept his hand over the floppy lock of hair that had fallen across his eyes. Then he recovered himself. Taking James/Anthony to the side out of earshot, he commented in a most serious tone,

"Too late dear boy, your house in Romford is being raided as I speak by the police. Don't worry all incriminating evidence, including your recordings of depraved sexual activity with the older women have been erased. You do not figure in any way, and James Pratchett is kaput, gone for good. You are from this day, Anthony Maitland Steel or Tony if you like!"

James was shocked and flabbergasted.

"Look, I have to dash. Bert Mountfield, my Personal Assistant, will show you to your room where you will find several suits and associated clothing. Nothing from you passed exists now. So, put it behind you, Anthony. I have also arranged a Penthouse Suit located at Canside Meadow Walk, Chelmsford with breathtaking views. Your office, of course, will be here and Bert will show you that this afternoon. "Now, forgive me, but I really must go."

A short, dry handshake and Lord Egbert Peter Gentry disappeared inside the chauffeur-driven Bentley.

A low, rough-edged growl brought James's attention back to the driveway. From the corner of the house, the noise of the BMWi8 emerged. It was like a predator creeping up on some unsuspecting.. It stopped by Olivia's left side, and a man in spotless brown overalls emerged from the driver's door.

"Thank you, Markham," she said, without turning, then,

"Goodbye, Tony. An absolute pleasure having you onboard I am sure."

She leaned towards him, kissed him on both cheeks and climbed down into the car, pulling the shallow door closed behind her. He heard the transmission protest as she shoved the gear stick into first, then with a short spurt of gravel, she was gone, the exhaust rising to an impatient yowl as she took the bend at the end of the drive without slowing. There didn't seem any point in lingering. The footman walked away, and James noticed he had a built-up shoe on his left foot that caused it to drag when he lifted it.

He retrieved the Maserati's keys from his pocket and took a look at the house. He was astonished what had occurred in such a short time. This was his new employment, and it seemed that his past criminal history was erased. He drove around the gravel road to the rear of the house, through the trees, a movement caught his eye. He looked to his right and saw a squad of four men, dressed in all-black military-style fatigues, jogging in a tight square through the woods. Ex-forces he thought, noting the easy way they carried themselves despite the heavy-looking Bergens strapped to their backs.

Bert was waiting for him as he came through the kitchen. It was the only way he knew from the garage. He said,

"This way Sir, I will show you to your office which has an on-suite bedroom should you have to stay the night at any stage in the future. Once you have settled in, I will take you to your Penthouse in Chelmsford. By the way, the Maserati's keys I need to have from you to dispose of the car. Your car is now a rather less obvious colour and make."

James was not too happy with this turn of events; however, he was prepared to go along with it for the time being.

Mountfield handed him a key-fob which had the distinct sign on the reverse of the four rings indicating it was an Audi.

CHAPTER 25
COCKTAIL PARTY

James Pratchet aka Anthony Maitland Steel had spent the downtime walking around the estate to familiarise himself with the surrounding area he now found himself. He was certainly impressed with the situation he soon found himself. The fact that his entire previous existence was erased. And now he had a new identity and seemingly tip-top accommodation in Chelmsford. He pondered if as Lord Gentry had intimated his possessions and all trace of him had been removed from Bruce Avenue, Hornchurch. However, he wondered if Mrs Robinson had been discovered, for if not in his absence, she would eventually starve to death. Gwynn had been an enjoyable play toy, but he was becoming rather bored with her to be fair. James, when he had tired of his plaything, would have ended up extinguishing her. He did, however, bear her no grudge and deep down has a little soft spot for the Good Samaritan, after all their entire aim is to help others who are less well mentally. The problem is that humankind is somewhat far from being human, and much further from being kind. After all, he had fed and fucked her for several months, and she was still in good health despite being drugged and isolated for over three months. But, just as his mind was about to wander elsewhere, he remembered that his killing weapon, his nine-millimetre Glock pistol complete with a silencer which he had secreted in a safe place within the house. His primary concern if recovered then it would likely prove his linkage to several paid for executions. That, of course, if he were ever caught and arrested.

James or was he, Anthony, looked at his watch and realised that Mountfield had informed him that Lord Gentry would like to see him before dinner at seven o'clock to discuss a few further details. He speeded up his walk back towards the house to be showered and dressed for the planned meeting. On arrival he entered through the main entrance, he noted that his car was no longer parked where he had left it that morning as Mountfield had secured the keys while seeing off Olivia.

On entering his room, he noted a Tuxedo White Jacket and immaculately pressed pair of black trousers with a matching satin two-inch piping going down either outside legs hanging on the hooks inside the door of the wardrobe. There was also a dress shirt, bow-tie and satin waistcoat. On the highly polished wooden floor was an equally gleaming pair of shoes. He checked the size, and as expected, they were his fit. It was clear that nothing during this complete change from being hitman James Pratchett to now being Anthony Maitland Steel, quite clearly nothing had been missed or left to chance. James had often had to assume different identities over his years in MI5. However, nothing quite ever came with this magnitude of preparedness. It seemed nothing had been left to chance. He was mightily impressed.

At a quarter to the hour he had a final look at himself in the bathroom mirror, content with what he observed, tweaked his bow-tie and headed for the door. He paused at the top of the first-floor landing and viewed his decent options. On either flank were the most magnificent pair of winding solid oak stairs with a handrail to accompany their route to the ground floor entrance hall. As he admired it all, his mind raced as to the guests' rank and level had entered Ingatestone Hall over the centuries. Peter Gentry as he insisted that James or Anthony address him was surprisingly informal. No Lord this or Sir, that! However, what he had been most importunate on was that James ceased to exist from now on, and Anthony would correlate, henceforth. He smiled and took hold of his double-cuffed white silk shirt purporting a set of gold links with the capital letter T showing on the outer side. Then under his breath, said to himself, Anthony, let's do it. Whatever, 'It,' is?

He selected the right stairway, making his way to the ground. He was met by Bert Mountfield who ushered him into the games room where Peter Gentry awaited him. He noted that on stepping through the door. Gentry looked at his Gold, Diamond, and Platinum Rolex watch. Anthony assumed that Peter was a stickler for time appreciation. This suited him, as he was never late for an appointment or an assassination. Attendance and punctuality were paramount in his world, and it just became evident that Lord Gentry suffered from a similar fate. Unfortunately, too many folks fail to appreciate this and can be fatal. As he approached Gentry, his host and now his employer spoke first,

"Anthony, how pleased I am that you reconsidered and now we form a team that will take out beloved great country forward to the Outstanding Reputation that existed during the reign of Queen Victory." He went on,

"Now, Bert, can you please pour us a glass of sparkling stuff and leave us? Oh, and return no later than 20.45 hours if we have not joined Lady Gentry was hosting the pre-dinner drinks. Thank you, Bert."

Mountfield carried out the requested task, pouring two

glasses of, Veuve Clique Effervescence easily recognisable by its distinct yellow label. He placed the bottle in the silver ice bucket, bowed his head, and left the games room.

Peter Gentry, took a sip of the champagne his new member of staff brought the crystal glass to his lips and permitted a good gulp to enter his mouth. He rather enjoyed the wetness of the liquid as he suffered for many years from hyposalivation. It reared itself when involved in operations in Iraq. Alas, the medics could do nothing to elevate the problem. He had to self-hydrate to survive.

Gentry was the first to speak,

"Anthony, first, I am so pleased that you have joined the team. The position you now occupy is one that requires, well a particular type of individual with little or no concern for his victim or victims. I am the leader of a cult who is determined to rid this country of its total lack of the will to win. Great Britain in the past was adored and applauded. This country is positioned at fifth in the world financially, and goodness knows, possibly in the low twenties concerning our military readiness."

Anthony assimilated all that was being preached at him and wondered where this would end. It was crystal clear similar to the champagne flutes that he was enjoying his refreshment. Lord Gentry having paused and took a sip, went on,

"I have to with the assistance of my followers need to take over the control and Government of this green and not so pleasant land. For decades, imbeciles have been elected and failed, and I intend that will cease immediately. Or as soon as I can take over as the ruler. But, First, you and I must fly to America to secure the weaponry required to succeed. Following the drinks party about to take place, you will be taken to your new Penthouse Flat in Chelmsford. I am confident you will be happy with it. You will spend one day there returning here on Sunday morning before our trip to California. We will meet some severe dudes and secure the weapons and ammunition we will require for the coup. The precise detail of which I will brief you about before we fly to the USA. I should warn you that tonight you will meet some very senor police individuals and Members of the Military and Parliament who are all on board. This Anthony is a resolute decision which will see our country become great again in the worlds eye. I should mention that there will be folk in this room you would have steered well clear of in your previous role as a hitman. Fear not as they are all on the side with your appointment. There is an acknowledgement of the necessity of having your ability and expertise on the team. Do you have any immediate questions before we join the others?"

Anthony, although slightly better off than he was before this meeting, had a mind that was racing but well controlled. The manifestation of racing thoughts was unapparent in his face or demeanour; no idea flights were apparent. James Pratchett was a calm person and had, on many occasions, proved this to a standard of excellence. No matter, his name's alteration meant nothing, and he was as ever was a highly trained individual and killer. Anthony looked at Lord Peter with eyes of steel and commented, "My Lord, you have nothing to concern yourself about. I am more than capable of conducting myself with anyone in a moment of crisis." Gentry, knew then he had made the correct decision to appoint him, he took his glass in his right hand, raising it towards Anthony proffering a toast. The glasses clinked as only crystal does. He then said,

"Here is to a very successful relationship!"

Steel, reciprocated, and they both polished off the final contents and moved towards the large double doors. As they entered the drawing room, it was awash with well-dressed people, the ladies in flowing gowns and their male counterparts in formal black-tie. Anthony noticed a gentleman wearing a red jacket and serge-blue trousers with an unmistakable broad red stripe on either side. Immediately he recognised this as an Officers Mess Dress and on the collar was the woven badge of a Scots Guard. Colonel James Craig holder of the Victoria Cross was an expert at working a room. Anthony was careful not to become involved in a chat with Craig VC as he may slip up during a conversation. Best to steer clear.

HE MADE a mental note to try and avoid contact with the said officer. Peter Gentry removed two glasses of champagne from the waitress's tray, passing one to Anthony Steel. He intended to work the room by circulating and introducing him to those he felt it necessary to acquaint them with his new Comminutions Director. Anthony had scanned the room but to no avail and did not fortuitously recognise anyone present. This was a plus point, for if he did not identify anyone, it was unlikely they could. There was a small gathering of three men together in what seemed available drinks party chit-chat. Gentry took hold of Maitland-Steel's elbow saying,

"LET me introduce you to a few important people?"

ANTHONY NODDED his assent following him towards the Bow Window where they assembled. As they approached the group, they separated to greet, Lord Gentry. In turn, he commenced introducing his new employee. Anthony shook Stephen Jones's hand, Chief Constable of Essex; then he was made acquainted with Superintendent David Bagley, Romford, and finally DCI Larry Donegan. Unknown to Anthony they were all senior members of Lord Peter Gentry's Rosicrucianism Cult. Also, they too were in total support of the coup and ruling the country.

There was a host of high-profile guests, none other than the Head of the Foreign & Commonwealth Office, Sir James Bleasdale. On being introduced to him, he noted that Sir James seemed to show in his face a sparkle of recognition, perhaps from his MI5 days. However, he need not have concerned himself as he was also part of the cult. Their entire aim was to overthrow the Government and take command of the British Isles. Farfetched but not in their view.

At eight o'clock, the room began to thin out; most people had departed as was the custom at drink parties. Anthony was gobsmacked and had no idea how the remainder of the evening would develop.

Once, there was only a handful of critical members present. They repaired to the games room for a private discussion. Anthony was not sure he was to be invited to join them as the newbie. On entering Mountfield was present with several decanters of quality brandy and cigars. Thus, ensuring the meeting kicked off properly. Steel was well aware that his presence among these very senior policemen could be detrimental to his survival. After all, he had assassinated many and would most certainly follow lengthy incarceration should he ever have to face the music. Once glasses filled, Mountfield looked at Lord Gentry, the latter nodded assent and Bert left the room. The assembled company took their seats in the leather-covered club chairs. Peter Gentry positioned himself in a central location with his back to the floor-to-the-ceiling book library. He then spoke in a determined voice to ensure that all present were left in no doubt about who was in charge.

"Gentlemen you have already been introduced this evening to Anthony Steel, my new Communications Director. I want you to be in no doubt that he will bring us to a new level of the promulgation of our ultimate aim. To this end, wherever necessary, you will afford him a safe passage in whatever mission he is involved." Peter paused and took a sip of his brandy before carrying on,

"Tomorrow evening, Anthony and I will depart this green and pleasant land and head for a destination where we will secure weapons and ammunition required to distribute to our various hubs up and down the country. As you are aware, we have cells in Edinburgh, Cardiff and Belfast. On the,' GO Day,' our teams will take over the ruling party in each of these central governance points. In doing so, we will be in absolute control. None of this will be discussed outside this room, until, I have secured and shipped the weaponry required."

Everyone in attendance was in full unison with this course of action, and to a man, there was a broad smile of appreciation. Sir James Bleasdale rose from his seat and commented,

"Gentlemen of, 'The ROSICRUCIANISM,' I give you a toast to our Grand Master and the next ruler of Great Britain, 'Lord Peter Egbert Gentry.'

. . .

The entire meeting rose to their feet except for Anthony Maitland Steel, as he was unfamiliar with such a show of collective loyalty, however, realising the error he got up and joined in.

The comment was audible and henotheistic, 'Lord Peter Gentry!" Almost in unison, they drank and emptied their glasses and except for Anthony, threw their crystal glasses into the fireplace in some ancient custom. Steel followed suit.

CHAPTER 26
POLICE WASH UP

The morning after Gwynn's Robinson rescue, should have been one of unbridled success at the rescue of her. However, this was far from that. DCI John Jenkins and his Team were assembled in the briefing room. The Wash Up Meeting would allow them to review the case. His Team of detectives was solemn faced when they should have been quite euphoric as the operation had yielded the rescue of the missing, 'Good Samaritan,' she was now safely reunited with her husband and son. The gloom existed due to their failed efforts to capture the suspect kidnapper James Pratchett were belated and sadly inefficacious. He had not returned to the house while it was under scrutiny, so the success rate was a mere fifty percent. He commenced the meeting by addressing his Team,

"Well, folks we had a good result and safely managed to rescue Mrs Gwynn Robinson who had been missing since Saturday the twenty-fifth of April. We should be proud of this fact. It was I am aware of a monumental disappointment that we failed to nail the person who abducted her. James Pratchett is out there, and we will do our absolute utmost to locate and arrest him. I have arranged with the Uniform

Branch to ensure that every policeman on the streets will have a copy of his, 'Boat Race -Face!' There was a laudable giggle throughout the room. John did not smile as he was seriously pissed off that James Pratchett had somehow slipped the net. Natalie Lewis was equally annoyed that the bird had flown the nest, despite the observation post having been set up to spy on him." John then looked at his number two; he addressed her request,

"Now DS Lewis will give you an update on Mrs Robinson's health situation. Natalie,"

She rose from her seat at the table in which she shared with him; it was at the front of the room. As she stood, almost everyone stared at her. DS Lewis was what men would call, 'A Head Turner. As a natural beauty, a clear complexion with long, curled eyelashes fluttering over her dreamy light-blue eyes. She wore a gorgeous shrimp-coloured blouse and her skirt tied at the waist with a thick brown buckle belt. The female detectives and there were three in the room, were quite used to her stealing the show and accepted her looks as she was also outstanding in her role as a DS.

Natalie, walked to the podium, placing both hands on the outer edges, her engagement and wedding rings sparkled in the fluorescent lighting. She then spoke with her soft but authoritative voice,

"As we are all aware Mrs Robinson was abducted from the Sarmatians Office in North Street at the end of April. It is now clear that the person who carried this out was one, James Pratchett, we have so far been able to trace him as a former member of HM Forces, Parachute Regiment, and SAS. On leaving the military he was employed as an agent for MI5 and took part in various clandestine operations on behalf of the British Government. It is however not clear why he left that employ. As is sometimes the case with such operatives there is a

'D Notice,' on his file so that is as far as we can research. It is thought he was used in locating Muslim t

Terrorists and extinguish them where necessary. So, we know he was a trained killer, why he fell off the edge is unknown. There exists no historical evidence of his whereabouts until our investigations came upon him some six weeks ago. By good policing, it was confirmed that he was renting a house in Bruce Avenue, Hornchurch. His movement in and out of that location was sporadic to say the least. From, tailing him with an assortment of operatives he seemed to be purchasing food, more than what was required for someone residing alone. We also possess various recordings of Mrs Robinson talking to somebody who went by the name of Jim or James. He was in short, attempting to persuade her to meet him. She wisely and bluntly refused to do so.

I hasten to add that he is a slippery character which sadly was borne out by our failure to capture him. It's clear from the hospital report Mrs Robinson has been drugged and sexually abused continually during, what I would term her enslavement. Her husband and son are grateful that we rescued her alive."

DS Lewis paused as she took hold of the tumbler of water and took a sip. She went on,

"It is clear from the searching of the Bruce Avenue address that his abduction of this woman was well researched and planned. He took the time to construct his lair, ensuring it was soundproof. Even to the extent that he had a Control Room with a recording facility. However, there was no recording equipment found during our search. But there was evidence of its existence. as there were various cables running to and from the lair, she was held in. In short, he or someone cleared the house of everything. There was no clothing, crockery or cutlery or information about who had occupied the house. The landlord gave a full description of Pratchett which failed to fit photos we had of the MI5 Agent. He seemingly paid the rent on time and always by cash. This ensured no trace of a bank account. So, we are no further ahead."

Natalie then left the podium and John replaced her.

"Well Team, that is where we are at present. The fact that our target managed to escape out planned snatch leaves us in the bad books with our Chief Super Bagley. We really do have to hope that we get a break, as we do need some large, Brownie Points. Either he was one step ahead of us and knew we were about to arrest him or he just got lucky. Let's now disperse and carry on our investigation."

CHAPTER 27
IDENTITY CHANGE

The phone in his bedroom rang for a long, long time. Slowly it insinuated itself into Anthony's brain cells and forced him from deep sleep into wakefulness. It was a fight against last night's champagne, and brandy to finish off. He lay listening to the shrill noise, not knowing what it was at first. Eventually, he threw off the duvet and went over to pick it up.

"Yes?' he croaked. "Pra (he almost used his former name) ... Steel here?' 'Yeah."

'This is Bert Mountfield here from Ingatestone Hall. May I confirm who I am speaking to?"

James now corrected, realising his slight error on answering the telephone and replied,

"This is Anthony Maitland Steel,"

"Lord Gentry has had to alter the flight details for your trip. It is now confirmed from Heathrow Terminal Five, checking in at three in the afternoon. Lord Peter has directed me to organised a taxi to pick you up from your apartment in Chelmsford at one o'clock. He has requested that you bring clothing to cover three days in Las Vegas, Nevada?"

Responded Bert.

Anthony asked,

"For security, what is the name of the taxi company doing the collection?"

Bert replied,

"It will be a Black Cab from Computer Cabs."

"Right, thank you, Bert."

He creeped out of bed by throwing the duvet aside. He was naked as he seldom slept with pyjamas on. It had been his first night in his new abode. He found it so much more acceptable than the house in Hornchurch. Okay, he thought no longer did he have the warm body of Mrs Robinson to satisfy his sexual urge. He was confident that he would alter once he returned from the Nevada Trip. Anthony entered his state-of-the-art wet room which also contained marble His/her washbasins a bidet and smart toilet. He depressed the button on the wall in front of him, the lid lifted in a slow, silent manner.

Relieving himself into the pan, then pressed the second button below the first, the toilet flushed and the seat and lid closed. He smiled at this innovation, wondering who the fuck would spend time devising a luxury toilet facility? He entered the kitchen, opening the Insta-view Refrigerator Door to his pleasure it was fully stocked. He located a water glass placing it under the ice provider, and automatically it dropped three blocks of ice. He moved the glass under the water spout and allowed the gentlest of water flow to fill his glass. As he drank, the cold water. Steel made his way back to the wet room. Opening the cabinet to the right of the His, the basin he was unsurprised to find it fully stocked with the shaving items, plus Men's toiletries. He shaved and immediately stepped beneath the showerhead, tepid water flowed down on him when he reached for the soap dispenser and had a good wash.

When opening the walk-in wardrobe, a complete set of

clothing, none of which he had worn previously. It was all new and not in style he would have chosen. Anthony assumed that Peter Gentry would be travelling, Business or First Class and chose clothing that would not set him out from his travelling companion. His ability to blend into a specific role was his modus-operandum. The travel arrangements had not been of his doing. He was concerned whether he would carry a weapon for personal protection and decided not to do so. After all, he was unaware of what lay ahead in the United States, notwithstanding that Americans were almost always armed. He made a quick call to his friend in Vegas. He arranged for a small Beretta 9mm Nano plus two ammunition clips to be delivered to him at McCarren International in Las Vegas. This way, he would have no security issues.

As arranged the Black Taxi arrival was twelve-fifty-five in a sunny Essex afternoon. He left the building carrying one small travel case containing as requested sufficient clothing to last him for three days. The driver was out of his cab, and the door was held open for him. The driver spoke first,

"Good afternoon Sir can I confirm that you are Mr Anthony Steel and I have also been asked to confirm with you that you have your passport and ESTA form.?"

Anthony reached inside his pocket and extracted his Passport with the ESTA Form folded neatly inside it. Removing it, he proffered it to the driver, who merely nodded and assisted him with his case into the taxi. Steel, settled down anticipating the ninety-minutes trip. The driver had placed several Newspapers on the seat to pass his travel time to Terminal Five. He was relaxed and settled back in the rear seat.

Romford Police Station was buzzing with John Jenkins team members as confidential information had been received from a source in London of a conspiracy being hatched. It was Top Secret, so much so that only three team members were aware of the situation. Neither, David Bagley nor Matilda Addison were made aware of the intelligence. It was a, 'Need to Know Situation!' They did not require this perspicacity; indeed, the triplet members selected were, DCI John Jenkins, DCI Bob Clarkson, and DS Natalie Lewis. SO15 had summoned them for a meeting with the CTC Commander, Deputy Commissioner Charles Telfer a bright, determined Scotsman who did not suffer fools. During the meeting with, The Counter Terrorism Command they all had to update their signatures to, The Official Secrets Act 1989 yet again. They were also left in no doubt as to the consequences of releasing the information discussed. The revelations disclosed by Charles Telfer cast a shadow over several senior figures in Essex, not least in the police.

Steel was content reading the Newspapers as the driver made his way to the M25 motorway, which would lead to Heathrow; he suddenly began to feel faint. The Taxi Driver had been hired for this purpose, and once he activated, the gas fed into the passenger seated area. Anthony began subconsciously to inhale what was a knockout gas. He suddenly realised what was occurring but too late. He was instantaneously knocked out, slumped on the rear seat almost like someone who had consumed over his limit in alcohol. The driver continued to the agreed location at 200 Harley Street where he was removed from the taxi, placed on a hospital gurney, then wheeled into a new operating theatre. The medical staff and anaesthetist were on hand to ensure he would remain in this comatose state. He inserted the cannula and intravenously administered Propofol the most commonly used general anaesthetic that maintained his sleep but permitted him to continue breathing independently. The theatre door opened and in breezed, the consultant plastic surgeon. He was gowned up and ready to commence the procedure. On the sizeable illuminated screen was a photograph of a former military officer and actor Anthony Maitland

Steel. Mr Keneth Speed, BAPRAS (British Association of Plastic Reconstructive and Aesthetic Surgeons, looked at his team of nurses and assistants and said,

"Let's get this show on the road and make this gentleman look like this photo. His patron has paid a lot of money to make this gentleman resemble his favourite British Actor. Mr Speed nodded his head and music broadcast within the theatre. David Bowie's Changes was rather appropriate. Some four hours later, James Pratchett no longer looked like his old self. Instead, he was very much covered in surgical dressings. Mr Speed was confident that he would look very much like Anthony Steel in the photograph in three weeks.

CHAPTER 28
NEW DEVELOPMENT

Their return journey from New Scotland Yard was pretty much completed in silence. It was well past seven by the time they reached the police station. As they all walked up the back stairs, they met the Chief coming down carrying his briefcase and an overcoat. He sported a surprisingly smart navy blue, pin-striped suit and looked rather pensive.

"Good night, Chief," they said in unison.

"Yes – good night."

He was a little surprised to see Jenkins, Clarkson, and DS Lewis together on the back stairs. He shrugged it off; perhaps they were using the stairs to keep fit.

Natalie stopped, turned with her back to the wall to allow him past, and stared after the Chief as he passed them on the stairs. She thought how strange he was using the back stairs. As a result of their meeting at New Scotland Yard, she was now suspicious of him. John noticed as he brushed past her his left elbow brushed Lewis left breast.

"Leave the Chief alone, Natalie."

Natalie, watched the Chief continue to hurry down the stairs.

Jenkins said when she caught up with him.

"You can make us all a coffee."

"I don't want one."

"Well, just Bob and I, then."

"You could make your own coffees?"

"I could, but then what would you pair do? "

"We could get on with our work. We must tie up the link between Chief Bagley and Matilda Addison and Chief Constable Steve Jones. Also let's not forget that Alan Boyd, the head of the Boyd Syndicate, is also allegedly aligned to them which was mentioned in-confidence by Assistant Commissioner, Charlie Telfer."

She smiled at both and commented,

"Oh well I suppose I am the coffee lady; I will head for the refreshment station and deliver the coffees to you pair of DCIs!"

John inserted the key into his office door, unlocked it, and they both entered his office. Bob place two flat-folding chairs in front of the office desk. John slipped onto his five-star based chair and picked up the telephone. He dialled his Team Room; the phone rang for a while before being answered.

"DC Paul Thompson, here,"

"Jenkins here, Paul, please contact the entire team I wish to have a briefing at nine o'clock tomorrow sharp, warn them latecomers will not be tolerated."

"Yes, got that Boss."

John, replace the telephone on its cradle.

Just as he has done so, Natalie entered the office with her rear-end leading as she pushed the door ajar while carrying the coffees on a tray. He could not fail to observe as he did her absolutely beautifully shaped derriere'.

Bob, moved aside as she placed the tray containing three

hot steaming mugs of coffee on the desk. She then took hold of the one at a time and using three saucers placed each in front of the two DCI's and one for herself. On dispensing them, she had altered her mind and decided to join them. Both men took a tasting sip and commented almost in unison,

"Thank you!"

John, commenced as he was the host and someone had to, (Nothing had been discussed regarding the revelations confirmed but already known on the return trip to Romford from London.)

"This is the most sensitive of investigations, and as such, we have to box very cleverly on how we play the investigation. As you are aware from my suspicions of Ingatestone Hall. We now know that Lord Egbert Peter Gentry has questions to answer."

Bob, then spoke,

"The situation regarding our Matilda Addison is also concerning, and we must also be careful on this subject. Otherwise, we could well alert the others involved. What has madam been up to and how involved is she is the prominent answer we need. We must not reveal this to any the team."

He paused to sip his coffee,

Natalie remained silent as she was concerned that she had a past friendship with Matilda, which could jeopardise her involvement. She made her mind up in an instant to withhold the strength of her association.

Bob, then spoke,

"I think we should profile each one of them as individuals with each of us inputting what knowledge we have of each. We must leave nothing out, even though we may perceive it is not of value. It is a harrowing situation, with two senior police personalities suspected of wrongdoing and another DCI involved. That aligned to a Peer of the Realm. Who knows at what level this corruption ceases? Anything that any of us can input could be paramount in solving this dilemma."

John then chipped in,

"Bob, as you allude, we must also bear in mind that a Lord of the Realm is incorporated in this potential scandal. His large estate just outside our jurisdiction. Indeed, well within the Essex Chief's area

Natalie remained silent, bearing in mind that she was the junior individual in this threesome. Then she decided to speak,

"Did you see the Chief's face as he bumped into me?"

"I'm not blind, Lewis. What are you saying?"

"When he took leave of absence a few weeks ago, and Chief Superintendent Michael Tuffney stood in for him, it was because of a personal matter. I bet it was something to do with his past, and I think that's what he's doing in this alleged crime. What is behind that locked door between his main office and the connecting door? It there something behind it about his past as well as his present?"

"We don't know anything about the Chief's past, do we? I am pretty sure that apart from Bagley's married life, we know little else."

Bob was reasonably persistent in his voice with this statement.

Natalie, now brimming full of confidence, mentioned,

"I did mention to Barrie Smith at that time it was rather strange that the Chief took that leave of absence, while we were investigating the, first 'Romford Tow Path,' murder."

There was a slight pause before she spoke again,

"Also, if my memory serves and we check the attendance diary, he was also absent on something or other, following the second young murdered female body discovered with similar markings on her body and her hand severed. Plus, her body was also bound by a similar cord to that of the first victim."

John screwed his face up and looked at Natalie,

"I thought I told you several weeks ago not to become involved with the Chiefs personal business!"

"Yes, I do remember that, Sir!"

Bob, quickly realised Natalie was being a little sarcastic and assumed John also realised this.

"When I give you an order, do you then decide whether it's an order you'll obey, or one you won't?"

"I obey all your orders, Sir."

"Clearly not, because here you are meddling in the Chief's personal business again that has absolutely nothing to do with you after I've ordered you a thousand times not to."

"Sir twice is hardly a thousand times."

"So, you admit that I've ordered you to stay out of the Chief's business twice?"

"I never said that."

"You said exactly that, which only echoes what I said."

"I agree that you might have mentioned something vague about the Chief, but I'm sure I didn't translate it as an order – more like a piece of friendly advice that could be discarded if more pressing matters came along."

Bob Clarkson was surprised at this notable, yet, a surprising shift of dutiable conversation. He wondered if John Jenkins was loyally protecting the Chief or was there something, he knew about that was detrimental to the Chief. Perhaps he had found evidence involving Bagley; he had concealed."

"My orders seem to be falling on deaf ears lately, Natalie. I don't know if you're aware, but the police force doesn't allow people with deaf ears to be detectives. I've told you to stop bothering the Chief, but you seem to be hearing something else. I do hope I won't have to tell you again."

"Oh, I'm sure you will," she said, with a full, friendly grin.

It was at this point from her smile, and Jenkins reciprocated smile. Bob concluded that this was light banter between two colleagues who were familiar with this type of banter and conversation.

DCI Clarkson then determined it was at this juncture to move forward because they were locked into John's office in an almost clandestine way.

"Let's put this shocking news we received at New Scotland Yard concerning very senior individuals who reside in London and our neighbouring county, Essex which we once were part of before becoming a London Borough. Commander Mary Wilhelmina Ward SO 19 and Assistant Commissioner, Charlie Telfer has named three very senior members of our local Constabulary society, two of whom we know extremely well. Our own Chief and the commander of the entire Essex Police Force,"

At that moment John interjected,

"As I think we all are aware, we have a mere two-thousand, six-hundred police officers looking after an area of some ten-thousand square miles. This has a substantial twenty-seven per cent of green area, So we are already stretched. Now we have the dilemma of investigating and evidential collation to prosecute them—our own Chief Bagley and Essex's overall commander, Chief Constable Steve Jones. Then, we have to investigate Lord Gentry of Ingatestone Hall, which is not even in our area. I have always suspected that they were off our local gird."

John Jenkins had not revealed that he had an undercover investigation of the estate by Harry Slessor, an Undercover Cop. He managed to obtain a good layout but was none the wiser. Lewis inquisitively looked at him. He was conscious of those in attendance, also that the church location had provided fresh evidence which pointed to cavorting's, which could lead to a severe scandal if it hit the News Media."

John picked up his coffee mug and sipped the final

refreshing drop of black liquid, He then looked at the clock on the wall, noting is was late, very late, way past, Grouse Whisky Late. He then brought the meeting to a close by reminding both,

"This, I reiterate strongly, is between us three and nobody else. Capiche?

The other two nodded in agreement, and they both went their separate ways out of his office.

John closed the buff folder, moved it to his secure safe. He turned, his head swimming with facts appertaining to this investigation, thinking where the hell is this going to lead us! As he was turning off the lights, his cell phone buzzed in his pocket. However, as he was about to answer, it stopped. He noted the caller's ID.

CHAPTER 29
WAPPING RIVERSIDE

The fog had descended early on the London waterfront, rolling in across the Thames at Wapping, a mile downriver from Harry Slessor's place, The Dark Man, where an old pier jutted out from Trenchard Street, an early Victorian pub standing back from it. A motor launch painted blue and white tied to the dock with two chains, giving it a permanent look yet allowing the launch to ease itself in the five-knot current running this morning. The name of the boat was 'HARVEST MOON.'

The fact that the painted sign hanging outside the pub indicated that the landlord's name was Harvest Moon amused many people. It didn't bother Harry, though. Since Queen Victoria's reign, the original family had owned the pub, which had made them proud, and he liked sleeping onboard the launch as he had the night before. But now there was work to be done, which meant a visit to his office. He went up the steps from the pier, a tall not insignificant muscular man in steel spectacles clutching his raincoat across his body, an umbrella over his head, and approached the front door of the pub. Two notices faced him, one of which pronounced:

FREE BEER TOMORROW: COME IN AND HAVE A REFRESHMENT

the other,

MOON ENTERPRISES LIMITED, LICENSEE Harold John Moon

Harry smiled inwardly at the 'Free Beer Tomorrow,' it caught many daft people out. The sign remained, and whenever someone demanded a free beer, they would receive the stock answer." Oh, that's tomorrow!" The problem was it was always tomorrow.

As he approached, the door was opened for him by Jimmy the Slasher, a hard, brutal-looking man with the flattened nose of an ex-boxer. He was the ideal person to have on board as the front of house barman. He said in his usual East London twang,

The pub was well known to the police as a location from which various drugs were available. The problem was that he had to keep the back story going as it was all part of his cover. The drug users seldom spent anything on alcohol, preferring to use their cash to buy fixes. When he took over the establishment, his first task was to clear the drug dealing. It took in all three-months; nevertheless, it was a success. The dopeheads were banned and moved onto the Wapping Streets.

Harry Slessor, not to be confused with, Harry the Hat, was an undercover cop whose identity was top secret. The habit of recording who was in this role had been abandoned by the Metropolitan Police higher command. The National Crime Agency, NCA and Metropolitan Organised Crime Partnership, OCP worked in conjunction to investigate, raid and arrest bad boys. During his three years in the job due to his investigations, and information supplied, officers, seized more than

£1.4million in cash, with at least £1.8 million more known to have been laundered by the criminal network. In short, DI Slessor was brilliant at what he did. His life teetered on the precipice of right and wrong. As well as life and death. The job existed twenty-four hours a day. There were no, 'Days Off.' His life treaded a ground of jeopardy between life and death. He possessed a very analytical brain and capable of scrutinising the most dangerous of situations. He was impressive to look at even when casually dressed as he was in peak physical condition. His hands were weapons of destruction. Harry Slessor was muscular in appearance and in a rough sort of way, handsome. He had a small scar of about two inches over his right eye, which enhanced his appearance to the opposite sex.

If ever his real identity was revealed death was a possibility. His extinction if actioned would, without exception, be violent and painful. He had to be very careful with whom he associated and strayed well clear of questionable women. At the age of thirty-two, he was a mature man with a sharp mind, and he needed to be. He was blade-faced, six and a half feet tall and an Aberdonian. He had moved from the significant and cosmopolitan city of Aberdeen to London; his intelligence and expertise immediately recognised early by the metropolitan police. Slessor was able despite his sharp good looks to blend into most environments; in short, he was a bit of an actor. This permitted him to melt in unannounced to the good and the bad of society. His soft well-spoken Scottish accent endeared him to most. The cover name of Harry Moon somewhat suited him.

The new development of high-end apartments along the Thames had opened a whole new world, and his portfolio was now considerable. Life was good. His mobile sounded, and he answered,

"Moon Enterprises."

"How great that sounds, Jimmy the asked him, Harry, are you coming to the pub this morning?"

"Yes, I am why?"

"I am so chuffed you're here this morning, Harry a Posh geezer called twice on the house phone. I informed him you were not expected until later today."

Harry was surprised, but not overly excited. It may well be one of his many underworld contacts looking for assistance.

He responded,

"Slasher, I will be in at about ten-thirty if he calls again."

To his astonishment as he ceased the call to, Jimmy the Slasher his mobile rang again, Harry was unclear whether to answer it or not as no caller identity was shown on his iPhone. That aside, he decided to answer it.

"Hello Moon Enterprises, how can I be of assistance and may I also inquire who you are?"

"My name is not relevant at the moment Mr Moon. I have a business proposition which I would like to put to you."

Harry had a habit of rubbing his nose with his left forefinger when he was unsure, and at this precise time, he was hedging his bets to discover what this caller wanted. Yes, he did have a very posh voice, as Jimmy, the Slasher had mentioned, but then he had met many folks who were good at putting on accents that were not their own.

"Fine, if you are unable to let me know who you are. I am happy to cease this conversation which is going nowhere."

With, that Harry cancelled the call, immediately pressed his iPhone, caller identity. The number, not surprisingly was withheld. He shrugged his shoulders, returned his mobile phone to his jacket pocket. As he did so, the fishing reel and bait had the desired effect. His phone began to ring, removing it he depressed the answer button and uttered not his name but just one word, but with authority,

"Hello!"

The posh voice spoke,

"Mr Moon?"

"Yes, could be, now will you stop pissing about and tell me who you are and the purpose of this call?"

The Posh Voice spoke again,

"I am unable to let you know precisely who I am due to the nature of the call. However, if you are available, I can meet with you this afternoon in London."

"You have the advantage of me, as I have no idea what you look like and how would I know I am actually meeting you, the caller? You will have to provide me with a little more than you currently seem unable to do. Let me also reiterate, without that this call will end as the last one did, Kapish?"

"Yes, I do Mr Moonr, and I am Peter Egbert, and I wish to hire you to carry out some personal and highly confidential work. I am reliably informed that you are someone that can be trusted to do a professional service. I can also tell you that the remuneration will be more than worthwhile!"

Harry, rubbed his nose again, this was intriguing, and his police skills and inquisitive nature led him to acquiesce, on this one.

"Mr Egbert, fine so where, when and how will I know who you are on approach?"

The posh voice replied,

"Can you please meet me at three o'clock this afternoon, at the City of London Cemetery and Crematorium, Alderbrook Road, Manor Park, E14? I will pay any expenses you incur to get you there."

Harry, being intrigued would have been an understatement.

"Fine, I will meet you there; however, you are yet to disclose sufficient information so that I can identify you as the person I am now talking to, please do so?"

"Apologies Mr Moon, I will be in a Black Cab awaiting your arrival. I know what you look like so there will be no confusion from my end. If you could also take a London Black Taxi, there will be no mistaken identity. Please instruct your black cab driver to bring you to the car park which is through the archway and adjacent to the Crematory."

Harry, knew the cemetery very well and in particular the precise rendezvous. He spoke into his mobile,

"Fine, Mr Egbert I will be there, please do not be late. Lateness is a sign of tardiness, and being sluggish has never been laid at my door, Kapish?"

Harry liked to use this word as it originated from the Italian Mafia and had a ring about it and fearsome connotations.

"Yes, I do, until we meet this afternoon. Goodbye, Mr Moon."

The line went dead, Harry mused in his mind as to what and where this would lead too. He looked at his wristwatch, which showed him that he had four hours until he would meet the Mystery Man.

CHAPTER 30
SAINT MICHAELMAS DAY

It was the fourth Friday of the month, it was a lovely autumn afternoon on Friday the 29th of September while the gathering of, 'Ordo Templi Orientis.' was assembling cloaked in white mantles; the chapter met at the grand temple which was an old church secreted in the grounds of Ingatestone Hall. As it was St Michaelmas Day, they sported attached to their mantles the Blue Daisy as on this specific day the special celebration was hailed as, The Blue Mass. Lord Peter Egbert Gentry, their Grand Master, led the procession into the old family church.

THE ENTIRE ESTATE had been cleared of the staff were given a special holiday except for Bert Mountfield. and the deployed security. Lady Gentry had been packed off to her friends in Chelsea, London. Bert's only task was to ensure that the vehicles arriving with guests would be parked following their seniority within Ordo Templi Orientis. Entry to the estate was in control of the Commandant of Security. Nobody would gain access to the grounds, that was assured.

. . .

This morning before first light the sacrificial lamb which would form the ritual part of the ceremony had been delivered to the church and stored, and imprisoned in the church's vault. This English Rose had been abducted from, 'The Old Bull Public House,' in the Market Square, Romford.

It would not have made little difference as the lamb in question had been fed so much of chloral hydrate, and alcohol, (Micky Finn) to render her unconscious. For as long as was required. The snatch was a simple exercise in enticement. This stupid young girl had fallen for the best chat up lines and the supply of numerous, 'Harvey Wallbangers,'

Yet again, the Romford and National Newspaper and Media would report in due course the missing teenager. It was of no consequence that this was the third celebration of the year and therefore, the triple offering of the sacrificial lamb for this, 'Ordo Templi Orientis Chapter.' She was in effect The Lamb of God, perhaps as the four horsemen of the Christian faith ride upon the Lamb of God's death and Lion of Juda. So, she would provide a similitude.

Once assembled, and the procession complete dressed in their mantels and headed by the Director of Ceremonies who held aloft, The Jewel Encrusted Latin Cross preceded the Grand Master, Lord Egbert Peter Gentry. The Officers were conducted to their pedestals. All present took their seniority positions, and the opening prayer was recited by, The Chaplin. Members then sat down.

THE MEETING TOOK place as it always had with much chanting and then the four senior working members, The Masters of the First, Second and Third Veil's carried the naked wench with their hands held aloft above their heads in the form of a crucifix cross and laid her upon the altar. 'Master of, 'Ordo Templi Orientis, The Academy of Alpha and Omega.'

THE GRAND HIGH Priest left his throne and approached the young naked wench whose legs had been spread apart and prepared her inners with Lovehoney Lubricant, thus ensuring easy penetration. Lord Gentry arrived at the altar, removed his cassock and entered the fictitious lamb and began to fuck her. While the congregation chanted the poem used on this third Horseman of the Apocalypse Day,

THE MICHAELMAS DAISIES AMONG DEAD WEEDS,:
BLOOM FOR ST MICHAEL'S VALOROUS DEEDS.

**And seems the last of flowers that stood,
Till the feast of St. Simon and St. Jude.**

He was the Angel who hurled Lucifer (the devil) down from Heaven for his treachery; however, that could not be the case as this was taking place on an altar of God. As he was about to ejaculate into her. The chanting rose to a crescendo, and he withdrew his penis, His sperm was decanted into the Chalice held by Principal Sojourner.

The sacrificial lamb was still insentient. The drug had worked a treat. She was oblivious as to what was occurring to her nymph-like body. Her hair was like waves of the pure earth, flaxen and softly reflecting the Autumn sun shone through the church windows and glistened on her. At that moment, in that fraction of time, as she lay spread-eagled on the altar, Peter Gentry was convinced that she had smiled in enjoyment. Of course, he was wrong; she was almost but not quite dead at this stage of the proceedings.

Both her arms were draped down by her side. She was in effect almost already dead as the drug inducement had been excessive, ensuring she would never awake again. Her right hand was lifted by the Inner Guard, armed with his razor-sharp poniard, which he passed to the Senior Warden, he then sliced through her right hand; her blood dripped into the Chalice. The Senior Warden, none other than Chief Constable Steven Jones, was well skilled in this action. Instantaneously the ulnar artery, which contains oxygenated blood gushed blood over the marble's white accentuating its colour. At the same time, The Junior Warden, Chief Superintendent David Bagley, had driven a wooden spike using the heavy maul into her left hand to depict The Lord Jesus Christ being nailed to the cross. At this precise moment of the sacrificial lamb symbol, the wind came in chilling gusts on his left side, whipping against his legs, it made him shiver. The Junior Deacon then approached the altar, where the corpse of this young lamb was. He took hold of the brandishing iron and burned her forehead with the Latin Cross.

She was now similar to all those who had gone before. A votive offering at the shrine of the Master of this 'Ordo Templi Orientis.'

Then to a man, those in attendance stood and beseeched,

"Satan represents indulgence instead of abstinence!
Satan represents vital existence instead of spiritual pipe dreams
Satan represents undefiled wisdom instead of hypocritical self-deceit!
Satan represents kindness to those who deserve it instead of love wasted on ingrates!"

Lord Peter Gentry, was presented with the ruby-encrusted Chalice by the Inner Guard. The Chalice was nearly full of the nubile wench's lifeblood. Lord Gentry turned toward the east where above the Master's chair was displayed the 'Ever Open Eye,' symbol. *(Their history claimed that Joseph of Arimathea used the cup to collect and store the blood of Christ at the Crucifixion.)

He held up the cup in both outstretched hands and announced to the assembly,

. . .

"Hoc Facite in Meam Commemoration.....Do this in remembrance of me!"

The now-deceased English Rose, with hair the colour of Crowned Crane would be similarly discarded as those who had gone before. Her two bare feet were bound together by a red cord taken from the drapes of the temple.

The meeting concluded, and as they left the church, not one person glanced at the corpse lying on the altar. The Disposal Team would discard her body as the others had. in an area where hopefully it would be some time before it was found.

CHAPTER 31
LONDON CEMETERY

Harry waved down the London Black Cab, and it was being driven by coincidence by a fellow Scot. As he entered the taxi, it was apparent that he had a result, the interior was immaculate and smelled of magnolia. It was clear that this particular Driver took real personal pride in his cab.

As he boarded the taxi, he was welcomed with,

"Good afternoon, Sir, where would you wish to go to?"

Harry, responded with the location and sat back to enjoy the expected twenty minutes or so it would take from Wapping to Manor Park where his rendezvous with the posh Peter Egbert was to occur. Still intrigued as to the nature of the meeting and what this fellow wanted him to do. The Driver recognising his accent and being himself from Edinburgh engaged him in conversation,

"Are you attending a funeral then Sir,"

"No, I am meeting someone there to discuss the preparations for a close friend who has passed away."

Replied Harry, it seemed like a plausible answer to deflect the intuitiveness of this fellow Jock. He did not want to know why Harry was going to the London Cemetery; it was just the usual cabbie chat to make the passenger feel he was being cared for.

Almost to the minute, the black cab pulled into Alderbrook Road, driving under the decorative archway constructed during the Edwardian Grade II listed building. Harry noticed the beautiful landscaped Memorial Garden, as his taxi approached the car park. He noted the location of another Black Cab parked at the opposite end of the car park. He assessed deliberately away from what he assumed was the private cars of those attending the current funeral. He spoke through the security intercom in the cab,

"Driver, could you please pull up next to that taxi as the person I am meeting I believe is inside it? If you could please wait and I will re-join you in due course for my return to Wapping."

There was no verbal response—however, the Driver done as bid. Harry alighted and walked the five metres to the other cab; It was a dry and sunny afternoon. The black cab was rather strange as it was completely blacked out, preventing anyone from observing the occupant. As he approached on foot, the Driver dressed in a Black Suit, with a white shirt, and black tie, sporting a peaked Chauffeur's cap saluted him and opened the door for him to get in. The occupant was equally well attired in a chalk-pinstriped suit, a man of about forty-five Harry assessed with immaculate hair and grooming. He introduced himself by proffering his right hand. Harry replicated and in doing so noticed that the hand he received had clearly never done a day's hard work, it was smooth and the nails manicured. He spoke,

"Good afternoon, Mr Moon I am Perter Egbert as I explained on the telephone. I have a task for which I am reliably informed that you are more than capable of carrying out for me for a given fee, I require complete confidentiality throughout, should you accept the task."

Harry, bit his lip, and rubbed his nose assessing the situation before replying,

"Let me assure you, Peter, may I call you Peter or would you prefer Mr Egbert?"

"Yes, of course, Peter is fine."

"If I do take on a job for you, that is what you will be paying for total discretion at all times."

"Good, excellent then, let me proceed to brief you on the contract as mentioned earlier. I wish you to carry out the extinguishing of a certain gentleman who has, may I put it caused me some embarrassment. He has in short been fucking my wife, and that has to cease forthwith. For this task, I will pay you the sum of one hundred thousand pounds sterling into whatever bank of your choice."

Harry, raised his eyebrow, contemplating this offer, before responding,

"Peter, that is an awfully lot of cash to pay for the erasing of one-lover. Are, you confident that the lady in question has only one suitor and amorous relationship outside your marriage?"

"Yes, I do."

Moon, being an undercover policeman, had to box clever with this request. It was evident that his reputation in the criminal underworld was of such standing that this gentleman felt confident that he would accept the hit contract. Harry, replied,

"So, who is the target?"

Lord Peter Egbert Gentry, handed Harry a rather expensive leather briefcase, saying,

"All the details of the individual are contained in the manilla folder inside. It also has an advance of half the fee of fifty-thousand pounds in cash with the balance on completion."

Harry opened the briefcase and extracted a buff folder that

revealed the man's photograph to be erased. The individual was dressed in an officer's uniform in the Brigade of Guards with a war medal row. One of which he immediately recognised as the Victoria Cross. He immediately realised that this was controversial in the extreme'. However, nevertheless, it was an exciting proposition. As a policeman, he was not in the game of wasting people for money. It was clear that this fellow Egbert had the real hump with the man in the photograph. He decided to go along with the ruse for the time being by answering.

"This is a serious business you wish me to perform for you. However, the sum of the fee is inadequate for what you wish me to implement. I will have to arrange to disappear for at least six months following this hit as the police will be all over it, like a rash. The person you wish killed is the holder of the Victoria Cross. If you believe his murder will go without serious investigation. You are not of sound mind."

Gentry, expected this response, for if nothing else he had done his homework on this one, He said in a rather stern manner,

"Mr Moon, I will agree with you it is a difficult task, but that is why I am prepared to increase the fee by another one-hundred-thousand, provide he is erased without scandal. In other words, he vanishes with no remains to be discovered. Therefore the authorities will assume that he has absconded from the Army."

Harry was about to reply when Lord Gentry went on,

"It was better if he just failed to exist anymore, and my cheating wife will not discover what has happened to her, 'Fuck Buddy!'

Harry, decided to go with the flow of this conversation traffic, and commented,

"I will accept the contract. However, I must inform you that once completed I need not meet with you from this day forth and that the balance in used notes is deposited in the place of my choice. I will furnish you with that location in due course. What is the time frame for this contract as I will have to spend substantial time in preparation?"

Gentry responded,

"No longer than one month and I do wish to know when complete?"

"That Sir will be fine by me. You will not hear of the said, gentleman's demise as he will disappear from his abode in the King Road, Chelsea, and life will be extinguished."

Lord Gentry, then offered his hand again to seal the deal but as he did so, Harry, interrupted his flow. He said,

"I will require your contact number so that I can send you notification that the contract has been completed."

However, Gentry was sceptical on providing this information but noted that failure to do so might be a ball breaker. He called Harry's mobile from his, this time the number was not withheld, and he saved it to his phone with the initials, GEPL.

They shook hands on the deal; Harry retained the briefcase containing the folder and the cash deposit. He alighted the taxi and walked to his waiting black cab and Driver. Once inside the vehicle, he remained until the Black Cab with the blacked-out windows had left the car park.

Harry, then asked the Driver to take him to New Scotland Yard.

CHAPTER 32
PRYGO PARK BODY

John Jenkins was just about to shower when he heard the alarm on his mobile phone, indicating, a message. He ruffled around his pockets to locate it. Once found he read the text message,

'Young female body found between the Deer Enclosure and the coffee stall in Prygo Park, Romford. Forensics are already on their way. Please call the Duty Desk?'

John was fully aware of this location as it was a public open space of about eighty-seven hectares close to the beautifully quaint village of, Havering-ate-Bower. It was one of the three main available family gathering spaces in Havering and Romford. The main entrance was in Broxill Road, and he was aware of its proximity to the Respite Hospital, St Frances Hospice. He also knew that it was part of Bedford's Country Park as they both blistered onto each other. They were both well used during the summer months, but, not so popular in the winter other than dog walkers. He decided nevertheless to shower first before calling the police duty Sergeant for an update. Once dressed, he called the Duty Desk Sergeant to obtain a verbal briefing. His worst nightmares were about to manifest again. The intelligence report on discovering the body was a young female with her two feet bound together and sporting a dried-up leaking wound from her severed right hand. The hand was as yet not found, therefore not present with the cadaver. Her feet were bare and kept together with a red cord.

He got into the shower. The hot water massaged his neck as he washed his short, wiry ginger hair. Once the shampoo had rinsed away, he opened his eyes. "Crap!" he said, covering himself up as best he could with his cupped hands. He dried himself and looked into the full-length mirror. The reflection did not please him. John's face these days was a repository for lines, creases, furrows, and ridges. He looked like a crumpled piece of corrugated tin that someone had thrown away – even more so when he was perplexed. As he did while contemplating what he would find when he arrived at the scene of the crime. There was little point in rushing.

Nevertheless, he dressed quickly; the police car was parked outside his house as he opened his door. He noted that Natalie Lewis was already seated in the rear of the vehicle. John entered and took his seat next to the police driver, and she greeted her boss,

"Good morning Sir, looks very much from the information I have received that it is another ritual duplicate killing of a young female. The verbal report suggests many similarities to the two previous young female murders. The body is dumped in the Deer Enclosure. Forensics are on-site, and hopefully, we will have a good brief and update on arrival."

Jenkins nodded approval and immediately reached inside his jacket for his mobile telephone, he dialled, letting the phone ring awaiting a response. Meanwhile, the driver maintained the moving car at the speed limit of the road he was driving. An edit was sent around the Police Station that excessive speed was not encouraged when attending non-urgent cases. As the report confirmed that the unfortunate cadaver was already lifeless, no haste was required. She was not going anywhere fast other than in a body bag in the rear of an ambulance. The Queens Hospital morgue was her next stop followed by a cold shelf in the bodies refrigerator.

JOHN WAS aware that Prygo Park had been an estate of that name for many hundreds of years. It also played its part in determining who became the sovereign of England back in its day. Henry the Eighth, King of England once occupied the Old Palace.

As the car approached the entrance gate, there was not unexpectedly a policeman preventing access, recoding the arrivals, and directing arrivals. John, immediately noticed that the area had already been cordoned off with blue and white police tape. A temporary car park had been designated, and they were pointed to that direction. The policeman determined where they should park. Natalie was enamoured by the number of Red Deer in the compound who had been separated from their permanent home to temporary ones in order that the crime scene is available to the investigating police. The deer were used to roaming freely so this restriction would not suit the animals.

John and Natalie approached the area, were signed into the incident logbook, and walked towards the white tent that was already in position. Doctor Cyd Loveday, was once again on site. They took the white suits and dressed in them, covering their faces they entered the tent.

The naked body of a young girl was laid out in the form of

Christ's Crucifixion; with her arms spread either side of her legs tied together by what appeared to be a red cord, which seemed to have been severed by some sharp instrument. The crimson line was also bound around her neck. The marking on her forehead was similar to the two other murders of the same nature. John, presumed, is not a copycat but very much perpetuated by the same killer or killers.

Dressed in his white forensic suit with his name tag around his neck Doctor Loveday nodded at them as they entered the tent.

John then asked,

"What are your initial views on this Cyd?"

Loveday replied,

"Pretty much the same as the other two we have had. She has suffered serious trauma to her body, the hand has been severed and nowhere to be found. There are indications of sexual activity. It is a murder, with the same ritual connotations. I will not be certain until I carry out the autopsy, John."

DS Natalie Lewis had a pensive look on her face and staring down at this poor deceased girl, no more than a teenager in her assessment. She raised her head with what was a melancholy looking expression. Her face was one of sheer desolation at what she witnessed the depicted crucifixion and punishment once more. Why oh why, did she and the others deserve to die in this way?

John noticed a tear had left her eyes as she commented to all present in a very shaky voice,

"The act of inflicting pain on other individuals is both psychological and physiological. Whomsoever is inflicting these horrendous murders, is truly incarnate with Lucifer."

John and Cyd looked at her fixedly. There was not much to be said. However, Doctor Loveday, aware of the moment, said,

"Well that is about all I can do here, and in turn, I will leave it to the Forensic Team to collate what they can evidentially. He snapped off his blue medical gloves, removed the hood from his head and mask from his face, commenting,

"I will carry out the autopsy at ten-o-clock tomorrow morning. I will see you then."

CHAPTER 33
HELL'S ANGELS ABOUND

The briefing was over. The team was ready to move. Natalie had been as honest as she could be about the situation, which pleased them all. Frequently briefings were couched in half-truths, downright lies, and need-to-know, which could put team members in unnecessary danger. Here, she had laid it all on the line, laid it on thick that Alan Boyd was a killer out of the top drawer, who knew how to have his men execute and kill well, they had been trained to do it efficiently and probably enjoyed it too.

They got the message.

"Do you have any further questions?"

She asked as she packed her notes together. The team leader, Sergeant David Drummond, a well-built officer over six feet tall, who looked as if he would take no messing from anyone, asked:

"Where has the information about the Hells Angels location come from?"

Natalie looked at the Uniformed Sergeant; She coughed and replied,

"From a reputable source in the East End of London - a man who's presently under-cover."

"And how much do we know about this Sandy Low fellow?"

"Very little, other than he's been in this country for thirty years, generally in the hotel or restaurant trade as his cover story. He's got a family connection with the Drugs Barron we're currently investigating - and family connections mean a lot to these people. It would appear that over the years he's given refuge to many overseas members, illegally entering the UK from either Italy or the Poland"'

"So, what do you think, Sarge?' Natalie asked.

"Ideally, I'd like to seal off the whole area, evacuate the surrounding buildings and then go in, preferably with a floor-plan of the location which they are hold up in."

"That sounds like a major operation to my way of thinking, and would I perceive require the deployments of several teams to guarantee success effectively."

Drummond a hugely experienced operator and commander

in these types of raids and as such Natalie wished to use that expertise to its fullest.

"May I suggest that I visit Boyd's, Hells Angels in the guise of a well-dressed businessman seeking an investment opportunity. By doing this, it may just afford us the intelligence required to launch a triumphant raid."

Although Natalie was handling this as designated by DCI Jenkins, she was well aware of the vast operational expertise possessed by Sergeant Drummond. It was in effect an easy decision to make, and she commented,

"I agree with that David; however, I insist if you go in alone, there must be back up close at hand should things turn pear-shaped!"

Drummond replied,

"Natalie, I would not think of entering a 'Lion's Den,' without due care and attention to my safety. And as such, neither would I put my wife and children's father at risk without it."

Natalie responded by saying,

"That's a goer then.

Following, changing into a slightly well-tailored pin-striped business suit David Drummond shook hands with her in the Romford Police car park and slipped into a sparkling racing green police jaguar. He left the station, not using the number nineteen, Main Road exit but the underground covert one into Oaklands Avenue.

His initial journey was uneventful, but as he picked up the motorway, he observed a car that seemed to be tailing his Jaguar in his rearview mirror.

It wasn't the next covert protection police car. It was some hothead in a Porsche flashing his lights. "Overtake then, arsehole!" David shouted.

"The road's empty."

But the 911 wanted to race. Any other day and any other cargo, Drummond might have obliged. The Jaguar was more than a match for the German sports car behind him. But the thought of being stopped for racing on a motorway didn't fill him with optimism. He signaled left and dabbed the brake to disable the cruise control. The Jaguar slid into the centre M25 lane.

The 911 got the message, and, after tailgating Drummond for another quarter-mile, pulled out to pass him. For a second, David seriously reconsidered his decision but then relaxed his grip on the wheel. With a harsh roar from its rear-mounted, six-cylinder motor, the Porsche shot past him. He took a sideways look, expecting some yuppie type in shirt and tie, maybe wearing high-end sunglasses. He was right. The guy looked about fifty, perhaps a little younger. Confident, chin up, looking straight ahead. Then he was past and accelerating away from the Jag. The howl from his car competing for undivided attention. Iy was then that David's mind flashed back to the photographs on the detective's wall. He was sure that the 911 driver was none other than Alan Boyd. Why was he in Romford!

Boyd was as dangerous, for sure. And he'd have the home advantage: his turf, his gang members. His muscle and leader of the Hells Angels Chapter was his meeting target, one Sandy Low. Hackney was his patch and thing could become dodgy. He was aware that Boyd, with his American cohort, smuggled large shipments of drugs into the UK for sale in London. He was a very dangerous individual. Even the Turkish Drug Dealers steered well clear of his patch.

Drummond decided he would go in with the Glock he had in his holster. But discreetly in the back of the waistband. The satnav was telling him he had about ten minutes, Boyd was immaculately attired wearing a tie. He was right. The guy looked about fifty, maybe a little younger. Confident, chin up, looking straight ahead. He was sure it was nothing to concern himself about, just another idiot on the road.

Then he was past and accelerating away from the unmarked police jaguar, the howl from his car competing with his for attention. And he'd have home advantage. His turf, his gang members. David decided he would go in with the Glock. But discreetly. Back of the waistband. The satnav was telling him he had about ten minutes to Hackney. Drummond pressed the button on the dashboard to silence it. The map was his friend now. He pulled off M25, motorway onto the M11 heading towards Hackney. After about a mile he saw the flashing roof bar of a police cruiser, stationary on the shoulder. He slowed, then pushed the Jaguar back up to sixty-five. No sense in drawing attention to himself by driving too slowly. As he passed the cruiser, he looked right and laughed at what he saw. Parked in front of the cop car was the Porsche, whose driver was no doubt getting a lecture about public safety, along with a ticket and a fine. He was looking for Reading Road. Sergeant Drummond saw it coming up on his right and slowed to make the turn. He was close now, heading south-east on another scruffy road. His destination was Hackney Gardens, and it was tucked away next to the ancient church. There were twenty-five luxury apartments, one of which was the Penthouse Suit occupied by none other than Alan Boyd, Drug Barron and enforcer for the entire area. However, he would be busy at present, explaining why he was speeding so fast on the motorway.

He pulled in to the side of the road and pressed the button to open the boot. He walked round to the back of the car and lifted the Glock out of its plastic case. Its weight was reassuring as he transferred it to the end of his waistband. He settled his jacket over the grip. He'd have to drive leaning upright and away from the seatback, but better that than arrive and not have a chance to get tooled up.

The gang's Headquarters was supposed to be down an unmarked road on the left just past the Esso petrol station. He passed the station, then he saw the sign, only as Natalie had described it on her copious instructions. Well aware that Lewis plus a well-manned back up team were in covert police vans hidden in close proximity if he required bailing out.

A small white steel square, of about eighty-one inches, painted crudely in red gloss, peppered with silver-grey circular dents where kids had been shooting at it with guns or air rifles. Risky, given who'd put it there. He made the turn into the narrow lane and cut his speed to a walking pace.

The alley was almost overgrown with bushes at the entrance, with just enough room for the Jaguar to edge through without scratching its pristine paintwork. But then it opened out – all the vegetation had been cut back from its edges – into a smooth stretch of blacktop leading towards a low-slung building with a giant neon sign projecting above the flat roofline. The sign read, 'Hells Angels Motorcycle Club' on one line and 'Flint Chapter' underneath. He parked what he judged to be a respectful distance from the building. Then he pushed open the door with his foot and stepped out of the car, squeezing the safety catch button of his weapon as he did so.

David approached the metal fence surrounding the Bikers lair aware that the CCTV Camera was recording his advance. Depressing the entry system, he announced that his appointment was with Sandy Low. Following a short wait, the metal walk-in door opened, and a moustached leather-wearing individual challenged him. He lied saying he was a Moto-Cycle Salesman. This bluff worked as the man stood aside to let him enter.

Facing him was a scene straight out of a biker film. There were fifteen or twenty Harley-Davidsons leaned over at lazy angles. To the left was another small door with the sign above, 'ENTRANCE.'

"Yes, who are you, and what do you want?"

"Good afternoon I have an arranged meeting with Sandy Low whom I have been advised lives here.!

Their kick-stands reminded him like drunks along a bar. Some wildly customised with high handlebars and flame-painted tanks. Others were off the shelf stock bike. Still, others had a distressed look, as they'd never been cleaned up since they were bought, matt with grease and road-dirt. The air smelled of petrol fumes, beer and cannabis smoke, thick, oily vapour that got into his nose and mouth, and onto the back of his tongue. Now and again a Harley would fire up from a workshop next to the clubhouse, its flatulent, coughing sound instantly recognisable. The harsh mechanical noise overlaid the southern boogie American guitar music floating from the main door – a band singing about a sharp-dressed man. Hells Angels milled around, holding bottles of beer, smoking, standing by their bikes, chatting.

David had always thought of Hells Angels as having long hair – heavy metal types. Most of these guys wore it short or even shaved, though there were a couple of guys with ponytails or just rats' nests of dank, greasy-looking hair. Quite a lot of silver, too. Some of them looked to be in their fifties at least. As he arrived, the Angels looked over, scowling or huddling to exchange comments while pointing at this corporate type in a suit invading their territory. But they didn't approach him. He supposed it was his move to make. He squared his shoulders and strode over to the stoop at the front of the clubhouse. He could smell something else now, a mixture of stale sweat, beer, and rank body odour. Like someone hadn't showered. Ever. Or had once, but decided he didn't like it. An immense man wearing the club uniform of greasy jeans, leather biker jacket and sleeveless denim jacket covered in patches, chains and metal swastikas strolled towards him. He was a couple of inches taller than Sergeant Drummond, but what impressed was his girth. He had a giant belly that stretched his black T-shirt tight. His biceps were massively over-developed, pushing his arms out from his sides and giving him the look of an old-school grappler about to fight. Which, maybe, he was. As he approached the lump, spoke,

"Help you?"

It was all he said, looking over David's clothes, which he now felt were ridiculous out of place, in this place of testosterone and high-octane gasoline.

"I'm looking for Sandy Low, who works for Mr Boyd, the proprietor of this establishment I believe?"

Meet brevity with brevity.

"Maybe so, son. A lot of people are. Now, what would a well-dressed gentleman like you want with a man like Low?"

He stared straight back at the man, picking up on a jagged double "S" tattoo on his neck and another reading "Aryan Nations" on his left bicep.

"I'm here to make a trade. So maybe you could let your boss know I'm here. Tell him it's Don Edmondson's bagman, David Drummond if you want."

The man's eyes narrowed, and his giant fists balled into clubs. He took a step closer to Drummond, close enough to have him within swinging distance, and leaned towards him.

"He's not my boss, you punk! He's our club president. I'm a full-patch; you know what that means?"

The man had raised his voice to an octave higher and more threatening tone. It was then that two or three other men were ambling over, intrigued by the sight of this out-of-state dandy. He was interested in who'd appeared in their midst on this hot lunchtime like an apparition.

"It means you don't get to walk in here and start giving me orders."

"Everything all right?" one of the other men asked his skinny frame a complete contrast to the grappler's bulky, gym-built muscles.

"Yeah, sure it is. I got this pissant Englishman disrespecting me, and I'm wondering whether to kick his ass straight out of here or throw him in the pond."

The other men laughed. A mean, expectant sound like they were hoping their friend might take both options. David spoke in a low tone, so the man had to lean in to hear him. He looked at the man's pupils, watching them dilate as the rhythm of his speech altered – as he was taught on one of the numerous police courses he was forced to attend. It permitted him to make assessments – and with it, the man's brainwaves.

"You'll fetch Sandy Low... out here and you will be ... pleased to do it. You'll tell your friends to ... get lost, and you and I will ... be friends. Also, go and get your president ... for me because he's expecting me, and he ... knows my boss and his name is Don Edmonston. Then you're doing what I want ... because you want to do it and tell your ... friends to go back to their bikes ... because this is all over for now."

It was an old trick, and he hadn't used it for a long time. The cadences and the unsteady flow of his speech coupled with particular tones and eye movements had distracted the man, subverting his focus by not conforming to any of his expectations. David Drummond shot out his right hand as if to shake, and the other man offered his own from instinct. But instead of taking it, David grabbed his wrist with his left hand and jerked it, then tapped him forcefully, twice, fast, in sharp succession on the forehead with digitus Secundus and digitus Medius manus. It had the desired effect by forcing his forward movement to reverse, from the blow's surprise and pain, it confirmed that David was someone not to mess with despite his physical bulk.

"Do it now. Fuck Features."

The big man rocked back on his heels, and looked at Drummond with a dazed stare, shaking his head like a dog with a flea biting its ear.

"Yeah, sure, whatever. I'll get Sandy Low for you. He's OK, boys. Get back to your bikes."

The other men, tensed to respond to the policeman's physical contact with their friend, shrugged at his change of heart and wandered off, grumbling, their hopes of a lunchtime cabaret thwarted.

The grappler turned and wandered into the clubhouse. The boogie band were now singing "She's Got Legs." David had hoped they were sturdier than the rubber items on which the Hells Angel was negotiating the stoop. An uncomfortable couple of minutes passed. He remained standing motionless still, feeling the hot sun on the top of his head. An American TV actor he'd once met in a bar in Pinewood Film Studios, Buckinghamshire had given him a lesson on commanding a scene.

'The trick is, OK, you do nothing. The other guys are all fidgeting or looking this way and that, trying to catch the camera's eye. But it's just motion, and it isn't an action. So what you do is, you just keep very still. Slow your breathing, hold whatever pose you're in and let the camera come to you. You're irresistible. And the audience knows it. You're the one still point in a screen full of movement, so they watch you. Then he'd drained his mojito and fallen sideways off his stool.'

David Drummond guessed keeping still is more comfortable to talk about than to do. A couple of the Angels were staring at him from the row of bikes, hands held loosely at their sides or resting on the throttles, but none approached. Presumably, they were waiting to see how the Big Man reacted. David had no illusions on the score. If he smelled a rat, then he, Police Sergeant, David Drummond, would simply disappear. Then the door to the clubhouse banged back against the wall with a loud crack like a dropped pile of books—show time. The man strolling towards him exuded power, authority, and control. He looked to be in his sixties. The other Angels watched him, not David, as he approached. He towered over him, and he was heavy, too. No gut, just a concrete wall of muscle. He wore no T-shirt like the others, just a scuffed leather waistcoat above his jeans and biker boots. His abdominal and pectoral muscles weren't the sculpted sheet of neatly quilted flesh sported by urban gym bunnies. These were cruder – slabs bestowed by nature and maybe bulked up by hauling timber around a sawmill, or bike parts, or something massive, hard and dangerous in a factory. Sandy Low his chest was a riot of tattoos, dominated by the winged death's head and the words 'Hells Angels' as recorded in the report. Cradling the winged skull was a loop of stylised wolf-heads, interlaced with complex plaited strands – maybe a Native American design. It looked like a chain of office.

Both his arms had full sleeves of inking – a fan of aces, more skulls, pneumatically breasted Amazons wielding swords, gothic letters. A rose was dripping blood, and Hells Angel's symbols, including a red 81" in a diamond – H and A being the eighth and first letters of the alphabet, it wasn't hard to decode. He remembered that the letter "H" is the eight of the alphabets, while the letter "A" is the first letter. 81 is "HA" an abbreviation for Hells Angels. Simple really, well it would have to be for them to appreciate it's meaning.

But it was his face that commanded attention. Trim, white-flecked moustache and goatee were framing a broad slash of a mouth, pulled down at the corners like he was disappointed at being called out to meet this foppish Englishman. Shaved scalp, the grey stubble was revealing a receding hairline. The right, eye was staring at Sergeant Drummond, the iris a pale blue, like a husky. The left eye was present, but not correct. Whoever had knifed him across the face had slit the eyelid and damaged the cornea. The lid was badly-healed, puckered somehow. It didn't sit right over the eyeball. The eye had a curdled look, maroon in places, iris, and pupil distorted into an oval. Low spoke, a softer tone than he was expecting. Maybe he did not need to intimidate with his voice, looking as he did.

"You Din Edmonston's boy?"

The con was working well. He obviously had no idea of David's fundamental role in life as an all-action police officer. Just as well he thought that discovery would end his life, for sure. So he continued the pretense.

"That's right. Are you Sandy Low, Boyd's boy?

This retaliation sufficiently pissed him off. The tall man stared down at him, his mouth hardening into a thin line, one right eye boring into David's eyes. Then he let out a huge guffaw, revealing a mouthful of big, off-white teeth, except for a shiny gold fang on the right eye-tooth

"You hear that, boys? Am I Boyd's Boy?"

The Greek chorus gathered around them either found this genuinely funny or knew it was acceptable policy to show their appreciation for their president's jokes. Either way they joined in the laughter, a mix of harsh crowing, high-pitched giggling and throaty rumbles, liquid with cigarette smoke and years spent breathing road dust.

"Who did you think I was, boy? Brad Pitt?"

This set off another riot of hooting and cawing. Drummond decided to take the initiative back.

"No. You're far too good-looking."

Low, paused for a split second and scratched his chin.

"Funny guy, huh? Yes. I am Sandy Low. Why don't you come inside, have a beer, and we can talk business?"

Low slung a heavy arm around David's shoulders and walked him into the shadowy interior of the clubhouse. He tensed for a blast of the other man's sweat but instead got an explosion of citrus, overlaid with aftershave. You just never knew.

The firearms team was parked up three streets away in their 'Battle-Bus': an armoured personnel carrier with one-way bulletproof windows which enabled occupants to see out but no one else to see in, giving the vehicle a sinister appearance. Natalie's car drew up behind. In the back seat, Torrance and the new member of the team, Peter Carew sat poring over one of the street maps, and they were muttering to each other.

DS Natalie Lewis having exited her car, ignored the battle bus and walked toward an area where the local streetwalkers were used as their pick-up location.

CHAPTER 34
INGATESTONE HALL

"Name please and your business!"

He removed his Met Police Identity Warrant Card and placed it toward the screen to enable the inquirer the ability to confirm who he was.

"I am Detective Chief Inspector John Jenkins, and I have an appointment with Lord Gentry."

The machine responded,

"Thank you; please follow the signs to the parking area to the rear of the building. There you will be greeted by Mr Mountfield, Lord Gentry's assistant."

"Hi I am John Jenkins, and I am here to meet Lord Gentry."

The Personal Assistant, Bert Mountfield responded,

"Sir, I am afraid his Lordship has been unexpectedly called away on business of the Realm. He offers his sincere apologies. However, he has arranged for her Ladyship to meet with you."

Jenkins was seriously, pissed off by this. That aside, he thought that perhaps the lady of the house would be more forthcoming. He replied,

"I am sorry to hear that Lord Gentry is not available."
"Then, please follow me?"

"Mam may I introduce you to DCI Jenkins of the Metropolitan Police.

He found Lady Gentry looking very charming in a light autumnal frock of lemon lace with a few printed red rose's set about it, and he thought that she seemed to be relaxed.

"Detective Chief Inspector, how lovely to meet you, welcome to Ingatestone Hall. I apologise for my husband's absence. He was called to the Palace of Westminster on urgent business by their Lordships and is not expected back until tomorrow evening at the latest. He asked me to give you his sincere apologies."

This turn of events peeved john Jenkins as he was looking forward to questioning Gentry. He forced a smile and replied,

"What a shame he is unavailable."

The detailed detective work on the white van's location involved in the dumping of the corpse in Romford had been tracked to and observed hidden in the adjoining garage. This provided evidence that Ingatestone Hall could do with a serious investigative look at. In discussion with his colleague Bob Clarkson, they collectively agreed that he should try and obtain a meeting with Lord Gentry, the owner. A drone which has flown over the estate provided a VCR recording which provided information that a relatively large church sat inside the grounds. They assessed it could offer a secluded location for dastardly deeds. That information accompanied with the fact that the murder of the two Romford girls intimated that a cult group could be involved.

On releasing his handshake from hers, he smiled and responded.

"Lady Gentry, I am so pleased to make your acquaintance; however, I must confess it was your husband whom I wanted to speak with."

"Detective Jenkins, well you will, unfortunately, have to put up with me. I do hope I can be of assistance in his stead."

"My Dear Lady Gentry, I am sure you will be of help, and I can return when his Lordship returns to speak with him."

She smiled with her full beauty in abundance, then she said in a shallow and inviting voice,

"DCI Jenkins, please call me by my Christian name Olivia? Also, without becoming too familiar may I call you by your first name, John?"

He was astonished by this familiarity, replying,

"That is most kind of you, Lady, Olivia. I will, however, address you for the time being as Lady Gentry!"

"As you wish. Well Sir, will you do me the honour of taking tea with me? I so need a good refreshing pot of Darjeeling? It comes directly to us here from the Happy Valley Tea Estate located in West Bengal. I can confirm to you it has the most delicious taste. Do please say, yes? You will not be disappointed."

" she acknowledged.

John immediately realised that this woman was hiding nothing as she was so forthcoming in both manner and speech. She immediately seemed to catch onto what he may well be after and continued,

John, could not resist this offer and her effervescent, bubbly, vibrant and enthusiastic personality shone through the smile on her face. It brought a receptacle smile to his own. He considered the offer for a brief moment and replied,

"Lady Gentry it would give me the utmost delight to join you for tea. All be it slightly against our normal procedure to do so!"

It was quite evident to John that she exuded an attractive charisma. Fortunately, for him, she had the patience to persuade him to join her against his better judgment for, Darjeeling Tea.

Oliva turned toward Bert and nodded, with that, he disappeared out of the room. She extended her right arm, and he noted that her fingers were manicured, that of a cultured individual who perhaps was a pianist. She beckoned him to take a seat on the sofa, saying,

"Please have a seat while Mr Mountfield brings tea to us please?"

John sat as requested on the comfortable sofa and was hardly seated when the door opened with Bert holding it ajar as two maids entered the room, the first with a silver tray containing the Pot of Tea and two cups. She was followed by the second maid again carrying another similar tray comprising of finger sandwiches, homemade scones with clotted cream and jam all stacked on a three-tiered silver cake stand. On the side of the tray was two porcelain side plates sporting two starched napkins and silver knife. A pair of crystal glasses containing Roeder Brute Premier Rose' A small circular table was rolled in from of them, and the waitresses proceeded to serve the tea to them.

John thoroughly enjoyed being spoiled in this manner, and conversation had been absorbing throughout the tea, however strictly uninformative. He abstained from drinking Premier Rose'. However, during their chat, he had arranged to have a guided tour around the estate. Once tea was over, he rose and was escorted once more by Mountfield to the Colonial Hall. He was introduced to Philip Ross one of the numerous footmen to accompany him around Ingatestone Hall Estate. This did not suit John as he wanted to have a look around on his own. Once they were clear of the main building, Ross showed him the

Horse Stables, as they passed them. These were not his main target for investigation. He aimed to have a good look at the Church which sat in a secluded part of the grounds. It was surrounded by trees which provided just sufficient to screen it to the human eye from afar.

Mr Ross was undoubtedly a fine fellow, and whenever John asked him a question, he was forthcoming with his point of view. As they cleared the stables DCI, Jenkins decided to inquire with Ross about his knowledge and experience of the church usage. As it was, he informed Jenkins that it was used sparingly for monthly Sunday Services. He was also aware but had no direct information that it was infrequently used on the fourth Friday of the month by his Lordship for what he described as, 'Perhaps Masonic Type Meetings.' He then persuaded Philip that it would be interesting to view the Church. As they both approached the church ground which was surrounded by grave headstones and several with massive, monuments in remembrance of the grave's occupier. John turned to Philip Ross and inquired,

"I suppose that the larger monuments to life are members of the Gentry Dynasty?"

Ross smiled and responded,

"That's true, Sir, and you will note that on the top of them, the hands are together in prayer, pointing upwards. This I was informed was a Victorian way depicting that the deceased has ascended to heaven. Also, they have received their final reward for a life well lived and confirmation of life after death for the faithful."

Jenkins, returned the smile, saying,

"For sure loads of folks do believe in life after death. From my point of view, I prefer the living to the dead. In my profession, it's my job to discover the guilty who illegally cause death!"

That said they together strolled up the shingle path toward the entrance to the Church. Both their feet made a distinctive crunching sound on the gravel walkway, for whatever reason neither knew they turned their heads towards each other and again smiled to one another. As they reached the Archway covering the Church entrance, there were two magnificent oak doors with highly polished metalwork. John suddenly thought what about the keys for access? He then asked Mr Ross,

"I am sorry Philip, but is there any way we can obtain the keys so that I may look at the inside of this magnificent structure?"

Ross looked at John and responded,

"I am afraid that would have to be authorised by Mr. Mountfield as he maintains access to the church's inner sanctum. Lord Gentry has issued firm orders that fetter anyone other than Mr Mountfield, and it would be more than my job's worth Sir.

DCI Jenkins remained silent for a good sixty seconds, which was sufficient in order to let Ross worry about what was coming next. He then reached into his jacket pocket, removing his Metropolitan Police Warrant Card. He flipped it open and held it directly in a threatening manner in front of Philip's eyes just close enough for him to read the print. Then he uttered the words of the famous Scottish Crime television program, and trying to emulate a Scottish Accent said,

"There's been a Murder. Now open these doors or I will call for the Police Black Maria to come and lock you in a cold dark cell in the Romford Police Station, comprehend?"

The look of concern spread all over Philip Ross's face, and, sweat appeared on his forehead. Silence remained between them which you could have cut through with a sharp knife. He stared at John, and then he surrendered to the abrupt Detective Inspector's statement.

"If you promise not to mention this to a soul, I will show you where the spare keys are kept within the graveyard?"

Again, John kept the Warrant Card reasonably far from his eyes, thus emphasising his importance and insistence. He without the Scottish accents responded determinedly,

"Show me the keys now!"

Philip wiped the sweat from his brow and said to John,

"I will, but it will undoubtedly cost me my job!"

He stepped off with purpose but with his chin almost on his chest and Jenkins followed.

At the rear of the Church, they arrived at what John assessed as a well-over-the-top monument with someone mounted on a white horse with a caption on the centre of the plinth the title,

COLONEL (THE LORD) FREDRICK DAVID CHARLES GENTRY,

44TH REGIMENT OF FOOT (EAST ESSEX)

The Fighting Fours
BORN May 1780 DIED Waterloo June 1815

He looked at Ross and wondered if this was some sort of micky take, Philip went to the rear of the monument and beckoned John to join him. He did so, and the Footman pointed to a not so obvious covered recess, which he slid open and revealed a digital key safe. He lifted the rubber protecting the safe from adverse weather. It exposed two sets of numerical numbers odds on the left and even to the right. Ross swiftly depressed four numbers and flipped the secure area, revealing an ancient large brass key. He removed it and passed it to Jenkins. He was about to close the key safe when John placed his hand over it, thus preventing him from closing it. He then asked the Footman,

"What is the code of this device?

Philip, for a change, looked far less concerned, and replied,

"WATERLOO, of course!"

John smiled and responded

"so, history again reveals all, one, eight, one, five, 1815!"

"Not quite.

Replied Philip,

"It is 5181 The Battle of Waterloo in reverse. And, when shutting, then it's the original date, 1581."

"Thank you very much,"

Replied the DCI.

John placed the large brass key in the door lock and turned it, the lock clicked, and he pushed the right-hand door open. He ushered the Footman to follow him, which he did. He bid him take a seat in what was apparently a quite large cloaking area. At the end of the cloakroom were two large bronze doors which were not locked, John took hold of the circled brass handles and turned both clockwise. The doors gave way to his pressure, and he went into the main religious Church. He was closing them behind him, thus debarring the prying eyes of the Footman, Philip Ross.

On entry, he was amazed at the opulence of this place of worship. He noted the gallery which surrounded the entire inside of the Church. Now have taken stock of this magnificent vestibule from the rear of the Church. He ventured forward on his own to make a cursory investigation. As he approached the marble, which he assumed was an altar. It was in the form of a crucifix. This somewhat alerted him as to whether he would discover any points of interest. He was not thwarted, dropping to his knees, and began to slowly inspect the white marble as it joined with the red and blue checked carpet of the surrounding flooring. He immediately recognised this to be a masonic colouring. There was a distinct odour of what he perceived to be bleach. He removed a small magnifying glass from his pocket, inspecting the base and finding what appeared to be faded dark marks. It would require forensic investigation and a team of experts. John removed his iPhone from his pocket and took several photographs of the altar and the precise location.

Once complete he returned to where Philip was and said to him,

"You must not mention to anyone that we have been inside this place of worship, do you understand to do so may disrupt police investigations and could lead to you being charged with perverting the course of justice?".

Ross nodded acquiescence to what was a command.

John returned the key to the location from whence it had been recovered from and personally locked the safe using the number 1815 as advised.

On return to the Hall, he was greeted by Bert Mountfield with a broad smile on his face. He informed him that. Lady Gentry had invited him to stay the night in one of the guest rooms as she was hosting a Dinner Party. Well aware her husband would not return home as was his wish when he visited London. Lord Gentry's London trips seemed to occur on the final Friday during February, April September, and December. It suited DCI Jenkins's plan to search the grounds and the Church for any further snippets of information he could discover. He was taken along to his room.

Bert who had escorted him opened the large ornamental door. He was astounded to behold the place as it resembled a small luxury hotel. Bert then commented as he guided John through the apartment,

"I just think white sheets in high-thread cotton are like no other for a guest room. They're just tried and true. And they help keep guests cooler as they sleep, too."

Jenkins smiled in a show of appreciation.

His usher returned the smile without comment. He then said,

"I am aware that you had not intended to stay the night. So, if there is anything you require Chief Inspector by way of toiletries, you will find them in the bathroom cupboard above the sink. They are all new and have never been used by another,"

"Many thanks for this."

DCI Jenkins and that point realised that apart from the suit he was standing in, he had no other clothing into which he could wear for a posh cocktail party. His introspection furnished no solution to his current predicament.

"The least that Lord Gentry would provide for his guests Sir if there is nothing else, I will take my leave of you. If you wish a waitress to serve refreshments before you come down? You need only pick up the phone on the writing desk, dial 111 on the in house telephone system. If you wish to make a call to an outside source, then it's the blue telephone. Will there be anything else?"

"Yes, there is, if you could please arrange the collection of my clean clothing from the Police Station in Romford, that would be most helpful. I will telephone the station and arrange it. I presume that the order of dress will be Black Tie?"

"That is correct, Sir, and we would not wish a member of Her Majesty's Metropolitan Police force to be improperly attired. Now would we?"

Jenkin's smiled saying,

"Talking of being appropriately dressed for the occasion I have this friend. When attending a Dinner Jacket event, he dresses up his Labrador dog in this ridiculous Black Dog jacket, accompanied by a bow ti around it's neck so that the hound blends in."

Mountfield broke out into a condescending snigger

John smirked rather than smiled as he pushed open an equally ornate door leading to the bathroom. When his eyes focused, the bathroom had an almost Baronial appearance with drapes of blue velvet, held in place by similarly impressive gold retainers. He turned to Bert and said,

"Thank you very much, Bert, and by the way, please call me John, there is no need for Sir, I am not your boss."

Bert received this instruction with some disdain and commented,

"If that will be all Sir, I will take my leave of you?"

DCI Jenkins assessed he had lost that point as the 'Gentry Household,' was quite organised and ran on a semi-military basis. He nodded assent at Bert as his Lordships personal assistant closed the door behind him.

John immediately the door closed and wandered over to the large bay window, pulling the lace nets to the side, thus enabling him from this second-floor advantage point to observe the expanse of this part of the estate. He could see the lawn's manicured green grass, which led to the thicket surrounding the church building, which was his,.' la raison pour laquelle,' for his visit to Ingatestone Hall. The 16th Century Church was half-visible breaking out of the west side of the woods. His visit with Philip Ross was most enlightening. It provided him with some assurance that he was not barking up the wrong tree. John was determined to confirm that the story that had been relayed through a former employee of the estate had mentioned the cavorting in the old Church that went on until the early hour of the morning.

At precisely seven-thirty, he came down the winding staircase to the ground floor. He was met by Bert to whom he was grateful for collecting his clothes from the police station. He directed John to the reception room where Her Ladyship was standing at the ornate fireplace with a clear liquid glass in a crystal champagne flute. As he entered the room, she turned towards him with a broad smile and in a sexy voice uttered,

"Good evening Chief Inspector, may I ask what you would prefer as an aperitif?"

DCI Jenkins responded,

"I would be pleased to join you in a glass of sparkling, Lady Gentry."

With that comment, the Victorian Attired attractive young lady appeared from nowhere, dressed in a black dress with short sleeves which ceased below her knees. Unknown to John it was the parlour maid, Helena Trustlove. Also unknown to him and Lady Gentry she had been serviced by Lord Gentry, and he was still paying her money to keep quiet about it.

She also wore a white pinafore apron; with matching cuffs and two tabs she wore. To complete the outfit, a white hat of which the frills covered part of her forehead, and visible two twelve-inch tabs descended the back of her neck. John, was aware that this was her evening order of dress, as she would have worn the coloured dress of a parlour maid during the day. She offered a silver tray to him containing a single glass flute situated dead centre. John removed the glass, and nodded his appreciation, turning towards Olivia he raised his glass, and she accepted it and in pure upper-crust form clinked his glass with her own and said,

"Good health Chief Inspector."

As John, was about to speak, Olivia interrupted saying,

"Oh, I almost forgot, we are being joined for dinner tonight by a real hero in the form of Lieutenant Colonel, James Craig, Scots Guards holder of The Victoria Cross. I am afraid that my husband has confirmed that he will be remaining in London tonight at his club, 'Whites, in St James,' which is his want when in the Capital. So, his absence is not unexpected Chief Inspector,"

DCI Jenkins responded,

"That is fine Lady Gentry; however, I am pleased to be with you and your guests this evening."

"We have a total of eight people attending this evening. They are Colonel Craig, Lady Penelope Tennant, Sir Ian Blair, Queens Council, and Lady Joanne Blair, his wife. Sir Rolf Resit the Swiss Banker and also Lady Diamonique Abbot who owns one of the largest betting companies in the United Kingdom."

The Drinks before dinner were an extraordinary experience for John, he thoroughly enjoyed himself. There was a obvious pairing that occurred. There were cleverly four adult males and females. It was evident to his detective's brain that Lady Gentry never expected her husband home that evening. He was seated interestingly next to the betting woman Diamonique. The entire evening went exceptionally well. However, he noticed how friendly Olivia seemed to be with Colonel Craig, VC. He wondered how far the adoration went!

For his enjoyment, he was sat next to Diamonique Abbot and had learned she was widowed. Her husband perished in a private aircraft accident In Australia He noted, what a striking middle-aged, mature good-looking woman she was. Interestingly to him, she was slightly out of place in this company. This he perceived from her non-posh accent. He assessed she was from somewhere up north towards Manchester. The dress she wore was crimson and her complexion, was strikingly attractive, however, not what may be thought of, as plain as a pikestaff. His assessment of her as not being beautiful. However, she certainly had an aura of attractiveness. He was aware that he got a kick out of chatting to her. Insisting he ceased using her full name Diamonique, instructing him to use the shortened version, Dom! John had to admit, that this was the first women he had taken too since the loss of his wife in the tragic road accident on the motorway; Dawn was very much daily in his mind.

As they departed from the dinner table as was the custom at this sort of upper-class dinner party, the men repaired to the games room for, Port and Cigars. John was thankful that neither of his three male guests was smokers. On re-joining the ladies, the small talk took place, but none of it was helpful to his investigation, other than the apparent closeness of Lady Gentry and Colonel Craig.

The men following their quaffing of port and a game of snooker in the games room re-joined the ladies. There was quite a lot of giggling going on as they entered. He felt as if Dom was trying to airlift him into being her friend. She quite obviously had little time for the others, being content to converse with him in many different subjects. The art of conversation generally seems to be a dying art. Not, this lady she was full of the most noteworthiness subjects. He sensed perhaps a little bit of flirting was forthcoming by Dom Abbot.

It continued until just after, ten o'clock when the majority departed the parlour room as their transport had arrived to collect them. To John's surprise, Dom sided up to him following her goodbye to Olivia and to his shock placed into his right-hand something, as she placed a small farewell kiss on his right cheek.

All left, with the exception being himself and James Craig. During the evening, he mentioned his apartment was located in Chelsea. Also, Craig VC would remain at Ingatestone Hall until the morning. It was not a surprise, but it did intrigue him.

After breakfast taken in the servant's quarters, he had insisted on no favours required or sought. John was still hopeful that more leads would have forthcoming. He telephoned Romford Police Station. There was no further information relevant investigative intelligence that had been forthcoming in his absence overnight. It wasn't proving easy.

John left the building by stepping out through the servant's entrance and walked swiftly towards the Church. Its decorative steeple broke through the tree line about seven-hundred yards to his right. As he did so, the noise of a horse snorting emanated from the stables. DCI Jenkins had always been fascinated by the equine sport, so he decided on a detour. On entering the yard, he slowly avoided a few loads of horse manure. The stable doors were wide open, enabling access without restriction. John wandered in and found the horse which was making a Naing noise; It was the most beautiful silver-grey which stood seventeen hands if it was one. It was to his untrained eye, doubtless a thoroughbred, he marvelled at its long slender legs with well-defined tendons which would carry its body over seven furlongs at Royal Ascot Racecourse. They were obviously, the legs of a racehorse, designed for speed and a smooth ride. As he looked around the stable, he thought to himself. I wonder if this location has any tales to tell? So, he had a proper search around the stables but found nothing of any note.

Horses communicate using snorts, nickers, whinnies, squeals, and neighs, if only they could speak, what would this beautiful animal provide? Alas, horses no matter how well-bred cannot talk, there is the old tail of the White Horse entering a pub and asking for a whisky, the barman asked any particular type, and the horse replies, 'White Horse,' of course, 'you're a numpty.'

He was quite sure that it would come sooner or later, possibly from the neighbourhood of discovering the second girl murdered, more probably from London. It was always possible that Mr Carrington, the lawyer, might find that some other legal beagle may have handled Lord Gentry's entanglement with Trustlove. The Master's recent movement to and from Ingatestone Hall was being tracked and reported to him if anything of significance occurred.

He retrieved the key from the monument key safe. On

entering the Church, his eyes beheld a magnificent place of worship. He noticed oddly in the centre of the Church a slab of granite about four foot in height, and he assessed about six-foot-long and, four-feet wide. This time without Philp, Ross's distraction would enable him to search the inners of the place of worship more thoroughly.

On looking upwards towards the ornamental roof, he observed what seemed to be a seated viewing gallery. John thought this was strange. Nonetheless, perhaps this was common back in the day. As he approached the slab to the alter, he could smell the odour of what he knew was bleach. Rather odd, he mused, in such a place of worship? Of course, bleach was used as a cleaning agent, and if so, why? His rough observance provided no concrete answer to this conundrum. He planned to obtain a search warrant to enable the forensic team to assess the presence of the smell of chlorine. When removed from the naked eye, he knew bloodstains the forensic experts, fortunately with the use of luminal or phenolphthalein, will show if haemoglobin is present. Also, if a shady criminal had washed a bloodstained item of clothing a dozen times, these chemicals could still reveal blood. It would take time, but if issued with the search warrant, John was confident he would succeed. Ross the Footman had provided credible information as to regular gatherings in the Church hosted by Lord Gentry.

He perceived clearly that the case was at a deadlock until he had more information. It was now becoming evident from his investigation inside the Church. That a forensic team was required as soon as possible to establish if his finding was indeed bloodstain.

In the meantime, his work at Ingatestone Hall was about done. He had exhausted its possibilities. There was no reason why he should not return to his office at Romford Police. After having conferred by telephone with Chief Inspector Bob

Clarkson as well as Detective Sergeant Natalie Lewis. He decided to leave one of the two detectives who had arrived on his request this morning to continue making inquiries in the neighbourhood of Ingatestone Village. All be it not his direct area of responsibility. However, the Essex Force was more than happy for him to deal with the second girl's murder as it copied the first found on the Tow Path of the River Rom. Two teenagers with similar signs, a cross on their forehead, and the right hand severed and not found. So, the London Metropolitan Police were in total charge of this investigation.

He found Lady Gentry looking very charming in a light autumnal dress of white lace with a few black bows set about it, and he thought that she seemed less under a strain than she had appeared the day before. He told her that he was returning to Romford; she expressed regret at his going. However, as he was about to leave her presence, he felt that he should unnerve her and said,

"I have a puzzle which you may be able to assist me with Lady Gentry when I was visiting the most beautiful chapel this morning. When entering, I noted a distinct redolence of bleach. I wonder if you had any information that would assist me in clearing this up?"

Olivia, with no hesitation, responded,

"Chief Inspector, the last time I was in that chapel was the day I married Egbert. I am not a religious person. I have never had the inclining to pray to God, and in truth, I am an atheist. You may wish to take that up with the estate manager who deals with the maintenance and cleaning of all buildings."

They parted on quite the friendliest terms. It was not as if he had met her before yesterday. However, she did seem a relatively bright and helpful sort of person for someone in such an elevated position.

As he came away, DCI John Jenkins thought it significant

that she had thanked him for attending the Dinner Party. His innermost thoughts wandered to the interesting dinner guest Dom, and his detective skills had ensured that the passing of the card as she left, he owned her mobile telephone number.

He observed that Bert Mountfield watched over his actual departure, he seemed less pale and haggard than he had been when questioned following his visit to the stables and the chapel. He could well believe that he was glad to see him go. John knew not why it was just a hunch.

As he drove through the estate parkland, he told himself that Lady Gentry and Mr Mountfield were hiding something between them. They would probably break down in any case under intense questioning although he was less sure about, Mountfield, as John opined to himself, that he was a tough cookie. He would not give much time or attention to the strange uniformed security team observed within the grounds. Bert had confirmed that they were all direct employees of the Ingatestone Estate when he inquired.

As DCI John Jenkins approached the park gates, he saw Bert Mountfield on the edge of the West wood, stopped the car, and walked a few yards down the road to talk to him out of hearing of his police driver.

"Hello again Bert, just one thing I would like to substantiate in my mind. When I inquired this morning on return from my walk, you mentioned that the security team members were all direct estate employees. Is that correct?"

"They are indeed Sir, and as far as I am aware they are all vetted before an appointment. Indeed, I can confirm that. His Lordship is looking to employ a new Director of Security. As he feels, one cannot be too careful these days. Perhaps you may be interested in applying for the role?"

John thought for a moment assimilating the conversation and replied, in a tone of warm approval,

"That's good,"

Bert then said,

"There is little cause to suspect anyone at Ingatestone Hall of being anything other than honest people."

DCI Jenkins mused at this comment, handed him a Metropolitan Police business card and said to Bert Mountfield,

"That as it is, you have been most cooperative, and the police always bear that in mind should something else arise to your knowledge. Please call the mobile number on that card and ask to speak to me directly. Nobody else must be informed. Do you understand this instruction?"

Mountfield replied,

"Yes, Sir."

John walked back to the car, pleased to have had this chat. He assessed that Mountfield knew more than he was saying presently. Bert would talk, of course, sooner or later, probably sooner. But he might have closed his mouth for a fortnight but, having a senior policeman stay at the Hall was as exciting as it was concerning.

CHAPTER 35
REVELATIONS ABOUND

Natalie Lewis was standing in the police car park awaiting John's arrival from his visit to Ingatestone Hall and the subsequent forced overnight stay. Her anticipation knew no bounds, as she expected revelations of magnitude. It was typical of an Autumn mid-morning in Romford. The slight drizzle of raindrops fell gently on several parked cars in the police compound. The droplets of moisture lay on the surface of highly polished vehicles. It was apparent that the molecules clung very tightly together. The waxed surface enabled rainwater to bead up rather than spreading out on the vehicle bonnet. Natalie had watched last week the garage staff apply the polish into the paint firmly and evenly across the cars. The garage manager who employed the Polish immigrants had real personal pride and competed with one another to produce these sparkling police cars.

While admiring the standard of the vehicles, she pushed back her left jacket cuff to reveal her Omega watch with her right hand. It showed eleven-fifteen, she expected her Boss earlier than this. However, as she was about to nip back into the building for a cuppa, the up-and-over metal gate rattled as it commenced with opening the access. The BMW nosed through the entrance containing the uniformed police driver behind the wheel and DCI John Jenkins in the rear of his conveyance. The automobile came to a stop where she stood. John alighted with a massive grin on his face; his eyes shot about in his head. An indication she observed that jubilant. His look was concealing critical intelligence appertaining to the investigation. Perhaps at long last, the perpetrator of the dreadful death of two young girls' bodies discarded on Romford Tow Path and the Raphels Park, Bandstand was close to being revealed.

As they entered John's office on the second floor, she made for the coffee machine, well knowing her governor would be ready for one.

Natalie decanted the black liquid into the two clean cups on his desk and passed one to him. He removed his notebook and pen from his pocket, placing them neatly on his blotting pad. The excitement was difficult to contain. So she said,

"Come on, Boss. Let's have it?"

"Well DS Lewis what I am about to reveal to you must remain within these four walls. They must, and I repeat, must not be disclosed to anyone, not even your pet dog, Is that crystal clear?"

She shuffled in her seat with real anticipation responding to his order,

"Your wish is my command, Gov!"

John slowly sipped his black coffee and paused for a substantial effect. Then said,

"I had an eventful time at the hall which included a useful conversation with one, 'Bert Mountfield,' personal assistant to Lord Gentry. He was most helpful, even supplied me with a change of clothing so that I was able to attend a most pleasant and informative dinner party last evening. Indeed the wine and port were most delightsome."

DCI Jenkins then paused for another sip of his coffee. It was apparent to Natalie that he was playing this for the agony. She was trying to maintain her demure exciting persona. However, impatience was mounting within. She could hold it no longer, and burst out with,

"For goodness sake! Stop stalling with the result of your findings and spill the beans Boss?"

"Okay, well on my return trip from Ingatestone I contacted Headquarters and insisted in a total clandestine top-secret operation. Not to be disclosed to anyone, including our Chief. I have sent Dave Torrance and a full forensics team to examine the old chapel and the stables as I have a distinct hunch, no it's more than that. Behind the sanctuary, is a semi-circular part that houses a separate chapel dedicated to the Virgin Mary. There is a granite altar in the centre of the nave aisle with a large type throne chair overseeing the chancery's entire area. The ornate chair is most definitely ancient; it is covered in gold leaf paint, and the carving looks to my untrained eye fit for a King or Lord. Indeed, Lord Egbert Peter Gentry must laud it over his parishioners from that position. I suspect that the grail has contained blood. The reason for this assessment is there is a strong odour of bleach, both on the granite altar and the font chalice. Some person or people has cleaned up these two areas of interest. So my thought is blood has been present before the cleaning took place."

DS Lewis was stunned at these revelations. She remained stum as her Boss had already cautioned on any disclosure would not only ruin the case investigation but could cause a significant and undesirable effect. As she was about to comment, the middle mobile phone commenced to buzz and move slightly from the vibrations. As was familiar with Detectives, he had more than one means of concealing information.

John reached for the Sony Xperia Z5, placing it next to his right ear. Then just before he spoke, placing his hand over the mouthpiece, he beckoned Natalie to leave his office raising his right-hand intimating five minutes privacy. She rose from the seat occupied and left, closing the door gently behind her.

DCI Jenkins then said into the mouthpiece,

"Go ahead, James!"

He listed to the caller with intense interest, the spoke again.

"This is without doubt shocking news, can you please confirm the names again of the three senior individuals that you have uncovered?"

The informant was a very high-ranking officer, whom he trusted one-hundred per cent — uttering the names once more, he assimilated the information.

John thanked him and depressed the end call button, cutting the call. He then went to the door and ushered Natalie to join him inside his office again. He apologised to her on their way to their seats previously occupied before the mobile call's interruption. As they took their seats, John said to her,

"That call confirmed beyond a reasonable doubt the names of three of the eminent as well as noble individuals. They are assessed to be connected with the death of the two girls found in Romford."

John was silent while he allowed this statement to ferment in DS Lewis's analytical mind. It was common knowledge within the force that some murders would never be solved and that it wasn't worth wasting time and money on them. With a limited budget, detectives, working hours, were paramount. However, given the latest development, Natalie made evident that progress was producing a severe predicament for her Boss. As she sat there using both hands to smooth her autumnal rust-coloured skirt, then changing her posture to one of uprightness she stared John in the face, eye to eye so that he was in no doubt as to her loyalty, saying,

"Gov, whatever you reveal to me will remain with me. You need have no fear of me informing my Labrador of anything, even if I did, I doubt he would be able to pass it on. So, your secret is safe with me."

My informant has......John remained deep in thought as to whether he should blow somebody's cover. He concluded that she was trustworthy and said,

"Lewis what I am about to disclose will shock you to the core. My informant, a retired former secret service agent and still a serving Army Officer has been investigating some prominent and extremely senior figures in society and the police. What I am about to reveal to you may put your life in danger. You are a mother, and I must stress the threat to your life that could occur. For myself, I am single and have looked death in the face on numerous occasions. Therefore, death holds no mysteries for me."

As he was about to.......continue his statement, Natalie raised both her hands intimating that she wished to interject. He ceased speaking, then with an air of confident assurance, made her pitch to assure John he had nothing to fear regarding her integrity.

"Boss, I want you to know that in my life, the danger has often visited me. It would be best if you had no fear of me not being totally supportive, and my mouth will be kept closed. So, whatever we have to do to succeed, in bringing to justice the evil people who murdered those two young girls in such a brutal manner. Let's do it together."

John rolled his tongue across his top lip, and the wet saliva glistened as he took hold of her arm, ushering Natalie out of his office door, along the corridor and into the Lady's toilet. She permitted his conducting of her physically and once inside the ablution, the DCI in true detective style, opened every cubicle door, thus ensuring they were alone. He turned to Lewis, and he revealed his secret intelligence when his mobile rang once more. John, answering had noted the caller's name on the screen,

"Hello, David Torrance. How's it going?'

"It's going better than expected, Boss."

His lip curled upwards. Ever the senior policeman he was sceptical. You've rung me David to tell me what?"

"Good News, the forensic team, has confirmed that they have found traces of fairly recent blood splatters on the altar of Ingatestone Hall, chapel. The inspection lamp immediately disclosed the colouration of bloodstains. Doctor Cyd Loveday has it for further analysis. There were also the remains of small droplets of blood inside a vessel. This chalice was also found in the nave. I have sent for police support from the Essex Police Headquarters, Chelmsford, as it's their jurisdiction area. We are only here with their permission and authority John so treading carefully as instructed."

Natalie stood and listened to John's side of the conversation as she assessed from his response it was DCI David Torrance. Strange that such a senior detective was dealing with what would have been a low-level search. She was surprised by this turn of events. Still curious as to what John was about to tell her, before the telephone interruption.

John began to speak once more into the mobile,

"David, I will leave the controlled security sealing of the estate to you. I have to give you a word of warning. If any policeman senior to you from Essex Headquarters arrives and tries to shut down the investigation, please keep me informed of any further developments. Meanwhile, I am seeking additional authority from New Scotland Yard as I may have to counter that attempt. As soon as I have that senior pre-eminence, then we are fire-proof. David, until then we are on a slightly sticky wicket. Please call me if anything which threatens this procedure occurs?"

The mobile went dead, and he placed it in his pocket, turning to DS Lewis he informed her,

"As you may have perceived from that conversation, Dave Torrance and the Forensic Team have discovered traces of blood on the chapel altar and in the cup of the chalice. It confirms my fears that at least one of the two girls were murdered in that location subject to proven analysis. Now what I was about to tell you is that my informant is a senior military figure in London. He has implicated that two senior policemen and a Lord of the Realm are suspected of being involved in a Cult with clandestine meetings in the Ingatestone Hall private Chapel. This establishes the reason I spent the afternoon there and subsequently overstayed to enable me to confirm the intelligence further."

Natalie still intrigued to discover who the senior policemen were that was implicated. She could not hold her patience longer and asked John,

"Okay Boss, you have teased me sufficiently although the telephone in your defence delayed the revelation. Who are the senior figures?"

"The following enmeshed are, our own, Chief Superintendent David Bagley, the head of Essex Police, Chief Constable Stephen Jones and finally as far as we are presently aware Lord Egbert Peter Gentry."

DS Lewis flushed immediately at this information. There was what would be described as utter astonishment on her face. Natalie remained silent her brain trying to compute this revelation. John well aware of her shock at this information had much more to disclose. However, caution was required before further divulgence. He turned to her saying,

"I believe we should consider the next step forward. That my dear girl is best done over a good cup of English Earl Grey tea. His colleague said nothing for she was still in shock at the avowal information. She pushed the door open, permitting John to step outside the Lady's toilet-less some passer bye may conclude something improper was occurring inside the Romford Police Station precincts. As he did so, his mobile telephone sounded its alert at an incoming call. As his thoughts strayed to the Lady Gentry gathering and more especially to one attendee, he chastised himself, namely the beautiful Diamonique Abbot.

As John sipped his tea, he permitted his mind to return to his brief time with his late wife, Dawn. It was such a short period of enjoyment in his life. What would have resulted from their partnership, would they have had children? Suddenly he realised that the lady guest had triggered this relatively warm thought process.

What was Natalie Lewis worried about as she too drank her tea? Her feeling of impending disaster that she couldn't shake off. Then, there was DCI Jenkins's exposure of dirty deeds orchestrated by none other than two of the most senior policemen with outstanding records. She asked herself what would happen if Chief Constable Jones and Chief Super Bagley were as revealed to be manifestly responsible for the three deaths of two young females. She also recalled the result of the autopsies on both girls. They disclosed that male penetration and seamen were found in the vaginal tract of both. If that turns out to match their DNA of any of them, it was curtains but worse still the reflected downfall of police trust. Also, with a peer of the realm involved. It all took place on his estate; it was liable to become an embarrassment to the British Establishment. She placed her mug of tea on the table, and she then looked at John saying,

"So, who is this snitch, who is a senior figure?"

John smiled again and then said,

"Natalie, suffice to say that he has provided me with first-class intelligence. All will be disclosed in due course."

CHAPTER 36
HACKNEY KICKS OFF

Eh The bells of some far-off church tolled out six chimes. Water Lane was narrow and dark, half the streetlights blown and broken. The cobbles slick beneath their feet. Not that it'd been raining. No, they were all slippery with

Dogs Shit. Yeah, probably best not to think about what he'd just trodden in. Or on. A tall granite building made a wall on one side of the lane, guttering sprouting weeds, lichen on the lintels, and broken windows. Boarded-up doors opened onto nothing but fresh air on the second, third, and fourth floors. A couple of trees had burst out through the windows high up there, like slow-motion explosions. The other side was more granite. Cold and unwelcoming. But then romance probably wasn't on the cards. Not even Jamie Doran of Fifty Shades of Grey would have affected these street walkers of Hackney. He would have wheeled any of the working girls here off to a swanky hotel for pampering and shopping fun. Two of them shuffled their feet, then looked away from the covert armoured wagon full of police dressed and tooled up ready to invade the 'Hells Angels Motorcycle Club and 'Flint Chapter.'

ONE LOOKED as if she'd never see sixty again, but was probably barely out of her thirties. Her friend hadn't been at the drugs as long, so she still had all her own teeth and nowhere near as many pin-prick bruises up the inside of her arms. But they were both pipe-cleaner thin. Natalie sighed and tried again, holding a snap of Alan Boyd.

"Are you sure you've never seen the man in this photograph?"

Both were chewing gum and simultaneously shook their heads, indicating that they had not. It was clear that they did recognise Boyd as he was, 'Numero Ono,' in this here part of London. She gave up on this inquiry line as she was to all intense and purpose, nothing more than a decoy. Anyone observing her line of questioning was in effect watching a plainclothes officer dealing with street prostitutes, nothing more than that. It was a tried and tested way to throw any scent off. The two of them shuffled their feet, then looked away from the picture in DS Natalie Lewis's hand. One looked as if she'd never see sixty again, but was probably barely out of her thirties. Her friend hadn't been at the drugs as long, so she still had all her own teeth and nowhere near as many pin-prick bruises up the inside of her arms. But they were both pipe-cleaner thin. Natalie sighed and tried again.

"Are you sure you've never seen him?"

BOTH ONCE MORE LOOKED IN the opposite direction, ignoring her once more. DS Lewis had the desired effect if she was suspected of anything other than routine inquiries; it was certainly not apparent to the casual observer. Indeed, if there was an observation from the Hell's Angels compound, it was not noticeable. However, she could not be too careful. The last thing she wanted was for the occupants to perceive what was about to go off.

Meanwhile, David Drummond sat with Sandy Low, the leader of the gang, and his life was on a precipice if his discovery took place. It was going well so far, and Sandy Low leader of the pack had swallowed his storyline of being Lord Peter's right-hand man. They were both enjoying a 'Budweiser,' and things seemed to be taking the route that DS Drummond wished. His decoy seemed to be working exceptionally well. He looked over the shoulder of Low at aa large clock on the wall, aware that on the hour things were about to occur.

At precisely 10 minutes before four o'clock the occupants of the covert police battle bus parked in Hackney Gardens under the direct command of Davy Torrance, they slipped out of the Battle Bus. Inside the Gold Commander Command Vehicle, DCI John Jenkins was a little apprehensive, aware that death and destruction were imminent. Fortunately, the video screens within the Hells Angels compound had been electronically interfered with. The observation screen was full of the actual movement of some twenty minutes which had occurred and was out of synchronisation with the exact time.

The entire party dressed in their black assault uniforms with Kevlar Body Armour, and black helmets with recording cameras fitted. They were armed to the teeth with Heckler and Kock assault rifles.

By creeping along the outside wall of the compound, their activity occurred unseen. Once in position, they ready themselves. At four o'clock the Old Church Bell chimed on the first stroke of the hour. By the fourth tintinnabulate the lead policeman placed the breeching explosive in position. As the fourth chimed, he activated the shaped explosive against the compound double doors. The explosion's noise was heard some four miles away as far as Saint Pauls Cathedral in the City of London.

The blast was so significant causing complete disorientation of the Hells Angels within the courtyard and blew every one of their motorcycles off their stands. Those inside the club once regaining their feet grabbed weapons and made for the exit. They were met by a fusillade of small arms fire from the H & K police weapons. Several never made it beyond a few paces outside the club as they were killed immediately. The firefight took place as those who had escaped the explosion plus the onslaught of police firepower attempted to take on targets of black-clad police charging towards the club. This reactive small arms fire took out quite a few police officers. During the confusion, David Drummond who was unarmed when he entered the Hells Angels Chapter managed to scramble to his feet and secured the nine-millimetre pistol which had been dropped by an Angel bowled over by the blast. Observing several of the occupants getting to their feet he fired several shots, bringing down at least three of them.

Sandy Low got to his feet and realised what had happened. He pulled his silver, Ruglar Six-Shooter from its holster and with his thumb pulled back the hammer, then proceed to empty the chamber in the direction of DS Drummond. The first-round missed his head but the second tore into his left shoulder rotator cuff with such force that the humeral head was penetrated and exited through his back. The second and third shots were slightly lower but entered his elbow with such force that lateral and medial epicondyle were severed. The result was that his left arm brachial artery splattered blood which exited in unison with his heartbeat. David was in severe shock and never felt the fourth-fifth and sixth .357 magnum rounds as they terminated his life. Detective Sergeant David Drummond slumped to the floor and bled out. Sandy Low was cursing himself for trusting the bastard with access to his Bikers Chapter, but at least he had seen him off.

Low was aware of the firefight going on between the explosion and the Metropolitan Police Assaulting Force survivors. He made his way toward the rear of the club premises. He avoided the small arms fire that was incoming the area from the outside. Sandy managed to escape the various bullets that whistled around the club interior to reach what appeared to be an old antique fireplace. It was decorated with silver candelabra on either side of the wooden structure. Sandy reached for the right mounting and tweaked it. There was a slow rumbling sound and the secret escape false door slid ajar. He looked over his shoulder, and there was nobody in the snug bar, he slipped into the void just as the automatic closer activated. To anyone on the other side, it was once more nothing more than an antique fireplace. The corridor was illuminated by small forty-watt electric bulbs which ran along the arched roof. He made his way swiftly in the knowledge that if discovered, his flight would be thwarted. He arrived at the egress, depressed the activation release button, and another door slid open to reveal a modern garage that contained but one vehicle. It was an inconspicuous low-profile VW Golf in grey and had been pre-positioned not to attract attention. It had deliberately not been kept clean and polished as part of its pre-planned get-away use.

He immediately discarded his clothes on the floor of the parking lot garage. On opening the VW Polo boot, he removed a dark grey boiler suit, dressed in the disguised attire he sat behind the wheel, activating the electronic parking lot door that slid apart permitting his escape to be complete. Pretty soon, his eyes were accustomed to the late September afternoon sunshine. He looked at the clock on the old church tower and noted the time was four-forty-five in the afternoon. The entire shootout had taken but three-quarters of an hour. He was now on Queensbridge Road, and as he passed the Victoria Public House on his left, he felt he could do with a pint of English Ale. He mused, not just yet; a beer could wait until he made the A10 and his way out of London to his safe house in Luton. Then he had numerous options of permanent flight via Luton Airport.

CHAPTER 37
ANGELS WASH UP

E̹ʰ The following day post the police raid of Hackney Gardens Hells Angels Chapter location. The Jenkins Team spent almost the entire day filling in forms and sorting out the mass of weapons, and cash that was found and confiscated. The team was busily employed logging the items found and interviewing those officers who had shot and killed individual bikers. The fact that several officers had sustained gunshot wounds; however, none were considered life-threatening. Sergeant David Drummond was their only fatality, and that occurred at the commencement of the assault.

As John sat in his office during the late afternoon, there was a knock on the door. He looked up and said,

"Please come in?"

The door opened to reveal Bob Clarkson who was holding a newspaper under his left arm.

"Hi John, I thought you might like a look at this afternoon's, Evening Standard Newspaper headline article."

Bob removed the paper from under his arm and passed it to John.

DCI Jenkins took it from him, and opened it, to read the front-page headline.

LONDON EVENING STANDARD

One of Britain's biggest ever crime busts has captured 26 crooked Hells Angels Bikers and foiled hundreds of plots after raids by the Metropolitan Police Force. It is reported that £6 million of dirty cash, two tonnes of drugs, and 77 firearms were seized after their phone network was smashed. Fourteen criminals were killed during a gunfight that took place during the police raid on the premises in Hackney, East London. The police report that one of their colleagues was killed during the attack. However, his heroic action during the assault was reported to have facilitated the operation's total success. His family and next of kin have been informed.

John opened the top drawer of his desk and extracted a bottle of Grouse Whisky and his two crystal glasses, placing them on the desk. He unscrewed the cap from the bottle and poured two large measures, handing one to Bon and lifting the other in a toast he said,

"Here is to the immortal memory of David Drummond who without his bravery we would never have gained access to the Hells Angels Lair."

Bob, clinked his glass on John's, and they both drank the whiskey measure in one gulp.

As they replaced the empty glasses on his desk, John said to Bob,

"I have been trying to get hold of Chief Bagley to no avail. I would have expected him to be the first person congratulating us on the Hackney Raid's success. His secretary has said he has not been in the office for three days. Nor has he answered his mobile telephone. She has spoken to his wife who has seemingly said, that she has left him, they are now no longer a couple.

DCI Clarkson raised his eyes towards the ceiling and looking straight at John, replied,

"I find that very strange if his assistant plus his wife and family have no idea where he is. I would suggest we need to carry out some police work and investigate where he is. Is he safe or has something untoward occurred?"

John picked up his desk telephone handset and dialed. He waited for the call to be answered, then spoke into the mouthpiece,

"Natalie, can you please pop into my office as soon as possible, I have a task that requires you to deal with."

Some five minutes later, DS Lewis arrived and entered his office. Alas, there was little Natalie could add to the problem. Bagley was missing. However, neither of them had any idea where he was. John poured a Whisky into a clean tumbler, recharged both his and Bob's and handed it to her, All three raised their glasses and commented not quite in unison "We Salute The Who Died during yesterday's Operation!"

They then sat on their chairs and were silent because Davy Drummond's braveness resulted in his demise. And the success of the operation. Bob said,

"The Evening Standard only depicts the little they know of the Shoot-Out! In Hackney, as their front page states. The actual result of removing 'Evil Bastards is not contained in the newspaper."

Natalie then commented,

"We were fortunate to succeed, and indeed we did. However, two bandits escaped. Alan Boyd and his Biker Henchman, Sandy Low. That we must bear in mind as they may return and cause more mayhem.

CHAPTER 38
NEW SCOTLAND YARD

Harry Slessor nae Mr Moon slammed his hands on the desk and the briefcase containing the cash handed to him by Peter Egbert. In front of him sitting behind the desk was his senior handler. He was none other than Assistant Commissioner Bas Neil. He was ultimately responsible for providing specialist policing capabilities including national security and counter-terrorism operations throughout the United Kingdom. It may be assumed that Harry was inferior to this highly appointed officer, but in reality, only in police rank. AC Neil was well aware of how outstanding Slessor was. He lived and survived with his life in jeopardy should it ever be discovered his real identity. Bas knew Slessor was in fact, Harry Slessor by birth and the son of a former senior policeman in the city of his birth, Aberdeen.

Harry went on having removed his hands from the desk, also having captured AC Neil's attention.

"I have to inform you that I have just accepted a contract from an individual who I suspect is not exactly who he said he was. I met him at the London Cemetery this afternoon when he presented me with this briefcase which contains the deposit of fifty thousand pounds in cash. Harry placed the leather receptacle on AC Neil's desk, flicked the lock catch and lifted the top turning it towards his senior handler. Bas looked inside the case and extracted the manilla envelope. In opening it, he tilted the contents onto his desk. The was on the top of each bundle of used notes each of fifty pounds, and there were one hundred containing a paper seal with the number displayed £500. His boss placed the cash to the side. He then took the manilla folder on opening it Harry spoke,

"By the way, I have not read the contents nor do I know who the target is other than that he is allegedly fucking this chap Peter Egbert's wife. He is willing to pay two hundred thousand pounds to have him exterminated. The envelope contains his details as you will note I have not had a peak at it, as it remains sealed.

The Assistant Commissioner took a letter knife from his desk and slit the envelope open. He then emptied the contents onto his desk, saying,

"Well, Kenney let's have a look at who the target is?"

There were two medium photos on his desk. One was of a rather attractive well-dressed female, immaculately attired. The other surprised them both, and it was of an officer dressed in the Household Division's ceremonial uniform. It shocked both of them. On his desk were many vellum paper sheets, each containing details and addresses of the female and the officer. Harry noted that one of the medals displayed on his chest was the Victoria Cross. He immediately realised that this gentleman was no slouch. The woman quite frankly was beautiful both in appearance and attire. Bas was also drawn to the VC and then inspected the second sheet of paper with the name and rank, Lieutenant Colonel James Craig, VC 1st Battalion Scots Guards, with his private address on a side street just of the King's Road, Chelsea. There was a further list of his friends and the London Clubs of which he was a member.

The fourth sheet of paper had the female's title, Lady Olivia Egbert, including friends, with regularly visited addresses.

Bas was surprised by the two sheets which contained the photograph of a senior military decorated figure. The fact that one Peter Egbert had taken a contract out on him was even more of a concern. The woman was less of a problem.

He spent some time musing the details of both named targets. Then he looked up at Harry nae Harry Slessor and said,

"You will have to leave me to contemplate this dilemma. I would like you to come back to my office in half an hour. I need to speak about this to various agencies and research the named individuals. Please go and have a teacup, and I will call you when I am ready to discuss this and ancillary details.

Harry expected something like this might be the result of the shock of knowing who the target was. He rose from the chair, and commented,

"I will do Sir, and I could do with something to eat and drink."

He left the fourth floor of New Scotland Yard, taking the lift down to the basement, where the Uniformed Police Canteen is located on basement one. He helped himself to a tray selected a salad meal containing smoked salmon and removed a bottle of Coca-Cola from the cold display cabinet. He observed a table in the far corner which he went towards. He sat in silence, undisturbed and enjoyed his meal. Once he had finished the food and the drink, he observed he had only been there for twenty minutes, he then went to the service area and dispensed and paid for a black coffee and a small plate containing cheddar-cheese and biscuits. He took a sip of the coffee and had just commenced removing the cellophane protective cover from the container when his covert mobile phone rang. He answered it,

"Harry Slessor, how can I help you?"

The caller being aware of the necessity to maintain secrecy spoke,

"Hi Harry, Bas here, can you pop in and see me when you have the opportunity?"

Harry knew precisely that he was summoned to the fourth floor again. He replied,

"I could be with you in five minutes as I am in the area. If that's convenient?"

The person on the line replied,

"That's wonderful. I look forward to seeing you!"

The line went dead.

One could not be too careful in the modern time as you never knew who was eavesdropping your conversations.

Harry or was he, someone else. The coffee was too good to disregard. He took the tray containing the empty plate and mug and left it in the area provided in the canteen. As he did so, he mused about his double identity. It was laughable that you'd be able to live two completely separate lives, often on opposite sides of the law, without someone figuring it out after a few months. Every character with a secret identity seems to be surrounded by nothing but oblivious morons.

On arrival on the fourth floor, the lift door opened and once more he was confronted with the security policeman on duty although this time it was a policewoman. He produced his warrant card, and once she had approved it, she screened it onto the electronic register. He was aware that anyone entering the fourth-floor sanctum was documented. He approached the office of AC Bas Neil. He suspected that his movement was caught on camera and every word recorded. This was the nexus of everything, 'Top Secret,' within the high-profile world of New Scotland Yard clandestine operations. The door opened automatically as he approached it. He knew that the pin-hole

THE ESSEX CULT

camera had clocked his movement, and AC Neil had activated the automated function.

Bas stood up from his desk and intimated with his outstretched hand that Harry should take a seat on the corner Perugia distressed leather Italian sofa which he had not noticed on his previous visit to the office this afternoon. He noted that there was a coffee pot with cream and brown crystal sugar. What did surprise him was that there were three delicate bone cups and saucers. AC Neil lifted the coffee pot and raised a cup and saucer with his free left hand placing it in front of Harry. As he began to pour the steaming liquid into his cup, the door opened and in walked the head of London's Metropolitan Police Commissioner Hogan-Howe. Harry stood immediately, and Bas introduced him to the Commissioner. He intimated that they should sit down and Bas carried on pouring the coffee, now into the three cups. The most senior policeman in the entire country sipped his coffee and then addressed Harry.

"Inspector, I have to congratulate you on the information you have relayed to AC Neil is extremely sensitive as you know that the contract you have been given to execute Lieutenant Colonel James Craig, VC. It is concerning but not because the target is a serving officer in the Household Division, plus he was frequenting the pleasures of someone's wife. This behaviour for a senior officer is unacceptable. However, that is not the major concern as the individual whom you met at the London Cemetery is not just the plain, Peter Egbert as you have relayed to AC Neil. He is actually, 'Lord Egbert Peter Gentry.' The force is aware that he has some questionable acquaintances."

Harry Slessor as he is known to those in Wapping suddenly concludes that with the Commissioner saying what he had and the rugged look on Bas Neil's face, things were developing in an alarmingly fast manner. Harry contemplated what result this would cause. A senior officer who guarded, Her Majesty and a Lord who wanted him dead!

Bas was next to speak,

"Harry, we are transparent that further investigation will have to be carried out. In the meantime, you will have to go about your undercover work as if nothing has happened."

Harry, picked up the coffee cup and sipped some of the liquid, he then replaced it on the table. He was attempting to remain calm and calculated to the two senior policemen present. Once his blood pressure was at the resting rate he commented,

"Sir I understand the seriousness of this situation, given the two individuals involved. Also, Peter Egbert wishes James Craig dead as he had been fooling around with his wife. All I have currently for the contact of Egbert or Lord Gentry as you have informed me. I have a mobile telephone number which he was loath to give me. As for Craig, VC, I have an address off King's Road which I have not investigated as yet. So, do I take him out as contracted, or is there another plan being hatched that I am not privy to?"

Bas Neil then responded,

"I have conferred with various departments and the Commissioner while you were having lunch. It has been decided that Colonel James Craig will be removed from the scene forthwith and that action is already underway. So, nobody needs to die, just yet. Craig VC will eventually be given another identity and moved to another country far away from the United Kingdom."

There was a pause while both the Commissioner and AC Neil permitted Harry to assimilate what was being proposed. Then Bas went on,

"You will be supplied with photographs of James Craig's

body with a gunshot wound to his forehead, which will be staged with the assistance of Colonel Craig."

Harry, butted in,

"What if he does not wish to go along with the plan?

The Head of the Metropolitan Police before Bas could answer his question,

"The photograph you receive to prove the execution will be so good that Lord Gentry; will be convinced that you have carried out the contract."

"As for Lord Gentry, you will contact him in a few days and relay to him that his contract has been actuated. You will provide the photograph as corroboration. If he requests proof that Craig is indeed dead, you will inform him that his body was disposed of in a cask of Sulfuric Acid."

Being an experienced undercover police officer, Harry was not that confident that would be a sufficient answer to satisfy Gentry. He then asked, and if he questions this story,

The Commissioner smiled and replied,

"You could ask him if he would like to try dipping his hand into a vat of sulfuric acid? That I am positive will shut him up."

You will relay the bank account for the balance of the payment to be made. That account will be set up in your undercover title, Harold J Moon; it will, of course, be a police account. The fifty-thousand-pound in the briefcase on my desk you had better take with you as it may well be that Gentry has someone keeping an eye on you. Have you ensured that on your way here you were not trailed?"

Harry had ensured that his journey to New Scotland Yard was unobserved. He confirmed that he had taken the underground to Liverpool Street Station on being dropped off by the black cab. It is a mainline hub there was safety in the numbers milling through the station. From there he jumped onto the District Line to

Whitechapel and changed onto the Electric Line to Wapping. On alighting there, he observed that he had not been followed. So, he got back on the electric line, returned to Whitechapel; and took a black cab to St James Park, the nearest public underground station to the Met Police Headquarters. And, as a further precaution went through the barrier as if to board another Tube Train. However, the platform plus the station were reasonably bereft of commuting Londoner's he was sure that his convoluted decoy journey was successful. He then voiced that to both the senior officers.

Bas, then spoke again,

"Harry if at any time you feel endangered then you must abort your cover story and make your way to the agreed recovery location. You are to take no risks, and if you require armed backup, please ensure you use that emergency number."

Slessor smiled and nodded, the acquiescence of the instruction issued.

Bernard Hogan-Howe rose from the sofa and proffered his right hand towards him, saying,

"Harry, please be, Argus-eyed at all times. You are a valuable asset, and we do not want to lose you."

Harry having extended his arm, shook his hand, saying,

"Sir, please be assured my life is important if to nobody else certainly to myself. Thank you very much for your concern. I will not take any undue risks."

With that, the Commissioner exited the room.

Bas handed over the briefcase containing the fee and also took Harry's hand saying,

"Be extremely on-guard from now on,"

With that, he turned and left the room on the fourth floor. He was booked out by presenting his warrant card to the duty policewoman who scanned it. He took the lift to the second level basement floor and left using the ramp of the car-park into Petty France. His disguise was still intact.

CHAPTER 39
AGENT DONALDSON

David Donaldson was a senior crime investigator from the Federal Bureau of Investigation. he was well known to his friends in the FBI as 'DDD,' Dangerous David Donaldson. He was in London and working alongside Bob Clarkson of the Met Police Serious Crime Squad. DCI Clarkson was attached to Romford Police. There was a serious concern, and rightly so, that Alan Boyd ran an organised crime family out of Hackney, East London. The suspicion was that his County Lines operation had infiltrated eastwards towards Essex and Suffolk and that the streets were awash with illegal, dangerous coke.

In a briefing room at Romford Police, Station David Donaldson briefed the assembled company consisting of Superintendent David Bagley, DCI Bob Clarkson, and DCI John Jenkins. On the screen was the photograph of a Caucasian, middle-aged male. D.D. as he was becoming to be termed in the Metropolitan Police as well as his own FBI. He used the electronic pointer to highlight the picture on the screen. Is the Texan accent of his birth he addressed those present?

"Gentlemen, or should I say, Fellow Cops,

The first photo is of David Cottage, and the second is of Alan Boyd, both U.K. resident criminals.

Boyd was involved with a big underworld player in New York. Who had connections with a massive Mafia boss called Tony Corelli? New Scotland Yard is well aware that La Cosa Nostra. The Organisation's name was derived from the original Mafia or Cosa Nostra, the Sicilian Mafia, with "American Mafia."

Specialist Operations Organised Crime SO6 are targeting up to seven American mafia gang members in London and the Home Counties who are flooding the streets with cocaine. SO6 Detectives have identified a specific suspect based in the capital with links to groups involved in a profitable trafficking racket. Police report these gangs are smuggling vast quantities of Class A drugs into London and the rest of the U.K. using the Channel Tunnel and cross-Channel ferries. The Detectives fear the soaring trade fuelled violence, including stabbings and shootings among street dealers as they vie for superiority.

Senior officers have reported individuals associated with organised crime engage in activities ranging from drug importation to people trafficking. They are linked to gangs based in London and the Home Counties and are thought to fix and enforce the cocaine trade.

THE CONTROLLING Godfathers remained in the USA but had their own Lieutenants working with Boyd. He runs an extensive cocaine supply network and has done for more than three years with links to other organised crime groups in London, Essex, and Suffolk. Those Americans seem to have disappeared from Boyd's criminal team, probably taken out and either wearing a cement waistcoat in the River Thames or supporting the concrete structure in a London building project. Needless to say, they are erased.

As I have already said, it appears that Alan Boyd used to work with Corelli but decided to go his own way and double-cross him by pulling off a drug deal with a Manchester criminal called Jason Brown. Apparently, Corelli had already been in negotiation with Brown but had failed to reach an agreement. Alan Boyd had seen the opportunity and done a deal himself the conservative estimate to be £10 million each! SO6 is hell-bent on catching Alan Boyd bang at it and using this as a lever to grass on Corelli, whom both the U.S. and British authorities had been after for many years."

D.D. paused and took the water decanter on the table poured a measure into the glass, and took a long refreshing sip of water from the glass before he continued,

"The story goes, Corelli was immensely upset that Boyd had done the dirty deal, and there was already a rumour picked up that a contract had been put out on Boyd. It does not take a great deal of imagination to guess that if this is true, then he may have also put out a contract on others within his crime family from Hackney. Boyd was always confident that his Hells Angels would ensure he was forever safe.

David Cottage, a well-known East End gangster, is believed to be the chosen hitman. Cottage is ex-Army and spent some time with the Special Forces. Therefore, he is highly trained in killing, using explosives, firearms, etc. and is very dangerous. He has no previous convictions as such. He was thrown out of the Army due to his liking for beating up prostitutes while serving in Frankfurt, Germany. He was also suspected of raping and murdering a woman officer in Herford. However, despite lengthy investigations, nothing was ever proven. He then joined

'BLACKWATER,' a private United States security company involved in Iraq, after the war.

He may have been recruited by Corelli's U.K.-based man about two years ago. Now that his I.D. is known, SO6 have linked him (via fingerprints and forensics) to eight other Mafia-related type murders across the United Kingdom. he was involved in bombs triggered by timers from pet-food dispensers. He's one lousy bastard. He can also be tied in with several murders of women mainly prostitutes. He, therefore, likes killing as a profession and a hobby. He seems to have been kept very secret by Corelli, with good reason. David Cottage is an elite killer, not your ordinary run-of-the-mill mobster-cum-gunman. If we can capture him and interrogate him and have him spill the beans. That will be precious to the Metropolitan Police. The story on the streets is that Cottage is the man to take out Boyd. So, over to you, Bob."

Bob Clarkson interjected by commenting,

"So Alan Boyd is the real target of the SO6 and the criminal works involving the Hells Angels shoot out in Hackney. His main henchman, Sandy Low, escaped the Bikers Shot Out by using the escape tunnel to survive.

I don't yet know much about him, but the SCS in New Scotland Yard do. He was a big player, into many legit things such as pubs, table dancing and striptease clubs, plus gambling joints. He was also well into drugs and had perfect connections in London where he is based, particularly in Hackney's east end of London. The deal he pulled with Alan Boyd was supposed to be for the importation of crack. Sandy Low was sighted and reported in Romford town centre a few months ago. But what was he doing in Romford? I don't know, but I'd lay odds he'd businesses there too, fronting his drugs-pushing activities was part of a loose criminal syndicate in Romford. But that's pure conjecture on my part. I will now hand it back to D.D. for his input."

David Donaldson stood and resumed his position at the front of the room, he commenced once more with his distinct Texan Drawl,

"Just a word about Corelli. He's a Mafia godfather (Yes, they do exist!) whose operations sphere is mainly Florida and the Caribbean. He runs an extensive criminal organisation that consists of drugs, gun-running, commodity fraud, tobacco smuggling, people smuggling, prostitution, and gambling. You name it he is involved. These illegal activities are fronted by highly lucrative legit businesses ranging from hotels, fast-food joints, nightclubs, building and transport companies and other leisure businesses such as deep-sea fishing trips, etc. His personal net worth cannot be accurately estimated, but he is believed to be a billionaire.

Having said that, most of this is purely conjecture by the FBI as Corelli has no convictions whatsoever. He once faced a murder indictment but walked out. He is continually investigated by the tax authorities but keeps his accountants and his accountant maintains Corelli's business books spick 'n' span. We don't know half of what's going on, but this international cooperation between crime syndicates worries law enforcement on both sides of 'The Pond! Prepare yourself for a crack epidemic in the north of England."

Bob, smiled and commented,

"That my friend is already well underway. It is significant, and often deadly, competition between rival organised crime groups at all stages of class A drug production and supply. There is also corruption at every stage of the drug supply chain, including that of corrupt naval port and airport officials. And, no matter how hard the National Crime Agency try to police it. Sadly it is a failure."

The meeting was about done they had covered all they

could and exhausted most angles. It was closed by Bob once again saying,

"Well folks that's about all for this meeting, I have no doubt we will be discussing this same subject for years and years. Let us all hope we get a breakthrough."

CHAPTER 40
STRANGE DEMISE

Sometimes death is simple for all intents and purposes, an open and shut affair. An older adult dies in his sleep, a child involved in a road traffic accident dies, and a well-attired woman on her own in a first-class train carriage commits suicide.

All tragic in their own ways, all mourned: all above board—no police requirement, except to confirm what her family already knew.

Except at times, looks can be deceiving.

Muffled against the night, two tall professional males dressed in suits and wearing black overcoats with smart-looking Marengo Fedora Hats in the same matching colour to their overgarments and pulled down over their eyes. One of whom had a physique of military bearing. Even under his coat and hat, he exemplified fitness. From what little part of his face exposed, he was the more handsome of the pair.

When they brushed into the well-dressed female at the local Ingatestone mainline, Anglia Trains rail station's ticket barrier, as she purchased her return ticket to London Liverpool Street.

Once she had gone through the machine and headed towards the platform, she had to rush up towards the train's front as it was already on Platform One and due to depart in two minutes.

The uniformed Anglia Railways guard was about to blow his whistle and wave his flag, signaling to the driver that it was safe to pull out of the station. She just about made it as the middle door was ajar, offering her the opportunity to enter. As was common at this time in the late evening, the first-class carriage was almost empty. This was apart from the two men who had accidentally bumped into her at the barrier. She took her seat, observing that oddly they were still wearing their hats.

She had argued with her husband hence the reason for the unplanned train journey. In normality, her chauffeur would have driven her to London. The trip was to meet her lover and spend a night of unbridled lovemaking. The two men seemed not at all to be engaging with the only other carriage occupant. The immaculately dressed and beautiful female removed a glossy magazine from her shoulder bag. It was the monthly copy. 'The Vogue Magazine,' as she pulled it from her Gucci handbag, one of the men noticed an open brown envelope which exposed brown fifty-pound notes. He assessed that the total value could be thousands of pounds.

The locomotive sped through the English countryside, but it was so dark outside the train window that all she could observe was the lights of the various stations it passed through. The train only had two stations to stop at on its journey to London. The first was Shenfield; the train passes through Romford and the Olympic station, Stratford and then Liverpool Street. However, before Stratford, a tunnel runs under the main road, and rail workers feel that they are followed or watched as they pass through it. One train driver reported seeing a blonde woman in a white dress; however, she has no face. But rather a bright shining appearance.

As the train entered the tunnel, the woman heard movement within the carriage. She was concerned and stood to see what was occurring. Almost instantly, as she got to her feet, there was something wrapped around her neck. She had no time to raise her hands in protection. The silk scarf became tighter and tighter, which blocked her windpipe. Her eyes widened in surprise. James tightened his grip as she started to scrabble to get a hold of any leverage she could to pry the broad, muscular hands from her throat. He could feel her pulse drumming as if she were a frightened rabbit, and the thrill felt good. He laughed maniacally aloud as she choked and sputtered. Almost at once, she was deprived of oxygen for several long, excruciating minutes before her eyelids slowly closed. James didn't release his python-like grip immediately though, for he knew she was merely unconscious, not dead. Once he felt her heartbeat sputter to a halt, he lowered the body to the seat. He then reached into his coat pocket and extracted a pair of blue rubber gloves. Immediately slipped his hands into them and tightened the fit by stretching his fingers as a surgeon might.

To the utter surprise of his fellow, he smashed his fist onto her face, not once but several times, thereby breaking her jawbone. Once content that the jaw was loose, extracting something from his pocket, forced her mouth open and slipped the object down her gullet.

James drew a deep breath to calm himself. His assistant was an experienced killer as the light at the end of the tunnel was about to appear. Thus exposing their actions which would be recorded by the CCTV security system. . The train was about five minutes away from entering the long recess leading into Liverpool Street Station. The taller of the pair carefully opened the first-class carriage door. With their united effort held the corpse until the train on the opposite track was departing and the station was gaining speed. Then let her go and pushed with all their might. The noise of flesh meeting inertia was excruciating as her body received the full impact. The shocked train driver departing the station was stunned as the body appeared on the reinforced panoramic glass before him. That impact caused instant blood and flesh to splatter all over the front panel and rivers of blood cascaded down the windscreen.

The driver pulled the emergency stop lever with all his strength. Instantaneously the breaks locked, it brought hundreds of tons of metal and passenger flesh to a screeching halt. As it did so the engine catapulted off the track, derailing and sliding on its side. The emergency alarm sounded and continued above the screams of passengers being thrown from their seats. They helplessly collided with each other, thus causing several casualties.

The driver of the incoming train from Ingatestone was blissfully unaware of what was going on in the wake of his train. He applied the safety brake and the train came to a halt on platform eleven. He commenced to carry out his final safety check before switching the power to the engine off.

Meanwhile, the leading carriage's first-class door opened. The two well-dressed gentlemen wearing Fedora's descended onto the platform, walked with some purpose to the exit barrier, and placed their tickets into the automated machine. The barrier opened outwards onto the concourse. Both men in no haste and unnoticed, walked towards the staircase leading to Bishopsgate while the entire station was in a state of emergency turmoil.

CHAPTER 41
LADY GENTRY AUTOPSY

John Jenkins and Natalie Lewis had arrived by car at,' The Royal London Hospital,' which lay between Whitechapel Road and Commercial Road, East London following the forty-five-minute drive from Romford. It was formerly the London Hospital and dated back to the sixteenth century. Of course, there had been several modernisations over the two-hundred and seventy years since it opened. Many of the Hospital's departments are still on parts of the former London Hospital Estate.

They were appointed to attend Lady Gentry's autopsy due to John's knowledge of Lord and Lady Gentry as he had spent an evening at Ingatestone Hall as her guest. It had enabled him to search the grounds of the estate. The British Transport Police provided evidence of suspected suicide.

"Okay, Guv we are here."

The Driver uttered as he pulled into the entrance area of this old Hospital, it was an old stone archway as Natalie observed the ancient stonework she commented,

"Guv, can you envisage that two hundred years ago it was coaches and horses that arrived under this archway?"

John, smiled at her and replied,

"yes, it was, and the staff would have rushed out to attend to the sick and injured while they tethered the horses. We are also fortunate that the archway is protecting us from the continuous downpour. Let us hope that the autopsy provides us with an assurance that Lady Gentry did cause her demise."

The Metropolitan Police Station, Bishopsgate were handling the immediate inquiry being immediately opposite Liverpool Street station; however, it would in due course be a joint operation with the Romford CID and Essex police as Ingatestone Hall was in Essex

The supposition was she had thrown herself out of a train door onto that of an oncoming engine to commit suicide was indeed a sheer fantasy. They knew she had more to live for rather than dying. Unbeknown to them and several other high-ranking police commanders many ranks above their pay grade were unaware that Lord Gentry had put a contract out on his wife's lover. He was sick of her philandering, notwithstanding that he was keen on young females. That with the aid of his cult had his fair share of them. He was in many views insanely jealous of her philandering. That was why he had employed the chap named Slessor from the east end of London to see off her suitor. Of course, he could have used his own man James now known as Anthony Steel to do that job. However, he had arranged for Slessor to deal with Craig VC. Tony would see her off in right style. He was assured that she would die the death he wanted her to suffer in such a manner. Her cavorting with the Scots Guards Officer was the last straw, and he too would die very soon.

As DCI Jenkins and DS Lewis entered the grand hallway, the painted ceiling's vastness above them was impressive containing blue, with white fluffy clouds and cherubs floating, apparently playing a tune on piccolos. They approached the reception desk and greeted by a uniformed Royal British Legion Security Guard dressed in a blue serge uniform with three chevrons on his uniform right shoulder.

"How can I help you, Sir?"

He uttered in what was a former military voice.

John, proffered his police warrant card proving his identity.

"Good morning, we are here to see Doctor Calum MacGregor, Pathology Department."

The security guard opened a folder on his desk, using his left index finger scrolled down a list of names, and responded,

"Ah, yes would you please take a seat and I will arrange for someone to escort you to him?"

Natalie and John had taken a seat when almost at once another uniformed individual dressed in an RBL Uniform arrive to escort them to Pathology. On arrival at this department, which not surprisingly was in the basement of the Hospital. Dr MacGregor kept them waiting for a goodly period. As he arrived John rose and commented,

"My name is Jenkins, and this is DS Lewis, were expected."

Calum MacGregor was dressed in a white hospital coat, wearing a colourful tie with a green coloured apron over his clothing. It had splatters of red over it which John assumed were spots of blood. He sported a relatively robust red moustache that coexisted with his red hair mop, which crept out from under his white cap. They were subjected to an eagle-like stare. His voice was not welcoming in the slightest, as he with a rather brusk Scottish voice said,

"This is highly irregular Detective Chief Inspector,"

Perhaps he did not wish to be rude, but it indeed came across to both of them in that way. Being a Glaswegian, his accent was more clipped than John was familiar with.

"My credentials."

The Scotsman took it without a smile, and brought the

'Warrant Card,' closer to his eyes in a manner that was unworthy of the horn-rimmed spectacles he wore. He spent an excessive amount of time deciding whether he was the person on the card photograph. Eventually, he said,

"Please step this way, and attire yourselves with the Personal Protection Equipment provided."

From the Doctor's attitude, it was clear he had been investigated very thoroughly indeed. It was evident that he had concluded that, despite his warrant card, he was not welcome. He stepped off, and they both followed it became clear that the good Doctor was a serious fellow. John was aware that they needed to prove their worth to this fellow as an equal. And, strange as John felt, he wished to do so. The Doctor said,

"When you are ready, please?

They followed the red-haired Scotsman toward the mortuary,

They waited dutifully for the man to lead the way, and then followed at a respectful distance. As they entered the cold room, they the brilliant light hit them on entry. John and Natalie blinked attempting to adjust their eyes to the whiteness that hit them. The metal tables a massive white butler sinks led them into a smaller, colder room, where a sheeted body lay on one of two tables in the centre of the room. His assistant removed the sheet covering the body. It was battered and bruised beyond recognition, and it was all too obvious that it was easy to conclude that Olivia Gentry had met an absolutely dreadful end to her life. John had read his preliminary report in the police car on the way to London. He decided that now was the time to say something,

"Your report is comprehensive, Doctor MacGregor."

John could tell that he was being assessed continuously by the Doctor.

It seemed that MacGregor was warming to him, and there

may just have been the sign of a smile upon his face. Natalie handed him a note pad that John, flipped it open, wet the pencil with his lips, and commenced writing some salient points on it. This action had the desired effect in that it reduced the Doctor to silence. John had the feeling that the red-haired man was attempting to unnerve him. Initially, he stood very close to John, trying to intimidate him.

However, he did not intend to fall for his ruse. The Scotsman move back to allow him to work unhindered. He also made some sketches of the corpse and then placed the note pad down in a position which permitted the Doctor to observe them. John took a pair of blue rubber gloves and snapped them onto his hands with excellent sound effect. He was running his hand over the ribs, arm and legs of the corpse. He looked up at MacGregor saying,

"Did you visit the accident scene?"

"I did." The Doctor responded.

"How much blood?"

"Given her injuries, insufficient. "

MacGregor conceded.

"Then she was dead before the oncoming train hir her body?"

"You have read my report; You ken damm well that's what happened!"

The Doctor snapped in his pristine English idiolect, smothered by Scottish anger.

Realising that MacGregor had misunderstood him, John said,

"I apologise Doctor. I am sorry. I was thinking out loud. DS Lewis will be familiar with my habit of thinking out loud."

MacGregor nodded, accepting his apology.

He asked him,

"Your report states that you found a particular item lodged in her gullet. May I please see it?"

"If you wish, it's on my desk?"

John looked at him for a reasonable length of time and questioned him again.

"What made you look inside her throat?"

MacGregor did not respond to the question but walked off, followed by Natalie and Jenkins. On arrival at his office, he opened a drawer and removed what appeared to be a white coloured tub, somewhat similar to that used in hospitals to store a patient's false teeth. He pulled the top off and handed the container to John for his perusal. Jenkins looked inside it and showed it to DS Lewis for her confirmation of the content. Natalie was somewhat taken aback at what she observed. He extracted a single cufflink and held it up to the light. It was gold and contained on the front edge a Latin Cross with two horizontal beams with the upper being more extended than that below, known in the religious circles as the Crux Immissa. John turned it over to look at the other side of the cuff link, and it contained the initials, 'IRNI.' John paused for a moment, but was interrupted by MacGregor in his Scottish twang, who provided the sought after answer,

"The four letters are a titulus, Latin label, inscribed above Jesus Christ on the Cross. They are the Latin initials for the phrase Pontius Pilate had written when he ordered Jesus crucified, INRI, **'Iesus Nazarenus, Rex Iudaeorum'** they translate to English as 'Jesus of Nazareth, the King of the Jews!"

Both Natalie and John were amazed at this explanation. The latter raised his eyebrows and said to the wise Doctor,

"How on earth did you know that Doctor?"

MacGregor smiled and replied,

"Before I decided to qualify as a doctor, I studied to become a Roman Catholic Priest. There lies the answer to your question Detective Chief Inspector."

John was impressed with this mans knowledge and questioned his expertise further by asking,

"I wonder, did you visit the site of the tragedy?"

"Yes I did, as I said earlier and like the police, I assumed she had thrown herself out of the train door onto the oncoming engine. She thus ended her life by suicide."

"Was the lack of blood that cautioned you to investigate her gullet?"

"No, not that!" he admitted slowly.

"I am ashamed to say; I decided that the poor girl committed suicide the moment I heard the authorities forum in her death by way of being hit by a moving train engine."

"Then what caused you to look beyond the obvious?"

The scan of her body indicated something lodged in her throat. I cut her open to investigated and found an expensive cufflink. I also believe it may have come from a club or religious sect."

Natalie decided following maintaining silence throughout the discussions between the two men to speak up; She coughed to interrupt them,

"I have to inform you that the sign is similar to that branded onto the forehead of the girls murdered in Romford. to which we have so far drawn an investigative blank."

Jenkins was delighted with this intervention by Natalie.

MacGregor was on a roll and went on,

"The facial bruising, even for someone who had fallen from a train, was extensive. In my estimation, this lady may have suffered a quite brutal battering."

"Your report stated that a cufflink was wedged quite someway down her throat. Perhaps a Calling Card? It intrigues me."

The Doctor responded,

Nobody would swallow something that size voluntarily! Thus, I conclude that the broken jaw was a deliberate act—quite a vicious one at that. Suppose you look at the crushed cheeks and the haemorrhaged eyes. I have already mentioned in my report, the person who killed this woman, hated her very much."

John said,

"So the work of a madman?"

Natalie spoke again,

"On the surface, yes. But why only one cufflink? Perhaps it was a warning to somebody else. However, for whom?"

The Doctor snorted in his Scottish accent,

"Surely, to show how clever he is. Like a needle in a haystack to discover to whom the cufflink belonged to!"

John responded again,

"A cat wearing gloves catches no mice!"

He caught the Doctor staring at him that suggested he had finally won over the' Red MacGregor!'

Just as they shook hands to depart, Natalie turned to Doctor MacGregor and asked,

"May I ask has the body been identified by her husband?

Callum replied,

"Not as yet, but he is booked to do so this afternoon.

John responded,

"Please ensure that that is recorded on CCTV doing so?"

With that final statement they left.

CHAPTER 42
MISSION CHANGE

Harry Slessor had a task to perform which he had already accepted part payment for Lady Gentry's lover Colonel James Craig VC's execution. However, following his meeting at New Scotland Yard with his senior handler and the Metropolitan Police Commissioner's presence, his mission had been altered.

He was resting on board his boat when his telephone rang. He answered it in his secure manner with the contact number only.

"7777, how can I be of assistance?"

The response was equally secret,

"949 here can we meet at the usual RV in one hour?"

Harry replied,

"Wilco."

He depressed the end call switch and ended the call. Harry looked at the time on his watch; it was close to five in the afternoon. Assessing that time was on his side, he filled the kettle with water and switched it on. Some four minutes later it had boiled. He poured himself a black coffee. He removed the lid and extracted a chocolate biscuit from the marked barrel. Harry wondered what was this sudden summons for! He ate the biscuit, slowly sipping the hot liquid. Once Harry had washed the cup and saucer, it was just about time for him to change into something casual and inconspicuous. These meetings were not commonplace but always significant. After several trials about what to wear, he opted for Levi's Jeans a blue Ralph Loren polo shirt in an almost matching blue. His shoes were black loafers which he felt blended in with his half-casual appearance.

At eight o'clock in the evening, the sunset over Cannon Street Station and London's City was going down. Harry had strolled over Tower Bridge as the lights commenced to illuminate the walkway. It was only a short seven hundred yards from the southeast corner of the bridge.

He entered the rendezvous, located on Butlers Warf, which was one of the most sought-after dining restaurants in London. The Thames River flows past the glass-fronted seated area.

Harry entered Le Pont de la Tour and was met by the reception staff consisting of two immaculately dressed people. The gentleman attired in a fetching coloured bow-tie and White-Tuxedo with immaculately pressed and creased black trousers. The stunning young lady was wearing a striking bright lilac satin blouse with high-waisted trousers sporting a cummerbund in a matching colour to the guy's bow tie. As he glanced around the restaurant's panorama, he noted that the colour of the tie and accompaniment were deep purple, matching the table decoration. Immediately he spotted his host located in the far-off corner of the oblong seated area. He greeted them with a smile saying,

"I am here to join Mr Smart for dinner; however, he can't be as smart as you two!"

The man smiled and looked at his bookings book, and with his pen ticked off his name saying to his fellow reception host,

"Chantelle please show Mr Slessor to Mr Smart's table?"

Slessor smiled and nodded, and he was happy to follow this young lady whose looks matched her name for he remembered it's associated with a song, and goodness knows her rear as she strode in front of him certainly was singing. As they approached Smith rose from his seat, he was angular in looks and sported a large scar which ran from below his right eye to his jawbone. He proffered his hand, which Harry shook using his strength to signal his muscularity. Garry Smart smiled and used equal pressure to confirm his robustness. he looked into Harry's eyes and immediately knew he was meeting someone of a similar disposition, He let his hand go and intimated to his guest with his right hand saying,

"Good to meet you, Harry, I have heard a great deal about you from Assistant Commissioner Bas Neil. What wine would you prefer with your dinner?"

Slessor looked at him promptly aware that Garry perhaps was a bit too keen on alcohol. He replied,

"I am happy with sparkling water. Thank you. However, before we progress, I wish to see your Warrant Card?"

Chief Inspector Smart, reached inside the rear pocket of his trousers, extracted a black leather wallet, and flicked it open, producing the information Harry requested. Slessor nodded assent to Garry Smart who replaced it from whence it came.

There was already a bottle of Highland Spring water on the table. Its label complimented the all-around purple effect of the restaurant décor. While the dining area was fairly busy, it was clear that his host had arranged a table out of earshot to other diners.

"Bas has issued me with new instructions relating to the mission that Egbert advised you on. The original target is no longer a problem. He has been removed to a safe house. He will be issued his new identity as the original reason for the ongoing situation has suspiciously committed suicide. In short Lady Gentry is dead. So, your new undertaking is enclosed in this folder,"

He extracted a buff-coloured folder from under the table, passing it to Harry.

On extracting the document, he noted that it contained several large photographs. He read through several pages of text. On then turning to the pictures, the new target was one Peter Gentry the same man he had met at the London Cemetery who had contracted him to execute his wife. It was indeed a change of plan. On looking up from the document and the photographs, he asked Garry Smart.

"What is the time frame of the survival of Gentry?"

Smart responded,

"You have ten days to plan and complete the mission. It is also well known that he has been responsible with other prominent folks for the murder of several young girls in the Essex area. However, you will have noted that he is a Lord of the Realm who contracted you to extinguish James Craig VC. He has been involved not unexpectedly with the Chief Constable of Essex as well as the commander of Romford Met Police. His wife has seemingly committed suicide, therefore that mission is null-in-void now. That has yet to be confirmed that she took her own life by jumping from a moving train carriage onto the front of an on-coming Railway Engine just as it entered Liverpool Street, Station. It is not yet confirmed that she took her own life. There is a suspicion that perhaps it was not a voluntary end to life! He has several friends in very high places. So, you have to be particularly measured on how you take him down."

Harry reached for his water as the waitress arrived at the table with their main course. They had opted for the same Rib-eye steak menu, grilled mushroom béarnaise with buttered French beans, and potato puree. The only difference is that

Smith preferred his steak rare. Following the afters, he sipped an enjoyable black coffee and avoided discussing the mission. He noted that Garry Smith only had one further glass of wine with the main course. They parted company at a quarter of the hour before ten o'clock.

As Harry walked over Tower Bridge, the moonlight reflected a long exposure as the River Thames flowed under the bridge. The water appeared smooth, and moonlight glistened as the greywater gently flowed and ebbed under the bridge. It resembled that of a glass mirror reflection. Harry mused as to what he had to do to satisfy Assistant Commissioner Bas Neil and Sir Bernard. He was pretty relieved he no longer had to kill someone who held the 'Victoria Cross.' However meet their orders, he would.

CHAPTER 43
GOODBYE DAVID

David Cottage was quite unaware that his life was about to dramatically alter. He may well have been Alan Boyd's favoured hitman, but that in itself would not guarantee existence or extinction. Boyd's other aid Sandy Low had left the country following the Hackney shoot-out and his eventual escape. Interpol had been alerted however their efforts to locate him were fruitless.

Unbeknown to either Boyd or Cottage the police had traced his hideout in the small Essex town of Gray's.

Essex Police headquarters in Chelmsford Its headquarters, the Force Control Room (FCR) (where emergency calls are routed too.) as well as the Essex Police College, are all located in Chelmsford. Strategically, Essex is an important force. The police HQ of Essex is located in New Street, Chelmsford in a modern built building that was opened in 2008. It is in some 27,000 square feet of prime location real estate and cost just over six million pounds sterling. A tidy sum even in those days. However, it is well documented that police today is a structure that is as appropriate to law enforcement as it is to the welfare of the public they serve. In short, he was found on several occasions to be found wanting and suspected of infiltrating corruption.

Both John Jenkins and Bob Clarkson had been summoned to a meeting by the Head of Essex Police for an in-depth review of the three atrocious murders of young girls from the Romford area. As they arrived and once security checks had taken place the unmarked police vehicle was permitted entry through the large grey steel gates. DCI John Jenkins looked at Bob Clarkson smiling at the distinct noise as the metal gate grated across the concrete driveway. Their driver drove slowly to the alcove entrance and pulled up at the door to Essex Police Headquarters.

The entrance corridor to the head of the entire Essex Force was nothing short of plush. Once more they showed their ID Cards. On entering the office sitting at a huge oak table was an imposing figure. Chief Constable Steve Jones was imposing in his appearance and dress. He rose from his chair circled those others present and proffered his right hand to John and then Bob saying,

"Gentlemen, let me welcome you to our headquarters. I am so pleased you are here. It is an absolutely disgusting set of murders we are dealing with, and I feel that your input will be invaluable."

Turning to the assembled investigators, pointing with his right hand he then ran through who they were. This is as you are aware your own Matilda Addison, the Acting Superintendent of Romford Police following the abhorrent murder of Chief Super Stave Bagley. This is DCI Larry Donegan who has also been involved in the ongoing murdered females from Romford. They took their seats and waited for Steve Jones to commence. Chief Constable Jones was a smooth operator, and both were aware of his reputation. Jones opened well aware that these pair were experts in their respective investigative abilities, so he had to box clever. His involvement in the death of these young women would if discovered would lead to him being locked up for life. And, worse still the inmates of HM Prisons would know his previous career. They would surely punish him and provide the recipient with a slow, painful death. His aim of this meeting was to throw in a few red herrings and hopefully deflect them away from the family church at Ingatestone Hall. He was unaware that both senior detectives knew all about that location and indeed John had spent a night there.

CC Jones, commenced with,

"Gentlemen, we are in deep trouble, the press and news channels are constantly running the stories of the three girls murdered plus their mutilated bodies abandoned in dreadful locations. Does anyone present have any clues where we may succeed in arresting the perpetrators of these horrendous crimes? It is apparent this is no single person committed these crimes."

Bob looked at John and smiled, he depressed the device in his right trouser pocket, and with that, the door to the Chief Constable of Essex burst open and rushed in were six uniformed and armed police officers. John immediately, instantly rose and swiftly removed a set of handcuffs. He took hold of Jones's right hand snapping one side of the cuff around one wrist. He then forced the Chief Constable of Essex's other hand behind his back. And, clicking the police cuffs closed and act he enjoyed.

He then repeated the similar words that Jones must have used as a young police officer,

"Stephen Anthony Jones, I arrest you on the suspicion that you collaborated and participated in the murder of Christine Mary Pearce of Romford, dumped in the Tow Path off Mawney Road RM7. *You* do not have to say anything. But it may harm your defence if you do not mention when questioned something which you later rely on in court. Anything you do say may be given in evidence."

Bob Clarkson looked at Chief Constable Jones's face and swore he heard the sound of a bird flapping its wings in a panic. Maybe it was his heart, he remembered having seen a wild bird in a cage, looking for a way out. The Chief Constable looked lightheaded and his facial skin was crimson with droplets of sweat commencing to appear on his forehead.

In short, he was well and truly nicked and in his own plush office, He was in sheer panic and shock He was looking for a way out well that was how his mind was reacting. As he looked around, he was not the only person present in severe shock. Matilda Addison feared she may soon feel the metal bracelets replacing diamonds on her dainty wrists.

After all, she was responsible for the death of her boss, Chief Superintendent David Bagley. She felt the noose was likewise tightening around her own throat.

Meanwhile, as this was taking place arch-villain and hitman David Cottage was happily sitting on the bar stool in The Wharf Public House sipping a pint of ale, a 300-year-old riverside pub and restaurant in Grays, Essex. Once known as The Sailors Return Inn. On the wall was an information plaque intimating that this was the first dwelling on this site dating back to the thirteen hundreds. This was his hide well away from the obvious locations that gangsters gathered. He had been raised in east London in the area of Bow within the borough of Tower Hamlets. Notorious for the age-old tale of Jack the Ripper.

He slid from his stool at the bar and headed for the gentlemen's toilet. As he meandered along the dark corridor he was in a good state of mind. David Cottage Boyd's top hitman pushed the door open. The first thing he did was enter the ablution, undo his trousers and let them lower to his knee. As he removed his appendage to urinate it was his very final conscious act.

With a silencer fitted, his killer fired three rounds of the undisputed calibre parabellum point nine-millimetre rounds in the back of his skull. The result of which was an entrance hole of no more than two inches in the rear of his cranium. The exit, however, was a full five obliterating and punching a cavity removing his nose and most of his face which scattered bone fragments against the wall and toilet bowl as blood spilt from the wound. David Cottage's body slumped against the wall. He was dead before this occurred. The perpetrator left quietly with no opportunity for anyone to observe her.

In the main bar, his seat lay vacant, it would be some time before the staff noticed his absence.

CHAPTER 44
DS LEWIS IS MISSING

John as agreed with Natalie was waiting in his unmarked police car waiting to collect her from the safe house she had been moved to out of her house in Emmerson Park, Romford to this apartment in Hackney, London. This had been well arranged and the collection times were always different to avoid prying eyes. He looked at the car clock and it was now reading ten minutes past eight on a bright Monday morning. It was not like her she was a stickler for time and in his experience, she was never late. However, he smiled inwardly, she was a woman, and they were sometimes liable to be a little behind schedule. So he decided to give her the benefit of the doubt and permit her another five minutes before he went to check on her shoddy lateness.

His mind drifted to her husband the doctor and her two children who for their own safety had been moved to a location in Devon. He sat in the car drumming the steering wheel with his fingers. Impatience was setting in quickly and he had to admit to his concern for his colleague. Strangely he had to confess he was worried sick. Should he call for backup or remain calm and visit the apartment, for surely there was a simple reason for her delay? Another ten minutes passed, and he decided on the latter plan exiting the car and heading towards Halcon Square, just off Richmond Road the two-bedroom penthouse apartment was well tucked away. The letting company SpicerHart Group had been well-researched and vetted. He walked into the square trying not to be conspicuous and attempted nonchalantly to press the buzzer for the safe-house apartment. There was no response. His heart was skipping a beat but yet again depressed the entrance phone buzzer. Once more, nothing. Observing the various names on the list he noticed at the bottom, Apartment Manager. He depressed it and held it for quite a while......eventually a rather posh voice was heard saying,

'James Nash, apartment manager how may I help you?'

'DCI Jenkin's of the Met Police I need to ask you a few questions?'

There was a pregnant pause......then the rather effeminate voice responded,

'Please wait to enter the door I will permit your entry. We are on the first door on the right with the title Apartment Manager. I will be there waiting for you Sir.'

The release buzzer sounded, and John entered the plush entrance hall which was decorated to an extremely high standard as may be expected. He arrived at the door and just as he was about to ring the bell, the door opened and a gentleman with fair wavy hear and striking good looks dressed in an expensive men's silk royal Teal Dressing Gown and on his feet was a pair of handmade slippers in the same fabric covering. This guy was dressed in expensive nightwear. In a similar tone, he looked at John's Warrant Card which he was holding up for him to view and prove his identity, he spoke,

'How can I help you?'

'I wish to speak with the lady in apartment twenty-six three. I have attempted to call her on her cell phone with no response, would you please escort me to that apartment immediately?'

The manager was a little hesitant......dwelling on his answer to this DCI request. He then replied,

'Will you please step inside, and I will quickly change into clothes appropriate to escort you to the apartment with the pass key?'

John nodded assent and was shown into a very plush reception area suitably decorated he was shown to an obvious waiting room furnished with, Violate Velvet Chairs in royal blue. He sat on one his mind was racing and concerned that Natalie had not shown up. In almost no time James Nash reappeared this time in a pair of red trousers, a bright pink shirt, and a deep red bow tie with a matching pair of suede moccasins with a branded trim. It was clear this effeminate individual knew how to impress. He spoke to John,

'Please follow me, Detective Chief Inspector?'

They both left the ground floor via the lift arriving at the twenty-sixth floor as they approached twenty-six-three John had butterflies in his stomach, he knew not why!

James unlocked the door and John called out,

'Natalie, are you here?'

There was no response so James went to walk further into the flat, John abruptly prevented this movement by placing his arm across his front. James halted, and DCI Jenkin's said,

'Please wait here and do not touch anything, do you understand Mr Nash?'

James replied,

'Yes, I do.'

John left him and entered the empty sitting room and moved into the kitchen again vacant, he opened a door which he assumed was a bedroom and was struck with a horrible sight, There on the four-poster bed was DS Natalie Lewis, naked and quite obviously dead! Her left breast had been removed and her stomach slit open, the bed linen was caked in dried blood. The shock was almost too much for John his beautiful attractive colleague and the mother of two children had been violently murdered. Both hands were tied with a crimson cord to the bed posts and her legs were similarly entwined with the same colour cord. Her right hand was missing her hand stump similar to the sheets clotted with dried blood. On coming closer he looked at her forehead.

There was also the sign of a crucifix branded on her forehead with a short arm followed by another which was slightly longer. As he went to her left side, he noticed that her left palm had been penetrated with a sharp instrument there was a distinct hole in her palm. He had seen and witnessed many a dreadful murder scene, but this was the worst it was one of his fellow officers and she had suffered a dreadfully painful death. He went back into the kitchen and vomited into the sink.

John cleaned himself up and taking out his mobile phone dialled New Scotland Yard to summon assistance and forensics which would hopefully provide information to the perpetrators of this atrocious crime.

He then entered the area where James Nash was waiting. Nash realised that something dreadful had occurred. John asked him,

'Do you have security cameras in all public areas?'

James responded,

'Yes, we do Sir, the recording system is in the basement and is downloaded electronically to Group Four Security Company.'

'Thank you, I must tell you now that what has happened

here is extremely serious, someone has been murdered so this apartment is now a crime scene. The entire floor and its occupants will be detained and interviewed in due course. I will inform the other three apartment occupants that they are to remain inside and only answer their door to the Metropolitan Police.

CHAPTER 45
THE CULL BEGINS

Detective Inspector Harry Slessor was well versed in training snipers and his choice this time he assessed was outstanding it had to be for the task that this person would have to complete.

The problem was that he'd known her before she became a drug user and a prostitute, and he could clearly remember her as a spirited, pretty and more or less honest girl. Given time, trouble and patience she could return to her former self. But there was no time. She had to do it soon. Steve Jones had to be wasted. The delay meant more lives were destroyed. Harry Slessor had purchased the murder weapon – a Bushmaster point five-zero bolt action rifle manufactured in the United States. It had bipod action legs to ensure stability and it propelled a point five-zero calibre round, its action bolt permitted a rapid reload if required. However, the sniper always ensured that the first shot counted.

Laura needed to get in close and that meant the Bushmaster, of a size and calibre she could hide and handle easily. And it had to be powerful enough to do the job. It was a wonderful gun to handle, though Harry found it too light for himself. It was in her large handbag, and she required about thirty seconds to assemble it, loaded the magazine aim and fired at the target. Harry had schooled her well in the countryside which nobody ever used. Following a detailed recce with Harry Slessor, they had picked the building opposite which on the entry had a flat roof overlooking the steps leading to the Civic Centre. The choice of the roof afforded her the best angle to take the shot.

Stephen Jones - Chief Constable of Essex – A Senior Cult Member, Senior Warden of the Ingatestone Rosicrucianism. The number two of the Essex Cult practising out of the old church at Ingatestone Hall Estate. The next target if she is successful would be His Lordship, Lord Peter Gentry. However, his hitman a former MI5 agent would protect his boss with all his expertise. His new name of Tony Steel has secured prevention from discovery however, Harry knew his birth name was James Pratchett for Special Air Service soldier. Taking him out may well be a job for himself. He was without a doubt a shrewd operator and killer.

Harry had a great deal of love for Laura indeed he had managed to get her off drugs when she was a habitual user in his cover public house in Wapping, East London. The DARK MAN. It wasn't too far from his launch on the Thames River from his little barge, The Harvest Moon one of the best on the river. He had trained her to perfection and while he had taken out many bad boys he had killed her in doing likewise. Her first hit several months ago while successful turned out somewhat troublesome as the target a bent policeman would have survived her attempted hit, but Harry Slessor being aware of her failure approached the wounded policeman, placed a high-visibility jacket over his head and extinguished any chance of survival. Following that she had proved great worth and snuffed out seven targets. Now she was ready for the biggest hit of her professional life as a hitwoman.

The Commander of Essex Police was visiting the Chelmsford Civic Centre in Duke Street to present a Police Chief's Commendation to Miss Gillian Cottage for services rendered for the most outstanding Help in The Community, Remus Group. The presentation was packed with a vast number of dignitaries including the

Thanks to the hard work of staff from a local business Remus Management - a property management company the Centre now has a much more inviting and welcoming appearance. Remus Management staff recently spent two days tidying, cleaning painting and even purchasing new children's play equipment for the Visitor Centre. The visit of such a senior police grandee was causing some real excitement. The crowds were gathering around the centre in anticipation of Steven Jones's attendance and the prize giving. The Chief Executive Chelmsford City Council Councillor Jeremy Vine was dressed to the nines in an immaculate dark blue with a chalk pin-striped suit and wearing the Chelmsford City Tie. He was attended by several flunkies and local notability hoping in anticipation of their details being included in the local newspaper and another step on the ladder to success.

James and his entourage were assembled on the steps to await the police cavalcade and as he looked to his left he viewed the unmarked police convoy approaching. Folks started to shuffle around in anticipation of the head of Essex Police's arrival. Slowly the vehicle came to a halt in the exact place allocated to enable the press photographers and the Look East Television News Cameras from Norwich to record the presentation for the local six-thirty evening news slot. As the car came to a standstill a uniformed policeman stepped forward and opened the limousine. He stepped back as Jones exited the vehicle. The policeman saluted his commander and Steven Jones returned the salute. He smiled at the constable and walked forward and ascended the small stairs leading to where Vine and his entourage awaited. As he approached Jeremy presented his right hand to welcome him. The smiles on both faces were wide and with a clear favourite and an obvious warm reception. As he did so the silent sound similar to a puff adder snake striking took place from the flat roof over the road, in milliseconds the point five-zero bullet entered the rear of Stephen Jones's head passed through it and continued its trajectory smashing Vine's face just by his nose to obliteration. He was propelled backwards onto the steps and was accompanied by the Essex Chief of Police on top of him. Neither would survive. The intended sniper target was successful but in effect, Laura could have been shopping in the local supermarket and bought two articles for the price of one. Both men's blood crimson red flooded the Civic Hall steps. The commotion that ensued was unbelievable with policemen looking to try and find where the shooting had come from but the immediate panic of the crowd prevented this.

Laura calmly stripped the Bushmaster, secured it into her bag collected the spent point five-zero-millimetre, empty case, and rolled up the mat she had used to ensure no clothing fibres were left behind for forensics to discover as instructed by Harry Slessor. Sill wearing her protective gloves so as not to leave any fingerprints opened the roof door and walked down the stairs/ As she did so the sound of the blue plastic shoe covers made a little squelching sound as she descended, As she approached down lift, confident and aware that the security cameras had been disabled.

Outside the noise of police sirens and ambulances arriving was audible to anyone within a mile of the Civic Hall. The ambulances and paramedics clad in the green and yellow high-vis uniform jackets with the words emblazoned on the rear,

'FAST RESPONDER.' Their swift arrival was just that, but alas pointless. Both men were lying on the steps, covered in blood but most certainly faceless as the one bullet had all but obliterated their faces beyond recognition. Mayhem ensued with additional police vehicle arrival and sheer panic of the assembled crowd

CHAPTER 46
IT IS ALL OVER

At the same time that John Jenkins and Bob Clarkson entered the police canteen for breakfast, the BBC 1 Newscaste was showing on the large 55-inch screens on the three walls not occupied by the canteen self-help area. Once they had collected their food, they took a seat at an unoccupied table. At that moment, Clive Myrie was informing those watching both in the UK and World BBC Service the latest update on the death of Chief Constable Stephen Jones - Chief Constable of Essex shot dead on the steps of Chelmsford Civic Centre.

John as he took a sip of his tea raised his eyebrow towards Bob, who in turn smiled, raising his eyes towards the ceiling. He took a bite of the slice of toast in his mouth, and said,

"John, how long before it is in the public domain that he was a leading figure of the Esserx Cult?"

DCI Jenkins raised his right index finger to his mouth in an obvious manner of expressing his action for Bob to keep quiet. With his fork and a piece of grilled bacon, he stopped halfway to his mouth, saying,

"We must be very careful as any leak of this would cause serious damage to the confidence in the Police force."

Clive Myrie spoke with a very distinct BBC voice reporting with a serious expression on his face,

"I regret to inform you of the sudden and tragic death of Chief Constable Stephen Jones on the steps of Chelmsford Town Hall. Our thoughts and prayers are with his family and the entire police force during this difficult time. Chief Constable Jones will be remembered for his dedication and service to the entire Essex community. May his soul rest in peace."

DCI Jenkins once more stared at Bob, there was a distinct silence between these two hardened police detectives.

Following what seemed like an age, Bob responded in his sometimes direct manner,

" The Bastard got what he deserved. How many young girls was he involved in kidnapping, abusing and disposing of their bodies?"

John Jenkins needed no time to respond, saying,"

"I hope this message finds you well. I wanted to bring to your attention some urgent information regarding a degenerate sniper murderer of Chief Constable Stephen Jones. We must discuss this matter further, as it poses a potential threat to public safety. Please let me know when you are available for a meeting or call to discuss the details. The Press is all over this. And you will be aware he was shot and killed yesterday in Chelmsford. Thank you for your prompt attention to this matter. Please call me back on my confidential Police Phone, Goodbye from John Jenkins."

Bob Clarkson stared at his immediate superior and remained silent. They finished their full English Breakfast and departed the canteen.

The Cult members were in deep shock at the killing of their second most senior member. None more so than Lord Gentry and his bodyguard were summoned to his baronial dining room where his Lordship was pacing the floor in angst. His world was about to dismantle in front of him and all the years of Igngastone Hall's history was imploding. He paced up and down the room from the door to the bay window looking out to the manicured gardens and in the near distance only five hundred steps from the conservatory door to the Family Monument and then to the entrance to the Church. His mind envisaged the sexual enjoyment he experienced from taking the local girls on the stone and bloodletting that took place and his enjoyment of drinking her blood.

As he pondered the moment and the excitement of remembering the kill the main double door swung open and Anthony Maitland Steel his trusted gunman and protector entered. His Lordship turned toward the plastic surgery-refaced Tony Steel reminding him more of the old British Film Star whose face had been copied during the plastic surgery.

Steel was looking very grave but as ever immaculately dressed in a dark blue chalk pin-striped suit, and with a white shirt that constituted the bedrock of every man's wardrobe according to sartorial historians. Peter Gentry raised the glass of blood-red port to his lips. With that movement, Tony decided that this was the opportune moment to brief him on how they were about to escape from Ingatstone Hall and more importantly the United Kingdom. Tony, explained that his escape vehicle was in the garage ready to leave the ancestral home for the last time. He had also planned a surprise for any interruption by the police. Anthony Steel was holding a captive in a strong embrace. The poor woman was unable to move. Steel the said to both John and Bob,

'HOW NICE OF you to join us,' Steel said, treating DCI Jenkins to a cold smile.

'And the show is just about to start too.'

He looked off-guard and relaxed, but John was not deceived. He knew from experience how quickly the ex-SAS man could move and how tough he was in a physical confrontation. He would stand little chance against him, yet he had to do something before it was too late. 'You're weighing up your chances, I think,' the psychopath went on. He tutted and shook his head. 'No contest, I'm afraid – as you well know in boxing terms, Red is too strong for blue haha.

'HOW NICE OF you to join us,'

Steel said, treating both senior policemen to a cold smile.

'And the show is just about to start too.'

He looked off-guard and relaxed, but neither John nor Bob were deceived. Both knew from experience how quickly the ex-SAS man could move and how tough he was in a physical confrontation. However, two against one Steel would stand little chance against both, yet they had to do something before it was too late.

'You're weighing up your chances, I think,'

the psychopath went on. He tutted and shook his head.

'No contest, I'm afraid – as you found out once before if I recall correctly.'

Steel's smile broadened and he produced a small oblong device from his pocket that resembled an electronic pager.

'And with this, I hold all the aces anyway.'

Before either could do anything, he flicked open a flap with his thumb and pressed something.

'It's been activated now, you see,'

he said, holding the device up to display a flashing red light.

'All it needs is just one little press of a button and a signal will be sent to a receiver on the explosive charge I have only just finished inserting in the petrol filler pipe of the Transit. Then it's Guy Fawkes Night all over again, but just in case your colleagues miss the show, I have ensured that the DVR here will capture everything in glorious colour, as it happens. Now, wasn't that thoughtful of me?'

Steel still had a firm grip around the throat of the parlour maid he had taken captive as part of his self-protection. Inadvertently Molly Jones passed him in the corridor. She immediately became part of his dastardly scheme.

'Let her go,'

Clarkson the former Scots Guard blurted hoarsely.

"She's done nothing to you."

Steel sighed.

"I'm afraid it's too late for that, Bob – may I call you that? I've invested too much in this little operation to abandon it now and besides, poor little Molly is a loose end from my past debacle, and I don't like loose ends – so untidy."

Bob caught sight of the time registered in the corner of the computer screen. It was four minutes to midnight. He tensed his muscles, preparing to launch himself at his antagonist in a last-ditch effort, knowing in his heart of hearts that it was pointless, but desperately hoping he could somehow gain the advantage.

"Your call, DCI Jenkins"'

Steel said softly, sensing what Clarkson had in mind, and giving him another cold smile.

"What have you got to lose?"'

It was the thudding blades of the approaching Police helicopter that changed the dynamics of the situation, for the noise provided a brief distraction and that was just enough. Even though Steel must have known that he would not be able to see anything through the windows of the room, his dead eyes instinctively flicked upwards and the next second Clarkson with all his might and it was massive cannoned into him. The detective did not have the stature or muscular power of the psychopath, but his strong body mass was still substantial, and it carried them both forward several feet. They burst through the half-open glass doors, locked together in a grotesque embrace, the remote flying from Steel's hand and into the short stubby grass, as they ended up in a tangle of arms and legs on the sodden ground, in the midnight darkness with the detective on top. But Bob's advantage did not last long. Even as he hammered Steel's face and body with his fists, the killer simply shrugged him off like an irritating itchy blanket, seemingly impervious to the blows he was receiving, one huge powerful hand gripping the detective round the face and forcing his head back at an impossible angle. Then suddenly there were flashing blue lights on the road beyond the field and the helicopter's blinding searchlight was fixing on them like the super trouper spot of a West End Theatre stage set.

With a snarl of anger, Steel hurled Clarkson away from him and scrambled to his feet, his eyes scanning the area around them for his remote. He saw the flashing red light among the tufts of grass and went for the remote at the same time as Bob – struggling weakly to his feet. Steel got there first, but before he could grab his prize, he was bowled over for the second time by the detective, whose determination to save the situation imbued him with a renewed strength, born of desperation. For just a moment Steel was taken aback by the unexpected ferocity of the attack, but, although the detective initially succeeded in gaining the upper hand, pinning the killer to the ground, the latter then recovered and hurled him sideways, kicking the policeman in the stomach before he could regain his feet.

Now the psychopath had the remote in his hand and, lashing out at Bob; 's head with his foot when the detective tried to get back on his feet, he turned towards the target Transit Van located in the area of hard tarmac at the front of the old Ingatstone Church as a convoy of police cars raced along the drove and skidded to a halt behind the doomed van. 'So the cavalry has arrived, have they?' he shouted above the roar of the helicopter still hovering overhead. 'Well, that's just more fuel for the fire, isn't it?' And in a fraction of a second later the night sky was blasted by an almighty explosion, which seemed to light up the entire sky and sent an end-to-end tremor surging through the ground like the aftershock of a mini earthquake. Steel was laughing inanely now, his usual dearth of emotion buried in an outpouring of psychotic glee, but it didn't last long.

The owner of the field in which the black bull had been kept should have known that the gate between his property and that of the derelict adjacent farm was rotten and incapable of standing up to a determined onslaught by such a huge, aggressive animal; his negligence was Steel's downfall. The creature, already wound up by the commotion was maddened even more by the roar of the helicopter some two hundred feet above. Clocking Steel standing in its path, it saw the opportunity to satisfy its pent-up fury, lowered its head and charged. Alerted by some kind of uncanny sixth sense, the psychopath swung round with remarkable speed, but, nimble as he was, he was much too late. The massive head of the bull slammed into him with the force of an articulated lorry, tossing him high in the air like an uprooted scarecrow.

Then, even as Steel's screaming writhing body plummeted back to the ground, one vicious horn speared him in mid-spin, slicing through his abdomen and practically ripping him in two when the enraged beast shook its head violently to free itself before it finished the job by trampling and goring his already dismembered remains into the marshy ground.

The whole thing lasted just seconds but for Steel, lying there on the sodden ground – only half-conscious and bleeding heavily as a result of the injury he had received to his head from DCI Jenkins boot – time seemed to stand still. It was Steel's immobility that probably saved his life too, for the bull showed no interest whatsoever as he headed back to his original field content with his kill.

John Jenkins and Bob had succeeded in not only saving the old church from extinction but had capturing this former SAS MI6 killer.

John handcuffed the broken body of Steel. Bob had regained his composure after the fight and went forward to assist John. As he did so he checked Steel's vitals. He looked at John saying,

"It looks like our not-so-friendly Black Bull has saved the

Crown Prosecution Service the trouble of dealing with this low life.

He is kaput, DEAD!"

DCI John Jenkins smiled at Bob and said,

"A close run thing my friend but we won in the end."

THE END

ABOUT THE AUTHOR

Ronnie Paterson was born to an Irish mother and Scottish father in Glasgow on 16th July 1945 following the cessation of the Second World War. On completion of his education, Ronnie joined the Scots Guards and completed his training at The Infantry Junior Leaders between 1961 and 1963. Joined 1SG before serving in Malaya, Borneo, Cyprus, and Northern Ireland, where he was wounded in action, resulting in the award of 'Mentioned in Dispatches for Gallantry'. He rose to Warrant Officer, Class 1, and, in 1989, was commissioned to the rank of Captain. The Falklands War saw him take part in the final battle of the conflict (Mount Tumbledown); watching from this advantage point he witnessed the white flag being raised by the Argentine Generals over Port Stanley on 14th June 1982. As his fortieth birthday beckoned, he decided to resign his commission and leave the army. He joined Brown Shipley, the merchant bank as an Administration Manager. Coincidentally, he was located immediately behind the rear entrance of the Bank of England's building, where he often had, as a young guardsman, mounted guard duty to protect the nation's gold. As with his military career, he did not stand still and was appointed Facilities Manager at the bank. He was head hunted into another financial company, Gerrard National Inter-Commodities in late 2004 to head up their Personnel and Administration Department. He left in 2007 to set up his own company. He eventually retired and was enjoying his life when a close friend and fellow officer from the military requested, that he assist in setting up what proved to be the most successful Private Military Company engaged in the reconstruction of Iraq following the overthrow of Saddam Hussein by the American-led coalition. Several years followed, with numerous visits to Iraq – perhaps he just liked danger.

Life is much more tolerable now as he resides in a picture-postcard bungalow located in Leigh-on-Sea, Essex. It is aptly named, Rose & Thistle. Rose, because his partner is an English Rose, Thistle, because he is a prickly old git. A far cry from his former life or lives, some say he had nine of them considering the number of times he could have died in military conflicts around the world.

His previous novel, The Romford Boys was a success selling 1,850 hardback copies and a number on Amazon Kindle to locations in the USA, Germany, and Switzerland.

Printed in Great Britain
by Amazon